FAITHFUL TO MY HEART

FAITHFUL TO MY HEART

ARI BASIL WAGNER

SAPPHIRE BOOKS

SALINAS, CALIFORNIA

using the production/publication for purposes of training A.I., artificial intelligence, to generate text that may replicate the author's style or genre similar to this work. The author retains all rights to use this work for purposes of generative AI training and development of any language learning system.

To the extent that the image on the cover of this book depicts a person or persons, such a person is merely a model and is not intended to portray any character feature in this book.

This and other Sapphire Books titles can be found at

www.sapphirebooks.com

Dedication

Faithful to My Heart is dedicated to all those who yearn for a fulfilling life with meaningful relationships yet find that journey hindered by an unresolved traumatic past. Though your struggles are heavy, they are also testaments to your resilience and your desire to embody your true essence. That peace can feel far away, yet there is simply a thin veil separating you from happiness. It takes much courage to explore our fears that unfold in the messy parts of love and life. This is for all of you doing your best in that quest. Even when it feels like you're sinking, remember that true healing is always an ascension.

As fate has it, healing is not achieved without unintentional and often profound hurt upon ourselves and those we love. The latter is one of life's harshest pains to reconcile. May you take those steps with compassion and grace. While they are yours to navigate, they are on the road of personal growth where so many of us gather. Me included. I hope that we can gather there with a tender gentleness for one another, knowing our stories are heard, and we are never alone. To your journey of healing, your courage to love and be loved, and your reach for your joy, I dedicate this book.

To Your Joy, Ari

Acknowledgement

I am grateful for all those who love me and allow me to love them back. My adult child who taught me how to be a parent also guided me to being a better person. Thank you, Mika! Your insights into writing, photography, music, and the art of being a present person are a continued source of inspiration and motivation for me. Your light in this world offers so much joy. To your other mom, Verna, what a lovely co-parent you've been all these years. Your kindness brings me home again, and for that, I will always be grateful. Along with Maria, whose kind heart offers so much care and love, I am so thankful to our family.

To my immediate family of over seventy-five people, I am grateful to you for being the beautiful souls you are and carrying the legacy of our ancestors within our gatherings and the way we love one another. Each day, I feel so cared for by you. You are with me always. Thank you for believing in me and supporting my choices in life. My siblings Marianne, Donna, Jerry, Jackie, and our brother who passed away, Bobby—thank you all for your absolute support and love for me.

I am thankful to you, all my dear friends from Nogales, who are as much family to me as those who I share lineage. Our bond is a daily joy and a torch in the darker times of life. Our friendship started in childhood when I shared my writings with you, and now, fifty-plus years later, your love and support were with me as I scribed this story.

And the Dear Ones, my friends who have entered this

stage of life with me, I am grateful for your support and warm friendship. Also, Wendy, thank you for reading this story and sharing your excitement for its completion.

Carol Ann, your belief in me and in my writing is unwavering. Thank you for always being a phone call away, for your care, and for your endearing and loving friendship. I am a better person for knowing you.

I'm unsure what good I've done to bring such love into my life, but I am humbly thankful for it and the energy it carries to my writing. All of which is within these pages with my gratitude to Sapphire Books Publishing, which believes in the power of lesbian stories and offers opportunities for writers to be heard. My sincere appreciation to Chris Svendsen, CEO and publisher; Tara Young, editor; all the staff and graphic artists; and to the other authors at Sapphire. It's a beautiful community of artists. I am honored to be one of them.

To Your Joy, Ari

Chapter One

Brooke Kent didn't realize she was clenching her fists. Nor could she feel the grains of white sand throbbing in the open wounds on her arms or the scratches along her thigh. At that moment, she tried to focus on her surroundings. She searched for anything familiar. But nothing on that hot day comforted her or helped her understand what happened or where she was.

"It's okay. You're going to be all right, sweetie. You're going to be fine. Do you hear me?" a voice asked her. "You're going to be okay."

Too tired to respond except to herself, Brooke thought, Okay? I don't feel okay. Where's Renee?

Again, she tried to open her eyes, but the sun smeared her view until everything was entangled in a blur of bright white and blue. She laid her head back and abandoned her efforts to her wandering thoughts of a time months before this uncertain day.

⁂

Brooke pulled her green convertible into her northwest Phoenix home precisely at seven thirty, like every other weeknight. Her regimented routine would make the most disciplined monk stand in awe. At five o'clock, she left the office where she worked as an analyst for the city's housing department. From there, she drove straight to the athletic club for a solitary game of racquetball. Pounding the small blue ball on the wooden court floor, she worked herself into a hypnotic rhythm of "ball-wall-floor, ball-wall-floor…" Her quick reflexes helped her stretch across the court to hit what looked like an unreachable shot. For a few moments, she became part of that rhythm and entered the zone that athletes try to describe but rarely do because it exists in a place beyond the limitations of language. Unlike those athletes, however, it was never Brooke's goal to reach any "zone," but it brought a pleasurable grin to her lips when it happened to her. Unfortunately, it didn't last long. Inevitably, an intruding thought about work interrupted her flow, causing Brooke to slam the ball into rubber shavings. At least she attributed that stress to her workday, but most of it came from tension she had not yet named. Her time at the club helped relax her, and she liked the way it toned her body.

Next, she took a Jacuzzi, showered, and got dressed to go home before the hordes of tanned Phoenix women hurried in for their maintain-a-size-four exercises. Sometimes Brooke thought about going to the club during the day, not at noon with the other ladies in suits working out during their lunch break, but rather during the business world's prime meeting times. That time of day would have a slower pace set by women who did not work outside their homes. Brooke wondered what the club was like when filled by those women. She couldn't imagine what they talked about or what could possibly occupy their minds if not the details of work and relationships with their coworkers. She never experienced their home life of leisure workouts, impromptu lunches, and afternoon movies—not even a glimpse of it. She began working in her early teens and kept going through what was now her early forties. Not that she financially had to start working so young. Her inheritance was managed so that it would take care of college expenses and well beyond. Brooke chose to work in her teens. Even then, she was too responsible for her years, and that early maturity caused her to desire a young life that was busy with something other than the emotional drama embraced by her high school peers. And once she started, she never stopped.

All the work and her education paid off with what she referred to as her little slice of the American dream, along with everything it afforded her. She loved the family home that was now hers. Walking into its iron-gated entrance and through the small garden, she headed toward the oversized front doors imported from South America. As she reached for the ornate wooden knob, she thought about grabbing a sun tea and hitting the hammock in the backyard or taking a quick dip in the pool. Maybe both. Her mind played through those relaxing scenarios while her body acted on a plan of its own. It was a habit to stroll into the kitchen, gulp down two pain-relieving capsules, make herself a quick pseudo-meal (tonight's was a bowl of cereal), sit down in front of the television, and watch a *Space Prairie* rerun. *Why can't I meet someone like that spaceship doctor?*

A familiar mechanical chirp interrupted her crush of a daydream. She looked at the old-fashioned phone replica on her grandmother's antique marble table. *One more chirp, and the answering machine gets it,* she thought while grinning at Dr. Wendy Powell on the large-screen TV. She picked up the remote and turned down the sound as Dr. Powell was giving the captain an experimental antidote to the illness he got during his space travels.

"Hi, you have reached 332-9981. Please leave the who, what, why, and when of your call after the beep."

Brooke made one of her ongoing but seldom-acted-upon mental notes. For heaven's sake, come up with a less nerdy message!

"Brooke," she heard Renee's voice start. "Brooke, pick up the phone. I know you're there. Come on, this is really, really important."

Reluctantly, Brooke answered. "It's always important, Renee, but when are you going to let me—"

"Brooke," Renee interrupted, "are you going to be home for a while?"

"Yeah."

"I'll be right over," her best friend said and hung up.

❧❧❧❧

Within twenty minutes, Renee Calderwood was pounding on the door. This time, Brooke put the TV on mute before leaving the room. She walked through the den, darkened by brown wood paneling. It had been her grandfather's room. Her friends thought it was too gloomy. "Why don't you put in a skylight or something, change this old carpet?" they'd ask. But she liked the feeling in the room. It was like Pops was still sitting there with her, even though he had been gone for several years. He was a man of few words, and in his den, she understood his silence.

The rest of the eleven-room house was much brighter. She walked down the hall with its showcase of family pictures. There was hardly a time when Brooke did not stop and spend time with them. She always began with her grandparents' black and white wedding picture. The one with the coral color added to their lips. Surrounding it were antique framed photos of her grandparents' siblings and their young children. Amid her ancestors were Brooke's treasured pictures of her parents. The photos scanned her mother's pre-marriage life, starting with her mom as a baby wearing that adorable smile. Then there was a picture of her mom as a toddler, which was right next to her photos of those classic awkward teen years when her mother looked like she had knocked something off a table or was about to.

These photos were Brooke's only visits with her family, and they gave her more than memories; they were her links to her origins. In them, she could see how she got her small ears and simple nose from her mom, and her crowned lips were pressed right from her father's charming smile. His photographic history started when they married. The picture of him with Grammie at the wedding, though, gave the appearance that they had known each other forever. Brooke believed her dad and his new mother-in-law captured that depth of familiarity because they both loved Brooke's mom so much. And that love gave their relationship more history than time shared. That picture also reminded Brooke of how her own dimples were the undistinguishable gift from her Grammie, as was her dark black hair, which waved back with a natural flow, always looking slightly windswept but professional enough for work. The mystery of how it stayed dark in the Phoenix sun or how it didn't show the birth of gray was forever between Brooke and her hairdresser.

Brooke's deep blue eyes connected her to one of

the few memories of her mother's voice: "Dear one, your eyes, the sea's magic lives in them."

Brooke looked at the picture of her parents with their first car. It hung next to the picture that saddened Brooke—her parents before their second honeymoon. They looked like they had just fallen in love as they stood at the airport before leaving for Europe. It was a look of adventure and romance instead of two people who would never return home to her again.

"Come on, Brooke," she heard Renee yelling.

"Okay, okay, come on in." Brooke flung the door open. Renee's light face was glowing from the Phoenix heat that didn't retreat even in the early evening. Beads of sweat gathered at the curly ends of Renee's short red hair. Renee was a typical Phoenician in a mad search for air conditioning, and she looked in need of it. Except for the cool expression in her eyes. Even the desert heat could not weaken the ever-present mischief in Renee's eyes. It was her trademark.

"Chicken teriyaki?" Brooke asked.

"You don't think I'm going to eat your famous cereal of the week, do you?" Renee rolled her dark eyes while working her way into the house.

The friends walked back to the den and ate this month's favorite takeout. They created a theme each month, and the Asian-made chicken had covered the last three.

"Thanks, Renee. I didn't realize how hungry I was."

"You never do, buddy. I have great news for you, me—us," Renee said as she watched Brooke's attention slip back to the television. "Will you turn that off? This is important."

"It's on mute. I'm listening. Go ahead."

"No. It doesn't matter if you can't hear it. I know I can't compete with that show. Besides, you've seen this episode before. Hell, you've seen them all before. Now turn it off."

"That doesn't matter. There's always something new to learn from these shows."

"Brooke, please," Renee pleaded like a little sister wanting her favorite toy.

Brooke reluctantly turned off the TV and leaned back in her grandpa's oversized chair.

"Guess what I picked up today," Renee started.

"A date with that woman you've been fantasizing about since you saw her two months ago?" Brooke guessed. She thought she had recognized that delight in Renee's voice as having secured an evening's date with a coveted stranger.

"No, better." Renee teased Brooke with her response.

Brooke stopped to look at her friend's eyes for a quick reading on the seriousness of this visit. Renee's voice had the "play" tone to it, but this wasn't like their usual conversations about dating. Brooke became more interested. "No date? But you have that spark, Rinkie," she called her, resorting to the name she used when in family mode. "What's up? What's in your hand?" Brooke took the paper in Renee's hand, but Renee pulled slightly back, wanting to control the tempo.

"Well, it's not a date yet," Renee reassured Brooke's instincts and her ability to interpret the tone in Renee's voice and the gleam in her eyes. "Brochures," Renee announced as she spread the information out on the coffee table.

"Is this another Meet-A-Date phone service? I know you didn't have me turn off Space Prairie for a lame dating service," Brooke warned.

"Like I put a gun to your head and told you to stay on that 'dial-a-dyke' number till three in the morning."

"Ouch. Okay, what is it this time?" Brooke asked with a hint of a blush.

Renee opened the colorful pictures of a large ship with women sunning themselves on the deck. It showcased a variety of women: young, middle-aged, and older. All were tan and beautiful. Brooke read the headline: "Escape to Paradise on Lez Cruise Line."

Brooke looked at her. "I've seen these before. A women's travel company, right?" Brooke perused the flyer.

"Look at the insert."

Brooke read out loud. "We are proud to announce our fifth all-lesbian cruise. The South Pacific awaits you and your dreams with lazy days at sea and romantic nights under the stars. This is interesting, Renee, really interesting."

"It's more than interesting, you data nerd. I called the travel agent. They've received over twenty-five hundred reservations, and more are coming in. The ship can take up to three thousand. This will be the greatest vacation of our lives! Brooke, I said, over twenty-five hundred lesbians out at sea together." She threw her hands up as if she scored a point in any sport.

"Don't you think most of them will be in couples?"

"Gosh, do you have to punch holes in it so quickly? No, I asked. So far, about thirty-five percent are single. Oh, sorry, I forgot who I'm talking to. That's thirty-five-point-seven percent, madam precise. Imagine, being out on the ocean, people waiting on us, entertainment, and single women! Oh, and you have to decide quickly, it leaves in four months, July 9, and it'll most likely be filled up by end of day tomorrow."

"That soon? How is it they have any rooms at all? This makes me suspicious of it," Brooke said.

"When I called, they said a huge posh wedding party canceled. I guess they broke up. Sad for them, happy for us. So, I, um, I…"

"You what, Renee? What did you do?"

"I didn't want to lose the suite, so I put down a deposit. And since it's so close, if you say no…I-I lose it." Renee ducked her head in anticipation of Brooke's unhappy response. But in hearing only silence, Renee continued. "Did I say that over eight hundred women on this trip are single? And if it's anything like couples at the bar, most of them will be single by the end of the trip anyway. Come on, buddy, let's do something fun. We're slowly morphing into these 'wholesome-polesome' dykes whose lives are nothing but work, racquetball, and looking at women from afar. Even our dating is less exciting than in our old Arizona State days."

"We are older. Most of our friends are in serious relationships. It's not like in our early twenties when everyone was content with dating. Let's face it, Rinkie, women our age are looking—no, desperately seeking— to be in a committed relationship. Now the first date ends with deciding whose house is more practical to move into and stopping by the rental company for a moving van. Everyone is looking."

"Aren't you?" Renee settled back into her chair.

"I'm looking, yes. I'm looking, looking for…"

"Yes, for what? What would make the incredibly beautiful and intelligent Brooke Kent happy? Please, the world is excitedly awaiting an answer to the million-dollar question."

"I'm looking for someone who makes me want to stop looking."

"Oh, the perfect woman." Renee rolled her eyes again. "That will ensure you never find her."

Brooke leaned forward in her chair. "No, not perfect, but someone who makes me smile at the mere thought of her. A woman who has me searching for her in a crowded room by the smell of her perfume in the air. A woman who makes me think twice about what I wear days before I'm with her. I'm talking about someone who gives me that glow of excitement that lasts long after the sex. I'll know her when I see her for the first time. I'll gaze into her eyes, the kind you make wishes on, and it'll feel like I'm looking at an old friend. Someone I've known through the ages, loved as long, and will continue to love into eternity."

"Sounds like a fantasy. A passing enchantment. Not someone you want to do the monogamy dance with." Renee giggled.

"No, Renee. When I look in her eyes, I'm not thinking about what it would be like to have our bodies naked next to each other like the image you approach most women with."

"What is it then? You want to wake up with her? Come home each day to her and raise kids with her? What?"

"I'm thinking about what it would be like to hold her hand. That's how I'll know that I've found my mate for life."

"Gosh, Brooke! Are you reading romance novels during your lunch break or what?"

Brooke flipped her off as only a best friend

could. "You asked. Sorry if I want to move forward, if I'm not stuck in some bar-hopping youth."

"That's right," Renee retorted. "I'm stuck there and damn proud of it. I miss our midday meetings at that deli by campus where we would solve the world's problems while checking out the women's swim team walking over to the aquatic center. We had life then. What happened to all that energy, that passion? We were ready to battle the institutionalized oppression of women during the day, dance at night, and have wonderfully intimate sex without settling into a lifetime of compromise and diminishing physical love. You bet I miss those days." Renee locked herself into her position by crossing her arms.

"I miss those days, too," Brooke almost whispered. "Mostly, I miss the dating. That was fun. I loved getting to know each woman, from the simplest, most superficial details of her life to all the complexities of her thoughts. All those unknown mysteries to explore in a single date." They smiled at each other at the memory of their college dating years, and Renee relaxed her arms.

"That truly describes you," Renee confirmed. "I remember when we double dated. Listening to how you got women to talk about themselves was like being with an archaeologist of emotions, slowly and carefully advancing through the layers of your date's life. Uncovering only the pieces of her being that she gave you permission to expose. And yet still finding out about her dreams and fears and hopes within a few hours of conversation."

"You make it sound like I stripped them of their inner beings. You missed the point. I had genuine interest in their dreams, hopes, and fears. I was honored that any woman would allow me to spend that time with her. It's the best intimacy. I truly enjoy hearing about another woman's life. I loved everything about those dating years, especially all those 'firsts.' The first time I'd ask someone out on a date, the initial decisions about where to go, what I'd wear, and endless wonder about whether there'd be that first kiss. Those firsts filled my life with excitement. Even though sometimes it was awkward, I miss that type of excitement now."

"You can still date. Those firsts are still out there," Renee reminded her.

"Yes, and I do date. Well, kind of. But the things we reveal to each other today are not as exciting or rejuvenating. When we were in college, women talked with optimism. Those enticing fluctuations have been preempted by complaints and worries. Unhappy at jobs, convinced they're not getting ahead because of all the sexism in the workplace, worries about paying back student loans, planning for vacations they never take. All that whining and woe is not the most attractive thing on a first date. It makes it hard to find her."

"The hand holder?" They both laughed.

"Brooke, before you choke on that self-righteous lollipop you're sucking on, let's talk about the fact that many women don't get advanced in their jobs because of sexism and that they have every right to worry about paying back loans because they make seventy-six cents on the male dollar. It's a statement of character that they work so hard to pay the loans back in the first place when many of their successful male counterparts dodge that responsibility. But we go forward trying to play by the rules and do the right thing."

Brooke responded calmly, expecting Renee's argument because she'd heard it many times before. And while Brooke considered it a recycled conversation, she was compelled to play out her part.

"And while we go forward, could we please spend time talking about things that are going well?" Brooke suggested. "I know the things you're talking about are true. But I also know that if misery is all you talk about, it's all you'll find. That's how we women cheat ourselves out of our right to peace and beauty. We fill our souls with our own pain so much that we leave no room for happiness. So, sure, tell me about your pain. I care about how that fits into your life. I absolutely care. But if you can't balance that with something positive, aspects of your own personal force, you'll give the gloom much more power than it already has."

Renee hardly let Brooke finish before she retorted. "You of all people know what that's like. Back then, we had each other to help find that balance. Hell, if we couldn't find it, we created it. In the college cloister, we knew where to find each other. We could room together, eat together, go out at night in large groups. It was all different then. Tell me, how many lesbians do you sit next to on the bus on those rare occasions when you take the bus to work? Or how many walk into the office with you from the parking lot? How many can you catch a quick lunch with? How many lesbians, work in the office next to yours, aren't hiding their lifestyle so much they can't even acknowledge that you have something in common with them? We're on our own. It's easy to get lost, down, and unbalanced. Speaking of that, how much of that balance did you achieve? Being an archaeologist of people was more like a one-way adventure."

Renee's argument switched direction and advanced before her common sense could stop it. To make things worse, she pointed her index finger at Brooke while unleashing those accusatory remarks. "You have that unique and deep understanding of others while only exposing the slimmest layer of yourself. You walk on the outskirts of people's lives, viewing, sometimes joining, but never becoming enmeshed with them. I never understood that." Renee stopped abruptly.

Brooke reached out and grabbed Renee's pointing finger, then leaned forward until they were almost face to face. With a cocked eyebrow, Brooke asked, "Is this your best plan to talk me into taking a trip with you?" Brooke ended the personality autopsy with this humor but got no answer. After a pause, they both laughed.

"Well, it's not exactly the bright and cheery cruise discussion I hoped for." Renee rolled her eyes. "We're sounding like those women you find so whiny. Let's view this as a positive thing. It might lighten things up with you. Come on, buddy, you've been so 'not you,' and it's…it's been over a year since your grandmother passed away."

Brooke's face grew hard, reminding Renee that she was entering a space where she already knew she was not welcome.

"Brooke, these are the words of a dear friend who loves you. Not someone trying to pry into your personal grief," Renee reminded both of them.

"I know." Brooke's face turned warmer. "You're half right. Part of my reservation is that loss and the sadness it has brought me. I guess more than sadness, I've deeply moved into my shell, not wanting to be part of it all. Hell, as you've pointed out, I was only half part of it before," Brooke conceded.

"Well, the more you're a part of it all, the more

you chance losing."

"Okay, enough of the psychoanalysis. How is it my best friend turned out to be fucking Anna Freud, anyway? Like I don't already know about loss." It was Brooke's turn to blurt out unedited thoughts.

"I swear, you're so turbulent," Renee said while acting scared. "I can tell right now that I want to back out of this conversation while I still have a reverse. Brooke, consider this, there may be 'balanced' women on the cruise. Maybe you'll find more of that for yourself. After all, there will be lesbians who are not thinking of a vacation, they're taking one—looking for fun, sun, happiness, and maybe a know-it-all to hold their hand."

"Do I have to room with you?"

Renee laughed. "No, you can pay double and get your own room. If you pay single, they'll put another solo traveler with you. Sweetie, it's a suite! One big bedroom with the option to split the bed into two, so I won't kick you all night. It has a living room area with TV, mini kitchen, our own bar, and large deck."

"It has been a long time since we went on a friends trip. Hell, you went into lockdown last year with all that Y2K Armageddon preparing."

"Hold the phone, my friend. While I may have been the only one of the two of us preparing for the complete shutdown of all electricity and computer-run equipment, we both know that had any of that been true, you would have come to live with me. I had the house generator, the gas stove, even the composting toilet. I was more than ready."

"That's right. We're into '01, what did you do with that thing?"

"I'll keep it for 2012."

"2012?" Brooke was confused.

"The Mayan calendar. Don't you read at all?"

"Apparently not survivalist journals. But I will think about this trip," Brooke said without emotion. "And I appreciate your wanting to get me back out into the world. But let's be honest. You want to go on this trip so you can meet women who live far away and who won't see you afterward. Those who can't make an honest lesbian out of you."

"Double ouch." Renee poked Brooke's arm.

"Got it. And I'll still think about it and let you know tomorrow."

Their conversation turned to more lighthearted things like stores they'd hit over the weekend and movies they wanted to see.

When they finished eating, Brooke walked Renee out, hugged her good night, and went into her shining kitchen. It was a large room where family members once met to cook and visit. Now it was just a sterile room for her to feel lost in. Standing at the sink, she looked at the oversized backyard and wondered why she didn't take that rest in the hammock. It swung so invitingly between the orange trees. Brooke looked over what was once a large orchard. She swore oranges only grew in California and Florida, and it must have been a mistake having these orange trees in her own backyard in Phoenix, Arizona. Of course, she was a little more accepting of the local grapefruits, but only because they tasted so good. Her thoughts mingled with the memories of her day as she contemplated this world of Southwestern citrus.

"Brooke, how's that cost benefit analysis coming along?" she remembered Arnold asking her, but she knew what he wanted to ask was, "Why are you taking so long? The executive housing meeting is in two weeks."

No, no, stop those thoughts. I'm on schedule with that report. Arnold was being his usual asshole self. He's so predictable, trying to convince me that I have a problem so he can help and play hero, but while he helps, he lets everyone else know why I need him so much. He does it to everyone at work. The new people get it the most.

Her thoughts darted between her workday and her home chores. I have to remember to get that new shower curtain for my bathroom. That fresh plastic reminds me of the smell of a new doll when I was a kid. Arnold asking me if I needed his help. What's with him anyway? Doesn't he have enough work of his own? He was a jerk like that in graduate school, and he's one at work. One of my past life karmas. I must have been ultra-mean to an insecure little boy, and in this life, we work together. What a nickel-dick. He sits in most meetings without an original thought and points out the deficiencies in everyone else. Why do other people like him? Or do they only act like it? Trying to stay on his good side so he doesn't criticize them, like anyone is immune from his eye for error. Jerk. The only time he's quiet at a meeting is when he takes a break and tries to secretly smell his fingers. Arnold? Doll-smelling shower curtains? Paranoid at work? Renee's right, I need to get away. Brooke sighed.

Chapter Two

Brooke looked out over the ocean, resting her elbows on the sun-warmed guard rail. The ocean was all she could see; the water melted into the horizon, mimicking her feeling. Her mind and spirit dissolved into each other, making her feel serene and connected to her heart. It was a long-awaited-for moment of peace and quiet in her otherwise noisy mind.

"Brooke, I finally found you," a familiar voice said. Brooke jerked back from her dazed position at the intrusion.

"Renee, you startled me," Brooke said, remembering that she inherited the term "startled" from her grandmother. There was a time in Brooke's life when those similarities embarrassed her, unlike now, when she felt proud to have any of her Grammie's mannerisms. "I've been here for a while. Not even sure how long. This is a wonderful place to lose myself."

"So you're glad you came?" Renee said eagerly.

"I already said you were right. What else do you need to hear?"

"Nothing. I love those words." They both smiled, and Renee put her arm around Brooke's shoulder. Both were facing the ocean with its vast bliss. Brooke didn't know if she wanted company even if it was her best friend in the universe.

"I've found a couple of potential dates for us. I saw a group of tanned and fit single women." Renee giggled.

"Fit? Renee, please stop talking about women as if they were ready to join the Army. You sound like a guy when you do that."

"Sorry. I guess when I see women that beautiful, it creates a pseudo-testosterone surge."

"You're incorrigible."

"So what does that make you, the best friend of an incorrigible dyke?"

Brooke answered with a slow half-grin. "Well, when do we meet all these single women?"

"I'm sure they'll be at the dance. It's the main event tonight. I guess they saved the big events until now. You know, things to keep us busy while we're out at sea. I don't think we get another port break for two days. It's weird not seeing any land, isn't it?" Renee didn't wait for her to answer. "Well, I still have time to scope out the ship. All these women and so little space in our tiny cabin! See you back at the room." Renee swung into her purposeful exit.

Brooke wondered how long it would take Renee to find every eligible single woman on the ship. She knew it would take up most of their conversations, and she'd let it. It was fun and a part of Renee's "playgirl" attitude, though it wasn't a part she liked very much.

Hoping for a quick nap to help get her through the night, Brooke went back to her room and dimmed the lights. *When did that happen? When did I start planning my daytime rest to ensure enough energy for the evening? I guess it was the same time I started taking all these over-the-counter precautionary drugs on my trip.* She looked at the "just in case" stomach and cold medicines crowding her tiny dresser top.

Brooke lay on her bed in disbelief that she was in

the South Pacific. I can't even feel the ship moving on the sea. The pillows smell like the ones at that Grand Phoenix Resort.

She reminisced about one of her date night hotel getaways. The kind that filled her with anticipation days before the date. She relaxed and slowly reached down to run her hand inside her shorts. Her fingers slid over her own juices, and she smiled at her touch.

It had been over a year since she had sex with someone else. And recently, thoughts of work sabotaged the enjoyment, and she mostly just drifted off to sleep. But not this afternoon, not after sitting by the sea and lying in a cabin that reminded her of those sexy hotel nights with loves that never lasted past checkout time. Her thoughts wandered into her favorite fantasy set in the athletic club back home.

Brooke walks into the racquetball court and plays alone as usual. She's wearing loose shorts around her small, muscular thighs. Hitting the ball to that repetitive rhythm, she turns around to make a shot off the back wall and notices that the door is ajar and that a racquet is poking in the court door.

"Yes, who's there?" Brooke asks.

"Hi, sorry to bother you, I was looking for a game. Interested?"

Brooke was rarely interested in a game. But this woman catches her attention, especially the way her bangs hang playfully at her eyebrows as a sexy introduction to her green eyes. Brooke glances away, concerned that this woman senses her attraction by Brooke's telling eyes. Trying to compose herself, she looks back at the stranger. Brooke's heart smiles as she notices the athletic woman's sculpted cheekbones, the kind Brooke likes to flutter her eyelashes over during foreplay. What is it about high cheekbones anyway? Is it some visual pheromone carried over from her ancestors dating back to Egyptian days? There's something about this stranger that makes Brooke feel like they've shared a tender intimacy. There's a closeness between them that fills the small court. Brooke feels a rush of excitement between her legs.

"Do you mind? I need the practice. My name's Cassandra. I was watching you play from the deck above. So are you interested?"

"Yes, very. I'm Brooke."

"Yes, I know. I've watched you play before," Cassandra says as she walks closer to shake Brooke's hand.

"A groupie, how lucky for me," Brooke nervously jokes.

"Give me a minute to warm up with a volley." As they practice, their bodies pass close to each other. Brooke can smell Cassandra's natural aromas, not loud with perfume or sweet with lotions. It's the smell that starts at the base of a woman's neck and wraps around her shoulders. Brooke tries to appear to be more interested in the game, but she's sure Cassandra can sense her distraction. They bump into each other and turn to see if harm has been done. At the moment their eyes meet, there's a loud explosion, and the lights go off in the entire athletic club.

"Must be one of those monsoon storms," Brooke says with an unsure voice.

"Best if we stay here," Cassandra agrees. She takes Brooke's hand and intensely guides her across the court until Brooke is against the wall and their racquets fall to the floor. Brooke can sense the vibrations from Cassandra's body leaning close to her but not touching her. She's breathing hard, half from the game and half from the heat of the moment. Cassandra's hands gently press against Brooke's shoulders as she kisses her lips lightly. With the next kiss, their bodies pressed together. Cassandra slides her thigh between Brooke's legs, and Brooke slides back and forth, sensing the strength of her leg. Cassandra moves her hand down from Brooke's shoulder and across her breast, stopping to stroke her nipple. Her touch is soft enough to be exciting and hard enough to make Brooke want more. They kiss again. Cassandra's tongue skates across Brooke's loosely parted lips, then tenderly enters her mouth until their lips tighten around each other. Brooke opens her mouth wider until Cassandra's warm tongue fills her. Cassandra reaches inside Brooke's shorts, teasing her tight clit. Brooke wants to slow and speed up to take in all of Cassandra at the same time. She spreads her legs and leans hard against the wall while stroking Cassandra's hair. Cassandra moves her hand deeper into Brooke's shorts.

The lock clicking on the bedroom door made Brooke jerk her hand out of her shorts and sit up, trying to appear as though she was simply sitting in bed.

"Hey, what's up?" Renee intruded.

Brooke's shallow breathing made it hard for her to answer. "I'm trying to find some privacy."

"Were you doing the nasty? Don't you hate it when your best friend breaks your rhythm? I'll leave." Renee turned around.

"No, you bitch, somehow I really can't recapture the moment now."

"I'm sorry." Renee laughed. "Gee, I can finish it off anywhere. Well, almost anywhere. There was the time…" Renee rambled on while grinning, which only made Brooke more embarrassed.

"Oh, I hate you," Brooke muttered as she brushed by Renee on her way to the bathroom. But they both knew that wasn't true. Renee was strong, fun, and honest. She spoke what was on her mind and walked the edge of being obnoxious during her quest for fun. It was what Brooke needed, this exact type of energy to pursue excitement. It could make Brooke get up off the couch, turn off Space Prairie, and do something. Renee was her real lifeline, a breath of fresh air in Brooke's introverted, thinking world. She was a dear friend. They'd shared fun times together and difficult tragedies. She was a love but never a lover. Brooke had never thought of her that way. Renee was too much like the sibling she never had. Though Brooke noticed Renee was attractive and almost too "cute" for Renee's raw personality. Brooke saw that unique Renee Calderwood playfulness in her eyes. It reminded Brooke not to take the world so seriously. Though she'd never admit it, Brooke really enjoyed being a tad taller than Renee. The sting of her best friend's teasing got muted as she had to look up to Brooke.

❧❧❧❧

Brooke walked out of the bathroom with a thick towel wrapped around her body.

"Okay, what's on tonight's agenda?"

"First, a formal dinner and then the dance and always the search for that perfect date. A 'good time' for me and a 'hand-holder' for you," Renee predicted.

"We should come up with a system for the bedroom," Renee continued. "I don't want to walk in on you in the middle of…" Renee made a noise that always bothered Brooke. She moved her tongue against the inside of her lower lip, sounding like a woman's juices as her lover's fingers moved in and out of her.

"That is so disgusting."

"It wouldn't be as bad as me walking in on you all by yourself," Renee replied.

"You butthead." Brooke threw a robe at her. "Anyway, whoever gets here first gets the room."

"What if the first one here is alone and the other brings a date?" Renee presented.

"Too bad. If I'm here first and you bring someone back, just keep walking. I'm not getting up and out to make room for you and a date."

Renee pointed her index finger at her. "Same if I get here first, and you, by some miracle, bring home a date."

"Deal," they said and did their own high five. Instead of hitting, their hands passed over each other, almost not touching at all.

☙ ❧ ☙ ❧

Brooke walked into the dining room wearing a pale white silk pantsuit with a sheer blue top. The style was made for her with its clean lines at the waist and tailored cut around her ankle. Her mom passed on that sense of classic style and the height to pull it off. She styled her silky black hair like a socialite in the roaring twenties. For this special occasion, she wore light lipstick on her crowned lips. And anchoring the whole classic style together were her sparkling blue eyes, made even more radiant by the matching shirt. She walked with a confidence she genuinely didn't know she had, so it was never overused.

The dining room looked like it was set up for royalty. Brooke was impressed by the fine details. The tables were covered with white silk cloths that shimmered against the soft lit room. They were set with the ocean liner's own silverware. Each large table had a candle centerpiece surrounded by small green and purple glass balls, making the room simply elegant.

It struck Brooke as wonderful and sad—wonderful to be treated with this attention and sad that it was the exception to her social dining life instead of the rule. She briefly thought of dinners at fine restaurants in Phoenix where she and a date were seated at the worst tables. I should quit my job and open a restaurant for women only, she added to her mental list of possible things to do with the rest of her adult life. Men can eat there once a week to deal with legal access problems. But it should be a place where lesbians are treated like they are on this night, like special customers instead of an embarrassment to the establishment. It was a new millennium after all. How much longer did they have to wait for their place in this type of heaven?

The room seemed to go on forever, filled with the ripples of beautiful tables. Each sat ten and as with every meal, staff escorted each woman to a randomly selected table. They always ate with someone new unless chance helped them to sit with the same person more than once. It caused the women to mingle in a way that didn't occur naturally. Of course, couples and groups were seated together. It was even possible to go in, get your food, and go back to your room. Usually, the seasick women had someone bring food to them in their rooms. Otherwise, everyone cherished the opportunity to dine with hundreds of other lesbians.

Brooke checked in on her feelings via her most

often used point of reference—a TV show. This is like I'm a character in an old black and white sci-fi flick. I'm the last person on earth, and I'm in a small town. The houses have perfectly arranged furniture, cupboards have food, stores sit with clothes on the racks, a school has books and desks, there are seats in houses of worship and historical pictures in the town meeting hall. Everything is clean and perfectly placed in this quaint place—quaint but void, empty place. My only companions are my thoughts, the echo of my footsteps, and the sound of my breathing. It's so strange, but more unusual is me not questioning where everyone else is. I'm just standing there looking at the varying shades of gray and white and listening to nothing as if it were perfectly normal.

Then one day, everything is colorful, and my house is filled with friends. Stores are packed with shoppers searching for that too-good-to-be-true sale. Children laugh on the playground. There's a choir practicing for service, and the town hall is filled with opinions from local politicians.

Yes, that's what this is like. A dead, dark town brought back to life by the company of other lesbians. Lesbians who are different, but who all share the fact that they, like me, once lived in that gray empty town and are now part of this floating colorful world of women.

Brooke and Renee sat toward the middle of the room. Three women were already at their table. Two were "wise women," as Brooke liked to call seniors. They appeared to be a couple, but at first sight, it was hard to know for sure. The third woman was athletic-looking and was about the same age as Brooke and Renee. She was wearing the white pin given to all the single women so they could identify one another. Renee proudly wore hers on her chest. Brooke refused to put hers on because it made her feel branded. Other women were gradually seated at the table until it was full.

"Let's jump right into the statistics," one of the wise women proposed.

"Statistics?" asked another.

"Yes, let's run through the answers to the usual 'getting to know who's at your table' questions. You know, name, place of origin, single or not, first cruise—the laundry list of questions asked at almost every meal or other encounter on this trip." They all laughed with acknowledgment. She continued while directing her comments at each stranger at the table, looking them in the eye without hesitation or discomfort.

"The sooner we get through them, the quicker we can get to the fun conversations. I'll start. I'm Kate, from McAllen, Texas. Retired now from the telephone company. This is my partner of twenty years—you can all applaud later—her name is Mildred, but everyone calls her Millie. She manages condos at a seniors gated community. Yes, in some ways, this is our first all-women's vacation. We travel a lot with a rather large group of friends, but this is the first one set up by a company. Yes, I love it. Yes, I would do it again. No, I don't know where next year's trip is going." They all laughed at how accurately she foresaw the first forty minutes of the evening, for those were the exact questions broached by every gathering of strangers on the ship.

Brooke noticed how much Kate and Millie looked alike. Both wore their graying hair short and behind their ears. Both had brown eyes. Their noses were different, and each were comfortably larger women. The sun was starting to turn their fair skin pink. They even reached for their drinks at the same time and placed them back on the table in unison. They reminded Brooke of that old saying, the one about how lesbians either start to resemble each other or their dogs.

"So what are the 'fun' conversations?" Renee asked. "You said once we get the stats out of the way, we'll get to the fun stuff. I'm curious what that means."

"Not yet, we have other people who need to run through their introductions," Kate said.

"Well, I'm Brooke, all the way from Phoenix, Arizona, where I work as a data analyst for the city's public housing department. Yes, it's my first trip. Yes, so far, I'm lovin' it. This introduction makes me feel like a game show contestant."

"Brooke?" asked Millie. "You're not wearing the single pin. Is your partner with you, or are you traveling incognito?"

"I'm pin shy, and yes, single."

"And I'm her single friend, Renee. I also work for the city of Phoenix in the parks department. I manage youth programs and special youth events. First trip, love it, and can't wait for the next."

"I'm Marie."

"Marie O'Brien, the golfer?" Renee interrupted.

"Yes. And I'm flattered that you recognized me. I've been on three other trips. My white pin also gives away my status. I think this is the only way to vacation. Spending time with other lesbians."

"Don't you do that on the golf circuit?" Renee was visibly curious about Marie's famous life.

"I should have qualified my answer. I mean spending time with lesbians who are out and doing all those secret dyke things they don't do on the circuit. Like holding hands and kissing and gazing into each other's eyes. Nope, none of that on the eleventh hole at the National Women's Classic. I love these trips."

"Me too. I play golf, but I suck," another diner joined in. "My name is Dawn. I'm working on my master's degree in business and have an undergraduate degree in architecture. I go to the University of Oregon in Eugene. I guess my game is so bad because you can only play golf in Oregon when it's not raining, both days a year." They all laughed. Dawn's long and thin sandy blond hair covered much of her narrow face. It barely showed her brown eyes and thick eyebrows. Her clothes were rather bohemian, or neuro-hippy, as Brooke liked to call it. "My parents gave me this trip in celebration of my doing so well my first year of grad school. They're cool people. Like all of you, I love this. I wish it would never end." She turned to the woman sitting next to her. "And you?"

"Me? I want your parents to adopt me. I'm happy to meet all of you. My name is Nina. I live in Nogales, Arizona, which is a border town with Nogales, Mexico. I own a small but growing import business. We bring curio items up from Mexico and sell to U.S. companies, mostly hotels and restaurant franchises that want a Latin theme. This is my second trip. I love being around other lesbos. I'm surprised by the diversity of women on these trips. Mostly, the age and employment differences and some diversity in culture like me. I'm glad my naturally tanned Latina hermanas are spoiling themselves."

But Nina was more than tan. Her skin had a natural olive glow. She was one of the few women at the table with long thick hair. The weight of it would have overshadowed her petite face, but she wrapped it up, which exposed her gorgeous eyes. She had a natural look that Brooke's straight girl friends would covet. Brooke could almost hear their voices. "How does she get her skin to be so perfect?" She was sure many would ask Nina that question upon an introduction. It was part of their unknowing insensitivity, a probing not many of them could keep to themselves or understand why white women shouldn't do that.

"I'm Amber, Nina's friend from Nogales. Glad to say I've met a lot of other Arizonians," Amber shared while gesturing toward the other Southwestern guests. She was the most animated in the group. "Not sure about the rest of you desert rats, but this trip was more financially workable for me. Some of the European lesbian trips looked inviting, but this was more in line with my teacher's salary. I teach elementary school." Amber took a quick breath. "So you can imagine, a small border town elementary school teacher doesn't get much of an opportunity to be out in the open with other lesbians, which makes me appreciate this trip. I can't remember when I had this freedom and honesty with myself." Amber gave much more detail than Brooke expected. Brooke thought Amber was a lovely contradiction. Her voice sounded young, more like a student teacher who was innocent and not sure about where to stand in the classroom rather than an experienced teacher. But her physical presence was commanding and sure of herself.

"Why do you stay in a small town?" Marie asked. "I mean, the social options are so limited."

"I've lived in larger cities. Lesbian elementary school teachers are in job-loss jeopardy no matter where we live. At least in Nogales, I get that small-town feeling. And it's predominately a Latino culture. I love that feeling, like I'm at home no matter where I am. Besides, Tucson is about an hour away. We go up there for our gay outings. It's not that big of a deal, not like two women together for over twenty years." She turned to Kate and Millie. "Now that breaks all the clichés. I'm impressed at the longevity of your relationship. Twenty-plus years, that's like thirty-five in gay years. You're a single woman's inspiration and hope! So I'll ask the obvious: How?"

Millie began, "We were best friends from the beginning, we grew together, and—"

Kate joined in, "We have great sex. What else do you need?"

"Okay, back up," Nina said. "Great sex after twenty years? My attempts at long-term relationships all have sex shelf-lives of half a year. Then it's like we become roomies. I have to ask you, how do you do that?"

"We buy erectile-dysfunction meds in a hand lotion," Kate joked with the group, and Millie lovingly rolled her eyes. "It's simple. We have the longest-running love affair."

Millie broke in. "She has a one-track mind. It's not all about sex, although I'm not complaining about that." She smiled at Kate and took her hand. "I think we found that balance between things we do on our own and joint projects we do together. It's helped us to make time for each other, and we keep learning new things and growing together instead of apart."

"What kind of projects?" Amber asked.

"Well, for one thing, we're working on a cookbook together. We're going to call it What Do Lesbians Like to Eat?" Kate replied.

Millie gave Kate a love pat on her shoulder. "Oh, we are not. Be serious for one moment, you goofball. In the past, we've done things like joining the Rainbow Runners, a group of lesbians who travel around the country in their RVs. It's fun. We've met new people and traveled together. We've done community projects, mostly around homeless issues, in different towns around the country. It's our way of giving back to the considerate people we met along the way. And now, we're working on planning a retirement village for senior lesbians."

"Yeah, we're thinking about calling it Bushwhackers Estates," Kate jumped in, sending the group into more laughter.

"We are not. Stop saying that. I dislike that term. You are such a goofball."

"I know. I just love to see people's faces every time I say it." Kate smiled and hugged Mille, who continued.

"Anyway, we know a lot of women who are retired or close to. The whole thing is such a new venture for us, but we'll make it happen."

Marie was genuinely interested. "Let me know. Even though it's about fifteen years away for me, unless I quit the golf world early, I still think about what I'll do. I would absolutely love to retire around other lesbians. Not too sure about Texas as my resting place, though. Don't they have lesbian hunting season there?"

"The 'where' is the biggest question," Kate agreed.

"Arizona!" Brooke, Renee, Nina, and Amber all said together.

"We thought about going to your desert state," Kate said. "But we don't want to live in such a politically conservative place."

Brooke smiled. "Yes, conservative, but also still clinging to the eighties me-ism era. Even twenty years later, folks are still so interested in their jobs, how they look, how tan they are, whatever, that they aren't aware of our presence, what we're doing, or even how many of us there are. It's great. You could build Lesbo World with all the amusement rides, and they wouldn't notice unless you either asked them to pay taxes for it or told them they couldn't use their sprinklers to conserve water for the complex. That would get their attention. Otherwise, dykes away!" The group shared more laughter.

"I'd suggest you check out Eugene, but it's not the best place for lesbians. Maybe other parts of Oregon," Dawn said, and her brief comment brought silence to the chatty table.

Everyone looked stunned until Nina finally asked, "What, Eugene? Everyone I've ever met talks about Eugene as a lesbian's haven. It's supposed to be like the P-town of the Pacific Northwest."

"Well, I was disappointed when I started college there," Dawn continued while pushing her hair away from her face, only to have it fall again, "for a couple of reasons. The scariest was how it threw off my otherwise keen gaydar. I would see a woman who I was sure was lesbian—short-haired, plaid flannel shirt-wearing, self-assured woman. Then she'd be with a man and kids. All those lovely down-to-earth women, and they'd turn out to actually be straight. It was weird at first, but then I got to know a few of them, and now they're the most wonderful friends I have, and I gotta admit, many of them are married to great husbands. That's the real secret of Eugene. It's home to the coolest guys I've ever met. They deeply cared about their wives and took their kids with them everywhere, bike riding, the movies, even the golf course." She nodded at Marie. "And when I talk to them, it's not like they're looking around to see who's watching. They focus on what I'm saying. They listen and respond with thoughtful comments. I would never fall for them. Not into men, but I get why those straight women do.

"So yes, in years past, Eugene was known as the lesbian mecca of the country. But its hidden claim to fame is being home to some of the best-raised men I've ever met. They found a key to unlocking the dichotomy of male/female roles and instead create a blending of loving people who care about others, and most of all, people who care about their family and friends. Knowing them helped soften my more jagged radical side founded on the principle that all guys are out to hurt women.

"But the lesbo stuff—please. That haven for lesbians in the fifties through the early nineties has been silenced. We don't even have a 'women only' meeting place, not even a standard issue dyke bar. There's one mixed gay bar, although a lot of straight college students go there. I'm not sure if it's fun or I'm desperate for queer company. Hard to believe that now in 2001, there isn't one place for women to be with other women in such a liberal place. I remember when I visited Phoenix," she gestured to the Phoenicians sitting by, "there were three women's bars in the middle of conservative cowboy country."

"It's that me-ism thing I was talking about," Brooke restated. "Don't ask me to support your rights, and I won't tell you to go away: the state's straight motto to gays."

Dawn continued, "Eugene's politics create

different issues. Its ultra inclusive environment with an 'everyone is welcome' vibe is a detriment to having women-only spaces. It's seen as segregation. A guy once sued the city for sponsoring a women's only dance. He felt that as a feminist he wanted to support the event. His legal maneuver is the strangest support I've ever seen."

"I'd have a hard time with that." Nina frowned. "I may have to travel an hour to Tucson to find a bar for women, but at least I can find one."

"It's like the rain, I guess," Dawn replied. "You actually like it, get used to it, or leave. It keeps a lot of the Californians away. And that's the goal of every Oregonian," Dawn added while laughing. "Anyway, it's worth it to me to live in a place of political fervor. Citizens get involved in everything from protesting tree cutting at a city park to opposing or supporting a major computer company setting up shop in our town. Everyone has an opinion, and they don't hesitate to voice it. I love that level of interest and involvement. We have other things in our favor that places like Phoenix don't," Dawn said, becoming defensive of her home, "like drivers who stop for pedestrians and slow down to let you merge into traffic, even in holiday traffic. And we can shower for over ten minutes unlike you in your drought seasons."

"Stop, stop," Nina cried. "Not the nice drivers and long showers. I surrender! I'm sorry I ever mentioned the bar!" They laughed for a long while; some wiped away the laughter-made tears from their eyes.

"Honey," Kate said, looking at Mille. "We should tell the Rainbow Runners to head to Oregon next summer and raise hell in Eugene by having an all-women's dance by the RV park. Or maybe instead of the retirement village, we should open a women-only bar in Eugene."

"No, sounds like we'd spend a lot of time in court with open-minded males," Millie countered.

Brooke wanted to change the tone. "Well, it may sound corny, but you two are an inspiration, not only for your longevity, but also for your obvious ongoing affection for each other."

"It's not corny," Millie said. "I'm proud of us. Of the fact we've been together so long, we've stayed physical—"

"Why don't you ever say sexual?" Kate half teased as she cupped her hands around Millie's cheeks. "You're an adult, you can say things like that."

"Hush, I'm talking now." Millie rubbed the top of Kate's head. "Anyway, we've been through all the joys of a long life along with all the grief it brings, especially in saying goodbye to those we've lost. By a grace beyond us, our journey brought us closer to each other versus pushed us into other women's arms. We also have similar interests and values. And like I said, the Fates smiled on us. It would all be perfect with our being able to legally marry."

"One day, my love. I know it'll happen one day."

"I hope we're here to see it."

"Me too." Kate wanted to lighten the moment. "And don't forget the never-ending attraction."

Millie blushed. "More importantly, that grew no matter what our bodies moods were—thin years, average years, overweight years. Whatever. We're drawn to each other. I know we're not skinny minnies like some of the youngins' here. But I enjoy every inch of her. And me too. Hell, I wasted too much time in life worried about my weight."

"It's sad that many of us still worry about something like that. I think that's hard for all women. Those relentless messages we grow up in—the ultra-thin dolls, the models, the starving actresses," Dawn listed. Then she pushed back her long hair, and everyone could see the seriousness in her face.

"Though it isn't as bad with lesbians," Marie casually commented.

"I couldn't care less about all that plastic-doll measurement BS," Dawn said.

"But-but," Renee challenged Dawn. "I mean, you are thin."

"Yes, but that's more a byproduct of my politics and eating habits, my choice. Not at all from something forced on me by a list of what women should look like. I'm one of those sandals-wearin', veggie-eatin', down-to-earth dykes," Dawn informed the group.

"Who's studying architecture?" Renee asked, suggesting it was an unlikely mix.

"Yes, my area of interest is low-energy, and even energy-producing homes and buildings."

"That's great," Brooke offered and cut off any more of Renee's attempts to call Dawn on contradictions she didn't have. "I admire women who try to live and work by their politics. I think it's a hard thing to do. Every day, we're asked to compromise. Sometimes in significant ways. Sometimes in ways we don't notice because we've made adjustments slowly and over long periods of time, so it feels normal. I know I face that in public employment all the time. I make decisions as best as my ethics will allow. I know I've gone too far when there's something in the mirror at the end of the day that I don't like. Fortunately, that doesn't happen often. And, yes, obviously, for me, those choices include being a thin person. But for the record, I preferred playing with the Ken doll."

"He was thin, too," Dawn joked.

The group continued to talk about body size and weight as if they were immune to the straight world's emphasis on the perfect appearance, though their toned bodies said otherwise. Brooke listened, and at some point, her polite grin turned into a genuine smile. The energy that night charged her with new emotions and gave a jump start to old ones that had been muted by her grief.

She perused the room and the women checking out one another. At a table next to them was a group of women who looked like soccer moms. She remembered seeing many of them at various social activities on the ship. The type who wore all the classic suburban clothes—any denim as long as it was expensive, white shirts with starched collars pointed up to their cheekbones, then out to the horizon, an array of expensive but classic-looking necklaces and bracelets that matched their beaded vests—it was all part of their gated community uniform. Their hair was always flawless, but their efforts were used by most of the women in that room. They didn't have perms or used an extra hour with sprays and curling irons of all sizes. The stylish cuts they wore required little effort. They paid to have it fall with elegance. On special occasions, like before this trip, Brooke treated herself to one of those cuts. Usually, she felt gawky at the hip salons. Each of the soccer moms was attractive; something about their clothes, that natural-looking makeup, and their self-assurance all combined in an appearance that ranged from cute to unbelievably beautiful.

Brooke glanced past Marie and then back to

her. A tiny spark grew into an enchanted glow in her soul. It was such a simple feeling that brought flutters of sexual emotion over her. Brooke fantasized about walking over to Marie, leaning her lips against her ear and saying, "You can have me for an hour or a lifetime." And she grinned at her naughtier side. Wow, where did that come from? She quickly knew the answer. Marie had that athletic sexiness about her, like a golfer who'd walked courses filled with sunshine and fresh air, a beauty that caught Brooke's weakness for that natural "country" charm. She was firm where it mattered but soft to Brooke's wandering eye and, she imagined, to the touch. Her sandy hair was short with a hint of a wave away from her natural look. No makeup, no fake tan, and a healthy look of someone who liked life and who was liked by it in return. A few friendly wrinkles rested next to her large brown eyes. Brooke looked for what she considered the most important feature for a lesbian—Marie's hands—and reacted with an unplanned but quickly concealed gasp. Marie had those long, sexy fingers with what Brooke could only imagine was a skillful grip.

Brooke liked those lustful feelings almost as much, maybe more, than actually having sex because they continued for as long as her daydream allowed. And it had been much too long since there was such a focus. She briefly thought about thanking Marie for rekindling that primitive feeling. She imagined going up to Marie and whispering, "Hi there, thanks for making me feel like a lustful teen again." But that would mean looking rather unstable at best and a sex addict at worst. Those fears, however, didn't keep her from smiling at Marie, who smiled back.

Brooke watched the famous golfer sign a couple

of autographs for women who approached their table. Some of them were shy and uncomfortable. Others ran up to Marie like they were meeting an old friend. The exchange woke Brooke up from her lustful dream because Marie gave each of them that polite, warm smile she had flashed at Brooke. It made Brooke feel like one of many nameless women Marie must deal with. Yuck, I'm not one of those types of fans. I'm not like that. I'm not interested in her because she's famous. I'm interested in her because…because she's… Okay, maybe I am like those women. Drawn to her without knowing her. But it's an innocent crush, not a fan thing. I'm different. Brooke almost blushed with the embarrassment of her commonality.

She turned her attention to the room full of women doing the rubberneck dance. So many of them were glancing past the person they were talking to and looking at who was at the next table. Heads were turning every which way to see who was there, who was looking in their direction, who they might want to meet, to crush on. It was such a high frequency that most forgot to conceal their wandering looks. Everyone, even the paired women at one time or another, glanced across the room to catch that warm glow of "wow, a universe of lesbians." Brooke thought about how that would be a felony if a room full of straight guys did it to their girlfriends. But on this night, in this place, there was an unofficial clemency for cruisin' granted by all here who understood the freedom of finally having this life, color in their otherwise black and white towns.

❦ ❦ ❦ ❦

Dinner was winding down. Kate and Millie were

the first to leave Brooke's table. They wanted to get to their room to get ready for the big dance that evening. Brooke watched Kate pull the chair out for Millie and help her with her dress jacket. Their relationship seemed to have everything she was looking for.

"I so much enjoyed meeting you. I hope we get together again," Brooke said.

"Oh, we will," Millie answered. "We seek out people we like to spend time with. Let us know if it gets bothersome. Otherwise, we'll invite you to all types of activities with us."

"Do any of them involve hand lotion?" Renee winked.

Millie gave her an endearing smile. "Now you remind me of someone I knew twenty years ago."

"You still know her," Kate said with a hug. "See you all at the dance."

"Hey, Brooke, want to head back to get ready?" Renee asked.

"Sure. In a second." She was still absorbing a perfect evening with new and old friends, crushes, and fun.

"Brooke, what's wrong? Are you feeling okay?" Renee asked. "Brooke, hello."

"Yes, yes, I'm fine. Let's get back to the room. I want to get ready for the dance."

"Right, the dance. What will I wear?" Renee muttered every woman's worry, even those who had already picked out clothes for the evening.

⁂

Back at their suite, Brooke methodically took her clothes out of the closet. She was sure each outfit would be perfect. But it wasn't, so she moved on to the next with the same expectation. Soon, several outfits were spread out over the bed. She tried variations of pants with shirts, jackets, and shoes.

"I'm going to take a shower," Renee said, "while I can still navigate my way across this room. I love your style, Brooke, but did you have to bring half your wardrobe? You've got clothes everywhere, and your closet is still filled."

When Renee got out of the shower, she found the room filled with clothes, shoes, and music that reminded her of college. They exchanged what clothes they could, mostly tops, and danced their way around the cabin. Brooke had only gone out a handful of times over the last couple of years, and each time, her pre-date preparations were banal. She would turn on the music, take a shower, let her hair air dry whichever way it wanted, put on a little makeup, and wear whatever wasn't too wrinkled.

This night was different. Her interest was back. Brooke embraced the lesbian evening-out ritual of finding the right outfit, taking a long shower while inspecting the strength of her own body, letting the hairdryer create her customized wave, finding the right outfit again and again. Brooke also created her fun to-do list as she got ready: go out more often, play more music in the house, dance like no one is watching, check out my naked body like everyone is watching. Again, she smiled at her impish thoughts.

She decided on a sage silk top with black jeans and black boots. Renee smiled at her choice. For her night out, Renee picked her "studly" outfit of jeans, white tennis shoes, black shirt, and her favorite white blazer. Brooke loved how Renee gave even that worn eighties look a hint of fun.

Women were scattered down the hallways on the way to the ballroom. Brooke walked down the hall with a light bounce next to Renee. She looked at most of the women and gave a smile that said, "Hi, glad to be here, glad you're having fun, would love to stop and chat with each one of you, but I'm having so much fun I have to keep moving to see what happens next."

As they got closer to the room, they could see the lights and hear the music. Without knowing it, Brooke began to lip sync to music she remembered from her bar-hopping days, unlike today's music, which she didn't recognize and certainly couldn't dance to. It made her happy just to be there. It all was like a surprise party, a night filled with unexpected gifts like this, the music of her college days, surrounded by happy lesbians and the scent of women, a mix of perspiration, perfume, and occasionally men's cologne.

She leaned over to Renee's ear. "This is great! Let's get a drink."

"I'll get them. Do you want your usual blue blood drink?"

"Yes, a cognac would be perfect," she answered and noticed the smile on Renee's face. She too was happy for all the same reasons and with the added joy of her best friend's rebirth.

Brooke walked around the large room with Renee, drinks in hand. The two of them embraced the fullness of the evening. Brooke loved to watch people. It reminded her of her early bar days when she would make Renee play the "guess the profession" game she made up. They'd point out a woman in the bar and try to guess what she did for a living. "P.E. teachers are a gimme," they used to laugh. Brooke was a champion at it. Not only did she guess the profession, but she'd also create lavish stories about their lives, where they lived, how many partners they'd had. Of course, they never knew if their stories were anywhere near reality. But Brooke's versions of those strangers' lives were always convincing.

Tonight, Brooke's inclination to categorize people was somewhat subdued, replaced by a desire to be a little more part of the group instead of the evening's commentator. But that role couldn't last long. It went against her natural calling, which was about to take over. She saw other women enter the room, alone, others in couples who were holding hands or walking arm in arm. All were smiling and excited to be part of something this grand, and their excitement filled the room with the energy of lesbians at their best.

Brooke watched people dancing alone along the edges of the dance floor. There were, of course, couples and even groups of dancers, so no one was sure who was with whom. Brooke watched those women who were trying hard to make the evening last while filling every second to the brim. There were older women dancing in a circle, moving into its center with their arms high in the air and then dropping them by their sides as the circle moved out again. Brooke noticed a young couple dancing and who seemed to forget that they weren't in a motel room, dancing the sex dance with their bodies moving to the rhythm of the music. She smiled. Gosh, you couldn't pour water between the two of them.

Then there were women like Brooke and Renee on the sides of the room taking in the dancers. Some of them tried to talk in each other's ears to be heard above the music. But not Brooke and Renee. They were happy with people watching, and one woman made it extremely easy. Brooke watched her walk into the ballroom like she was the evening's mascot. She wore clothes that made a room full of lesbians turn their heads in lust. Her jeans rested on her hips with comfort—loose enough to be welcoming, tight enough to be alluring. When her suede vest fell open, there was a small designer emblem on her well-pressed shirt. Her clothes moved with her as she walked through the room with a sexy confidence and a secretive smile. Brooke watched the entire room turn to follow her as if it were a natural part of their dance moves.

How can these be the same types of women I know back home? Here, they're relaxed and wanted, but back home, at family gatherings, they can be so painfully out of place. How can that same suede vest make a woman longed for here and yet shunned at her parents' Christmas dinner? "How could you wear such a thing tonight of all nights? You look like a boy. You knew we were having company." One family member's critique, at some point, belonged to every lesbian in that room.

Brooke knew many peers who had to deal with those emotionally brutal inquisitions. They believed they were dressed wonderfully, and tonight's lesbians proved them right. But at that holiday meal, their closest family members announced otherwise and put a burning spotlight on something intended to be stunning. Then Brooke smiled again. Fortunately, the echo of those families' voices could not be heard here. The music was much too loud, and the crowd of strangers were lovingly more accepting than their kin.

Brooke turned to Renee and unexpectedly hugged her. The two of them were giddy. They walked around until they found the premium bar table, one positioned so they could watch the dance floor action but maintain enough distance to hear each other. "As I promised," Kate said as she and Millie joined them. "Told you we'd keep an eye out for you all."

"I wish they'd play more Motown," Kate reminisced. "I love that music. It's much more fun to dance to than this."

"I'll request it for you," Renee said and left the table.

"Requests, now that's a lost art of the dance floor," Millie said, and she and Kate hugged. "Hey, look, there's Marie."

Marie was standing by a rail looking at the dancers. Some women came up to her for autographs, and she smiled and signed them. She even hugged many of them. Brooke thought that was classy. Marie wasn't a rich jock who thought she was too good for the little fans. She was nothing like Rosewater, the other famous women on the trip. Rosewater, a musical duet, was part of the cruise entertainment along with a comedian and an up-and-coming actress. But Rosewater was by far the most famous. The two of them were legends in the women's music business. Every lesbian had a favorite Rosewater song, the one that was popular when they first came out of the closet or the one they played the first time they made love with a woman. Rosewater was so much a part of that lesbian blossoming time that most were sure they knew the musicians in a way that was as intimate as the memories their music created.

By Brooke's observations, however, Rosewater wanted no part of that association. Brooke watched them on the trip as they ate alone at their private table. All the other entertainers ate alongside the passengers. It wasn't only their choice of dining places that bothered

Brooke. She thought they went out of their way to be rude to the women who made them famous. Brooke even overheard one of them telling the rising comedian entertainer, "You'll have fun, but the fans can be a pain. You'll sit there after a performance and hear the same thing over and over." She mimicked them to make her point. "'I love your work. Are you two together? Are you single? I can so relate to your song Freewoman.' It gets so old. Just sign the autographs and get through the line as soon as you can to keep a piece of yourself private."

Brooke wondered what made them so hard over the years. Perhaps it was too invasive of women to treat the singers like their best friends because one of their songs was an important part of their history. Perhaps it was rude of the fans, but did they have to be so cold in return? The contrast between the famous duet and the world-known golfer was extreme. Then Brooke added another note to her often forgotten list: I must spend less time being so critical and simply not spend time with people I don't respect.

"Hi again," Marie said, pulling a chair up to Brooke's table. "Enjoying the evening?"

Brooke smiled. "I haven't seen you dancing. Don't you like to?"

"Is that an invitation?" Marie suggested.

"Yes, as awkward as it sounds."

The DJ played the song Sisters Are Together, and Marie slid her hand into Brooke's, leading her onto the dance floor. Smiling at each other, they danced close, then moved apart, and close again, though their bodies never touched. Brooke was moving with the tempo and enjoyed finding a "zone" outside the racquetball court. She glanced at Marie to watch her dance. Brooke had a theory about dancing. She believed you could tell how people made love by the way they danced. Stiff people on the dance floor were traditionalists in bed, according to her theory. People who moved wildly no matter what song was playing were overaggressive, the type who started yelling during foreplay. Marie moved to the music like she was part of it. Her rhythm inspired by the tones. Fully with it and not distracted by anything else in the room. Brooke was thrilled.

Several women danced up to Marie and mouthed, "Are you that golfer?" Marie nodded. Others walked up to say hi like they knew her. Marie always smiled or waved. Once, as they moved close to each other, Marie whispered, "I hope this doesn't bother you."

"No, does it bother you?"

"I'm proud of my profession and honored people recognize me and take the time to talk with me. It gives me the opportunity to meet other people and get brief intros into their lives. I love hearing about their struggles and accomplishments. Women are so amazing, aren't they?" she said.

A fellow archaeologist. We have a kinship.

They danced through several songs before Brooke said she needed a break.

"Sure," Marie replied. "I enjoyed dancing with you. I need to go now anyway. I told some folks I'd sign autographs tonight. Can I catch up with you later?"

"I'd like that."

Brooke walked outside to the spot by the rail she called her own. It was as if no one else on this or any other cruise had ever stood there. A moment shared with none other and she connected to like she was the linking piece between the horizon and the sky. She looked out over the night's sea and took several long, deep breaths.

It's been a long time since I could fill my belly with air. My breath always stops mid-chest. Well, on those rare occasions when it gets past my throat. Tonight, away from work and grief's cradle, I can actually breathe deeply and clearly. Stepping out of that thick grief fog, will I miss its constant companionship since Grammie died? Maybe before then, maybe when Mom and Dad… I don't need to fall back into the fog. I'm stepping into life's light in this dark of night.

Brooke smiled a slow smile because she knew that for the first time since Grammie's death, she was doing something that would have made her grandmother happy. She was letting joy touch her again. And in that moment of her joy, for a second, she thought she felt her grandmother's hand on her shoulder. A light touch of love and pride, but mostly of peace. She responded by whispering, "You can rest now, Grammie, I'll be fine. I know this is what I need and the only thing you ever wanted for me. So I'm learning to be happy again like the young child that lived in bliss within your loving care. I'm learning to be happy again for both of us. I'm sorry I fought it this long. It's just that I miss you so."

Something out of the corner of her eye caught Brooke's attention. She turned as many thoughts rushed through her mind in a second's time. "Grammie? Is this one last goodbye? Is it a gift from the universe? Are you truly here as I hoped you'd visit me one day? Is this the sign I've begged for?"

At first, her eyes could not focus on the being in the light next to her. "A ghost?" Please let it be.

Brooke's thoughts told her body to turn quickly before the spirit was gone, but her body moved in slow motion. She noticed a woman standing against the rail.

Is she real? Brooke stopped and focused on her with intent and hope. "Is Grammie finally visiting me?" The stranger moved and looked toward Brooke. She was not a spirit. She was real. Brooke may have been more disappointed, but any disenchantment was restrained by what she saw.

This stranger caught her eye and took her heart far away from any thoughts of lost loved ones. Even the wonderful view from the deck and the sound of the party in the background became muffled. The sky darkened except for the thin light on this woman. Wow that's certainly not Grammie, but she is someone's angel. Brooke's full attention drained away from everything and pulled to the stranger looking back at her, or so it appeared. Brooke noticed this creature standing there in full softness. She wasn't close enough to fully see them, but Brooke thought she had light freckles around her eyes. Eyes that might be green or blue, but for sure, they were friendly. This woman was fiercely feminine and seemed to come together in an unassuming way. She was lovely. Lovely and familiar. She stood there calmly, looking at—or past—Brooke, who was sinking in captivation quicksand.

It was like Brooke had known her a long time ago and then somehow lost her. This is weird! What is it with tonight's lust flood? Get a grip, focus on one thing. You're too old for this pinball game reaction to attractive women. It's the golfer, no, it's the ghost. Grammie, I said I'm happy. Stop sending these gifts before I do something stupid!

Brooke turned back, but the woman was gone. Did she imagine her? She frantically looked around, but there were only a few couples holding each other or making out by the moonlight. Was it a daydream? Some pent-up lust that meeting Marie set free? She walked to where the haunting stranger had stood and looked around. Brooke silently stood there, almost feeling the remaining energy from the woman's presence, but no one was to be seen.

"Hey, Brooke," Kate called out, "want to join us for a game of pinky swear?"

"What's pinky swear?"

"Girly, it's the sort of game where you only get the instructions after you agree to play."

"Sounds like the games we played in junior high. Who's playing?"

"I rounded up the dinner group. Come on, it'll be fun."

"Okay, I'm in," Brooke said.

❧ ❧ ❧ ❧

Kate and Millie had one of the coveted suites on the ship like Brooke and Renee's, complete with the mini kitchen and wet bar. Brooke scanned the room as she watched the women find their places of comfort with new friends.

Dawn, the college student. Funny, at what point did lesbians replace their last names with job titles? Then Brooke observed the way Dawn sat on the floor, propped up against the small couch and cross-legged. Her long hair still covered her narrow face, but unlike her manner at the dinner table, she tried less to push it back. Her nose came to a small point, and her lips were so thin and pale that the top lip barely showed. Her gangling arms and legs might have been awkward for her as a teen, but now she moved with them in a graceful rhythm, adorned by her carefree hippie style.

Kate and Millie directed everyone to their places. Brooke thought they served as models for many achievements in the lesbian world, like the loving couple with an enduring relationship, or the kind and generous neighbors reaching out to these women. Again, noticing their similarities, Brooke grinned. But she also saw the subtle signs of their individual styles, like the way they both wore their salt and pepper hair short. Millie, though, wore longer bangs, while Kate had them cut blunt at cheekbone length. Or the way they both dressed in lightweight tan pants and short-sleeve shirts, but Kate's shirt had thin stripes and Millie's had polka dots. They both even wore brown leather sandals. Kate's had small crosses, while Millie's had two large bands across the instep of her foot. And they both were wearing reading glasses, but Millie took hers off more often. Brooke couldn't decide if they were two old dear souls or the cutest couple she had ever met. Most likely both.

Nina and Amber sat close together on large pillows on the floor. Brooke noticed Nina's almond-shaped eyes and naturally full lips. They made Brooke think of the women she knew in Phoenix who paid big bucks to replicate those lips. Nina was the real thing other women fruitlessly attempted to copy. Like they tried to replicate her skin by tanning themselves or use the volumizing hair products to simulate hers. This was a beauty Nina didn't have to buy or spend weeks planning for or a lifetime coveting. It was hers by nature. Brooke wondered what Nina did with all that extra time, if not spending it trying to acquire the things she had naturally. She probably spends her time and energy dealing with the unrecognized biases of those women working so hard to copy her features.

Amber sat by Nina with comfortable informality, like they were more than just friends. Amber reminded Brooke of that famous fifties actress. The innocent-looking one who made all those comedy/romance movies. She had that milky skin, green eyes, and the perfect button nose. But she also had a commanding physical presence and obvious strength to her physique that made her seem more like the actress's stunt double if she ever needed one.

Renee and Marie were chatting, which made Brooke feel both good and scared as she was never sure what her friend was up to. They smiled as Renee nestled in by an end table. Marie walked over purposely to sit next to Brooke.

"Compared to this, our room is a closet," Nina observed. "I'm fixing the drinks."

"I'll have a Sea Breeze," Amber said.

"Water with lime in it for me," Dawn called out.

"Plain old gin and tonic for me," announced Marie.

"Beer sounds good to me," Renee called.

"I'd love a cognac, if that's okay with our hosts," Brooke said.

"More than okay, sugar. I'll have one of those pipe cleaners, too." Kate laughed.

"I'll stick with red wine. Thanks, Nina," Millie added.

Nina laughed because she realized that she'd forgotten each order just as soon as the next was made. "Okay, was that gin and cognac or a beer breeze?" They all laughed and went through it again but more slowly. Nina poured, and Renee served the drinks. Soon they were all situated, some sipping nervously, still not sure what the evening held in store for them.

Kate instructed the group. "Okay, folks are sittin' in a circle. This is good. Let's get started with the pinky swear. Everyone lock pinkies and repeat after me: Whatever we do or say tonight goes no farther than these walls. We will never repeat or ever talk about the events that are about to transpire, except with each other."

"I'm so curious," Amber offered after they all repeated the words like a Scout pledge. "What is this about?"

Kate responded, "It's a way to get past all the boring, predictable dyke chitchat and get to the good stuff."

"You have a science for doing that, don't you?" Renee half asked and half observed.

"Yes. As much as we've traveled and met other women, we've seen the same things in the relationships. As wonderful as they are, it takes a long time, much longer than the time it takes to be on a cruise, to get to know people. This game gives us permission to say the things you might tell a friend after knowing her for a long spell. We don't have that kind of time on this ship. Of course, most folks don't have that type of time in life, but they live like they do."

"A spell?" Renee questioned with her cocked eyebrow. "I find most women, lesbian and straight, pour out the pain of their lives in the first five minutes of meeting them." Renee mimicked these monolithic women, "Hi, my name is Janean, my dad was an alcoholic, my parents divorced when I was ten, I have a lot of difficulty with relationships…"

"Very true," Kate agreed. "But I'm not talking about that style of sharing, which isn't sharing, it's pain projectile. I'm referring to the fun secrets we keep to ourselves."

"So how does it work?" Amber asked as if she were eagerly talking to her grade schoolers.

Millie answered, "Well, we ask each other anything we want. Like truth or consequences without the consequences. I'll start and ask, hmm, Renee a question. When she's done answering it—completely and honestly—then she chooses someone, and either asks her the same question or comes up with a new one and so on."

"Shit, I should have asked for something stronger to drink." Amber exhaled, which surprised Brooke. Amber's innocent persona didn't seem to have a cursing drinker behind it.

"Renee, here's your question." Kate didn't allow time for more side talk.

Renee straightened out her slightly slouched back to look as attentive as a debutant who always sat with good posture. "Yes, yes, I'm ready."

"Tell us about your first time." Kate bowed her head and peered over the top rim of her glasses.

Brooke smiled at that perfect question for Renee, who loved to talk about herself almost as much as she liked to talk about sex.

"This is good." Nina was captivated.

The women moved around as if to find a position that made the game more comfortable for them. For Amber and Nina, it was just a slight move—changing how they crossed their legs. Dawn pushed her long stringy hair behind her tiny ears. Marie was even more subtle; she changed her drink from one hand to the other. It might not have been out of nervousness, then again, there might have been even more nerves behind the gesture. Brooke would have been much more fidgety, as Grammie used to call it. But like so many other uncomfortable situations, her own reaction was preempted   by observing what everyone else was doing.

Renee, on the other hand, didn't move at all but launched right in without hesitation or thought, "My first. I was fifteen—"

Kate interrupted before she could stop herself. "Fifteen? I swear I was born at the wrong time. When I was fifteen, we didn't even talk about our periods with our friends, not to mention eating each other's pussies."

"Honey, please, must you be so bold?" Millie grimaced.

"Sorry, my heart's joy." Kate leaned her head on Millie's shoulder.

"That's better. Remember, in the future, use 'muff' or nothing at all," Millie said in a surprised comeback.

"Well, for better or worse, I was fifteen," Renee continued. "Sometimes, I think it was worse. If I were older, it would have meant so much more. Come to think of it, maybe we should start a lesbian abstinence program in the schools," Renee joked, continuing her lesbian coming-of-age story. "I was on the tennis team at my high school in Springfield, Illinois. My school was in the farmlands where I would sit in class, stare out at the cornfields, and daydream of kissing the prom queen or one of my teachers. What is it about English teachers anyway? I'd have thoughts about my first woman date, first kiss, first touch, and—"

"Renee, I've heard this story more times than I can count, and even I'm on the edge of my seat waiting to hear the good stuff," Brooke teased her friend. "Plow through that cornfield of your youth and tell us what happened!"

Everyone laughed, including Renee, who continued, "Funny! I just wanted to highlight that I entered my first time with highly neglected and raging hormones, along with unnamed desires."

"Honey, I think that's true for all of us." Millie laughed.

"Oh, so true," Renee said. "Sports helped me channel all that energy and kept me from falling into isolation. I loved tennis. We had an away game, an exhibition at an all-girls' boarding school in Chicago. We were sure it was a gesture on their part. A kind of challenge-a-hick tournament or something equally insulting. But we proved to be the David of Goliath and were amazed at our win. Our team was so pumped after the game and wanted to head home for a good old bonfire, drinks, and to get high. However, severe thunderstorms hit, and we ended up staying at the school.

"I roomed with Patty Elizabeth Scott. She was a senior. We talked about our families, our studies. Teachers we hated and loved. Tennis, tennis, and more tennis. And she talked about Josephine Ride, J.R., as the world of tennis called her. The woman who put women's tennis on the map. Patty talked about reading that J.R. was living with another woman for several years. She even had a couple of pictures of them together.

"I asked Patty where she got the pictures. She said she reads this woman's magazine Out and About and threw a copy at me. I'd never heard of it. I looked through the pages and didn't even clue into the name. I saw women standing next to each other or holding hands or with their arms around each other. At first, I thought they were modeling clothes. Then something told me there was more in their pictures.

"Finally, I saw an article, 'Lesbians in Miami,' and saw pictures of women holding each other on the beach and dancing in the streets. All the pieces fell together, and I felt dumb for not getting it sooner. I didn't think I'd even see another lesbian until I moved far away from home. But then, in that room, I was far away from home.

"We stopped talking. I was both scared and excited. I had wanted that moment to happen in my life, but now that I was there, I wasn't sure what to do. I'd never seen or read about two women together. Even my own daydreams didn't go much past kissing. I didn't know what two women actually do or even what I wanted to try other than to kiss the girl. So I kept looking through that magazine over and over as if I were memorizing each page.

"Patty finally told me I could take it with me. I told her I better not.

"She sat by me while I talked on and on without finishing a single sentence. She brushed my hair back away from my eyes and around my ears, leaned over, and kissed my cheek. I stopped talking, looked at her soft brown eyes, and leaned into her confident lips. My old life stopped, and my new one began with that kiss. I went into this uncontrollable skirmish with my thoughts, feelings, actions, and reactions. I ran my fingers through her hair like I'd seen in the movies. We lay on the bed side by side. She was moving her hand down my back as I ran my hand over her breast. I worried it would seem weird or something, but it was wonderfully natural.

"Then my insecurities melted away. I swear I heard her body telling me what to do. I unbuttoned her shirt and slipped off my T-shirt. We lay closer, our young naked breasts slipped together as if bred to do so. Her softness guided me. I ran my lips over her nipple and stomach. As my tongue circled her bellybutton, I could smell her. Her essence floated out of her pants and around my nose, inspiring me with its power. My mouth slid back to her breasts, and I was sucking her farther and farther into my mouth until my tongue had little room. I pressed it against her welcoming body.

"She reached down and moved her hand inside my pajama bottoms. She moved over my mound and stroked my thigh without touching my clit, the hint of that wetted me in anticipation.

"She told me I have the softest thighs, and I said it's because I'm a girl, and we giggled.

"Her finger slightly poked inside me, and we both knew how wet I was. She wet her finger in me and, finally, stroked my clit, swirling my own juices over me. I made noises I'd never heard before. It was… perfect. I wanted her to continue to do so much more, and I wanted her to feel that same pleasure. I took off her pants and gently kissed her body, moving toward her thighs. Her pubes tickled my face. I took my hand and separated her, exposing her clit. Her smell, it enticed me in ways I'd never imagined. I placed her in my mouth and moved my tongue over her in ever-changing motions, each one made her harder and bigger. I knew what that felt like, I knew exactly what she was feeling. Even my young life appreciated the profound experience of that shared knowledge. It spun us into a hot and wonderful excitement.

"She begged me to come inside her, which made me hesitate in naïveté. I wasn't sure what that meant, and she must have sensed my uncertainty. She turned me over on my back, spread my legs, and went down on me, bringing me to the point where I had left her. While licking me over and over, she spread my legs farther and started to move her fingers inside me. In rhythm with the stroking of her tongue against my clit, she moved her fingers in and out of me, going deep with each lick. Her fingers and tongue were so well versed in this lust massage.

"Oh, I thought, come inside me. I get it.

"But then she did things I wasn't sure how to replicate because I had no idea what was happening. Truly, I no longer cared about understanding. I was out of thoughts and curiosity. She brought me into full ecstasy. Throbbing pleasure inside me and over my clit joined in a union of excitement, and I came all over her hands and face. My thoughts were stuttering. Before I could even catch my breath, she was on her back, and I placed my mouth back on her.

"She was harder and wetter than I had left her. My fingers slid effortlessly inside her vagina. I had to force myself to go slow so I could feel her, feel what it was like to be inside another woman. In all my daydreams, I could never have imagined that thrill. The softness, openness, how her throbbing smooth walls responded to my touch as if my fingers and her body were breathing life into each other's skin.

"Her body would tense and then relax in a rhythm of intense quivering. I heard her whisper, 'I'm going to come,' and I knew I controlled that pleasure by the movement of my tongue, the stroke of my fingers inside her. When her body reached complete ecstasy, she came and held her orgasm, stopping time between us. As her whole being fell into a sweaty relaxation, I laid my face on her thigh, smelling my fingers that were inside her.

"And that was my first," Renee matter-of-factly finished her story.

A stunned silence greeted Renee. They were all just staring at her with a mixed look of joy, excitement, envy, and nostalgia. Kate was the one to break the stillness.

"Okay, ladies, it's been fun, but you all need to leave so Millie and I can have vicious lesbian sex." Kate fanned herself.

"I like this game!" Amber yelled.

There were hoots and hollers from the other women.

"This room is OOC, out of control," Nina joked.

"There's one thing I don't get," Amber joined in. "Earlier, you said something about regretting having sex at age fifteen. What the hell fuck did you regret?"

"Hell fuck?" Renee asked. "What caliber of a schoolteacher are you? I didn't say it wasn't great sex. I said that had I waited, it might have meant more. It was like I was waiting for that special twenty-first birthday party—it was supposed to be the best party of entering adulthood. And then someone threw me that best party when I turned fifteen. It was a great party, but I was so looking forward to the one in six years."

"Where did she learn that much about sex that young?" Millie asked.

"A teacher from her sophomore class," Renee told her.

"An English teacher?" Amber wished.

"No, the P.E. teacher."

"How fucking predictable." Amber dropped her head.

Silence revisited the group, and they sat there, thrilled and exhausted for a while.

"I need another drink," Brooke finally said. "And I've heard this story before."

They laughed, poured new drinks, and took turns in the bathroom. Renee sat with what was now an explainable grin on her face. Amber gave her a hug and thanked her for sharing that intimacy with the group. Marie stepped out on the patio and lit a thin cigar. She thought the sea's stars were even brighter than those in the desert sky, which she watched after the Palm Springs Golf Classic. Like many of the women in that room, she was reminded of her first lover, Sue, and smiled; she wondered about the journey Sue's life had taken her on. Marie thought about calling her to say hi, but as in the past, she never acted on the thought. The fresh air was so peaceful. Marie thought of it as an internal body massage. The cool air rubbing her tired cells and muscles.

Brooke sat in the room wondering how to get out of her question. Group sharing, even as a game, was uncomfortable for someone who shared her thoughts with an ounce of calculation.

"Want to join us, Marie?" Nina asked. "We're starting again."

"Okay, Renee, you get to ask someone a question," Kate reminded her. "Either the same question or something new."

"One thing before Renee does this." Nina became more inquisitive. "You asked Renee to tell you about her first. But you didn't say her first what. She could have told you about her first time with drugs or even her first day at school, right?"

"Nina, you go to the head of the class. You caught on to the game." Kate laughed. "But her story was so superb, Renee also gets to go to the head of the class."

"Well then, I shall be thoughtfully specific with my question," Renee said. "And this one is a roundtable question, which means each of you has to answer it. Who here is a 'gold star' lesbian?"

"You know I'm not," Brooke was the first. "I had sex with a couple of guys in my early twenties. I thought I should at least give it the old college try. See what all the fuss was about. But each one confirmed my desire and preference for women."

"In my day," Millie began, "I always sound so old when I start that way, but when you're close to sixty-eight, it's just true. So, in my day, lesbians weren't out and about as you say. I even did the marriage thing. I have three children, none of whom were conceived by artificial insemination like you techno lesbians. Now I have seven grandchildren. I adore my family and don't regret that time. It wasn't my time. No regrets and no gold star here, not even a tan one."

"Nor here," Kate added. "I didn't get married, but I was engaged."

"Sex before marriage in your day," Marie joked.

"Now you all know you didn't invent that," Kate joked back.

"Sorry, no star on my chest," Nina said. "Though I wish there were. I, too, thought I should give the other side a try, and I'm so sorry I did it. To think I wasted four precious minutes of my life."

"Four? That should at least make you a gold twinkle," Amber told her friend. "I dated in college. I was in a sorority, and even though I had visions of panty raids within my own house, I did the straight walk for a while. Some of it was nice, gentle, caring intimacy. Even wonderful sex. I met a couple good male souls at college. But none of them, none…well, I didn't mesh, as Renee said, with any of them like I do with women."

"I have gold golf trophies, but no stars for me," Marie shared. "Like Amber, I had pleasurable experiences with men. One of whom is still a close friend of mine. I call him often for business advice. Hell, I'm even godmother to one of his kids. But as good as it was, it wasn't the real thing."

It was quiet for a moment. "Dawn?" Renee probed.

"I hate being the youngest and the only gold star lesbian. It's so cliché. Like some of you, I've thought about giving the other side a try. You can't help but wonder what it's like. I grew up with all those images and messages about straight sex. But then it strikes me, how many straight women think, "gosh, I really should try lesbian sex today to see what it's like?"

"I bet a lot of them do," Renee said. "Actually, I know they do because I've helped to end their curiosity. I think it's common for them to talk with their friends about, 'I wonder what it's like' and other curious straight women's stuff. Or to wonder about that friend they were so emotionally close to, think about what it would be like to take that emotional closeness to a level of physical intimacy. They probably wonder about it much more than they act on it. There are, of course, those flaming straight women who not only don't wonder about dykedom, but the mere thought of it makes them lose their lunch."

"Perhaps. Perhaps I'll give in to my curiosity," Dawn said with her head down. But then she looked up with a big smile. "And then again, maybe I'll die a happy, fulfilled, gold-star-one-hundred-percent-true-blue real lesbian, and I'll laugh at the rest of you wanna-bes." She laughed.

"Dawn, since you were the real winner of that round, even though this is a non-competitive game, why don't you ask the next pinky swear question?" Kate directed.

"Okay, another roundtable. How long did your longest sexual experience last, or what's the longest you've gone making love?"

"With someone else?" Renee clarified with a long laugh.

"Yes."

"What do you consider from start to finish and how do food breaks play in?" Nina asked.

"From foreplay to the last orgasm."

"Five hours," Nina said as if she had rehearsed the answer. "I kept track of that myself."

Brooke went next. "Eight for me."

"Eight's about right for me, too," Renee said, "but it wasn't with Brooke. We're just good friends." Brooke wondered if Renee's repeated description of their relationship from the dinner was a not-so-subtle replay for Marie in case she didn't hear it the first time.

"Four," Kate said.

"Then it better be four for me, too." Millie laughed, and they kissed.

"Eleven," Amber said while stretching out on the floor.

"Amber, do you want to add anything to that?" Renee asked.

"No, I answered the pinky question. Eleven."

"Eighteen," Marie said. "Eighteen of the most wonderful hours. And then we ate and slept for ten."

Her comment brought up a wave of lust in Brooke.

Renee added, "Eighteen hours! That must be a fucking record."

"Literally," Marie replied, and they all laughed again.

"You're at an unfair advantage from the rest of us," Renee said. "All that golf exercise takes you to another level of eye-hand coordination."

"Well, who wants to start off the next round?" Kate kept the game rolling.

"I do," Dawn said quickly. "Marie—"

"Oh, no." Marie dreaded the question.

"What's the kinkiest thing you've ever done during sex?"

"Oh, there's so much to choose from. This may take me a while," Marie said, trying to buy time.

"We're not going anywhere," Dawn told her.

Marie looked right into Brooke's eyes and calmly said, "Once, during my early years of college, I was at a friend's house. There were about a dozen or so of us. All women, all lesbians. We were sitting around a coffee table, drinking, rolling joints. Wow, that was a long time ago. I haven't gotten high in years. Anyway, someone finished her bottle of beer and spun it on the table. The first two women it landed on got up and kissed as if we were back at a seventh-grade game of spin the bottle. Then they spun it repeatedly. The kissing got longer. Clothes came off, and, well, we kind of had an orgy."

"Kind of?" Renee jumped in. "What does 'kind of' mean?"

"Okay, it was an orgy." Marie blushed. "At one point, we moved the table and were all over the living room floor. There were hands, tongues, breasts, butts, and sweet pussy, sorry, Millie, sweet muff all over the place. It was undoubtedly the kinkiest thing I ever did. Most of us stayed friends. Some had sex with each other off and on. I never did it with any of them again. It was a one-time experience and a pretty hot one at that. It was such a crazy time."

"I bet you had a lot of crazy times with all those dykes on the professional golf tours," Dawn said.

Marie thought for a second. "I'm sure the young players have that breed of fun, but I'm not chasing that folly anymore."

"But there must be lots of women on the tours, the fans who want to be closer to the famous golfer than their gallery seats allow." Renee seemed to reject Marie's claims.

"Sure, that's part of it. But I don't take it seriously. They don't even know me. Besides, I want something different now."

"Someone to hold hands with?" Renee ribbed her friend.

"Hold hands? I guess. It's ridiculous, but I date less now that I'm quote, famous, unquote than when I was a rookie kid in college. I either intimidate women or attract women who want to have sex within a few minutes of meeting me. Or others who see the hype of my life but not the real me. They see it as a dream life. And I'm not complaining. I love my profession. But there's much more to me that gets lost in all the 'dreamsville' those women see me in. I'd like to have meaningful conversations, balance in how we connect."

Brooke bore guilt again for having that instant lust for Marie, but it didn't last long. After all, it wasn't all about the "famous golfer," she rationalized. She was attracted to her. And the more she heard Marie talk about her life and interests, the more she liked her. It was warm and scary.

"Well, I'm going to have to call it a night," Brooke announced. "Can we continue this tomorrow night?"

"Your question will go first, Brooke, and that gives us all twenty-four hours to think of something extraordinary," Kate teased.

"Okay. Let's do this. Tomorrow, Rosewater is playing right after dinner, and then most everyone is going to the disco to dance. Let's meet up there, dance for a while, and then head back to this suite," Brooke said. "I mean, if I can volunteer your place again."

"We'd love it," Millie replied.

"Sounds good. I want Millie and I to talk more about Renee's first," Kate added.

They finished their drinks and started the good night hugs. Brooke observed the women, smiling at all the fun. It was a perfect evening of dinner, dancing, and new friends. She was in awe at the camaraderie women could conjure up with a few simple ingredients picked from their female spirit of sharing and humor, and the indefinable spirit of woman-dom.

Chapter Three

Brooke strolled down the hall to her room, still thinking about the night's magic where she was part of a female troupe who performed unscripted acts of fun and laughter. The boat moved, reminding her she wasn't at a downtown grand hotel, but far out to sea on a lesbian voyage. She walked down the lavish corridors with the evening's smile on her face like it was part of her attire.

"Hey, Brooke, wait up," she heard Marie call out.

"Hi. I can't believe what happened. Was that a fun evening or what?" Brooke shared her excitement with Marie, whose alluring gaze rested on her. Brooke welcomed that stare. It was part of Marie's country charm that made Brooke want to know her more. Marie was so peaceful and enticing.

"Yes. I don't think I've ever known kinship with women I just met. Not sure I've experienced it with women I've known for a long while, either," she realized aloud.

"Kate was right about that game. It helps strangers bypass the usual and safe 'getting to know you' chitchat," Brooke said, still immersed in Marie's eyes.

"I'd say by years. Would you like to go to the concert with me tomorrow night?" Marie awkwardly switched topics. "I thought we could meet for dinner and then head over to the music hall."

Brooke had a quick ebb and flow of thoughts. I love the idea of spending more time with Marie, but no way do I want to go to Rosewater. Our time is so limited. Maybe I could sit through the concert. I don't want to compromise my beliefs here. She finally broke out of her mind trap and responded in her honest charm.

"I know this may be a lesbian federal offense, but I'm not a big Rosewater fan. Would you mind if we skipped the concert and spent that time talking on the deck? Or something?" Brooke hoped.

Marie smiled. "A much better idea. Everyone will be at the concert, so we can hoard the stars for ourselves. If I don't see you before, let's meet at the main entrance to the dining hall at six thirty."

"I'd like that. See you then," Brooke said and walked away thinking, "An actual date! Wow. A real date with Marie."

❧ ❧ ❧ ❧

That night in their room, Brooke and Renee whispered about the happiness they found on the ship and giggled about the fun.

The next morning, Brooke got up at daybreak to take an early dip in one of the ship's two massive swimming pools. She had the water to herself for several laps. She wondered if everyone else was that hungover or having a hot morning, which gave her a surge of energy seldom seen before ten. She swam for what felt like a long while and then wrapped her cooled body in a thick terrycloth robe, stood on the deck, and looked over the ocean's morning sky. The clouds wore hints of colors like a favorite old baseball cap. She knew it wouldn't stay that way for long. The sun would gain strength and burn off any reminders of this thin overcast. It would all be gone about the time the rest of the vacationers woke up. Funny, they'll wake thinking it's just another predictable sunny day, oblivious to the fact that the sky had already been so busy. How often do I take such things for granted? Will I ever remember that all I see is not all there is or all that has been?

With each deep breath, she enjoyed taking in more of her surroundings and scattered thoughts. An extravagant blue owned the ocean that morning. Brooke wondered how something so vast and far-reaching could also be so calm. Other women slowly joined her on deck. Some for the group tai chi, others for brisk walks around the teak wood. Eventually, other women started to swim in the pool.

"If we could only start each day like this," she heard someone say. Brooke turned and had to hold back an audible gasp. Standing next to her was the mesmerizing woman from the night before. Brooke had convinced herself that it was a dream. She shook her head as if to clear her eyes of a mirage. But this was up close and three-dimensional. Her disbelief was quickly replaced by intrigue with this woman.

Brooke confirmed what she thought she saw in the night's haze: The mystery woman had light freckles around her green eyes. She was shaped like a Greek goddess wearing the full curves of womanhood, and Brooke could have become lost in her beauty had she not been fluent in guarding her reactions.

"I'm Heather," the woman introduced herself.

"I'm Brooke. It's nice to meet you."

"Good to meet you, too." Heather extended her hand, and Brooke gladly shook it.

Brooke smiled at merely hearing Heather speak her name. Then something unusual happened. Brooke felt nervous. So much so, her hands trembled. She let go before Heather could notice.

"What did you think of the dance last night?" Brooke asked, searching for an introduction to a conversation.

"I didn't go. Except for meals and daily morning jogs, I mostly stay in my cabin or on its balcony enjoying the view."

"Oh, are you feeling okay? I mean, I know when women get seasick out here they stay close to their rooms."

"I'm fine. Nothing like that. I feel…reclusive."

"Oh." Brooke stumbled and wondered how many times she had said "oh," fearful it made her sound immature.

"That's one of the nice things about these trips, you know. You can be with as many women as you want, or you can hide from the world. Is your partner reclusive, too?"

Brooke almost bit her lip at that painfully obvious probe.

"No, my partner didn't come. Actually, we're on a trial separation, after ten years of being together."

"Oh, I'm sorry, I didn't realize."

"It's fine, really. You're the first person on this trip I've told," Heather said, staring at the morning horizon instead of Brooke. But Brooke didn't mind. It gave her more time to gaze upon this enchanting woman. Brooke didn't know where Heather's powerful influence over her had come from, but she was sure the attraction was older than her own memory.

Heather continued, "We told our family and friends that my partner could not get away from work, and I was taking a much-needed vacation from my job.

Wow, that feels good for me to say it out loud. Admitting to the lie somehow doesn't feel as bad as when I told it."

"What type of work do your friends think you're resting from?" Brooke asked, trying to steer the conversation away from the homebound partner.

"I own a printing company in South Carolina. We deal mostly with textbooks and instruction manuals. Not a glamorous job, but busy. Well, it was nice to meet you, Brooke," Heather cut off their talk.

"I enjoyed meeting you, too, Heather," she said and thought about what it would be like to hear that Southern accent whispering in her ear. Then she made one last effort to keep the connection. "Oh, the disco is a lot of fun, if you feel like hiding from your thoughts tonight."

"Thanks," Heather said and walked away.

Brooke let free her self-critical thoughts. Gosh, how dorky can I be? Oh, I'm sorry. Oh, there's a disco. Oh, shit, was I nervous. She was sure Heather somehow saw her obvious fascination.

I must have worn my interest on my face… just like when I met Tammy in college. Tammy. I haven't thought of her in a long time…not a good comparison. That turned out to be one of the unhealthiest relationships I've ever been in. And Heather was in a long-term relationship and is dealing with the emotional pain of a possible breakup. What am I thinking anyway? There's Marie, who is amazing. Marie…we have a date tonight, and I encouraged Heather to come to the disco. Shit. This is my isolation coming back to haunt me into dating hell, I know it. Where's the simple 'Cassandra on the racquetball court fantasy' when I need it?

But all those worries didn't keep Brooke from developing an unsubstantiated crush on Heather, and the adrenaline it created was exhilarating. Suddenly, she had a new level of excitement for the day. This is like a shot of confidence. Confidence shot with a happiness chaser. I feel so hopeful like the moment right before someone bursts into song on one of those old musicals. No wonder people have affairs. This is such a pleasurable intoxication. The type of rush that drugs come close to but never replicate, even though the misguided users are sure they'll get there with the next dose.

For a brief moment, Brooke wasn't sure what to do with her thoughts and feelings. Go to the gym for a good workout? Or back to the room to work the excitement off? Find friends to talk to? Join one of the ship's daily activities and interact with this lovely crowd of lesbians?

All this seemed too overdone for her, as if the activities would cause the joy of her titillating feelings to escape out her pores. She wasn't eager to let that joy go. A lounge chair on the ship caught her attention as if it knew her dilemma and yelled out, "You want to lay on me all morning and let the sun help you bask in your roaming feelings for women?" And so began Brooke's day, a comfortable spot on the Pacific Ocean with a heart and libido filled with attractions.

She spent most of her time alternating the lounge chair between the shade and the sunlight, as she had learned from living in the Phoenix heat. But this place didn't bake her like the desert did. Here, she was warmed by the sun and cooled by the ocean breeze. Brooke would spend a long time in her lounge chair. She read magazines the steward brought her. Though, looking through the dyke magazines made Brooke feel a little unfaithful to her principles. She once vowed never to read the magazines at the grocery checkout line or watch tabloid-type shows on TV. These decisions were all part of her life's journey. They were small but telling parts of a much deeper spirituality. Beliefs and rituals she borrowed from pieces of world religions and indigenous practices. She cultivated those practices not as a scholar who would become fluent in their meaning at her life's end, but rather as someone at a religious smorgasbord, someone passing by the spread, perusing the various schools of thought and practices of the heart. She picked items up, studied them for a while, and if they made sense to her, put them into her growing dogma, a way of living, her own code of ethics.

After many years of this, Brooke felt an integration among the compassion of a true Christian, the commitment of a Jewish scholar, the presence of Zen, the patience of Quan Yin, the connection to earth with a pagan's soul, and the indigenous people's practice of calling upon their ancestors for strength and support. She was not part of any but grateful that each found a place in her beliefs. She trusted the guidance that came with it if she could just be silent long enough to hear it. But that was often blocked by the consuming noise of her trivial and rambling thoughts. And she had enough humility to admit she was far from mastering any of these practices and knew they were simply part of a long continuum of her personal faith. A faith rarely discussed with others, for she believed it was the practice that gave them truth, not the talk.

Brooke's spiritual life existed in an undercurrent in her life that she drew upon to make decisions and "regroup" when she got lost in her hectic world. Part of her journey was led by her belief that she needed to unlearn the lessons of this world like fear, hate, and insecurity, and get back in touch with the innocence, love, insightfulness, and intuition she believed everyone was born with. Self-solidarity before connecting with others. There were many ways in which she integrated this into her life. One way was her sense that what she put out into the world was what came back to her. Some people called it karma, but for Brooke, it wasn't that linear—you do a good thing, and you get a good thing back. Instead, it was woven into her entire life, and she believed the tone of her overall actions created the experiences meant for her.

One of her decisions was that personal embargo on tabloids. She once read those magazines and watched tabloid TV to help her relax after work, but she realized it made her more tense. And when she meditated on it, she found it was simply wrong to seek entertainment from the sordid details and pain of other people's lives. And by being an active spectator in that exploitation of others' suffering and sorrow, she was inviting those things into her life, which was not at all revitalizing or healing. With that revelation, she turned off the tabloid shows, stopped buying the magazines, and tried not to engage in conversations with her coworkers about the tabloid headlines or even gossip about other employees. The latter proved more challenging at work as her actions were not always as strong as her beliefs, and fresh gossip was the focus of most work break conversations.

Like those moments, this day abated pieces of Brooke's convictions, and she allowed herself a retreat from her own code. In the pages of the gay tabloids, she found a sneaky but satisfying joy in reading about a famous woman rumored to be lesbian. But her reading proved not to be a total retreat for her. Her beliefs occasionally wrestled with the fun she was having, and she wondered why she didn't feel more guilt about compromising her principles.

She searched for an acceptable rationale. *Perhaps this vacation allows me time for common pleasures. Common pleasures, listen to me, like I'm above this. Hell, if I'm going to fall for two women within a day of meeting them, I might as well break all my rules.* She unsuccessfully tried to convince herself. But somewhere inside, she knew better. Instead of confronting that knowledge, however, she tried harder to make sense out of nonsense. *And it's not like I get this type of information in any of the mainstream media. That's it, I'm starved for the gayness in life. There's no credible gay news. Not like we have Queer News Network, QNN, now that would be cool. Then I wouldn't have to resort to this trash. This is the only print information about our world. I'm either exposed to gay exploitation while I try to read other news about us in these magazines, or I don't read about our lives at all.*

Brooke's thoughts were rescued by a moment of clarity. *I can't believe I almost fell for any rationale with the word "exploitation" in it. How real are my values if they jettison at the first sign of vulnerability?*

She put the magazine down with appropriate shame and grinned at her choice to change the direction of her day.

While reclining in the lounge chair, Brooke watched the growing number of women go by her. She was reminded of the beauty of their lives and was happy to find a more acceptable way to spend her time. She saw many women she had already met during meals, by the pool, or at the disco. In her typical manner, she could not remember any of their names, but she did remember what she considered more important things, like what they talked about during their interlude. They had exchanged answers to all the typical questions when meeting fellow lesbian vacationers. The "stats," as Kate called them—where they lived, if they were single or in relationships or in-between, their varied types of jobs, and other usual chitchat.

The soap opera director from New York walked by and waved at Brooke. Brooke remembered her from their weight room conversation, where the director boldly introduced herself to Brooke. She told Brooke that she had been on every lesbian cruise. She was single and struck Brooke as being too restless to ever settle down. Not only restless with relationships, but with everything — her job, her family, her friends. She seemed led by an uncontrollable force to roam.

The doctor from Kansas passed by and yelled at Brooke, "Hey, make sure you have enough sunscreen on." Brooke smiled with a thumbs-up. They once shared a table at breakfast. Brooke thought the doctor had one of the gentlest speaking voices she had ever heard. And her concern for people was obvious even during their short visit. Brooke thought of her as an old-fashioned country doctor held hostage in an HMO system. She was also single, though Brooke got the sense there had been a significant relationship in her not-too-distant past. It was visibly too painful for the doctor to talk about. Brooke remembered how she got all choked up when talking about someone back home, so she didn't pursue the conversation. Instead, they had talked about how women in their kind of jobs should learn how to golf.

Then Brooke noticed the camerawoman from a local news show in Orlando running by on the way to the pool. What a hoot, Brooke thought, smiling. She told Brooke outrageously funny lesbian jokes. She was starting to date and met someone just before the trip. "So far, so good," she told Brooke, "but they never show you the shitty side until the middle of month five. Beware the ides of month five," she joked.

A group of cops from Washington passed by next. Brooke met some of them in the bathroom at the dance. They were wearing either blue or tan shorts and slip-on shoes. They walked with more purpose than other women, even though their destination was the same. They marched on, while talking and laughing. Brooke couldn't help but give them the once-over and linger on their muscular bodies. For the most part, they stayed within their pack. A few were in relationships but none with other cops on board, which Brooke found interesting.

The women in some type of mysterious work from the L.A. area strolled by and saw Brooke, but they didn't recognize her from the lunch table they shared earlier in the trip. Brooke could understand why. They didn't talk much at lunch but displayed a loyalty to one another, a type of protectiveness that was obvious even during their superficial lunchtime conversation.

The pilot from Denver walked by with two women, one on each side of her, and they were enthralled with whatever the pilot was talking about. She was a striking woman, and Brooke wondered if she'd ever get the nerve to talk to her or the ability to get past the other women.

Her two companions were trying to make as much eye contact with the pilot as they could. It looked almost dangerously funny to Brooke, seeing their necks stretched and turned up to the pilot's face, trying so hard to appear interested in every word the pilot's glib tongue produced. Brooke was sure one of them would bump into something. The pilot, however, didn't seem concerned or even aware. She looked forward, waving her hands as she talked, intently making some point.

The pilot made reference to being in a couple of relationships around the country when she talked to Brooke in the buffet line on the first day at sea. Brooke had mixed feelings about that, even though the pilot told her that all the women knew about one another. Brooke never bought the story that simply being honest about one's behavior made it honorable. But she didn't dwell on it much. At the time, she had been more interested in the salad bar than the pilot.

The gardener from Salt Lake City, a white woman whose partner was Black, passed by. Brooke didn't know any biracial lesbian couples and wondered about all the "isms" they had to deal with. Then she thought it probably wasn't as difficult as being a lesbian couple living in Utah.

Intermingled in the growing deck crowd, Brooke spotted a couple of women she met who worked in the domestic violence field. They were counselors, agency directors, even a couple of lawyers who specialized in defending victims. The lawyers most often described their clients as women who found themselves on the wrong side of the law because of desperate actions, like those who fled with their children when the divorce proceedings looked as though they were headed toward giving the abusive husbands sole custody. Or cases where women had tried to kill their abusers—and a couple who succeeded.

Brooke's thoughts drifted as a couple of them passed by. Why do lesbians work in this field? Yes, some may have experienced partner abuse, but their conversations were all about their working with women who had male partners and spouses. It's like my friends working on abortion rights. So many lesbians fighting for the rights of straight women. At some point, it didn't matter to her what causes women immersed themselves into. Their fierce bonding together is what mattered.

She wasn't part of the lesbian collaborative approach to social change. Brooke's support took form in annual donations. She felt for women in an environment they couldn't control but had no personal experiences with that type of harm. Even within her vague family memories, she

knew for sure her parents didn't fight like that. Dad never called Mom names, and Mom never talked about all the things he wasn't. They were the opposite. They had lived the real deal of love.

The deck became crowded with women passing by. Brooke saw women she had not yet met or seen, which she thought strange. It wasn't as if they bused new lesbians in at night.

Smiling again, Brooke watched all the diverse walks of life passing by in lesbian packaging. The women were from so many different professions, economic backgrounds, ages, races, and ethnicities. Though, they were not as diverse as the people at her job in Phoenix. But according to Dawn from Oregon, it was much more racially diverse than in Eugene. The ship's culture must be somewhere in between the rich diversity in Phoenix and the racial drought in Oregon. Brooke had heard about a cruise for Black straight people. And she wondered if there was one for lesbians. In one way, she hoped not. She would like to believe that the sisterhood of lesbianism could serve as a bridge, albeit weak, but a bridge. But she knew those were naïve white-girl thoughts. Then she thought that even trying to rank such things was a sign of her overactive logic and her habit of looking at categories instead of complex people within her own biases. She tried to learn about those complexities and had a long way to go. She switched to her ongoing list of personal improvements. Try to make fewer assumptions about what other people prefer. Take more time to ask individuals how they feel. Of course, what kind of an ass would I be? Excuse me, would you prefer to be on an all-Black lesbian trip? Oh, that's a great way to meet people, sounding like the great white dope. There's that "oh" again.

"Hi, is anyone sitting here?" a woman asked while claiming the lounge chair next to Brooke.

"No, you're lucky. It's one of the few available chairs left on the deck. But the choices improve around lunchtime."

"Thanks, I'm Maureen."

"Hi, I'm Brooke. It's nice to meet you." Brooke couldn't help but watch Maureen pick up and adjust the wood-framed lounge chair as if it were made of toothpicks. She was tall and full framed and looked like a giant from Brooke's reclined position. She reminded Brooke of a female discus thrower, but her face was softer than Brooke would expect from someone throwing heavy metal balls. And she was showing the signs of an older athlete: muscular in some places and sagging in others, all the beautiful ways women show time.

"I love your bathing suite, Maureen," Brooke said. "Where did you get it?"

"There's a little shop by where I live that sells vintage-looking clothes. I just fell in love with these green and white stripes."

"It's fantastic."

"Thank you so much. Oh, my, this is the life! How do I get paid to do this?" Maureen's far-reaching voice broadcasted.

"I'm with you on that one. What do you do when you're not in this ideal world?" Brooke asked.

"Well, not a lot, but I'll have to look for something soon."

Brooke felt a big story behind that.

"Oh, what type of work have you been in?" Brooke tried to find a way out of this for both of them.

Maureen looked at Brooke as if she were trying to guess her dress size, then said, "I guess I can trust you. Actually, it doesn't really matter, I've told so many people while crying in my beer at sea, I won't avoid any trouble by not telling you. I worked at home. I was a partner, a lover, a friend, a hostess, and more for who I thought was the most wonderful woman in the world. Then she dumped me. You see, I was involved with a famous lesbian who's in the closet. I won't say her name because, well, I can't say her name. The gag order won't let me. As my lawyers describe it, if I say the name, I lose the settlement. I hate that word. It should be my alimony. We were as married as any other couple with the legal document. Hell, even without the legalese, I would never tell—the name, that is. Somewhere inside me, there's a trace of loyalty to that bitch. Anyway, I was with an aspiring actress who became a late-night talk show host."

Brooke wanted to laugh but controlled herself. So much for taking the higher road away from the tabloid magazines. She said, "My keen perception for the most obvious tells me it was a bad breakup."

"Yes, it was bad in all the ways bad can be. I stayed with her during the hard years, more than sixteen of them. I was there while she struggled to find gigs. There was a commercial or two, but mostly, I worked several part-time jobs to keep the asshole landlord from locking us out of a crappy studio apartment door. And she was touring those lousy comedy clubs while I picked up whatever jobs I could. What is it about being waitstaff anyway? Why do people think they own you when you're bringing a burger and fries to their table? Then she gets a small but meaningful role in a breakout movie, then a TV deal, and me? I'm history. Oh, sure, I got a lot of cash out of the royal dump, like I said, but what I really wanted was to have it all work out with us, ya know?"

"Yes, at one time or another in our lives, we all know. But aren't you afraid of losing the money by talking this way?"

"Fuck it. I didn't say her name, and that's what the lawyers told me not to do. It's not my fault there's only one female late-night talk show host." She paused. "Only one on the networks anyway."

They both laughed.

"I'm not surprised," Brooke said, adding, "Folks in the community have been talking about her for a long time. Lesbians mostly filled the audience of those comedy clubs. And we did a major write-in campaign when her first TV show was canceled. In some ways, I guess we all feel a little betrayed by her silence. But then again, I always say it's not for me to dictate another person's safety zone. And our sense of betrayal doesn't compare to yours and the intimacy you shared.

I'm sorry."

"Thank you. That was the biggest issue for me. I'll never be silent about who I am. So, eventually, she would have been outed by association, which ultimately scared her too much. She was afraid of losing the show, contracts for movies, all that stuff. Of course, she does great things with her money. She does a lot for charities. She has a limitless sense of compassion for others in need, especially the elderly."

"Your memories are not all terrible. You still see the good side of her."

"How could I not? I couldn't have been there for her all those years if the good wasn't wonderful. I hated the ending and the self-denial." Maureen's voice dropped.

"Well, I'm sure her fears are real. She might lose her show and fans and all that stuff. While I've always been out, it's not for me to tell others what to do. You two seem to have had different safety zones," Brooke repeated.

"As long as people like her know what a luxury it is to be so silent in this world. I mean, think about it. Did Carmen Rios, the queen of all those inspirational TV shows, ever decide to say, gee, I'm going to hide the fact that I'm a Latina woman so all those racists in America don't put me out of business? No, she celebrates her culture in a way that educates people. I know I owe it to people like that to live out of the closet."

"Owe it?" That puzzled Brooke.

Maureen scooted her chair closer to Brooke's, so they touched each other. "Okay, here's the second-saddest story in my life. You're lucky, most people must know me for five years or more before they hear it. But, hey, this trip won't last that long." She snorted.

"My life is not secret and certainly not unique. It's the life shared by many of us when we were young— young and lesbian, that is. I was confused, ashamed of who I was. If it wasn't enough to be hiding my gay life, I was also too poor to even have the right clothes to help me feel more comfortable while on that playground of screaming, name-calling, and haunting whispers: tomboy, lesbo, he/she, they would say. And home was no comfort, either. It wasn't safe enough there to ask for help. And by my early teen years, I was often too tired with the whole thing to even go on. Although I never considered killing myself, I don't know if I would have objected if the Fates had taken me. You know, in a car accident or something. There were many times when I was content to get out of the parade of life and sit on the curbside watching others go by. I thought if I sat there long enough, I'd fade into a being as insignificant as I felt in my own heart. Once there, I'd wait for a breeze, even the slightest one, to blow me away into the nothingness I knew I was. But before I'd get to feel that small, someone from that moving crowd would stop in front of me, reach down, and take my hand. I'd feel their strength and compassion. Somehow, something greater than me would help me find the strength and courage to stand up. And that stranger would put her arm around me, and we'd stroll away from the curb and back into the crowd of life. And it didn't end there. Somehow, she'd help me find the gifts in my life that made me feel special and important. That happened a couple of times from the time I was a child into my young adult years, and often, that hand of rescue belonged to a person of color.

"It was a superhero thing. The kind where someone's struggles gain them the ability to see the pain in people like me. And even greater than that is the fact that, in spite of centuries of pain inflicted by people who look like me, they still stopped for me. Stopped without hesitation. Many of those people who helped me are no longer here. And even if they were, I know of no words that would come close to sharing the deep gratitude and love I have for them. Of course, the greatest thanks are not through words but through actions, so that's how I try to show my thanks, by being part of the good white allies' team."

Brooke was listening to Maureen with all her might. She thought about how Maureen's words were so simple yet full of meaning. She talked of things bigger than Brooke and outside her own immediate thoughts and struggles. It was like Maureen was knocking on her forehead and saying, "Hello, anyone in there? There's a big world out here with lots more than your efforts to put everything in its proper cubby."

Maureen kept talking, unaware of her effect on Brooke. "It's not like they teach you what makes an ally in school. And lord knows we are surrounded by good examples of how not to do it. But where's the blueprint on how to be a good one? I had to figure it out on my own. Not sure I figured it all out, but I have learned that it can mean going to marches or meetings, donating money, doing the work, or other ways of being a steward of the work. It's about being part of the struggle. And sometimes it means accepting the fact that there are times when I won't be asked to the meeting, the times when people of color don't want me there or my contributions. That was a hard thing for me to imagine, but then I grew up. Like me, everyone needs time to be with people who share a common background. Time to play, to plan, to strategize, and to do the work they need to as only they can identify.

"Those are some of the ways I try to thank those who would not let me sit out on this great life. But most of all, and here's the important part, Brooke, the one thing I can do is be out—out when it's not convenient, comfortable, or even safe for me. Those are the times it's critical for me to be out. And allow my life to be real and face the prejudices they cannot hide from by running into a racial closet."

Brooke nodded; all the while, Maureen talked about her childhood isolation, but less so when she talked about the wise souls who saved her. Brooke didn't have that history with strangers, but she could relate to those same comforts from her grandmother.

Maureen continued, "White queers in the closet have a luxury that other discriminated groups don't. The choice to be safe by hiding who they are."

Brooke thought for a moment. She had several responses but wanted to speak them carefully. "It sounds like your life's pain has been relieved by the help of people who have been treated horribly by people who look like you...like us. Their act of love is real grace. I don't know that very well," Brooke started. "You met loving people, but do you think those individuals represent all people, of any race? What about the many racial and ethnic minorities, who say we don't have something in common with them and even get insulted at the comparison of prejudices? I'm sure you've heard it—'You're not like this at all...you've made a choice to live a life that the Bible condemns.'"

"Well, it would be a show of appreciation for me to find a way to help them, too, now, wouldn't it?" Maureen stared directly into Brooke's eyes.

"Okay, this is too deep for me." Brooke smiled.

"I see your point, your uncompromising devotion, and your sorrow. But this conversation has caused me to face two opposing and passionate views I have: lesbians' right to feel safe by staying in the closet and how we make a statement about human rights and solidarity with other people living in the margins of life. I hate that image. It sounds like I live on a giant legal pad and others are off to the side."

"Pushed off."

"But you know what I mean." Brooke struggled to find her words, comparing herself to this newfound orator.

"Yes. How about if I go get yummy snacks and drinks to treat us while you're examining life's contradictions?" Maureen asked.

"I think that's the least you can do since you made me look at them. Actually, that's especially nice. A virgin Bloody Mary sounds wonderful."

Maureen moved her large body from the recliner with an elegant swiftness and was quickly swallowed up by the now large crowd of passers-by. Brooke was thirsty for more of their conversation and enjoyed the time with the sun and surrounding sound of the waves and women's chatter. Maureen had trays of treats and drinks. One of the ship's helpers was with her.

"Thanks for the help," she told the steward as she tipped him.

"This looks great," Brooke said. "How thoughtful. So what has been your favorite part of the trip so far?"

"Trashin' my ex has helped." She laughed. "It has been good to talk about her. I think I can go back to L.A. with much less residue about things. Start new. Some women have asked me out, but I was too preoccupied to engage with them. Now I'm looking forward to it.

So my favorite part has been a relationship cleansing. And you?"

Brooke was silent while she searched herself for her feelings. "Something like you, finding joy beyond the difficult time of grief. My grandmother died about a year ago. It was unexpected. She was old, but I thought healthy. I was wrong. She raised me because, let me warn you, this is the three-hankie part. I lost both my parents when I was ten. They were on a second honeymoon, and their bus in London crashed. People who survived were badly burned, so I'm glad my mom and dad didn't end up like that. When Grammie died, it was like I'd lost my parents all over again, and her."

"My God, I am so sorry." Maureen's eyes filled with tears.

"Thanks, it's been so difficult for me. But the fact that I'm even talking about this with you shows how the trip has helped." Brooke was sure that stating the list of losses was the same as sharing her feelings about it. "I've not discussed it with anyone, not really, since her death. Everyone asks how I'm doing, how I get through it, what I'm going to do around the anniversaries, and I come up with generic responses. I haven't been able to or wanted to talk about it. I mean, how many times do you have to pull a scab open on a wound?"

"I guess that's your call. Has it helped, I mean, leaving all those feelings alone?" Maureen simply asked.

"No. I feel like I'm in a kayak maneuvering the rapids of grief."

"Isolated and lonely," Maureen said. "You could be on one of those big river rafting boats with other people helping you move through the water. Why the kayak?"

"Because the pain is vastly profound, I feel I'm alone with it."

"Of course, you are. Hell, even with support from others, you'll still find that at some point it's a lonely pain. The difference is, you'll have that support. You deserve it. And as long as we're total strangers and I'm talking to you like we're as close as cloister nuns, I'll add, I bet your grandma and parents would want that for you. No one could love you and not want you to find that support."

"I know." Brooke struggled to hold back the tears. She hated crying in public. "I'm afraid I don't know how anymore. They didn't teach you to be an ally, and they didn't teach me how to ask for help."

"You absolutely do know how, just like you did with me. Say what you can and keep the rest in your heart. It will help you believe that you have control in all this." Maureen stroked Brooke's hand. "But if there's one thing I learned from loss, it's that any control we think we have is a false security. You never know when or how, you only know about now." She stopped for a moment, eyeing Brooke. "Funny, that's your favorite part of the trip. Seeing through some of that gloom. You've started to open the door, not much left but to keep pushing it open, with gentleness—you need that gentleness. One day, you'll walk through. Not like you'll leave the hurt behind, but that's not all you'll have. Yes, like you're finding on this trip."

"Well, Doc. What do I owe you for the consultation?" Brooke said while blowing her nose. "And I can't believe anyone would let you go. You're a sensitive person."

"Thanks, and no charge. This one's on me. I guess it wasn't so much that she didn't love me anymore. I reminded her of where she's been, and that's the part she didn't like." There was a respectful pause. "Isn't being a woman wonderful? I mean, can you imagine two men who just met each other having this conversation?"

"Nah," they said in unison. Then they sat in silence, eating their snacks and letting the sun warm their sore souls.

Maureen broke their stillness. "We should discuss a few good things, things that are wonderful in and of themselves. You know, make it a balanced exchange between strangers."

"I love that idea. I'll even go first. I've met a lot of dear, fun, intelligent, ultra-amazing women on this trip, including you, Maureen. You've listened to me, and I dearly appreciate your thoughtful insights. This trip has been the best. I love being around other lesbians and meeting so many women. I cherish this genuine time together."

"Don't know what I can say after that. I'll add my appreciation for our lesbian sisters here and their spirit to go on despite the dark stuff. We have emotional strength and persistence and daring as solid as our love for women."

"Well said," Brooke replied easily.

"With that, I'll wash up for a delicious late lunch. These appetizers have made me hungry for the real thing. Perhaps I'll see you at Rosewater tonight." Maureen rose and stretched in the sun.

Brooke looked up at her. Maureen's body blocked the sun.

"No, I won't be at the concert, but I will be at the disco."

"Then maybe we'll share a dance."

"Great, and I'd like to introduce you to my old

and new friends."

"I look forward to meeting them. I knew there was a large boat with friends somewhere on that river of yours. You're too friendly to be alone all the time." She gave Brooke a sociable kiss on the cheek and went off.

How did that happen? There are so many female caped crusaders flying around me. Not merely flying, saving me from the emotional boulders in my path. Thank you, oh, divine creator, God, whatever you are, thank you.

Brooke collected her things and headed to a quick lunch, wondering who she would meet next. What would they talk about? How many crushes would surprise her? And how many old souls like Maureen would challenge her?

Chapter Four

Kate, Millie, and Dawn stood at the dining room entrance rounding up their pinky swear friends for dinner. They found everyone except Nina and Amber. Brooke's face wore a giddy smile and a gleam in her eyes that said Brooke didn't care if anyone noticed her happiness while walking arm in arm with Marie. The rest of her wore a crisp white shirt, jeans, and burgundy boots. Even in the casual attire, her look was classic Brooke. Her blue eyes were vibrant with clarity. Her full lips distinguished her small and beautiful face. Brooke's skin, bronzed by the Phoenix sun, was flawless. Back home, her look caused men and women to turn their heads and stare, but she only noticed the women. And tonight, there was a gala of them looking her way.

Marie stood a few inches taller than Brooke. Her short, sandy blond hair bounced with each step. Her brown eyes were soft and comforting. A delicate pink hue warmed her lips, which rested on her kind face framed with a hint of rose in her cheeks. She was confident in her powder blue pullover shirt and white pants. Her natural beauty glowed next to Brooke's uptown features, making the pair stand out like city lights shining under country skies.

It was International Night with three long buffet tables of worldly foods laid out with an elegance that was almost too attractive to eat. Each section represented a different country's food. There were feasts from Italy,

Mexico, China, Germany, India, and Greece; each table had a chef from its country standing behind it. The chefs answered questions, served the food, and guided people through the tables. They were the only men on the ship, and Brooke enjoyed seeing them wait on the women. Their charming accents and humor were as artful as their cooking. They acted as if it were a pleasure to help her instead of a duty or job. No egos or points to prove. Just talented chefs doing a splendid job, including interacting with these lesbos. They were enjoying themselves, which made the exchange even more adorable. Brooke spent purposeful time with each chef, talking to him about where he was from, where he studied his culinary art, ships he had sailed on, and places he had visited. One was gay, but the others were straight and quick to point out they didn't have a problem with the women's lifestyles. "But fewer dates on this ship, right?" Brooke joked, which made them blush. Marie seemed to enjoy Brooke's interaction with the chefs. They were at ease meeting and talking to new people.

Millie and Renee were following them in the food line, each individually lost in the sight and smells of the delicacies.

"Why do they do that?" Millie asked.

"Do what?" Renee answered.

"Put the dessert table in the middle of everything. Those chocolate éclairs are calling me."

"Oh, it doesn't bother me. I wear the 'chocolate patch,' so cocoa is time released into my bloodstream throughout the day."

"Renee, you are unrestrained and cute. I love it," Millie told her.

"That's me, U and C." This was too contemporary

for Millie at first, but then she caught on and smiled.

Marie had to wash up and excused herself as the other women sat down. Unlike the others at the table, Brooke did not eat right away. She tried to secretly scan the tables for Heather. Several times, she thought she saw her, and each time, she got that rush of fun.

"Looking for someone special?" Renee caught on.

"Someone who plays golf?" Kate added. "She'll be right back, you know? The bathroom isn't off the ship or something."

"This is why I don't play poker." Brooke laughed. "Hey, there's someone I'd like you all to meet," Brooke said while standing and motioning to her new friend. "Maureen," she called out. "Come and join us." Maureen approached the table; she looked elegant in a black chiffon pantsuit.

Brooke exposed the telltale sign of someone who worked too much by introducing everyone by their occupations. "Maureen, this is Kate and Millie from Texas. Let's see, Kate is retired, and Millie manages condos, but mostly, they raise hell in a lesbian seniors' version of the dirty dozen, except instead of hogs, they ride RVs. Dawn is a student in Eugene. Dawn, was it architecture you're studying?"

"You have an excellent memory," Dawn said. "My undergrad was in that. Now I'm working on my master's in business." She stood and shook Maureen's hand. Marie, meanwhile, came back and sat next to Brooke, who continued with the introductions.

"And this is Marie, the most out professional golfer. And this is my dear friend, Renee, from Phoenix, who runs wonderful youth programs for the city." She stopped at a new woman sitting at their table. "I'm sorry, I didn't get your name." Brooke gestured to her.

"I'm Adair. It's nice to meet you all. Uh, they escorted me to this table, but if you all are having a reunion of sorts—"

"Not at all," Renee jumped in. "It's nice to meet you, and you're welcome to join us."

Brooke continued, "Yes, Adair, it's nice to meet you. Everyone, I met Maureen on the deck today. Be careful, she has a way of making you tell her your deepest and darkest secrets."

Renee jumped on that before Brooke even finished her sentence. "You mean you got the disciplined and emotional recluse to tell you something about herself?"

"Sorry, I don't listen and tell," Maureen retorted and changed the subject as she sat down. "Adair, I love that name."

"Thanks, I gave it to myself. I changed it from Jane. I was the seventh of eight kids. My parents ran out of name ideas, so when they asked my older brother and sisters what they wanted to call me, they said Jane. She was their favorite babysitter. All my life, I wanted something a little more special."

"Well, you found it," Renee said. "How did your family react to the name change?"

"My parents experienced a bunch of hair-graying times with the older kids. My sibs got caught with drugs, one burned down part of his junior high school. He was on probation for three years, and my older sister thought she wanted to marry at sixteen, which they threatened her out of. So by the time I came into my rites of passage, they were relieved I was just an average dyke who wanted my own name and to go to college."

"Now that's a Father Knows Best story for the nineties," Brooke said. "Did you go to college?"

"Yes, I'm a dentist."

Kate jabbed, "Are you out at work? Is that even possible in your profession? I mean, do any of your patients say, 'Sorry, Doc, but I know where those hands have been,'?" and they all laughed.

"You'll have to excuse my partner." Millie patted Kate on the shoulder. "She has a corny sense of humor. I stay madly in love with her out of pity."

"That's okay. I like dentist humor. And, yes, I'm out to my staff. Patients rarely bring that up. But if they ask if I'm married or whatever, I tell them the truth."

"What reactions do you get?" Renee was interested.

"Most everyone has something to say about it, but I usually can't understand them because my hand is in their mouth." They all laughed again.

"Now that reminds me of a time..." Renee started.

"Guess Kate has a protégé here," Adair smiled at Renee, "but I asked for that one. What about the rest of you?"

They went through their various statuses at work. Most were out or willing to be if anyone asked.

Marie leaned over and whispered to Brooke, "Do you mind if I catch up with you after dinner on the deck? I promised some women I'd take pictures with them and sign autographs. I feel bad because we talked about dinner together, but I'm concerned that if I don't do it now, I'll miss out on fun at the disco later." She pointed to a group of women across the room waving at Marie and gesturing with their cameras.

"No problem. I'll see you later," Brooke said and kissed her cheek.

Then Maureen told the tale she wasn't supposed to tell while being true to the court order not to name her famous ex-partner.

"I knew she was a dyke." Renee pounded on the table. "She has dyke clothes, dyke lips, dyke gestures, and especially dyke hair. That 'trying to grow it out' thing made it worse. Can I ask, what is she like as a lover?"

"Renee," Brooke said. "That's off the mark."

"It's okay, I've been asked that before. But, well, I don't eat and tell, either."

When the chuckles calmed down, Dawn asked, "Is everyone going to Rosewater tonight?"

Heads nodded, and Brooke added, "No, I'll enjoy the quiet night sky." She thought it best to keep the Rosewater sermon to herself. She knew if she shared it, they'd all turn on her as if she were a national traitor. But the group's excitement over the evening eclipsed Brooke's absence.

"I love them," Kate said. "They were the first out lesbian singers. I came out shortly after they became so popular. I found bravery in their music and inspiration in their songs. Millie, remember the night we danced to their first album? We were in our living room with all those candles." She took Millie's hands in hers, and the two looked as though they were the only ones at the table. "We danced all night. I still have that album, or vinyl, as they say today. The cover is a bit worn, like us." She leaned over and kissed Millie. They gave each other a loving look, one that was finely aged in caring hearts, and then they kissed again.

"I go for the atmosphere. Women together singing along with songs they've heard many times before. I prefer music from current women singers,"

Dawn said, referring to their dated music. "But you can't replicate the atmosphere you find at a Rosewater concert."

Brooke nodded and grinned. Yeah, right, an atmosphere of has-beens treating their fans like shit. What transparent hypocrites who haven't had a hit song in almost two decades. Then the words escaped her temporarily monitored lips.

"Have any of you sat at a table with them for a meal on this cruise?"

"No, but I sat with Leslie Curr, that comedian. She's so nice and down to earth. She's making a movie with several big stars and talked about it like it was no big deal," Millie said.

"We also ate with Cirene. Wow, a real actress on this ship. You know they nominated her for an Academy Award. I can't believe it," Kate said. "Everyone wanted to know about her life in Hollywood, and she talked about a few things. But, get this, mostly, she asked about us. She wanted to hear about our lives and not only in a chitchat sort of way. She was genuinely interested in us and as friendly as friendly can be."

"But what about Rosewater?" Brooke repeated. "Has anyone eaten with them? Has anyone seen them at all outside their rooms talking to the women?" Brooke tried to hold back a challenging glare, but it escaped out of her blue eyes.

It was quiet for a moment. The women were blankly staring at Brooke. A small part of her saw the clues on their faces warning her to back off. She would later wish she paid attention to those clues. She knew the other women were not connecting with her. What is my motive to continue with this? But she ignored that inner voice, convincing herself that her point was an important one—one that needed to be clarified and shared, never mind what was motivating it.

"I'm saying they're the great entertainers who have filled our history with glorious memories and that blended our histories with their songs. But they seem so…so…"

"Okay, so they're not the most interactive folks." Kate rose to their defense. "They travel all year and work hard. They need R&R, vacation time, too."

"Some, sure," Brooke continued. "But have you seen them at any event so far?" There was no response. "My point."

"Boy, Brooke, how can you go after a lesbian legend?" Millie brushed her off.

Brooke blushed. "I'm in way over my head here. Sorry, I didn't mean to go after them. Not sure how to talk about this. But, well, they were rude. I just pointed it out to you all. It doesn't change the fact that they're icons of women's music. And I think it's heartfelt that their music is like a soundtrack to every older lesbian's coming out story. I would even thank them for all those memories. And sorry, but no, I can't talk about how wonderful they are now because I don't think they are."

"I see what you mean," Dawn said. "Like you said, they're good for the nostalgia. I'll go for that and the atmosphere. And I understand why you don't want to be there. So what type of music do you like?" Dawn didn't realize it, but she had changed the course of Brooke's doomed conversation.

"I listen to the top 40 and the oldies station. I love music from the sixties. Now that's soul."

"I agree," Kate said. "I've got CDs in my cabin. We'll have an oldies party."

They smiled, turned away from Brooke's

disturbing comments, and replaced them with their individual conversations while the room filled with other diners. It became difficult to hear the people on the other side of the table. Brooke looked around, still searching for Heather.

Adair leaned over to whisper in her ear. "I need to ask you, are you and Renee partners?"

"No, we're only close friends."

"Is she with anyone?"

"No. Do you want to switch seats so you can be next to her? Ask her to the concert or something?" Brooke smiled.

"Won't that be too obvious?"

"Perhaps, but I don't think she'll care about an obvious move. She may even like it." Brooke knew for sure that Renee would like that bold gesture.

Adair was someone most women would like: smart, fun, and down to earth. The fact that she was gorgeous added to the allure. Brooke thought, but for Renee, it would be the first thing she would notice—how could anyone not? Like Brooke, Adair was a smidge taller than Renee but not so tall as to make the two clumsy looking. Adair had darling brown eyes and a sparkling smile that accented her Roman-like features. Her nose was a tad large, but her rose lips called most attention away from that. Brooke noticed some similarities between herself and Adair: the light eyes, thick eyebrows, or women-calling lips. She also noticed enough of the differences between herself and someone who Renee might want to date. That seemed important to Brooke.

"Thanks." Adair smiled.

They changed seats, and for the most part, no one seemed to care. Brooke used the opportunity to look around the room. While she didn't see Heather, she was still in awe at the atmosphere in this dining room filled with beautiful women sitting at stylish tables. There were women whispering, yelling across tables, laughing, kissing, holding hands, toasting with wine, and dropping their heads into their cupped hands with uncontrollable laughter; others giggled, trying all the different foods and smiling with comfort, happiness, and outright joy. There's that peace again. Will there ever be a time when this feeling will always be with me instead of sticking out as the exception? How can I get it from the people I'm close to as easily as from a room full of these strangers? Do I give those feelings to others? Certainly not with that verbal assassination of Rosewater. I need to fight the urge to tell all the lesbian Virginias that there isn't a Rosewater. Either shut up or say something noncommittal.

Brooke was quieter at this dinner, her attention directed at the crowd. The women at her table started to clear, and everyone said goodbye as they headed to the concert.

"See you at the disco and later at our place. Right, Brooke?" Kate reminded her.

"I'll be there."

"Hey, Brooke, I'm going to the concert with Adair. Too fun," Renee whispered in her ear.

"Have fun and remember to share the details," she whispered back.

"I hope there are details to share." Renee flashed her mischievous smile.

※ ※ ※ ※

Brooke stopped on the deck by the rail she thought

of as her very own. She looked over the calm sea lit by the moon. Her thoughts wandered. There must be a star in the sky for every person who ever lived from the beginning of all time. Wonder which one is mine. A big one? One of those hard-to-see small ones? Yes, that's mine. That one so small I'm not sure if it's a star or a brief sparkle from a larger one. No matter. It may seem insignificant, but even a tiny star can bring together an entire constellation.

"Making a wish upon a star?" Marie asked.

"Making a wish on my star," she answered. They stood at the rail for a while in easy silence, scanning the night for nothing. In the faint background, they heard Rosewater, not enough to make out which song was playing, but enough to sense the energy in the theater, that of women transported back in time to each of their Rosewater moments.

"Glad you found me." Brooke focused on Marie now.

"Good. I know we agreed to meet. But you looked so peaceful, I was worried I was crashing in on your private time."

"No, I'm glad you're here."

"Yes? I may be reading too much into this, but I thought I noticed a hesitation. And at dinner, you were somewhat distracted."

Brooke looked into Marie's eyes and, for the first time, saw the depth of her kindness and modest qualities. She also thought about the treasure and curse of being with such a woman. Marie had a finely tuned intuition that heard Brooke's unspoken words. Even more refined than the innate talents of most women. She knew some men with that skill, too, but not many, and few with the knowledge of how to handle the range of responses that could follow "I noticed a hesitation." Marie had said those words perceptively and with enough confidence to hear the response. Now Brooke knew she had to answer with the same caring and genuine style.

"Yes, there was a hesitation, but not because I don't want you here. I do want that, so very much."

"Then what is it? Can you talk about it now?"

God, she's good at this. "Yes, I want to talk to you about it. I'm scared, and I feel somewhat foolish."

"I hate when that happens," Marie joked, easing her a bit.

"Well, it's not often I find myself in this situation. It's been a long time since I've wanted to spend more time with someone the way I want to with you. Hell, it's been a long time since I've been with anyone, period. I'm finding that I really like you, and I want to explore what that means and if there's anything else there."

"Sounds good to me. So what's the 'but'?"

"Not a 'but' an 'and.' All the things I've said about you are true, and I've seen someone on the ship who I keep searching for." Brooke was quick to get those last few words out.

"You mean you've found someone you've been searching for?"

"No. I saw this woman, and ever since I saw her, I keep searching for her to see her again, to talk to her. I'm pulled to her like an uncontrollable fucking magnet. Oh, bad choice of words."

Marie's eyes were friendly. She stood with her arms at her side, open to hear all the things Brooke was presenting.

"I see. One of those 'I looked at her, and the room went dim' magical occurrences."

"Not sure about the magic, but yes. That's the part I feel foolish about." Brooke lowered her head.

"And what's the part you feel scared about?" Marie asked, not looking hurt or disappointed as Brooke imagined she would. Her face was relaxed, understanding, and even a little amused.

"That now you've heard this, you won't want to spend more time with me."

Marie looked at her, and without a blink said, "Well, I've heard a couple of things. You like being with me and want to see if you have more feelings for me. You don't have the same heart-stopping attraction for me as you have for this 'searched-for' woman. But it doesn't sound like you're repulsed by me, either."

"No, not at all. On the contrary, I find you wildly attractive."

"Okay, after hearing about this woman, I did need to hear you're attracted to me because I'm attracted to you and want to get closer to you. We just met, and you don't owe me any kind of promise after an introduction. I said I'm interested in you and now even more. I adore your honesty and how in touch you are with your feelings, even the ones you're unsure about. That's refreshing and somewhat cute to me. Also, I'm glad to hear you want to spend more time with me. I'm a silent but fierce competitor. It's a professional hazard. So if I continue on this path of liking you more the more I see, then I don't mind competing for you. The only way I can do that is by spending more time with you."

"You really are wonderful."

"And I'm betting, or hoping, that my true self proves to be more attractive than some crush flash."

Brooke looked back into her eyes. She thought

about Marie's words and the calm way she spoke. She put her arms around Marie's neck and, while thinking about this made-to-order date, she kissed her with the softness of exposed affection.

"With all that out of the way, tonight is our date," Marie said. "Let's get dessert and coffee and enjoy nature's theater for two."

"Sounds wonderful. But, well, is there anyone I should know about during our date number one?"

"There's no one special in my life. Occasionally, and I mean in a great once in a while, I sleep with someone on the tour. There are fans who want to be with a star athlete. I guess I fit the bill. They get what they want, and it works for me because on those nights, well, I'm lonely and horny. Now if that confession isn't enough to make me feel foolish, nothing is. And I do feel foolish. Still want to get that dessert?"

"Yes, and I'd like to feed you a couple of pieces."

Marie reached over and kissed Brooke. This time, she used her tongue, giving both of them pleasure and closeness. A warmth rippled over her body, awakening sleeping organs.

❧❧❧❧

Most of the women made the way to the disco later that evening. They were still whirling from the concert and ready to dance their emotional high into the night. Brooke and Marie went right to the dance floor. They moved close, then farther away while smiling at each other, looking down, looking into each other's eyes. Brooke thought about her dance theory. She smiled thinking about how sexily Marie danced and noticed Renee and Adair dancing their way around the floor.

Brooke had a fun memory of her and Renee in their college days: dancing at one of the lesbian bars to the pulse of disco music and finding women on the dance floor they wanted to meet.

"Hey, Renee, see the one with the curly blond hair?" she would whisper in her friend's ear.

"Yes. Her dance partner is so tall."

"Can you handle her?"

"No problem" was Renee's typical cocky response. Then she'd go over to the tall woman and ask to cut in, telling her she wanted to dance with her. It was both arrogant and insensitive by Brooke's current standards but was perfectly acceptable for someone in her twenties after several drinks. They knew one of a couple of things would happen. The tall woman would either tell Renee to get lost, tell her that she was with her date and wanted to be left alone, or she would say "sure," and she'd leave her partner dancing by herself.

The latter would give Brooke an opportunity to dance up to her, talk for a while, ask her out, or at least get her phone number. Then Brooke and Renee would exchange roles. Brooke did a good job with the initial "cutting in" role, but she was not as masterful as Renee, whose break-up success rate was in the eighties. There was something about that cocky attitude that made women say yes to her. Many times, the couple was on a date. But that didn't matter to their carefree fun. They would dance for a while, then dump the two connivers and go back to their dates. The flashback made Brooke laugh at herself.

"Are you glad you came?" Renee called to Brooke, bringing her back to the present.

"Yes, you were right," she answered on cue,

smiling at her.

Soon after, Brooke and Marie stepped outside for some air. Kate and Millie joined them as they tried to corral their new friends out of the disco and into one place. They wanted to take them back to their room for a repeat of last night's pinky swear game. Maureen even joined them as the group talked on the deck.

"We should do this every year," Nina announced.

"Agreed!"

"Also," Nina continued. "I'll give you all an open invitation to visit Amber and me in Nogales. We'll show you a great shopping and eating time in Mexico and give you the chance to compare the desert stars to these ocean heavens."

"We may take you up on that," Kate said. "We'll bring the dyke-o-home on wheels and turn the town on its ear."

Maureen leaned over to Brooke. "Do I still have that dance or is this a 'bad' night?"

"Never a bad night for a new friend." Brooke smiled.

She kissed Marie on the cheek and whispered, "This really is just a friend."

"I'm not worried," Marie whispered back. "Have fun."

"Marie, I hope this doesn't seem as busybody as it may sound, but it's wonderful to see my friend so happy and like my old friend," Renee said.

"I'd think nothing other than a friend who enjoys seeing her buddy happy. And you should know you have more information than I do. I wasn't aware this is so different for her, and from the sound of your voice, I'm thinking it may be something Brooke needs to tell me for herself."

Renee stood a little straighter and crossed her arms. "It's even nicer to know there are two of us looking out for her. I may get obnoxious at times, but I don't tell my friend's stories."

"I didn't mean to imply you would." Marie put her hand on Renee's shoulder, which helped Renee unfold her arms and relax a bit. "Sorry if it came across that way. I didn't want you to unknowingly believe I knew something I didn't."

"No need for an apology. I appreciate your thoroughness, and I'm sure Brooke would, too," Renee said.

"As long as the rest of us don't know what the fuck you two are talking about, perhaps we can interrupt," Amber said.

"Don't you mean hell fuck?" Renee replied.

"You brat. I'm going in for more drinks. Can I get you all anything?"

"I'm going to stop the drinks," Marie said. "I don't like the way I feel when I drink too much."

"I'll wait, too," Renee added. "I'll save myself for the pinky swear."

"What's that?" Adair asked.

"Can't explain it, deary. You'll have to come to our room and see for yourself," Kate told her. "We're going to get things ready. You know, tidy up the room, hide the toys. Please invite Maureen to join us, too. See you all in an hour or so." The couple walked away arm in arm.

"Marie," Brooke called out. "It's a slow song. Come dance with me." Marie almost skipped back to the dance floor, and the others followed back inside.

They held each other on the dance floor, their bodies on the edge of touching. "I'm having a great time," Brooke told Marie.

"So am I. But I do have to check in. I'm an understanding date but a curious one, too. Is she here?"

Brooke put her cheek on Marie's and whispered in her ear, "I don't know. I haven't seen her, nor have I looked for her. I said I felt foolish earlier, not mean. This is our date. This is your time with me and mine with you. I'll deal with that mystery on my own time, if at all. And you should continue to ask what you need to when you need to. I will let you know what's happening with me. I hope you do the same with me and continue this extraordinary type of communication we've started."

"Agreed. This is what's happening with me," Marie said and softly pulled Brooke's body close to her. "I'd like to spend time with our new friends at Kate and Millie's, then take you to my room for the rest of the evening, bring you breakfast in bed, and stay with you there for the rest of the day."

"Yes, take me to your room, and I'll take you to much more than my lips," Brooke said, and they kissed and kept kissing even after the song had stopped, while everyone else was waiting for the next song. Even after the crowd whistled and the deejay put a light on them, they kissed, and when they became aware of their exhibition, they laughed with the rest of the women. Brooke saw Renee and the others huddled by the door pointing and laughing, and she blushed.

Chapter Five

Kate and Millie arranged their suite so everyone could sit comfortably on the floor against large pillows. Nina and Dawn helped to make drinks while everyone visited. The women had changed into more relaxing clothes—sweats and T-shirts. Brooke's arm was around Marie's shoulder as they snuggled close.

Renee and Adair were holding hands. They had an innocence about them, and as Brooke watched her friend, it reminded her of the gentle loves back in junior high school. The love culture most young lesbians only got to observe. Acting on them had to be postponed until later in life when their peers' reactions would be less brutal and their own inner strength more sophisticated. Brooke watched Renee embracing that crush, and she heard echoes of those pre-teen years.

I remember kids at my middle school dances. Renee and Adair have that look, that early adolescence "getting to know you" kind, the one shared after the first date at the after-school dance. The dance that lasted from three to five thirty. Those were such delightfully awkward times. Kids spending the first two hours staring at each other and waiting for someone to start dancing in a gym that smelled different. Not like dirty ropes and old gym mats like during P.E. The dance had an aroma of too much cheap makeup on girls unsure of how to apply it and older brothers' cologne on young boys' unshaven cheeks. That was the first date followed by the first walk home. Kids with puppy love walked with an even three feet between them. Renee and Adair are like that young couple. A gym dance and first walk home behind them. On their way to the second date. Their real nighttime date at the county fair. It started rather unassuming with one of their older sisters dropping them off at the fair's entrance formed by those oversized white and yellow lights. That was an evening when things could happen. Things girls giggled with their friends about. Things boys bragged about. Somewhere between the giggles and the brags, they'd hold hands on the Ferris wheel. They would sit close to each other and hear all the sounds of the fair, louder at first when they entered the ride, but having an off-in-the-distance tone as their seat made its way above the smells of cotton candy and corn dogs to the top of it. That's the look Renee has, the "things could happen" look. Things that would never have happened at the school dance in the gym, things that could only happen at the top of the Ferris wheel on the second date, a nighttime date.

"Hello, Brooke. Are you with us?" Marie joked.

"Yes, I'm here, thinking about a carnival ride I never rode. But my friend is telling me it's never too late." Brooke confused Marie, but not enough for Marie to ask.

Suddenly, Brooke was much more aware of the room. She noticed Millie resting her head on Kate's chest as if she had molded a place there over the years. It was a place where no one else could ever rest and feel at home.

"Looks like the couples are multiplying," Nina observed.

"Have you two found anyone interesting?" Kate

asked Nina and Amber.

"I met someone tonight at the dance," Nina answered. "We danced like we owned it, talked, and laughed together. All good ways to spend time with someone. I liked her, and because I did like her, I didn't invite her here tonight."

"We may have just been insulted." Millie told Kate.

Nina laughed. "No, friends. I think it would be dangerous to bring someone you recently met to an evening game of pinky   swear. It might totally scare her off."

"Not sure how to interpret that comment," Adair thought out loud.

Renee was quick with her response. "You can interpret it as my being more adventurous than the average dyke."

"Well, I'm rationally scared," Maureen said. "What's a pinky swear?"

"Oh, I'm sorry, Maureen," Brooke said. "Have you met everyone?"

"Yes, I have, either at dinner or at the dance. I even met Amber before the disco at the afternoon water polo games."

"We sure did, and, boy, did we suck like the master suckers," Amber said.

Amber's choice of words again surprised Renee. "What school did you say you taught at? Drunken Sailors Elementary?" Everyone laughed.

The group explained the pinky swear game to Maureen and Adair. They all joined pinky fingers and repeated the oath. "I swear not to repeat anything I hear or see tonight with anyone who is not in this room, ever."

Then Renee remembered. "I believe it's Brooke's turn to get a pinky swear. Does anyone remember who gets to ask her?"

Kate answered, "Well, Marie was the last one to tell us about that unplanned and exciting time. So she gets to ask Brooke a question. What a difference twenty-four hours makes." They all laughed as Marie moved her arm from Brooke's shoulder and rubbed her hands together.

"Let me see, something, something, well, I want it to be something different, but my creative gene is fairly dimmed tonight. So I'll ask you the question I got. What is the kinkiest thing you've ever done—sexually, that is?"

"The sad part is I kinda do think I did something kinky, but I don't know what it was," Brooke replied.

"Come on, you're stalling," Renee ribbed her.

"No, I'm serious. It's the kinkiest thing I think I ever did. Anyway, I'm sure it will satisfy this game, though. Once in college, of course it had to be in those wild days, I tried LSD. I had never used any kind of hallucinogenic, and my friends bugged me to at least do it once before our college fun days were over. The idea of being out of control was never appealing to me. And while I didn't have a bad trip, what I experienced kept me from ever trying it again. I did enjoy some parts of it, but overall, I was right. It was unpleasant not having control of whatever was melting around me. Anyway. I was at a party at the Lesbians R Us home, as they used to call it. About five dykes rented out this house near ASU. They had some of the hottest parties I've ever been to. There was always a theme to them, like 'edible underwear night' or the 'bobbing for dildoes in a bath of gin' party, don't think those need any explanation.

"This was a small exclusive LSD party. I decided to go at the last minute because I thought my friends had a good point. College would have been wasted years if I didn't at least try it once. They had a large backyard with a high fence, so there was a lot of privacy, and we spent most of the night outside talking to trees, bugs, whatever. I was engaged in solving the world's problems with the wisest blade of grass I ever talked to. You know, all that psychedelic crap. It was fun but not what I wanted in terms of it being so unpredictable. Then the next morning, I woke up with a garden hose in bed with me. I don't remember what the hell happened, but it must have been kinky. At least my fantasies about what happened were pretty kinky."

"Wow," Adair roared. "Most of us go to the sex shop for toys. You probably visit the garden section of home improvement stores." They couldn't stop laughing. Brooke didn't mind, even though it was at her expense. She saw Adair's playful humor and liked it.

Then Brooke's voice rose above the laughter. "Okay, Adair, you're next."

"Oh, shit."

"I'll stay with the theme. What's the kinkiest sexual thing you've ever done?"

Adair was quick. "I'm assuming you mean with a human and not our in-ground sprinkler system."

Brooke looked at her friend. "Renee, I think you've met your match. With whatever you'd like to tell us about, dear Adair."

"When I was in dental school," Adair began, "I went to—"

An earsplitting explosion interrupted Adair's story. The ship rocked violently, and the turbulence continued with more explosions intermingled with screams. Women were thrown into disarray. Items in the room flew at them with the ship's quick and erratic movements. Brooke's mind raced through snapshots of thoughts.

Noise. Firecrackers on deck? Why are we moving? Not firecrackers? What's wrong? The ship's going down? Screams? Others are screaming. Renee, where's Renee?

Brooke saw her friend holding Adair. Both were sliding across the floor in what appeared to be slow motion. It was a predictable but unstoppable slide, and Brooke concluded, "That's not firecrackers, what's wrong?"

"Everyone, let's head to the deck. Stay together," Maureen yelled. "Grab those lifejackets in the closet. We'll get more on deck."

Brooke was paralyzed, unable to express the questions racing in her confusion. Lifejackets? Why, what's happening? What does Maureen know?

"Honey, take my hand. Stay with me," Marie told her.

"Renee, Renee!"

"Buddy, it's okay. I'm here. Stay with Marie. I'm here," Renee called back.

Kate and Millie had on lifejackets and were passing out the other two to Nina and Amber as the four women huddled together. Brooke had all but forgotten the need for the jackets. She was lost in a vertigo of sounds and disjointed images flashing by her.

There were more explosions. Some seemed smaller, but it was hard to tell. Were they softer or just farther away? They opened the cabin door and saw the hall packed with women. The corridor was jammed with bodies pushed from one side of the hall to the other as the ship continued to toss violently. Alarms were blaring in a rhythmic tone of high and low pitches. A red light flashed from the ceiling over those desperately trying to get to the top deck.

Maureen used the force of her large body to clear tiny spaces in the hall. Each woman from the cabin disappeared into a space. Some tried to hold hands and stay close. "Come on," she called to Brooke and Marie. "Get the hell out of here," she warned as the crowd sucked her away. There were more screams, faint ones and others in loud stereo. Brooke stood in the doorway with Marie wondering how they could possibly get into the packed crowd, unsure if she even wanted to.

"We can't go in that." Brooke shook her head.

"Yes, we can. Trust me." Marie tried to sound reassuring.

Marie locked arms with Brooke. "I'm not leaving you," Brooke thought she heard Marie say over the melee.

Brooke choked on her own fear, gasping for breath. Marie fought their way into the crowd. They were wedged into the group with pressure coming from all sides except the top of their heads. Brooke tried to get some air by tilting her head back, but the bodies pressing against her made it impossible for her to maneuver even that simple move. Are we moving? It was as if they were standing still, their bodies compressed together. She thought she smelled smoke.

No, it can't be. It's from those women who smoke. It can't be, I'll die. I'll suffocate. Please, please, not that family curse. Not the burning fire, not my parents' fate. Grammie, help! Help, Grammie!

Brooke's thoughts were hard to hold on to. The smell of smoke got stronger. She gasped. She couldn't feel her legs or hands, and her face was tingling. Her cheeks were numb, and her thoughts were screaming in her head.

It is smoke, I can see it. Black swirls of smoke reaching out for me right there, floating over my head. Death riding on black smoke, it searches the halls for me. It doesn't care who else it takes, but it won't stop until it takes me. I don't want to die. Please, not like this!

She tried to turn and run from the smoke, but the crushing pressure of bodies forced her into the black haze.

❧ ❧ ❧ ❧

Brooke took several long, deep breaths and stretched out as far as she could. She did this over and over just to make sure she could breathe and move again. Moving was still slightly restricted, but she could breathe again and took it in like drinking from an oasis in the desert. She opened her eyes and saw Marie looking down at her. Brooke's head was in her lap.

"You rest, honey, the storm is over. It looks like smooth sailing from here," Marie reassured her while stroking Brooke's hair.

From where? she thought, but all her scattered questions were quieted by the joy she found in breathing and feeling freed of that crowd.

"Shit, shit," Brooke heard someone say. She looked around and saw many women sitting close together and even lying on top of one another. It was hard to make out all their faces. There wasn't much light left. She noticed the life jacket wrapped around her chest.

"We're in a raft?" she realized.

Marie was soft spoken. "Yes. The ship went down. We're okay. The sun is almost set. It'll be dark soon. I won't leave you. Rest. You really need it."

"Did I burn?" Brooke ignored all the other information. "Did the fire burn me?"

"You're going to be okay, Brooke. But you need to rest now," Marie repeated.

"I heard if you hit it in the nose, it'll turn away," another woman said.

"Fine, you jump in the fucking water and hit the mother fucking shark in the nose!" the other argued.

Shark! Brooke's heart was pounding. For the first time, she noticed the cold damp rubber bottom of the raft against her body. It smelled like plastic and mildew.

"Where?" Brooke tried to get up to see over the side of the raft.

"Someone restrain her! Fuckin' great time to get up," the mean voice yelled.

"It's okay, I have her," another answered as she put calming arms over Brooke.

"Brooke, lie still. We need to keep the raft calm. We need your help to do that. Can you do that?"

"Sure."

"No one move. Be still," they whispered.

While still not sure she believed in her surroundings, Brooke was aware enough to lie still. She held on to Marie's leg, then immediately thought of Renee. She wanted to jump up and see if she was on the raft but had to fight off that urge. "Renee?"

"I saw her get on another raft. Shh, we'll talk later. Seriously, this is not a good time." Marie held her hand.

Brooke's thoughts came and left her. This is too calm to be in the water. I must have misunder...

Misunder… Not gotten it right. I don't want to be here, either.

A slight movement bumped the bottom of the large rubber raft.

"The shark, the shark," she yelled with what little strength she had.

"Yes, it dove right underneath us," an icy voice acknowledged.

"Is it…" Brooke tried to ask when hearing a single scream and then more.

"No, no, help, please help m—" a voice called out from the ocean.

"What?" Brooke managed to say, and her words were mixed with the soft crying of the women on her raft. She struggled to look up over the top of the raft.

"It-it got another raft. There are many of us out here," someone told her. "Some of the other rafts you can see. But there's more out there that we've lost sight of. The screams seem to come from everywhere. It's been three days of this hell. A week of storms, and now three days of shark hell. You'd think they'd just eat us up or move on. I'm sick of the daily screams."

"Go help them. Maybe it didn't get everyone. Find the others." It was difficult for Brooke to talk. She was weak and didn't understand why.

"Brooke asked us to go and help," Marie said in a more commanding voice.

"Help? How the fuck are we going to do that?" that stern voice answered.

"Brooke's right," another joined in. "We should move over that way to see if there are any survivors."

But the mean voice answered them all in elevated anger. "Move over there? I can't believe I got on this plastic boat with you people. Let's talk about this. A few minutes ago, someone said sharks are attracted to movement, and we should be still. We also know that they're sensitive to the smell of blood. I hate that this has happened to those women. But now you're asking me to move our little boat around in bloody shark waters where there's probably going to be a feeding frenzy."

"Help!" they all heard.

Brooke gathered up her strength. "People are alive over there, and we need to help them. So you either help move this boat, or I'll swim over myself." As she spoke the words, she realized it was a stupid threat. She obviously didn't have the strength to move, not to mention swim, and the mean woman wouldn't have given a damn if Brooke jumped out of the raft.

"Tracy," another woman said. "You need to shut up. You need to shut the fuck up and do it now! We're going. If you don't want to go, get out and swim to another boat."

A much better threat, Brooke thought.

"Doesn't anyone think this is fucking suicidal?" Tracy tried to argue.

No one answered; they were too busy moving the oars and turning the raft around. Tracy started to help, cussing all the while. The raft only traveled a short distance when they came upon the carnage.

"Help!"

"Over there, she's over there."

Brooke could hear the stranded woman being pulled into the raft. She could smell the blood in the water and feel the fear in their helpless little raft.

"I don't see anyone else. Let's get out of here." That was the last thing Brooke heard before she passed out.

Chapter Six

Brooke tried to focus her eyes, straining to find anything familiar. Unaware her fists were still clenched, she noticed the throbbing in her arms and along her thigh. Fine sand covered her eyelashes, and when she tried to wipe it off, the sand covering her hands made it worse. It stung her eyes like the time her grandmother shoved a spoon into a grapefruit and shot the juice across the breakfast table into Brooke's left eye. "Ouch," she said over and over each time, increasing the volume. This place felt and smelled different. This wasn't that hell life raft she last remembered—were they home now?

"It's okay. You're going to be all right." She heard a voice.

"Who's saying that? None of this has been all right. What is this place? It's hard to breathe. My eyes," she mumbled.

The voice answered, "Yes, your eyes have a lot of sand in them. We ran into ultra-nasty weather. Remember, on the raft? We're on the beach now." The voice was calm.

"Beach? Where are the lifeguards, ambulances?"

Brooke was so fixed on seeing where she was and what had happened, she didn't notice the blood running down her sunburned calf. Many women's bodies had cuts and scrapes from hitting against coral before they washed up on the shoreline.

"What about that cut?" someone asked.

Another replied, "I don't know. Try to bandage it up with torn clothes. It's okay, sweetie, you're going to be okay."

That voice. Okay? Okay from what? Who is that?

"There are others a lot worse than her. Give her antibiotics from the first-aid kit and clean the wound with alcohol. It'll hurt like hell, but she won't get an infection."

Brooke tried to place those voices. They seemed vaguely familiar. Was it Dawn? She was so bad with names. If only she could see the face—faces she could remember.

"We can help her more by using this stuff on her eyes," another voice commanded. "You hold her gently, and I'll squirt fresh water in them."

"But the water. We should conserve it," a second voice whispered.

"Please. That makes no sense. What would a couple of squirts in the eyes buy us? It'll help orient her, and that will make it easier to deal with the cuts that way."

Brooke felt a gentle hand on her shoulder. "You can help us. Please lie back. Trust me. Your eyes are full of sand. We can get it out, and then you'll see what this is all about. But we can't get there until you help."

Finally, someone who senses my thoughts.

Partially induced by exhaustion, Brooke surrendered to the confusion, too tired to make sense of it. She lay there and tried to open her eyes while they squirted water into them. But her eyes clamped shut.

"I'm sorry I have to do this, but..." one woman said and used her fingers to pry Brooke's eyes open one at a time. "Breathe deep. It'll help you."

It seemed like forever, but after a few moments,

Brooke sat up and looked around. Even though her eyes were still stinging, her surroundings came to her in soundbites of thoughts.

There's so many of them, lying there moaning. Others sitting up with heads resting in their hands. Why are those other women trying to walk? They're stumbling. Blood on my leg, how did that happen? Will I lose my leg? Everyone looks so…so beaten up. These can't be the same women from the ship. They're all messy…confused… fearful. You can see the pain in them, too. I don't recognize a one of them. Clothes torn, some without shirts. They're so red, sunburnt. Ouch. My arms, too. Or is that a burn from the ship? That's right, there was smoke. I'm burned? No, must be a sunburn. Where's that pain coming from? Cut on my arm…ouch, is that ugly? Those two women coming toward me…Amber? No, they're like a couple of those soccer moms from the ship. They're helping. The soccer moms are taking care of us? They combed their hair. How'd they do that? Renee, where's Renee?

As the women got closer, Brooke noticed more sounds around her, as if her hearing was coming into focus along with her eyes. The first sound that captured her attention was the choir of crying. Some deep, painful tears. Others soft with sniffles.

The soccer moms approached her. Brooke heard one say, "Here. I made makeshift bandages, we've used a lot from the first-aid kits. I rubbed disinfectant cream right in it. This will help her cuts." Her voice was compassionate.

The other replied, "Good. Too bad I don't have some of my essence here. This kit will have to do. I like the way you prepared the bandages," she complimented the other woman, and they both talked to Brooke. "Is your vision better? What's your name? Can you hear us, honey? What's your name?"

"I'm Brooke. Yes, my eyes are better. Still sore, but better for sure. Where's Renee?"

"Well, I'm glad to hear that. About your seeing. I'm sure the blurry part will continue to get better. Let one of us know if it doesn't. And, yes, they will be sore. The important thing is your sight is getting better. We'll do another wash in a bit. The pain will go away, be patient. I'm saying that a lot today. Not too many of us have had a chance for introductions since we washed up on this island. I'll ask around for your friend…Rena?"

"No, Renee. Yes, find her." Brooke looked at the two women like a photographer superimposed on the tropical scenery. All the other women were so disheveled at best and outright mangled at worst. These two barely had a scratch on them. Their clothes were wrinkled but not at all ripped like most of the others. It was so out of place that, for a moment, Brooke doubted she was still alive. "Are you the soccer moms? We're alive, right?" Brooke uncontrollably asked.

They smiled. "Well, we've been called worse than dead soccer moms. Brooke, we are alive. We've washed up on this beach, and right now, we're helping to take care of the injured. Rest now. We're going to help some of the other women."

"No. Don't leave me now," Brooke pleaded.

"You go ahead, Claire. I'll stay with her for a while. Brooke, I'm Lillian. You can call me Lillie. I'll stay here for a few more minutes. Then I need to go help others. I know it doesn't feel like it, but you're going to be okay. There are other women who are a lot worse off, and I need to help them."

The sun was much too hot. So hot, Brooke was sick to her stomach. She lay on the sand and curled herself up like a child fighting off the flu.

"Where's Renee? Where's Renee?" she whispered over and over.

She fell back into a sick sleep until familiar voices woke her.

❧ ❧ ❧ ❧

"Adair," Marie called out, "how's Brooke? Is she better?"

Adair was calm. "Physically, she is. Claire and Lillie took care of her. She's lucky she doesn't need stitches. That cut must hurt like hell, though. Emotionally, like I told you before, she's been in shock, like on the raft. It confuses me. I mean, it seems so much worse than what her wounds would indicate. The good news is she's been more coherent over the last several hours than in all the time we were at sea. She's able to answer simple questions and stuff like that. Oh, and I'm not absolutely positive about this, but I didn't see any new cavities," Adair tried to joke.

"Thank you so much. I know we've all expected a lot of you, perhaps more than your dentistry teachings prepared you for." Marie hugged her.

"It's okay. Hold her now and talk to her." Adair smiled.

Marie sat and gently placed Brooke's head in her lap. Her long fingers stroked Brooke's hair in a rhythm that was equally soothing to Marie.

"Brooke, it's me, Marie. We were on the cruise ship—remember?—and played fun games with some other women. There was an explosion. Or a couple.

We were at sea for several weeks on the raft. Now we've been on this island for a couple of days. But the important thing is, it looks like you're going to be okay. Did you get that? You'll be back to your old self soon." And Marie started to cry.

Brooke opened her eyes and looked at Marie, who had a bruise on her forehand and a small cut on her cheek. Brooke was fatigued but not tired enough to miss the concern on Marie's face. Brooke lightly touched her bruise and tried to blow her a kiss.

"I heard," Brooke whispered back. "How are you? What about Renee?"

"I'm fine. A bump on the head, but I'll be on the golf course by next week."

"Renee?" Brooke repeated more desperately.

Marie's answer finally brought some relief to Brooke. More so than any first aid. "She wasn't hurt at all. I think she's made of rubber or something. She's been by a lot to check on you, but you were always out. She's been running all over the place, helping the injured and working with a group assessing this place, you know, finding food, shelter, and all that."

"That's my Renee."

"Yeah, she's a regular Florence Nightingale. Really, she's been wonderful. You'd be proud."

Brooke smiled. Renee was okay. Marie was holding her. For a moment, her world was perfect, even in her painful body.

"All right, you're up!" she heard Renee's voice. "Here's food, some fish, fruit, and all that good stuff. Sit up, visit with me, and thank those Caribbean-born dykes who know how to spear fish."

"Renee!" Brooke called as Marie helped her to sit up. They held each other as if they'd been apart for years.

"I'm so glad you're okay. It's unimaginable to think of something happening to you. I've been asking for you, or maybe I thought I asked. I couldn't lose you, too," Brooke cried.

"It's okay, buddy. I'm not going anywhere," Renee said while gently rocking Brooke in her reassuring arms. "It's okay. We're here together. We're all alive as alive can be. Now listen, I'm worried about you. Can you eat something?"

"I'm not exactly hungry. Just hold me for a while." Brooke would not let go of her and was confused by Renee wanting to talk about food at their tearful reunion. She was oblivious to how weak she really was.

Renee tenderly rubbed her back. "I'm here with you. I'll be here for you. And I need you, too, you know. Brooke, you were out of it most of the time on the raft and ever since we washed up on this place. It's not like we have a cure for extreme dehydration, and I'm afraid you're headed there. You've had so little to eat or drink. So, please, eat this. Eat it now," Renee begged.

"Yes, ma'am. You're right, I need to eat," Brooke conceded, still ignorant of her own endangered health.

"You're right. I love it when you say that." Renee smiled through her own tears.

Renee looked up at Marie, who was interchanging smiles with tears. The two of them were much more aware than Brooke that not everyone had shared their luck. Both of them had been helping the sick, holding women separated from their partners, comforting the worries of what had happened to women not on the island. The list of pain was longer than either of them dared to imagine.

Brooke was up and around after a couple of days in time to attend the castaways' first full meeting. Up until then, they had acted like ants setting up a new farm. They instinctively knew the group was going to have specific needs and joined in small groups to take care of the others. But it had gotten to where the initial shock and caretaking were over. The focus changed to multitudes of tasks in what they now considered part of their long-term survival.

The women who were able gathered at a clearing near the beach. It looked like a section of the palm trees had been carved out in a half circle. They sat with their backs to the ocean. Though she couldn't be sure, Brooke thought there were about seventy-five, maybe even a hundred women there. It was hard to tell among all those faces.

Brooke sat with Renee, Marie, Kate, Dawn, Adair, and Maureen. Her friends were scruffy versions of the women she knew on the ship. Marie's bruises were starting to heal. She carried a soft sadness, but her eyes were as alluring as when they met.

Kate was the worst off, if looks could tell anything about a person's feelings. One eye was opened larger than the other, and everything about her looked—lost. One hand had a small but constant shake to it. Her pants still had bloodstains.

Dawn's natural bohemian charm fit well with the island's primitive accommodations. Her loose-fitting clothes swayed with the island's breeze. She greeted other women with a caring smile and hug. Sometimes, she gazed out into the ocean like she saw hope in the horizon; most everyone did at some point.

Brooke knew Adair and Maureen less than she knew the other women. Adair's striking good looks, like a Roman goddess, were subdued by the sand and dirt on her cheeks. Maureen, like Renee, had the deepest of sunburns on her fair skin, which added to her tall frame, made her stand out like a warning sign.

Brooke looked out over the crowd and back again at her friends. In many ways, the members of this small pinky swear group were strangers to one another. But compared to their relationships with the full group, they were old friends. Brooke was glad to be with them again. Renee told Brooke that a few of the women from Kate and Millie's room had made it to the island and that they were well, but this was the first time she had gotten to talk with them other than tearful hugs she'd had with so many women over the past few days.

The crowd's faces told her a lot at this gathering. They were searching, worried, brave, comforting, heroic, sad, calming, disturbed, tired, hurt, and all women. They sat in small groups like Brooke and her travel companions. Others were obviously couples. Many sat alone or lay on the beach by themselves, looking up at the sky. Brooke could not tell if those women were resting or too sad to make eye contact with anyone directly.

"Glad to see you up and about. Are you feeling better?" Nina asked Brooke as she joined the group.

Brooke smiled. "Yes, much. Not as confused anymore." Without thinking of all the possible answers to her question, she turned to Kate and innocently asked, "Where's Millie?"

"She's not on the island, so I don't know what's happened to her. I imagine her on another island or rescued. We got separated while scrambling into the lifeboats. I told her, 'Hold my hand. Hold it tight.' She stopped to help someone who slipped on the deck. Others were running over her, but Millie stopped and tried to pick her up. I could see them over my shoulder as I was carried off the boat by the rushing crowd. So I don't know. I'm sure she's been rescued. I feel half here, Brooke." Kate's voice was weak. She had a tearless sadness about her.

"We're here with you, honey. Take a long deep breath. You're right, she's probably home heading our rescue party," Maureen told her as she secured her large arm around Kate's shoulder.

"I bet she's got all your RV friends to launch a search effort for us. I bet she called it the dykes by air 'n sea rescuers," Renee joked.

"Thanks, Renee. I hope so," Kate said with false conviction.

"I don't know about Amber, either." Nina was crying. "I fucking hate not knowing. I can't believe this has happened to us." She waved her arms about.

"This thing doesn't happen to us. It happens to goofy characters on a boat with a fat captain and a skinny slapstick first mate. It happens to young boys from a private school who regress to animals. It happens to the family Robinson or an overworked overnight shipping employee who has a fucking cosmic lesson to learn. It even happens to a group of people competing for a million dollars, but it doesn't, it does not, does not, not, not…happen to a group of lesbians on a fun cruise!"

"Though, it has," Maureen said evenly. "I know it's unbelievable, I know it's scary, but here we are, and we need to be here for each other." Now she was comforting Nina with her arms around her and ever so slightly rocking back and forth. Brooke looked at the woman she shared afternoon deck chairs with and conversations about her ex-partner. She still looked like a giant to Brooke. Her face was worn, but her reassuring voice and calming presence made it through the tragedy and onto the island in all its beauty. Now she was using it to comfort strangers brought together by two dear, wise women and one pinky swear game.

Nina was running her hands through her hair. "I'm so hot."

"Here." Maureen continued to help. "I made these hair ties. We'll bunch it up. Or we can cut it short."

"Cut? Do you know how long it took me to grow this? This is my Latina Rapunzel hair, thank you very much. Cut?" Nina lowered her voice and smiled at Maureen as they pulled up her hair.

Brooke saw a woman walking to the center of the crowd, and her presence quieted the group. She stood there, hands on her hips, looking around as if to inventory the group. "My name is Shelby," she announced in a voice as large as she was tall, which was a good thing, for a small voice would have been lost over the soft waves and rustling palm trees.

Brooke smiled. "Shelby's dad was probably a race car fanatic. She was all tomboy, grew up without brothers and got all her father's attention. Her smile caught all of Brooke's attention. Shelby had a sizeable grin and perfectly white teeth. Her healthy lips seemed to wrap around them with ease with a shy smile. Shelby continued talking with what Brooke thought was a Midwestern accent.

"We thought it best to get together with everyone to share what we know and what we don't know and to decide what to do next. There's a lot to discuss." Shelby talked slowly enough for folks to follow, even those who were still not sure they believed all this.

"But first, the hardest and saddest news. We've lost three of the women who made it to the island. No one seems to know two of them. The third woman was Tonya. She was Shavoon's partner." Shelby motioned to her right. "Shavoon asked me to thank all of you who have offered your support and thoughtful words. In the early evening, we're going to have a service for these women. Let's take a moment of silence to pray, meditate, send out white light, or whatever it is you do to show respect for the passing of these lives and for the gifts they left behind them.

"Next." Shelby cleared her throat and wiped her eyes several times before she continued, which reminded Brooke of the softness inside tomboys. "I'm sorry. My heart is full of sadness for those who have died and for those grieving. Give me a minute." And they did. They all took a long minute of silence and tears. Some cried for the losses, others out of fear, and many because it was a good time to cry.

"Well, next we need to deal with rumor control." Shelby cleared her throat. "There's been more speculation about what happened to us. You've probably heard the more popular theories—there was an explosion or that we hit something in the water or something hit us. I've even heard the one about us being attacked by a prehistoric giant sea serpent. The truth is, we don't know the truth. There were several explosions that ripped up the ship. No one here knows for sure how many lifeboats were usable. At one point, I remember counting over fifty women in the water. I know we lost many to shark attacks. I was close to that, and I've tried to remember lost faces, but I'm having trouble with that. I know many of you are counting on me to remember. I'm trying. But keep this in mind: If someone isn't on this island, that doesn't mean they're gone. The waters were choppy that night. And as you know, we went through bad weather in the days following the accident. Other lifeboats were most likely scattered in different directions.

"One raft that brought us here may still be seaworthy. Tomorrow, we're going to discuss the wisdom of setting back out to sea in it. Anyone is welcome to join in that decision."

"How will we decide?" a voice called out from the crowd. "I don't want to go out there again. Not ever again. Not to the heat, the sickness, the sharks." Others cried out when she mentioned the sharks. "Not again, don't ask me."

Shelby responded calmly but assumingly, "No, no one will ask you to do that. You're on the island now. You'll stay here on land with the others. Actually, I don't know how we'll decide who should go or even if we will go. We'll have to see how the conversation goes. I've tried to serve as a town crier so to speak, keep folks informed, start off our meetings, but I'm not the self-appointed leader. You are all the leaders. You decide how to decide, I'll help you get there. Though, from what I've seen so far, you don't need a lot of help. You all deeply listen to each other, try to take care of each other, and come to agreements with or without voting or by processing yourselves into a new acronym. There isn't even an impenetrable alliance to using consensus. Everyone naturally comes together. I hope that continues. If it doesn't, we'll figure how to go from there," Shelby directed.

"Yeah, fuck Robert's Rules," someone yelled, and

for the first time, they clapped.

Shelby moved to the next item. "Most of the injured were finding relief and healing pretty well, thanks to Adair, our dentist-turned-M.D., Kerri, the nurse who hasn't slept, and let's not forget our herbal healers. Bless you, Claire and Lillie. Any questions before I go on to the next subject of living needs?"

"Yes," a woman called out. "First of all, I'd like to give my sympathy to Shavoon for her loss. Also, I was wondering about the other two sisters. If no one here knows who they are, how will we let folks know about them once we're rescued? I'm assuming the service will include a burial."

Shelby informed everyone, "The group had several discussions about the two lost ones. We've written a description of them, and a couple of women drew pictures as best they could. We're going to bury them on the island somewhat away from where we've set up our living space." Then, Shelby bent over to talk with Shavoon, who nodded in agreement at whatever Shelby had said. "Shavoon has asked for Tonya to be cremated at sea. So we're putting together a raft of sorts to launch and set afire." She paused for another moment.

"Okay, let's talk about the island for a minute," Shelby continued. "The scouts are thinking it's a couple miles long and about half as wide, to be as nonspecific as possible."

They all laughed.

"Maybe we can get a scout to fill us in on some details." Shelby gestured.

"Sure, my name is Madison." A woman stood, towering over many with broad shoulders and sparking eyes. "There are no large animals that we could find.

Though, as you can see, the vegetation is super thick in the center of the island. Not sure what's in there. We found fresh water from a small waterfall right under the hilltop. A couple of women are there with makeshift containers. We're also using the desalinization tools we found in the lifeboats. That process takes a while, with a small yield of fresh water, so trips to the waterfall are critical for a group this size. We didn't find anyone else on the island, but there's scattered evidence someone has been here."

"What does that mean?" a woman called out.

"We found a hint of a campsite. Someone worked hard to clean it up, but part of a fire ring is still there."

"How do we know they're not still on the island?" another inquired.

"Could it be drug smugglers hiding out?" was another's concern.

"We don't know," Shelby joined in. "Boy, this group has watched a lot of Miami Vice reruns. Okay, we're thinking if that person, or persons, were still on the island, it would be a fresher campsite. If they're drug smugglers or another type of asshole, I'd say we severely outnumber them." She motioned to the large group, which responded with laughter and screams of "Yes!" and quickly became quiet.

Shelby just kept going. "On to living needs. Renee, stand up." Renee rose. "That's Renee. She's the lead on living needs. Take it away, Renee."

Brooke noticed her friend's face was sunburned, all red and blistered in some places. It looked like a permanent squint had been placed on her somewhat small eyes. Though, she still carried herself with a solid look as though her body did not feel the pain of the life raft trip or even the wreckage, for that matter, but her powerful frame was slimmer now. Also, she had a less mischievous flirtation about her when she talked. She was more mature.

Renee spoke with a supportive tone even as she gave out details of the work groups. "Hi, everyone. I'll tell you about the work groups we've come up with so far, ask you if we left anything out, and finally allow you time to volunteer for a group. The food group is working on, well, feeding us. There's a group working on our shelter needs. The pee group—you all have to find a new name—has been setting up outhouses. In the meantime, please do not piss in or near where we meet or eat. Go into the thick trees with a friend and bury it. We need to get this under control soon to minimize it turning into a disease zone.

"Okay, what else? Oh, yes, there's a group of counselors if you want someone to talk to. Also, a couple of professional massage folks offered to set up shop over the next couple of days."

"Hey, sign me up for a back rub," a voice announced.

"Okay, okay, I can see the massages rank over the pee group. But how long can you go without a massage? Now how long can you go without taking a shit? You see, we mostly need help with the outhouses.

"You all have heard this, there's a group of scouts who search the island for more clues about any past visitors, mapping the place out, that kind of thing. And lastly, the rescue group takes turns on watch and managing our flare guns, the bonfire, etc. By the way, each of you should thank them for their fire-starting talents. All they learned as kids, how to rub those sticks together, start sparks. It's helped in many ways. I don't know about the rest of you, but I'm so glad these women were more interested in learning about survival techniques when they were young than they were about selling cookies. Of course, we would all be a lot better off if part of their education included learning how to fix waterlogged cellphones, but still, we're thankful for the fire.

"Also, there's a superbly intelligent, a.k.a. egghead, group that will review options about using the lifeboats." She pointed at a woman and added, "You know I'm only kidding, we love ya. Of course, none of them is smart enough to make a radio out of coconuts, but they understand water currents, stars, all that stuff. Guess that's about it, except you should see me if you want to join any of these groups. Did I leave something out?"

"If there was a search group, wouldn't they have found us by now? Or maybe they've stopped looking?" A worried voice ignored Renee's agenda and asked what many were thinking.

"Stop looking?" Renee smiled. "I guess you haven't met my mom. The whole Navy fleet couldn't keep her from finding me. Now multiply that by as many women as you see here." Her response seemed to reassure the worried faces on several of the women.

"What do we do if we have our periods?" someone else called out.

"Stay out of the ocean," another screamed.

"Actually, that's good advice," Renee said. "Hell, we don't have a moon group. What are folks doing about that?"

"I ripped up clothes and made a pad. And I wash that out in the ocean."

"Okay, will you get with others and decide on period options? Maybe you all can combine and form a pee and bleed group. Any other items not covered?"

The women were quiet and looked around at one another. Brooke could see the confusion rising. While Renee gave them good advice, it was as if they expected more clear-cut answers about how they got there and when they were going home. Someone besides Brooke must have sensed the same thing. Someone with the knowledge of how to help, because with one simple question, she pulled the plug on the stress bottle. "Hey, Renee. What are folks doing about birth control?" she yelled from the back of the group, and the women happily followed suit.

"I have some rubber gloves if you're worried."

"I pull my fingers out early."

"I pull my fist out early."

"We only have oral sex."

"I jump up and down after sex."

"I jump up and down during sex."

"My partner had a fingerectomy."

"This group is wild, do you hear? Wild."

The women laughed and cried and held one another, and with time, each one intentionally made her way to Shavoon for a hug and to say something to her. No one left that site until every woman had talked with her. But it was Kate who particularly caught Brooke's eye. She seemed so lost, even more so than Shavoon, who at least had sadness in her face. Kate had the blank look of the unknowing, trapped between the fear of what might be and the hope of what should be. Her gaze fixed on nothing, longing for the blankness to be filled by Millie. And Brooke, who had experienced such deep loss herself, didn't feel competent to know what to say.

❧ ❧ ❧ ❧

They spent what was left of the day getting involved with groups and helping with food for the evening. After they ate, they met as a group again by the Landing, as it was now named, to say goodbye to Tonya. The early evening sky had scattered thin clouds with hints of pink and purple in them as if to set the tone for the service. Tonya's body lay on rotting driftwood. She was wrapped in white cloth, mostly from people's clothes. Brooke could see the outline of her body in the wrap, and she imagined what she had looked like. The ocean breeze brought an unpleasant smell of decay, which drifted among the crowd. Several women coughed, trying not to show their gagging. Brooke wanted to let it pass, but she couldn't. She thought it was horrible that Shavoon would have that smell to remember.

Uncontrollably, Brooke was attacked by the memory of reaching down to kiss her grandmother's body goodbye at the funeral parlor. She saw the events of that night as if she were at a disturbing play. Her lips pressed gently on Grammie's forehead, and Brooke tasted something unexpected. Her grandmother's cold, hard skin had something strange on it, a drop of something, with a noxiously sweet and salty taste on it. Brooke wiped her mouth quickly, trying not to call attention to herself while ghastly thoughts from the dead filled her mind. Was it powder they used in her makeup? Could she have tasted the chemicals they used to prepare her body? She gagged and was overcome with dizziness. The lightheadedness became worse, so she ran outside for air, but that taste and smell escaped with her. It was now part of her lips, absorbed by the fullness of their skin. She remembered how that sensation, that taste, along with the weighted sadness engulfed her—not into a rage or a wailing cry, but rather into a horrifying nothingness. For a moment, she wondered if that was how people went crazy. Not in a slow gradual slipping of the senses, but in a quick chain reaction from a single event, which on its own would not lead to this confusion. But there, under the ceiling of a parlor that had covered hundreds, maybe thousands of dead bodies, it led to that unexpected nothingness. She remembered thinking, Did a single sick taste on my lips push me into insanity, just like that—gone? Is this it?

Brooke could not answer. She did not know, and the fear of even a "maybe" kept her impotent in thought.

But something with a force that matched her confusion, something that came as unexpected as the nothingness, pulled her back into a clearer moment. She did not know where that saving force came from or where it went. It was something from within and beyond her own will that released her from slipping completely away. She knew right away she hadn't gone insane but she did visit it. Even for that blink in time, she was unrecognizable to herself. It was as real as if she had grown up in it. But she couldn't dwell on how close the detachment really was. Instead, she composed herself enough to go back into the parlor to watch them close the casket, sealing in her beloved Grammie forever.

Now the taste was back on her lips. Brooke wondered if she'd ever be able to go to another funeral. It seemed to be where that memory lived. Brooke thought in a selfish moment while trying not to throw up. Hurry up. What the fuck did they do in the olden days? Maybe being around that smell made it easier.

Maybe it gave them a sick and clear message that their loved one was gone. And like people of not so long ago, here on the island, friends and her lover were with her when Tonya died, heard her final breath being released from her body, saw the life leaving her, helped prepare the body, wrapped it in that makeshift robe. Now getting ready to push her out to the waiting sea, all that sure makes the point. Death isn't something that just happens to old people. It doesn't only happen in hospitals, it's happening here…among us.

Shelby stood before the crowd. "Shavoon asked me to say a few words. Tonya believed in the power and force of our Mother Earth and in the cycle of life. So I'll call to the great powers of the directions. Air from North, Fire from the East, Water from the West, and the great Mother Earth from the South. We'll ask the ocean to evoke the love and comfort of Tonya's ancestors. Those lovely people who came before her are the reason she was with us. We ask them to take her back home in peace to the unconditional love that lies in the hearts of all women. The gifts we are all born with. And finally, we'll call each other to find ways to celebrate her life. Go back to the mother sea, dear Tonya, go back to where we all have come from and find peace in your next journey."

Brooke turned away as they rowed the floating tomb out to sea and set it on fire, not wanting to see the body burn. The thought of cremation had always been difficult for her, though she respected others' choices to do that.

There were wails coming from the crowd, which Brooke found reassuring. Death never seemed complete to her without a deep and echoing wail from the crying souls of women. And the castaways who had gathered that evening gave a profoundly sad wail.

Shelby continued, "Shavoon has asked to be alone tonight, to say goodbye in her own way, but she will welcome your support tomorrow and over the coming days. Again, she thanks you for your kind words and acts of sympathy."

The women quietly left the site. Brooke, Marie, Renee, and Adair sat silently on the rocks. Brooke cried the tears of someone whose soul had fallen to its knees in sadness. Marie gently rubbed her back, not wanting to stifle the tears with a hard hug. Renee took her hand with the same sensitivity.

"Honey, what do you need? Do you want to be alone with Marie now?"

"No, Renee, stay here. I want you all to stay. I'm fine, really. Just so sad. My heart hurts." And she cried some more.

"It's this whole thing, the whole fucking thing. Why this... It..." The jerky weeping kept her from continuing. Brooke had long sobs fueled by shallow and shaken breaths.

"The whole thing was a lot, you know. The accident, that explosion, or whatever. All that smoke. I was so confused, scared. The noise, screams, the blaring alarm, it was what I had always imagined my parents experienced that afternoon in Europe. On that bus wreck. Is that what they heard? Did they smell the flames of burning people? Were they the burning people screaming? Is that how Mom and Dad spent their last seconds on this earth, screaming with fear and burning pain? I choked on the thoughts until I passed out. I wasn't brave like the rest of you. I wasn't helping others or taking charge. Renee, I'm so proud of you. You're like a hero with the way you've brought things together.

Where was I—in shock from a noise, a sound, a smell, a sweet taste? I wasn't even badly hurt! I was overcome by a non-memory, something I think happened to my mom and dad when that bus… I don't even know what happened to them. I don't know what happened to us. But one of many thoughts about what happened to my parents crushed me into a little nothing as if it were real. I barely remember the days in the lifeboat. I have some glimpses of a storm, the hot sun, people talking, and you all holding me. Marie, you held me…holding my weakness in your strong arms. This is too much. I don't want all this right now. I've never wanted all this. I hate being weak." Her body shook from the deep cry, and she buried her head in Marie's lap.

The other women looked at one another as if their eyes would silently tell which one of them knew the best thing to say. But the woman with the suitable response was not revealed by any of their faces. In fact, their looks showed that their lives' experiences had not taught them what to say. No one trained them for this. They didn't expect to need such wisdom at this time of their lives. They thought they still had time to search for the answers, not provide them. But they spoke anyway.

Marie was first. "I hope this doesn't sound patronizing because I don't mean to say this to soothe you. I mean to say it because I believe it's true. You weren't weak during those horrible days we had. Not on the ship or the life raft and certainly not during your recovery. If you hear nothing else, hear this. You were not weak. You were taking charge of a fear and sadness that caught up with you. When your parents died, you were just some kid who was told about a horror she couldn't possibly understand. It takes incredible courage to stare that demon in the eye and pull through it."

"Is this that little-child-within-me-hurt stuff?" Brooke was more embarrassed.

"I don't know about all that. But I do know you. You were a kid who lost both her parents in a violent accident. If the ship's wreckage set your memory off, then I don't see a weak person. I see a formidable and wise woman. An average person would have easily gone over the edge and never returned. You're here to tell us and share your tears with us, that takes strength. And it took strength on the boat. You just didn't hear folks talking, you heard them talking about sharks. You were the one who insisted that we go to the other boat after the shark attacked to get a screaming woman out of the water. I don't see a weakness in that."

Brooke wiped away her tears and raised her head.

Renee spoke softly. "I don't have a lot to add to that except that for all those reasons, I think you're the hero, and the person without strength was the one hiding from her feelings since her grandmother died."

Brooke cried like she lost her grandmother again.

"This is good, Brooke." Renee smiled. "I see in you right now someone I haven't seen in a long time. Someone I've missed, who I've mourned the passing of. I see my deeply feeling best friend who watches way too much Space Prairie."

"I like your versions of me a little more than mine." Brooke was trying to soak in the compliments. A part of her understood Renee's point.

"That's what friends are for. A new version or two of the same old you." Adair smiled. "And it's not like there aren't other opportunities to help. You still have time to be someone else's hero. Other people here still need you. Our castaways' needs have not gone away. The scout troop could use someone like you: aware, keen, sensitive with strong marching legs. Oh, I forgot the scout women hate the military analogy—strong strollin' legs."

Brooke looked at her. It was as if she opened a sealed box in Brooke's life. "Thanks, Adair, for that extra reminder that I can still be there for others. In a sick kind of way, it's almost comforting to know that there are a lot of things and others' drama going on outside of the noise in my head. What a great idea."

"Glad the rest of us and our woes bring you some comfort," Renee joked.

"Renee, I love you."

"I love you, too."

They sat in silence as the smoke rose from the ocean. It materialized thick and impenetrable as it rose from Tonya's body. Then, when it reached the beginnings of twilight, it became a faint haze in the open sky. Not too much later, the sky grew darker and the stars brighter. Brooke made her nightly silent wish on the first one she saw like Grammie had taught her so many years ago. Star light, star bright, the first star I see tonight, I wish I may, I wish I might, have this wish I wish tonight. I wish Mom, Dad, and Grammie are at peace.

"I'll catch up with you both tomorrow, but for now, I'd like to be alone with Marie," Brooke said. Renee and Adair hugged Brooke goodbye and walked off hand in hand.

Brooke laid her head back in Marie's lap, and Marie brushed the hair off Brooke's forehead, looking at where each strand fell as if she precisely accounted for each one. She kissed Brooke's forehead, then her cheek, and lastly her hand, as if she was trying to heal a child's booboo. They looked into each other's eyes. Brooke fidgeted, too full of emotions to look deeply at Marie. Marie, however, kept her gaze fixed on Brooke with a streaming compassion and affection without pity. It covered Brooke with warmth that melted any remaining hint of shame Brooke may have had about her emotional display. Brooke reached up and ran her fingers over Marie's lips.

Marie started, "I didn't want to talk about this in front of everyone, but you have a profound valor in the midst of what you call weakness. You just went through it all. I admire that. I learned something especially important from you."

"You did?" Brooke was noticeably stunned. "I mean, you seem so together. You know what to say and when to say it. You speak from your heart. What could I have taught you?"

Marie's face shifted a bit to a less comfortable look. "You showed me how to be raw with your pain. When it was my turn to face my demons, I drank too much and had more one-night stands than I care to discuss."

Brooke's eyes showed that she was making some connections about Marie's life. "Was that all during the time you weren't doing so well on the circuit? I remember the newspaper headlines: 'Has Marie said goodbye to the golden touch?' They were so ready to write you off, those bastards."

"Oh, yes. My dear friends in the media. I got much more coverage during my drama compared to when I was on top of the game. The story we gave out about dehydration problems was such a farce. An old lover of mine from college died by suicide that year. She had tried to contact me. She left a message that she had to talk to me and that it was important. I, of course, was so busy with being the best and believing my own press that I didn't have time for such things—reminiscing with old lovers, that is. I thought, and despite all the counseling, I still think I might have helped her had I just taken the time to call back. That was my lesson. I was so sure that all my fame gave me control and predictability. Now I know that predictability is a comforting but false security we wrap ourselves in until the Fate Sisters change things in the blink of an eye."

Brooke agreed. "They sure can, especially when those bitches are low on estrogen."

Marie held her tighter. "You and I have a lot in common."

"You mean the horrible losses?"

"Some, but mostly, the immeasurable survivals."

Brooke looked at Marie with a love you could only find when at peace with yourself. "The last evening we were like this, we were going to spend the night together," she reminded Marie.

"I know and look what happened." Marie smiled.

"I'm not really feeling sexual now, but...but," Brooke stuttered.

"Me either, but I would like to sleep with you tonight and hold each other."

"Yes."

"My sand pit or yours?"

Marie took Brooke's hand and headed for another part of the beach away from the burial and talk of loss. She found the perfect spot, far enough away from the water to keep them dry and close enough to hear the waves serenade them to sleep. They lay together in the cradle of the ancient sand. Brooke's head rested on Marie's shoulder while she held Marie's hand. Brooke could smell Marie's scent, hear her steady heart, and feel the tenderness of her touch. She fell asleep in the safety of Marie's silence.

Chapter Seven

The island spawned its own way of life for the women, complete with survival jobs, recreation, and rituals. Brooke spent her time focusing on healing her body and soul. Lillie and Claire helped heal her wounds and got her back in shape. Other than their caring, she was reclusive, working hard on her soul's spring cleaning. That was what she called it. Like the times she emptied all the items out of her closet. Then spent days deciding what to discard and how to arrange what was left. This was her decision now—selecting the joy she'd keep in her and the pain she was ready to give away. Brooke spent some time with Marie, but not much. She was on an exploration of her own thoughts and feelings, which she called "Brooke time," but that was about to end.

"Hey, Brooke, wait up," Renee called out as she ran up the hill toward her friend.

Brooke stopped her daily run and flashed that competitive grin while Renee struggled to catch up with her.

"Gosh, I know you've been working to get your strength back, but you're in the Ironwoman training league now. I can't believe how you've healed." Renee panted.

"Thanks, Rinkie, I feel most iron maidenish. But the healing award goes to Claire and Lillian and their island magic. I think they're witches or something."

Renee agreed. "I've worked with them a bit.

They've asked the scout group to find specific herbs, roots, and sometimes plants. Not sure what they concoct with them, but they seem to have magic, all right."

"They have brews mixed with much more than magic. I'm in awe of them. I'm not even sure what adjectives to use to describe them! I've known yuppies, I've known women into alternative medicines, but these women are a hybrid, wiccans trapped in those soccer moms' bodies.

"They boiled herbs or plants or whatever and soaked cloths in it, then wrapped the stinky-ass compresses on my leg. Then they changed the wrap about three times a day. Look, look." Brooke pointed at her thigh and calf. "You can barely see the scars from those deep wounds. And they gave me intensely gross, awful-tasting drinks. Who knows what the hell they make it from? I swear they tasted like formaldehyde. But it gave me this." She gestured at her body. "I'm stronger than ever and don't remember ever having this much energy. Oh, and you know what else?" Brooke didn't wait for Renee to answer. "I got this horrid yeast infection. Well, the witches made paste to heal that, too."

"Okay, no need to show me that." Renee laughed. Brooke jabbed at her shoulder when Renee added in a more engaged voice, "I agree with you. They do sound like they know how to use their inner spirits to heal. But 'witches' doesn't sound right for them. That's a term for our barefoot friends living in communes in the desert outside of Yuma, dancing naked under the desert moonlight. But these ladies? Come on, they're soccer moms. They're the only two to go through the accident, get tossed around at sea, get washed up on this island, and look like, well, see for yourself. Their clothes are still in one piece. Their faces are flawless even without makeup. Hell, I swear they're still wearin' it. And their hair…how the hell do they do it? The rest of us have either makeshift cuts, hair stickin' out all over the place, or tied back. Theirs looks like they're coming out of a beauty shop." Renee was running her hands through her own shortened hair. "I mean, even their names, Claire and Lillian. They sound like some mail-order catalogue with expensive Christmas sweaters in it. You know the kind with a picture of Santa in the forest in hand-sewn sequins on cashmere."

Brooke put her hand on Renee's shoulder and used a fake, condescending voice to respond, "You've been thinking about this for a while, haven't you?" Brooke laughed. "I know it's hard to reconcile—that much spirituality and medicine women in these soccer moms. For a while, I couldn't accept it myself. Now, well personally, I like to imagine them as new healers. The kind who come from the coven on the cul-de-sac." And they both laughed.

"Works for me." Renee put her arm around Brooke. "Whatever they are, I'm glad they found you and you're doing so much better. We need you."

"Need me?" Brooke questioned.

"Yes, the scout group definitely needs support. Hell, you look good enough to be the whole scout group by yourself."

They sat together and allowed their conversation to take away any awareness they had at that moment for the tropical beauty surrounding their friendship.

Brooke continued. "Thanks, I did tell them I'd catch up with them in a couple of days. Guess I've been enjoying my season of no responsibilities a little too long."

"Well, you know you don't have to give it all up. All the groups alternate workers," Renee informed her.

"No, I hadn't heard about that."

"Honey, this isn't work as usual. You work out your schedule with other members of your team, so you get as many days off as you work over a month's time. We're trying to make as much time for leisure stuff as for work."

"How Plato's Republic of us." Brooke smiled.

"No, more like Lesbo's Dreamland. We don't want to go sour like the republic. We're not into failure. So you're looking particularly glowing. Done the vicious lesbian sex thing lately?" Renee changed the conversation with a matter-of-fact tone.

"Don't beat around the bush so much, just come out and ask me if you've got something on your mind."

"Defensive. I guess that means no," Renee came back.

"The glow is because I'm happy, Rinkie. I'm thrilled. I feel better than I ever remember. My best friend is here with me, and yes, I'm spending time with a wonderful woman."

Renee patiently looked at Brooke, waiting for her to get to whatever was behind this flattering, uninformative preview.

"We spend time together but not all our time. We still do things with other people, and I've needed a lot of time alone. It feels so…so normal being with her. What I love the most is the way she talks and listens to me. She listens with all her might, not thinking about what she's going to say next or interrupting to tell me how she had a similar situation, which, of course, switches the focus from what I'm saying to her. She hears me with her entire being. And when I'm done talking, she waits, thinks, and then says something meaningful and to the point while being caring. It makes me feel truly—"

"Loved?" Renee interrupted.

"Yes, but more than that, I feel, I feel…"

"Cared for?"

"Yes, that too, but more than even that, I feel… important."

"Okay, the hair is standing up on the back of my neck. This is all touching and stuff, but you know what I mean. How's the sex?"

"Thanks for bearing with me through all that superficial stuff till I got to the sex talk."

"No problem." Renee laughed. "My heart is happy for you, buddy. I can see that you are dearly cared for. But I'm not hearing anything about how amazing the intimacy is. I know the island has changed you, but— come on—it can't be that much. You have had sex, right? Of course, you have. That sounded so stupid. I can't believe I even asked."

Brooke was silent.

"Brooke, you have, right?"

"Okay," Brooke said. "We have spent some evenings together, holding each other under the stars. We've gone far with our intimacy, but we stop as we, well, before we… Why am I suddenly so shy about this?"

"I don't know. We've shared everything," Renee reminded her.

"This feels more special than our tell-alls. Marie and I have gone far, but not all the way. There, I said it."

Renee searched for her sensitive side. "It's been enough time since you two met. And you've been on the mend for a while now, feeling well enough to… You are all healed, right? There aren't other parts of you that don't work properly, are there?"

"No, I don't have any bad parts."

"Well, is this really okay with you?"

"Yes, of course, it's okay. It's more than okay. We've talked about it and everything. We feel like teenagers. You know that experience you never got to have in high school? Well, most of us never had it anyway." Brooke lowered her head and raised her eyes at Renee.

"Now that's uncalled for." Renee blushed.

"Sure, it was," Brooke jokingly jabbed at Renee. "We both want to enjoy the anticipation for a while. And that tells me a lot. Marie is someone who doesn't have to rush into sex. But more than that, it's how we spend our time together. I love it, and I'm surprised when I'm alone. Surprised that I don't spend all that time thinking of Marie. It's like I've gained this wonderful girlfriend but haven't lost myself. This is the 'hand holder' and a lot more." Brooke's blue eyes were shining almost as bright as her smile.

But Brooke's happiness didn't stop Renee from rushing into reality. "This is it? Everything you've waited for, but not enough of it to have sex? After all this time? Like in high school? Sweetie, high-schoolers have sex, so I'm not buying this story you're telling yourself. Brooke, that's not 'not rushing,' that's basically not having sex. Not having sex at all." Her voice rose at the end.

"Well, 'all this time' for you could be a normal courting time for others. Besides, I didn't read the Most Have Sex by Now rulebook. Like I said, it's like those teen years I never got because I couldn't date girls when we were young. You know, the virgin time of being together, but not 'doing it' because you're almost too young."

Renee cut right to her point. "Sure, that sounds innocent and romantic, even nostalgic. But I'm so confused. You've dated before. You've had those loves. Virgin time? Seriously? I gotta ask. Do you think you're avoiding sex because this is the one, the one you settle down with? Is this your way of avoiding finding the complete answer to that question?"

"Could be," Brooke answered softly and without hesitation.

"Could be. Could be?" Renee put her hand on Brooke's knee. "Honey, everyone in that kind of love doesn't have to have a tragic ending. Some couples stay together for a very, very long time. For others, it's too long." The sarcasm sneaked in. "And you know, not everyone you get close to is going to die on you, either. After all, I'm still around, and then there's, there's… Give me a minute…well, there's… This is a sign you need more people in your life, so there can be more of us who outlive the ones who die."

Brooke smiled and looked at Renee in the eyes as if she were looking for a guarantee. Instead, Renee took it for one of those brief and much-sought-after times when Brooke opened up and let Renee in.

"I think you deserve Marie, and Marie, well, Marie is like no one I've ever met. She's got to be the healthiest person in the universe. She's so balanced, she should do one of those public broadcasting specials. You know, like during their fundraising campaigns, The Nine Steps to Complete Lesbian Happiness, or maybe…" Renee slipped into her irreverent side.

"What's the point?" Brooke brought her back.

"You know my point, she deserves all of you, and

if you're not ready for that, then tell her so."

"Gee, Renee." Brooke moved Renee's hand off her knee. "We should do this more often. I love having all the magic dust blown off my dream. Especially by my best friend."

"Sometimes it's not magic, it's just dust." Renee didn't retreat.

Brooke caught her angry retort before it lashed out of her mouth, stopping it before Renee could be hurt by her bitter reply. She stopped it because she knew Renee was right. Marie deserved more than the "nostalgic" rationale Brooke had talked herself into.

"Okay, you're right. I'll tell her." Brooke surprised Renee.

"Tell her what?"

"I said tell her, not you. And what about you, my dear friend? Can we take me out of the friendship microscope long enough to hear about the many adventures of maverick lover Renee?"

"My many adventures have been replaced by one: Adair. I love that dyke dentist."

"Really makes you open wide and say ahh?" Brooke brought their friendship back to its playful side.

"In the worst way." They laughed. "She is perfect for me, Brooke. I know what you mean about the feeling when you're apart. She leaves me with so much of her, she's always with me. I don't think of other women. Did you hear that? I don't think about or seek other women. I just want her. Is that the last fuckin' thing I thought I'd ever hear myself say? Now don't get me wrong, I loved all those chasing days, none of that has changed. But there will forever be this unexplainable grin on my wrinkled old face because the truth is, all those fancy-free times put together don't add up to five minutes of what I have with Adair."

Brooke never thought she'd hear the maturity in that type of confession. "Wow. I'm so happy for both of you. I like her, too, Renee. She's a good soul. One thing, though. I have to sing at the wedding."

"You can't sing worth shit. I'm not having my best friend fuck up my wedding, but I would like you up there with me when it happens." Renee didn't flinch at the word wedding. It was heartwarming and surprising for Brooke. She was seeing a new person. The closest thing she would ever have to watching a little sister grow up.

"Nothing would keep me away. At least I know where you get your glow. Seriously, you look younger."

"Well, no poker faces here. But my happiness comes from more than Adair's talents in bed, and who knew I had things to learn? But more than the great relationship with the highly skillful lover is that it's all happening here." Renee motioned, and they broke out of their intense focus on the conversation to be reminded of the peace that surrounded them. "I've finally found that place in my life where things are coming together. Remember how we used to talk about the forty syndrome? You know, how we always heard other women talk about how they came into their own at that age, like they reached a new plateau in their lives. A time of more security with who they are, less concerned about what other people think. They slowed down enough to put things in perspective."

Brooke nodded. "Yes, I remember those conversations. Mostly, I remember thinking that, while I was so close to forty, I felt nothing. I wondered if I had to wait until the actual birthday, and then, like some midlife rite of passage, it would happen just after the clock passed midnight. I would officially become forty and one with myself."

"Well, I'm there early. I'm in a late thirties forty syndrome."

"Good for you. I'm not that surprised, either. You look it. As for me, I'm starting to feel it come my way. Like I can hear it off in the distance. No, that's my stomach. Hey, do you mind if we head back for dinner now?"

"Sure," Renee said while giggling and walking back to the gathering. "I'm feeling a kinship with this place. It's familiar now, not a strange and messy jungle like when we first got here. It feels like my neighborhood. I recognize the leaves brushing against us. Those same plants from hell that used to scratch and make me itch are now reaching out to greet us as we walk by like a neighbor. When did that happen? I know that particular coconut tree among the zillions here. That one tells me we're almost at the clearing. I know it from its gentle arch to the west. I'm home."

Brooke nodded in silent agreement.

Chapter Eight

Brooke and Renee reached the clearing in time to help set up for the second round of dinner. It was papayas and "tastes like chicken" snake tonight. Surprisingly, Brooke liked the snake but could not get herself to even try the cooked rats. Only a few of the women could. Adair joined them with a big hug and kiss for Renee, then turned to Brooke.

"Hi, Brooke, you're looking great. Hey, Marie asked me to tell you she will not be here tonight. She spent too much time in this humidity from Hades. She took a cool dip, ate, and went to bed early."

"Is she okay?" Brooke worried.

"Yes, she wanted me to tell you how she took care of herself, so you wouldn't worry. The extra sleep tonight is only a precaution. She said she was feeling much better after she ate. She didn't puke or anything, just started with the headache and mild chills. All the warning signs, so she did the best thing."

"Thanks for letting me know, Adair. Maybe I should check on her."

"Not like I want to tell you what to do," Adair hesitated. "Okay, I guess I am telling you, but she asked not to be disturbed tonight. She needs some alone time. She spent the day doing water runs. She's tuckered out."

"I'll check in with her early in the morning before I meet with the scouts," Brooke thought out loud as she watched the women coming together for the evening's gathering. Someone lit the torches, which flickered in the early twilight. Brooke loved this part of the day when everyone came together. And almost everyone attended their now famous fireside chats. Only the most die-hard loners missed this part of the day.

Brooke sat with Renee and Adair, and without intending to, she inventoried the women by placing them into neat categories. She never even noticed the fine skill, which made her so good at her job, cheated her subjects out of their uniqueness. If she was aware of it, she would never have done it. It was not at all in her nature to shortchange other women, only to group them.

Brooke liked to watch the women sit in mini social groups. What was most intriguing to her was how easily the women transitioned from their eclectic work groups during the day's chores to these enduring high school social cliques at the daily gatherings.

She first noticed the group sitting closest to the beach. They had proudly adopted the nickname "space heads," which most of the other women endearingly called them. One was an engineer with the Johnson Space Center. Brooke thought that talking to her was like having a raging conversation with a bowl of oatmeal. While Brooke didn't understand most of what the engineer said, Brooke had complete respect for her intelligence. She seemed to understand the ocean currents and talked about the best time to launch the most seaworthy life raft, if folks agreed that someone should give it a try. The space heads also included a biology professor, a high school math teacher, and a genetics researcher. Brooke smiled. She found them positively innocent and brilliant at the same time. Brooke couldn't keep her playful thoughts still.

She imagined them in their teens getting ready

for a wild Saturday night. Dressed in straight-legged jeans with their brothers' button-down shirts, they would throw a dark sweatshirt over it so only one side of the collar stuck out. They'd tell their parents they were going to the library but drove to the other side of town, the "bad" section next to the railway tracks, where the train cars stood empty. Their rebellious instincts fully came out of their otherwise studious lives. With only the moonlight to guide them, they'd spray the sides of the boxcars with unintelligible calculus graffiti.

Brooke laughed out loud at her own daydream. Renee and Adair were confused, and Brooke laughed more until her attention went back to her own visual scanning.

Sitting close to the space heads but hailing from a social group far away from the isolated intellects were the ultra-professional women. The Wall Street tycoons who talked a lot about how their careers represented the last of male bastions. Though these days, any woman in the world of work said that. The ultra-professionals also had some ex-straight-wives-turned-lesbians who lived off healthy divorce settlements. Brooke thought of them as professionals by proxy. Of course, there were also several successful businesswomen who had either inherited a family trade or started one and worked their way up from the ground floor. It made no difference. These women were not particular about how each got into this group. The point was, they were all there.

Brooke also noticed the women from the coven on the cul-de-sac. Aside from her deep appreciation for their helping her, she had a profound respect for the way these women effortlessly combined things that seemed impossible to blend. They were part medicine woman, part counselor, and part prophet behind those

European facials. One of them even predicted things no one could have guessed. There was gossip that one asked the captain to turn the boat around the day of the accident because she had a nightmare about an explosion of devastating proportions. These women were sought out for health care and emotional advice by many women on the island. This group was more popular than the counselors when it came to helping women cope with what had happened. Brooke stared at them in awe, and her mind raced with ideas.

They combined the enlightenment of Zen with the compassion of Mother Teresa. No, it can't be, are they really? They are. What did they find to use as makeup? Not only did they find something to give them that made-up look in the middle of this "hotter than the coals of hell" jungle, but they found something that still looks fresh at the end of the day. Real makeup doesn't even do that. I'm convinced they're witches. "How do they do it?" Brooke unknowingly said out loud.

"Do what?" Renee asked.

"Oh, nothing," Brooke muttered and kept looking around.

"Come on, Brooke, if we're bothering you or something, Adair and I can go somewhere else," Renee teased.

"Don't be ridiculous." Brooke brushed her off while looking at the wise women gathering around the campfire. Brooke thought they wore their years gracefully.

Some look like dykes in their forties, even though they're much older. Okay, so their skin does hang a little lower, and their wrinkles are a little deeper, but I still see the youthful sparkle in their eyes. Like that one, pushing back her hair like a dyke in her twenties would, catching the strands between her ring and middle finger and moving them back as if they were going to stay to the side. How is it I can love that gray on other women and continue to weave it out of my hair? The wise women aren't as eager to squeeze an answer out of all life's mysteries like my peers. They often say, "You did it this way because that's the way it was done. You got married to a man because that's the thing we did then. You had children with him because that's why we got married. You joined the Army because you knew you were 'different,' and you hoped that's where other 'different' women were."

Oh, there's Kate, who's been reclusive, lost looking, not at all the lighthearted woman who rounded up everyone for a game of pinky swear. Her eyes now have a hollow, flat stare. I don't know what else I can do. I tried several times to spend time with her, but she always seems to have a reason for not wanting to join me. Talking to me must remind her of that last evening with Millie.

Brooke saw Maureen with them and smiled. The wise women adopted her, their apprentice. She's taller than most any other woman on the island, but she's so much smaller framed here than on the ship. Until she speaks, of course. Her voice can still carry like a sonic boom. This tropical wilderness must have taken its toll on her. You wouldn't know it by her energy, though. I only know it because I saw her before…before…

Brooke got teary-eyed with that memory and with thoughts of Millie and Grammie. She wiped tears from her eyes.

Renee and Adair were frowning as they stared at her. "Brooke, honey, are you okay?" Renee sounded worried, having watched her go from laughing to talking out loud to tears without any visible means of support.

"Shh, I'm thinking," Brooke said.

"Oh, okay, sure," Renee whispered to Adair loud enough for Brooke to hear her. "Shh, she's on a mental archaeological dig. See, can't you tell? She's got that surveyor look to her. Oh, and that noise you hear? It's her probe gears turning. She's using mental powers only known to her to peel the layers off the lives of all of us around her. Now mind you, she'll never know if what she's thinking is an actual portrayal of their lives or a concoction she dreamed up. But it doesn't matter if it's a real treasure or fool's gold. That's not the point. It's the dig that's important."

"What are you talking about?" Adair was thoroughly confused now.

"Shh," Brooke repeated and rolled her eyes at Renee, who knew her better than she thought.

"It doesn't matter," Renee added to Adair as she sat behind her and wrapped her arms around her new love. "It really doesn't matter. It's Brooke, at her best."

Brooke noticed Renee's attention turning toward Adair. It reminded her of how happy she was that Renee had finally found someone. But her warmth for Renee was brief as she scanned past the wise women and over to the buffest women she had ever seen. While she spent little time with them, Brooke had a lot of fun with the athletes. They were so willing to drop everything and help someone else, especially if it meant doing hard physical work. The athletes helped Brooke by showing her how to build her muscle strength back. This evening, they were by the rocks and seemed to be in constant motion, like hummingbirds, having to move all the time to be still. They took turns sitting on the rocks, standing on them, playfully pushing one another off, and holding one another. Some of them reminded Brooke of early college days when she would watch the women's rugby team, another sure way to be around lesbians. She thought it was a confusing game and never understood when or how they scored points, but she liked to watch the physical contact between the coeds. They would all go out for drinks after the game. Brooke loved joining them, as they could party like no other group of women she had ever met.

Sitting close to the athletes was a group of the radical lesbians, or trailblazers, as they liked to be called. Brooke credited them with the benefits she enjoyed, though she found them the most difficult to relate to. She watched them holding hands while lying on their stomachs. They were the most physically affectionate with each other, so much so that it was hard to tell if any of them were in couples. Brooke flashed a smile slight with envy at the ease of physical contact they shared. Often, she agreed with many of their views, which surprised her because she didn't consider herself political. Brooke didn't limit herself to any label except "Brooke." She never related to any single group, only to individuals within them. Also, it was much easier for her to categorize other people into neatly arranged factions than look at her own common attributes.

She admired how the trailblazers tried to live true to their politics. They had taught her several lessons about women supporting one another, but she never could completely, or even mildly, understand separating one's self from men as the ultra-separatists did or vehemently tried to do. She wondered how they would have dealt with male staff from the ship on this island with them.

❧❧❧❧

"Well, here's today's update," Shelby stood before the group in her matter-of-fact stance. Brooke wondered how she did that, how she looked like that, like she didn't carry the residue from her last conversation about how much more food they needed. Nor did she have that anticipated worry of how to answer the questions laid before her by each woman at the gathering. She stood so tall with that playful tomboy stance that said, this is where I am now, even with all the uncertainty. She scratched the buzzed-off hair on the sides of her head and ran her fingers through the longer light brown hair on the top. Shelby counted the day's inventory on her long fingers, one at a time.

"We have food, fresh water, and no sign of a rescue." She flashed her generous smile.

The crowd cheered, and she continued.

"Our more learned friends here are under the thinking that we can expect storms over the next couple of days, perhaps weeks. So we've postponed any plans to send the boats out."

"Fuck the boats. I don't want to go back," someone yelled from the crowd.

The women were cheering. Brooke started a smile but withdrew it quickly when she caught Kate's face. It reminded her that there were women waiting to see what happened to their partners. But they were a minority, and their sadness was dimmed by the others' joy. Brooke was not sure when it happened, but it was obvious that most of the women did not want to leave the island. They were smiling and dancing, waving their hands to the sky in thanks for their marooned destiny.

After they all settled down a bit, the testimonies started. It was now part of each day, a part Brooke loved in others but never found secure in herself: their ability to wear their feelings on their sleeve. Brooke called it being raw with their feelings and thought of the women who had it down to a science while others, like herself, left their feelings swirl inside. They carried them in deep pockets, letting them out slowly as trust grew with others. One dyke joined in.

"My name is Lorna, and I'm with her. I hope we stay here forever. This place puts the shine back where it belongs."

"Like that tropical sun, do you?" a voice called out.

Lorna shrugged them off. "No, no, it's much more than a good tan. One of the greatest moments of my adult life happened on this island."

"Okay, who was she?" They all laughed.

"She was me." Lorna brought the laughter back to her important point. At least Brooke noticed the importance on Lorna's face. She also noticed that Lorna was otherwise exceptionally average-looking, like someone she would pass on the street without noticing.

Lorna continued, "Who is she?" She paused and looked around at the group who settled down. "She is me. It was the greatest gift, and I gave it to myself."

"You mean this is the first time you ever did the hand dance?" the same voice called out, and there was more laughter.

Lorna motioned again for the crowd to listen. "Not like that, you sillies. It was totally unexpected and no, not sexual. The lovely part is it wasn't a grandstanding moment witnessed by all. I didn't have to wait for some cheap fifteen minutes of fame. It happened quietly, one innocent day."

"What?" someone else called out. She finally had their attention.

Lorna gazed over the crowd, allowing their anticipation to grow a bit, a payment for the jesting they had given her. "I got 'me' back," she announced with conviction and grinned.

"One day, I looked in the still of the morning waters, and I saw something that made me run to find a mirror, for I was sure it was an illusion. But it wasn't. It was true. In that image of myself, I saw someone I had not seen for more years than I care to mention. It was the 'me' I remembered being when I was fully living. For a second, I thought it was someone else. But then I remembered, that's the face of a youthful me. The clear shining eyes, excited about my world and whatever the day's fate has in store for me. Of a face not contorted by the pressures of the day, but rather, wearing a restful and clear look. I looked and felt cute, something I hadn't experienced in well, now, I've forgotten how long.

"Now I have it back. Goddesses and Fate Sisters, I have it back! I'm that hopeful young adult I left back in high school over thirty years ago when I was full of dreams, energy, and courage. That's the 'me' I remember being. I looked at that image and said it out loud: 'I've missed you.'"

"What did the image say? Where the fuck did you go?" someone yelled, but it didn't sway her position, and no one laughed this time.

"I know where I went," Lorna almost scolded the voice. "That same place many of you got lost in."

"Oh, no," someone next to Brooke whispered.

"Here comes the rape story or another abused-until-I-lost-myself story." Brooke could not believe what she heard. Why does she think Lorna is talking about past abuse? And what if she is? What a cold thing to say. And why say it out loud? Like I'm going to agree with her or something. What rude dark hole did you climb out of?

Brooke turned; she didn't notice when the woman had walked over to her. But there she was. Brooke flashed her a noteworthy frown and hoped it would keep her from saying anything else, or better yet, encourage her to walk away.

Lorna did not appear to hear the rude whispers and continued telling the group, "I detached from myself through years of sacrificing my soul to work and chasing things I thought were going to be fun, like the cars or vacations or shopping trips. But I was always too tired or stressed to really enjoy them. I didn't get it, you know, I just would think, well, maybe next time."

Brooke turned to the woman next to her. "No," Brooke whispered back in defense, "she's talking about the American dream abused." She turned at the cynic next to her and realized it was Tracy. Her mind raced. Tracy from the boat. You, you're the one who didn't want to go back to look for others during the shark attack, even after we heard the screams. I remember you, your face, that scratchy voice yelling at me during my somewhat managed delirium. This feels gross. I should walk away.

Brooke's heart raced enough for her to notice her own discomfort with the situation. There she was next to someone she had heard so much about and liked so little.

She doesn't recognize me. Then again, I wouldn't

have recognized that thing hurt on the raft who resembled me, but her face is one I wouldn't forget. She wears that history of a 'hard life,' as Grammie would say. She's worn, with a hard round face, like she's trying to hold her lips on. Like they'd crack off if she relaxed. She would be pretty if she could wipe away the hardness. I'll go now, but then I'd be the bitch. Be polite but unengaged.

Brooke directed her attention back to Lorna and scooted closer to Renee, who didn't seem aware of Brooke's discomfort or of Brooke at all. She was busy snuggling with Adair, who had her face resting in Renee's arms.

Lorna was elaborating on her insights. "My inner light was sucked right out of me by my job's tentacles. No wonder I ate antacids for lunch, wore a night guard to bed to protect my teeth from all that grinding. Now I see why I counted the days till the next long weekend. I was submerged in the work swamp. I did it all, worked evenings, weekends, rejected social invitations so I could do extra work to try to get ahead. What was I trying to accomplish, scratching out my identity in the work world? I was a slave to proving the improvable. I was successful by what I did. But what I did was never enough. There was always more to prove. So, in turn, I would never think of myself as successful. I would have continued chasing that dream that kept me from getting a good night's rest. But no more. This place, the distance from work. I know it's not my job that defines who I am. It was my job that lost who I am. This place helped me find it. And here I am."

The crowd's reaction was mixed. Some smiled and nodded. Many had silent tears sliding down their cheeks. Others stood up with a cheer and applauded.

But Brooke was reeled back in by Tracy, who whispered, "Wonder how far the software king would have gotten with that attitude."

Brooke's head spun to the side to tell her to shut the hell up. Oddly enough, it was Tracy who stopped her. Brooke saw Tracy's hardness and felt more compassion than anger. She wore a thin layer of sadness over a scowl that must have been years in the making. Brooke speculated on their origins.

The deep lines between Tracy's eyes must have been forged by life's cruelest of branding irons. Did she lose someone she loved? Someone who died or left her…for someone younger? Was it years of hurt, abandonment, disappointment? Did she carry the shame of a childhood memory? The shame of enjoying things children should never enjoy? Whatever it was, she can't escape it. Did she ever try? Even her hair looks like it's in pain. Her thin lips look stretched back by an unforeseen force that forbids her to smile or even frown. She even moves her body as if she is wrought with subtle but chronic pain…pain that should make her frail-looking, but she's too big for that. Fighting that level of pain would make anyone else tired, but Tracy's constant anger fights off the weakness, giving her unusual energy.

Then Brooke thought about Tracy's cruel remarks toward Lorna. Regardless of the reasons, Lorna didn't deserve that type of sarcasm. Brooke knew her challenge was to let Tracy know that without attacking her any more than she clearly had been.

"I know you share a different perspective on this, Tracy, but I'm interested in what Lorna has to say. So please, keep those comments to yourself or to someone else who may appreciate them. There's no appreciation for that here." Brooke smiled and looked in her eyes to prove her commitment to her point.

Tracy stared at her for a moment and then said, "How do you know my name? Have we met? Oh, wait, you're the one from the raft. The one who made us turn around in that shark water. Of course, you don't share the same perspective as me. I like living." She huffed and walked away.

"Could have fooled me," Brooke couldn't help but whisper.

"What was all that about?" Renee became interested.

"About me being as self-disciplined as I can be," Brooke half-answered. "Let's listen to Lorna. Her words resonate with me."

Renee responded silently but in agreement.

Lorna was waving at the group to sit down and let her finish. A few still clapped for her and made comments about their own jobs. "Now I know many of you know exactly what I'm talking about. It's a little sad, isn't it? Thinking about all those lost years? If you haven't already, and I can tell by the cheers many of you have, you'll smile, too—smile at getting your lives back with enough time to enjoy them. Isn't it an incredible lesson to learn? What a long journey to find out our destiny lies at the beginning of life's journey, not the end. That's the new shining me, the shine of returning to me, and I'm not going to let me go ever again."

"How?" Brooke didn't see who called it out, but she could tell by the raspy voice that it was Tracy.

"How? I'm not letting go, that's how." Lorna was certain.

Now Tracy moved in front of the group so Lorna and others could see her. "Come on, if it were that easy, you never would have lost it to begin with. It happens while we're not looking." Tracy's voice of depression continued, "The worries of work and everyday details secretly choke out the spark in our eyes, and if we don't actively do something to keep that from happening, we go back to survival mode before we know it. How can you not? How can you teach your palate to savor the fruits of the moment, keep their thoughts out of tomorrow's worries long enough to enjoy the day? Here it's fucking easy. You know what will happen after we're back home. It'll be like returning from a two-week vacation. By Wednesday, you'll be fully fighting work's invisible vortex, a tunnel of pressure that sucks you out of vacation's joys and into the reality of daily chores. You'll look at your weekly calendar and wonder how you'll get through it, never mind about enjoying anything."

Brooke wondered why Tracy didn't let it go. Let Lorna finish her talk and let the gathering disperse. What motivated her to challenge someone's found spirit?

"Maybe it's merely your job," Shelby offered, and talked to the group in a way that offered a different view without sounding defensive about Tracy's comments. "I won't go so far as to say I miss going to work every day. But I miss the people I work with. I miss what my job gave me. You know, at home in a place of constant change and increasing isolation, work is one of the few rites of passage left in our culture. It's right up there with that first car, first kiss, and first job. It seemed like yesterday rather than twenty-five years ago, but during one of my college jobs, my boss said something to me that changed my life. It was during an evaluation. He commended me for the work I was doing and suggested

I use my leadership skills more…my leadership skills. It still echoes in my mind. I certainly never thought of myself as a leader. No one ever talked to me like that, not at home, never in all my years of public school, not even in college. But that boss, almost a stranger in the larger scheme of things, saw something in me. He saw a leader, and in that quick observation, he opened up a whole new realm of possibilities for me. I think bosses can be your worst nightmare or your hero. He was one of the heroes."

Tracy didn't let a second pass between the "o" in hero and her next comment. Brooke figured she must have been planning her comments the whole time Shelby was talking. "How many people had boss heroes?"

There were a few claps.

"How many people can relate to what I'm saying?" Tracy raised her hand as she spoke.

The applause was much louder, and women hollered.

One woman from the coven on the cul-de-sac stood. At first, Brooke wasn't sure which one it was, Claire or Lillie. She was far away, and they looked so much alike. They were both blond now; the sun had bleached their hair almost white, and both wore it straight back, showing off their full Grecian faces. They were both perfectly tanned and about the same small build with sparkling eyes. They still looked like they had stepped out of a salon. It still surprised Brooke. Their elegance was so far away from the bohemian women who usually worked with herbs. Then Brooke realized it was Claire.

"It doesn't matter what job you do. The 'right job' isn't the answer to it, and I think that's part of what we're talking about. The problem lies more in what we tell ourselves about our jobs than what we actually do at work. Somewhere along the way, we bought into the big lie. The one that made us believe that who we are as people is defined by what we do at work. You know, you're an okay person if you manage to stay employed, you're a good person if you get promoted along the way, you're great if you get the better office, and you're important if other people recognize you by what you do even—or especially—if they don't know you at all. But if they relate to you by your work, you're famous. Of course, you know what that means for women who don't work or who are not sure what they want to do. Yes, we bought the lie. And you know what we used for payment?"

She had their full attention. "We handed over what all women know in our souls. Who we are isn't about what we do or what our partners do. We are, each of us, the wonderful gifts we're all born with: the gift of insight, keen perception, depth of feelings and compassion, motherhood, sisterhood, perseverance, we are thoughtful, we give friendship at all hours of the day and night, we are sexual, wise, contemplative, aggressive, caring, hopeful, we feel deep sorrow, limitless joy, contagious laughter, and the ability to do any of these things despite cramps from hell. This is who we are. Not something you'll find in the want-ads or the promotion list, but everything that's worth something." Claire spoke as if she knew life's truth and never questioned that knowledge.

A new voice spoke out from among the athletes. "I propose we start a vortex protection group. We're creative women. We'll find ways to protect ourselves from that fate when we return home. We'll create a plan, so we don't crack up on re-entry, a way to reintegrate back into our jobs without losing ourselves. We'll keep us from being engulfed by that madness and remember the joy of fully being in the day, to 'live in the present' as this island has taught us. All those who want to help me bust a vortex, see me tomorrow under the bent palm tree."

"I'll be there," someone else called out.

"Count me in," still another cheered.

The women were clapping and giving each other high fives. They talked among themselves for some time, comparing notes about their jobs. Then they nestled into an early evening rest along their sandy home. Brooke smiled at the way they created a team of problem solvers and had high confidence that they would beat the work vortex. It would have been a good time to move on or do nothing at all, but someone got her second wind and took them all along with her.

"Hey, while you're doing that, please, please, please come up with a plan to deal with the she workers." A soft voice came out of a woman who stood up. She was like several women who put together whatever clothes they could find from what they put on the rafts. Brooke thought this woman looked like a bicyclist: thin round calves like someone who rode in marathons, composed and direct, and a smile of someone who liked an after-work martini.

"She worker?" Claire asked.

"Yes, you know the women at work who could make Gandhi forget about creative nonviolence. My name is Irene, and don't get me wrong, I like my job, no, I love it. I like the people, the work, the pace, the money is enough, and the benefits are great. What I don't like—and I get embarrassed to talk about it because I think of myself as someone who gets along with almost everyone—however, I've known women in my career whom I call the she workers. And if you've ever worked outside the home, you've met them.

"I'm talking about the women who put as much time into pissing off people they work with as they do doing their own work. The she worker is highly controlling, manipulative, deceiving. She uses her intelligence to betray you. She is competent at what she does, but that's not enough. She has to be the only one who's good at it. She views any other woman who is also competent as a threat, someone the she worker marks as an enemy, and she spends boundless ugly energy trying to undermine that person. You know, make her seem less competent than the she worker. Jealousy is a crazy drug."

Most of the crowd nodded. They all knew someone addicted to the influences of jealousy.

Irene continued with her tale of work woe. "There is at least one she worker at every job. Sometimes two or more, though never too many of them at once. They need to spread out for survival. They're in every type of industry—private, public, nonprofit, or volunteer agency. Not only are they at every type of job, but the she workers are at every level of an agency." She went on with her exposé of difficult women to work with.

The honeymoon is over, Brooke thought, and without considering what would happen, she joined the conversation with her goal of changing the direction of the evening. With perfect timing, she interrupted the discussion with a new and alluring topic. In a confident voice, she said, "Perhaps our expectations are too low. I mean, geez, what we settle for! We think it's a big deal we have Mother's Day or International Women's Day. Oh, how about Take Your Daughter to Work Day. Maybe we're getting so little because we ask for so little. So we get a couple of days during the entire year. We should dream bigger. And I'm not talking about a special week or one of those honorary months. We should ask for— no, demand—much more recognition. An appreciation fitting of what we give. Like, the Millennium of the Woman!" Everyone roared with excitement.

Then Claire brought them all together. "That's it! Reach high. Keep our promise to come together with the best of us and not lower ourselves to women whose hurt spews out on the rest of us." They cheered again. Claire had successfully muted their interest. They lay in one another's arms, rediscovering the soothing feel of a woman's touch. Her inspirational words would have been enough on their own, but the ocean's ambiance added a mild breeze to blend with her warm words.

"Okay, if we're done with all the world of work woes, then can we get on to the important stuff, madam facilitator?" Maureen winked at Brooke.

"Of course, we can," Shelby answered.

Maureen's comments pulled them further into fun. "I don't know about the rest of you, but I'm relearning how to have sex all over again. I mean sex without my battery-operated toys, that is."

Women cheered and gave hoots and hollers.

"I'd forgotten how creative my girlfriend's fingers could be," another announced.

"Well, I'm lovin' that, but I sure miss my little buddy-girl. That's what we call our toy. She moves in two directions, different directions, mind you, inside me and another part is an external massager. I loved when Gwen strapped it on and made me hers," someone else said.

This is more than I need to know, Brooke thought as she walked away from the crowd, smiling at the raunchy conversation.

Brooke thought about the beauty of women bonding over and over again. As she listened and watched the group grow into almost solving these work, stress, politics, and sex issues, she wished Marie had heard this evening's discussion so they could talk more about it. Looking over the group again, Brooke thought about all these women. She contemplated where Marie would have sat. With the athletes? The thirty-somethings? The professionals? She could fit in with almost every group. She's a mix between the professionals and athletes. She's so talented with people, listens to everyone with such a caring ear. Why am I letting her stay on the margins of my life? No more. I need to be as close as I feel toward her. Tomorrow… tomorrow night, we'll have vicious lesbian sex, sharing everything with each other, things I haven't even explored before.

Chapter Nine

Brooke started her day with great expectations. She gave a moment of thanks to the divine creator for all the new gifts and old reunions in her life. She took a deep breath. That feels so splendid. I keep forgetting I can do that whenever I want. No more short breaths amid a busy day. No more lumps in my throat. The best of all self-pleasures, breathing deep, filling my belly with all this air. I don't have to wait for some type of break. I can do this anywhere, anytime.

She smiled at her affinity for her own self, at her heart being filled with more than grief, and with the promise of a new romance.

Tonight, I tell Marie I want to share all of me with her. No, that sounds too dime-store paperback. I want to go all the way. Too junior high. I want her to fuck me. That sounds too much like Renee.

Her thoughts excited her, and she noticed her clit rubbing against her shorts. It became a pleasurable walk. She wondered how she could think of anything else today. But there were things to divert her attention. This was also the first day of working with the scout group. Yes, this truly will be a remarkable day in the life of Brooke Kent.

Brooke briefly stopped by Marie's, checking to see if she was okay and would be available in the evening. She wrapped her arms around Marie's neck and followed the embrace with a big kiss. "I was worried about you, but Adair kept telling me to leave you alone."

"Sorry to make you worry. I ran too many trips to the water in that humidity. It kind of crept up on me. I wanted to rest and think about things for a while. If it makes you feel any better, one of those things was you." Marie blushed.

Brooke looked into her warm brown eyes and at Marie's natural beauty. The sun on the island had brought out even more of her freckles. Her hair was much more blond than brown now, and she kept it back in a short ponytail with her bangs resting on her forehead. Brooke tenderly moved her fingers over Marie's cheek, which was as soft as she looked.

"I thought a lot about you, too. I'm hoping they were parallel thoughts."

"Easy to find out. What were you thinking about?"

"About how wonderful you are, how much I love our time together—"

"How much you love me?"

"Yes, and I hope it's not too late to show you how much. I talked a little with Renee. She thinks I'm scared to get really close or that kind of close."

"What do you think?"

"I don't know how to get that close. Somewhere along the way, I took a road away from it, and now I'm hoping I can find a way back. But I do know this, if ever there was a person I'd like to learn it with, it's you. I want to be with you, Marie. I want to make love with you and break all my endurance records. Is that what you were thinking?"

"Partially." Marie smiled at hearing Brooke's love and courage. She looked down, then back into Brooke's eyes. "I'm so glad to hear you say that. And yes, I want us to be together, but I know how scary it is for you. I spent a lot of time wondering what I can do to make it less scary. Then I realized that it's not me, it's so many things from your past. I can't change those. I can tell you I've fallen in love with you. Being with you is the best thing for me. Other women I've known were too dependent on me or so distant I was a bystander in the relationship. You're somewhere in between. You need me and lean on me now and then, but then you catch your breath and work things out on your own. I feel happy when I help you out, but I'm always honored to be there to watch you go through challenges on your own or with the help of your dear friend. Whatever, it's incredible to be a part of. Your strength of character is inspiring. Oh, and did I mention the part about being attracted to you? I don't want you to think I just want you for your personality. Those dimples at the end of your smile call to me, and those lips of yours, those full, crowned lips are almost impossible to stay away from. But what finally caught me is that look in your steaming blue eyes. There's magic in them."

Brooke cried softly. "My mom used to say they held the ocean's magic. You made me feel more beautiful than anyone else has ever done. Thank you. And I would love for you to see what I'm going through and how you give me the time and space I need. But I don't think I'll ever be completely ready. I've gotten to the point where I feel it's okay to move forward. And with you, it's more than okay. It's something I deeply desire. I don't want my fear keeping me from doing something my heart knows is so right."

"I'll see you tonight at the bonfire. Good luck on your first day on the job."

Brooke kissed her goodbye, feeling both proud of saying as much as she did and remorseful she had not said it sooner.

⁂

Brooke walked to the scouts' morning meeting place with a rush of excitement and a confidence as if she could accomplish anything. The love and lust for Marie were part of the wonder of emotions going through her. She anticipated being part of the scouts as she imagined being a modern-day Margaret Mead in search of clues to this place. The group seemed so adventurous to her, and her daydreams began.

Maybe I'll be the first to spot the search plane or a rescue ship and send the flare to signal our trip home. Or maybe I don't want to be that one, after all. I'd be a hero to a few but definitely a villain to many others. After last night's conversation, I doubt many would even leave this place. Maybe with time, the scouts will turn into a warning team. See a boat or plane and warn everyone on the island to go and hide. The team could be for finding exotic hiding places on the island, like in caves and caverns. A scout would send a signal with a huge seashell and all the women would scatter. Hiding together, never to be found by the civilized… No, Brooke corrected her own daydream—by the uncivilized world.

"Brooke, is that you?"

She got close enough to the scouts to see Nina. "Nina! I haven't seen you since that first night or so. I can't believe all this time has passed without seeing more of you. Oh, do I need a hug." They held each other for a long time, patting and rubbing each other's backs. Then Brooke put both her hands on Nina's cheeks. "I am so glad to be with you again," she said and cried.

"Thank you. It's wonderful to see you again, my pinky swear friend. Not too many folks have seen me after those first couple of days. I was with one of the first groups to hike over to the group called the settlers on the other side of the island."

"Settlers?" Brooke asked, aware of how much Nina had changed. She had cut her long thick Latina Rapunzel hair. She had also lost a lot of weight. Like so many of the other women, she was down to a lean frame. Her wonderfully brown skin looked at home on the island, unlike the others, who were often painfully red. Her complexion was still so lovely. Brooke remembered her own thoughts of Nina on the ship. How she had that appearance so many women try to achieve at the spas. Her lips were full of rich colors of the soil with a perfectly nature-drawn dark liner around them.

Brooke looked into her brown eyes to see the other signs of the woman she knew on the ship, the one from that border town in Arizona who was a sharp contrast to her friend Amber, the Doris Day look-alike teacher who talked like a drunken sailor.

"Yes, the settlers. It's where the more—what's the word in English—'reclusive' women set up camp. They stay up there on that highest mountaintop. It's a beautiful place for sure. A beautiful place that's nearly impossible to get to, that is. They like to live away from the clan. That's what they call the rest of you."

Instead of being confused about a group she'd heard nothing about before, Brooke was concerned about Nina. She wondered why Nina was camping with that group. "Are you okay? I mean, did wondering about what happened to Amber make you want to be away and live with those, those…settlers, you called them?"

"Yes, no…yes, they're called settlers. No, not out of distress on my part. I know she's alive. I can feel it. All the women in my family, we have these senses about us. And when I get off this place, I'm going to find her and never let her go again."

Brooke had several reactions and wondered which one would be the most appropriate. She inventoried her options. I didn't think you two were together as a couple. No, too much over-generalizing. Should I be more neutral? I'm glad you're keeping the faith. No, too distant. What do I feel? My feelings, where are my feelings? I'm always on the edge of knowing them. It's so good to see someone else from that night. Even though we all had just met, I sensed a connection with you. No, she's talking about Amber, don't run from that.

Brooke's sense of her own ineptness was keen. She knew she was searching for her feelings the way someone else looked for lost keys. Then she stopped and took one of her newly rediscovered deep breaths. "Then you two will have to have me and Marie over for an evening of pinky swear and something to eat other than fish and fruit." She smiled and placed her forehead against Nina's. They stood there with their hands on each other's cheeks.

The scouts gathered. Some were eating the morning fruit, others were pacing and looking at the sky, trying to judge the heat of the day.

"Brooke, let me introduce you to the group," Nina said. "Ladies, we talked about a new scout. Well, this is Brooke. I met her briefly on the cruise. Brooke, this is our sometimes leader, Gail Arnez. I'm sure you know her, you being from Phoenix and all. She's the famous senator from back home."

"Of course, it's a pleasure to meet you, Senator

Arnez."

"It's Gail here. And nice meeting you, dear. It's good you're here, as we're a medium-sized group today. There are days when we have twenty-plus, which helps to cover a lot of ground. With this size group and the increase in the humidity, we probably won't do as much today. But I guarantee ya, the conversation is always an adventure." The group laughed. "This is Madison, Leslie, Nina—sounds like you know each other—Carolina…"

"Cody on the island."

"Sorry, Cody." Gail continued, "Cody, Claire, Lillie, Naomi, Joey, Shavoon, and Tracy."

Claire and Lillie. Brooke smiled. My favorite people from the coven on the cul-de-sac. Tracy, my least favorite witch. She may be the island's only she worker. This is going to be fun.

"Well, enough with the formalities. Brooke, in short, we walk for a while as a full group. Then we break up in twos or threes—ladies, today looks like twos—then cover a certain area and regroup as a full group. I hate using the analogy, but it's like a football team. We're in a huddle, we break up to move the ball, then we huddle again."

"I like to think of us as fireflies whose chore is to light the dark and discover mysteries in the night," Lillie said.

Gail broke off the conversation before everyone joined in with their renditions of the group's choreography. "Okay, I'm sure we each have a version of what we're doing out here. Why don't you say we talk less about it and just do it? Brooke, I say this every day. Take lots of breaks…" The other women joined in. "…and drink plenty of water and watch each other's backs."

"She's the task-oriented one." Lillie smiled.

Brooke's confidence in the group grew as she watched Gail at work. She knew of Gail's reputation in Arizona and was awestruck to be in her presence.

The scouts went along the perimeter of the island and then worked their way into different sections of the thick tropical vegetation. It was hot, but unlike her native Phoenix, it was not a dry heat. The intense humidity and treacherous landscape made for a demanding and dangerous excursion. They stopped several times for water and snacks. They moved quickly, keeping an eye out for critters and clues to this place. They talked, asking about one another's escapades on the island, about family back home, their favorite meal, pets they loved, and even the shoes they missed wearing.

"Ladies," Gail commanded, "looks like a good place to pair up. Let's unhuddle, firefly up, whatever you want to call it, and regroup up on the waterfall for some fresh water. We've all noticed the increased heat today. So let's make it an early day. Walk safely and take extra care of each other. Give out a call at the first sign of heat exhaustion or any other type of emergency. Choose your own partner. Brooke, you can join me today."

Brooke felt like the new kid being treated with extra care and rather liked the motherly attention, though she wondered if someone else needed it more. So far, she was strong, like she could go on for a long time. They walked for a long while in silence. Without intent, the two of them developed a natural rhythm while searching their environment. One would inventory the treetops while the other meticulously charted the thick brush. Then they switched their line of sight. When the path allowed, Brooke walked beside Gail, then fell behind her when it narrowed again. Sometimes, as her gaze shifted from the treetops to the ground, Brooke caught a glimpse of the back of Gail. She tried to focus on her surroundings, but she couldn't help noticing the way Gail's sweat matted her white shirt against new muscles in her middle-aged back. Gail's short salt and pepper hair swung at her neckline with each step. Brooke thought about how she had seen Gail on TV, dressed for political battle in her tailored suits. Here, Gail had the same qualities Brooke saw in her TV interviews: the leadership tone in her voice, dedication in her eyes, and that unwavering commitment in her stance, but she looked so much more comfortable in the sweat-stained clothes. The tattered attire acted like permission to free her up, which allowed her other leadership qualities to breathe easier. I wonder how we'd all perform at work if we could wear anything we wanted. But she couldn't let her mind wander too much, which was a harsh task for her. The thick jungle walk demanded her attention. She had to be careful not to trip on thick vines at her feet or get hit in the head by the large leaves pushed back by Gail. She looked up and marveled at the blue sky peeking through the vegetation. There wasn't a place on the island where clear sky couldn't be found. The heat made her sticky, like she'd been "rubbed in egg and dipped in salt." To her, it was like the sound of rustling leaves or the surf. All were ever-present, and you either got used to it or it would drive you out of rational thinking and the sounds and that heat would become a tropical torture.

"Let's rest for a while up here on this. It should let us see what's crawling toward us," Gail suggested as she climbed up a rock. "Well, not seeing anything different today."

"I'd say we can report back to the group that we're definitely on an island," Brooke said, and they both giggled.

"You don't talk much. That's fine with me, different from what I'm used to on the trail," Gail said almost as a thought out loud.

"Well, it's most embarrassing, but I'm feeling somewhat like a shy fan around you."

"I'm flattered. Okay, ask away."

"Ask?" Brooke didn't track Gail's point, even though she said it as if Brooke were waiting to ask her something.

"Yes. Think of a question you'd like to ask the Senator Arnez and make it personal. I'll answer it honestly. Then maybe I'll be more than the mystery of a high-profile politician. Maybe you'll see the person behind all this lovely sweat and sunburn."

Brooke smiled. All lesbians must have a bit of pinky swear in 'em. Then she did not hesitate. "Is your job as lonely as it sounds?"

Gail's eyes widened a bit.

"I'm sorry, is that too personal.?"

"No, not at all. I didn't expect you to start off with such a serious question. Given the chance, most lesbians want to know all about the gay life of a senator or other such dyke drama. Of course, they're usually disappointed when my answers don't match up to the fantasies they have swirling about my life. Actually, I appreciate such a purposeful inquirer."

Brooke wanted to explain. "It's not that you give off lonely vibes, you look great, I mean, comfortable with your esteemed role. But you're one of the few political leaders, and probably the only one in Arizona, advocating for the rights of undocumented workers. You seem like, well, all the right stuff in the absolute wrong place."

Gail looked out in front of her. "But it's the place that needs people like me the most. Of course, it can be lonely, especially on those days when I feel beat up in D.C. on the Hill. On the Hill, even in describing that place, we try to put it high above the rest of the world. But then I go back to my home state and…and…you need to see the big picture to completely understand where I'm headed with all this. I grew up in the border town of Nogales. You know, Nina is also from that area. Small island." They both laughed lightly.

"I've been there a few times," Brooke said. "Though it was mostly for shopping and eating in Mexico."

Gail smiled. "I love that area so much, and the border has its own special magic. Although folks I meet in D.C. think of it as a flat tumbleweed ranch."

Brooke sounded almost appalled. "What? It's not flat. I love the landscape there. Those rolling desert hills. They sit with a patient wait—a timeless wait. And when I pass by, I feel like I become part of their ancient meditations," Brooke said with conviction.

"Brooke, that's beautiful. You must be a poet."

"No, I'm a city analyst for Phoenix. Just a data nerd."

"Please, we both know that's not true." Gail put her hand on Brooke's shoulder and said, "When I was a kid, those two countries were one large town except for a small chain-link fence separating them. I can still smell the aroma of home-made Mexican cooking. And I so remember the times with my cousins there. It was like the town was our personal playground. I have wonderful memories of walking with my cousins in downtown Nogales, all three blocks of it, and going to the candy store. We'd get those rolls of dot candies and see how much we could eat in one try without ripping the paper roll. We'd stop at the drugstore, put our nickel in the photo machine, and get those funny black and white pictures made. I still have one of those pictures. I carry it in my appointment book.

"You know, we didn't even have a fast-food place there while I was growing up. And the only place to see a movie was a drive-in theater. I'd take my parents' oversized T-Bird there. Back then, we still had to take chaperones on dates with us. I remember those nights at the drive-in with my cousin sitting in the backseat. Of course, we paid her off to sit in another friend's car." She knocked Brooke's shoulder with her own as if to gesture, and you know what happened next.

"That was my home. Can you even imagine a place where friends, neighbors, other relatives would just stop by without scheduling a visit? Well, it happened almost every day in Nogales, especially on weekends. Friends would come by with their friends, and everyone brought food, ready to eat or ready to cook. They'd put on the aprons, start up the barbecue, whatever it took to create a weekend feast where a late lunch turned into dinner, and if everyone was still there, it became a midnight snack in between dancing and drinking.

"In that kind of a place, you were welcomed wherever you were, and I understood that at an early age. Once, my friend took me and my cousin to her home for lunch. It was a small home with barely enough room for the people who were there, and there were a lot. There must have been eleven people around the table. They all moved over, made room for the two of us, and we sat down like we'd done it a hundred times before and joined right in whatever conversations were going on at the time." And then Gail looked down. almost talking to herself. "When was the last time you saw such generosity from people with so little to give?"

She paused for a moment. Brooke watched her silence and wondered if it was the start of a cry. But there weren't tears in her brown eyes, only the sun shining through her long dark eyelashes. Her round cheeks and beautiful smile looked more peaceful than sad.

"It was that old-school type of town. The kind where the only pharmacy had the same name as the pharmacist, right next to the grocery store also named after its owner.

"Now the pharmacy is a small law office, and folks get their drugs at the chain drugstore over by the fast-food restaurants. The drive-in is an empty field. Still no movie house. But the hardest part hasn't been the changing of the stores as much as the changing of the guards."

There was something different in Gail's voice. The lullaby of her childhood memories began to sound like a speech at a prominent podium. "The meaningless and small chain-link fence that used to divide the two countries was replaced by a twenty-something-foot high, rusty fence that looks like someone welded old soup cans together. Its ugly face stretches the border as far as you can see. It looms over the ugly things happening there. Never revealed violations of women in the "search" rooms, families torn apart, it's crimes against humanity. The once-friendly border patrol has turned into an army of masked secret police. The once-gorgeous night sky that served as the official arena to the desert stars is now filled with helicopter lights flashing across the countryside in frantic patterns of hate. They've taken those hillside meditations into a frenzy of worry." She looked down, and her voice lowered almost to a whisper.

"If all that wasn't bad enough, then the phone calls started. Friends and family telling me about the increase in abuse by the border police. There had always been unchecked use of intimidation and violence committed by those entrusted to protect. But the atrocities were increasing.

"The stories I could tell you. I'm sure you've heard it on the news, but they don't begin to tell the real-life horror experienced by people living there but mostly by undocumented workers.

"Don't misunderstand me. I'm the first one to say we need the border police to enforce our immigration laws, protect our borders, and stop drugs from coming into this country. We have to have safety through a strong presence there. They would have my full support if they did that job with integrity and fairness. But that's not what's happening. They have a choice in terms of how they perform those jobs, and by the calls I get, some of them have chosen their own rules, rules that violate every dignity of humanity. It's heartbreaking. They take parents away during the day so when their kids come home from school, they don't know where their parents are. They bust into businesses the day before payday to do a round-up of undocumented workers so parents can't buy food for their families, and those calls I get—so many young women saying the border cops raped them and other horrid stories of what happened in those non-windowed search rooms.

Unchecked authority—abuse against women and children—that duo is related.

"As I keep saying, it wasn't always like that. When the border police hired more local people, they did their jobs, but they treated people with respect. It was after they brought in the forces from other states like Texas that it turned…unchecked, shall we say.

"That's what it's all about, isn't it? That's why my job can get lonely. Because most other politicians use the 'Mexican fear' as their platform. You've heard it—'Stop them before they take our jobs, increase our welfare, bring drugs into our communities, and put trash on our farms, blah, blah.' That grandstanding led to millions and millions of dollars being poured into the border towns. Of course, the issue of needing a more secure border needs strategic attention, but they're not using a smart response. Our government turned the tragedy into a barter chip—you give me your rights, and I'll fund more false security.

"No money to help the kids, families, or the schools there, just to build bigger fences, buy helicopters, and increase the people power by hiring glorified security guards without limits or accountability. If this were happening anywhere else in the world—no, I mean when this happens anywhere else in the world—we call it a violation against international human rights. Here, we call it law enforcement doing their jobs."

Her voice raised. Brooke was aware of the things Gail spoke of, but it was like hearing them for the first time. Gail struck one hand against the other. "I don't believe the people of this country expected them to hurt so many kids, women, and families in ways that, if done by anyone else, would be illegal. Where is their due process, where is our compassion? These are children they're rounding up like dogs!

"So my lonely fight is one to reform their practices, to create community review boards, even have a full, independent investigation into their behavior."

The conversation entranced Brooke. It pulled her into a promising description of what could have been in that small town and the horrors of what was.

"This is so sad," she finally said.

But Gail would have none of it. She held her head up high and looked at Brooke. "It would be, except the town's soul is still there. You know, it didn't get bought out when they had to sell the old pharmacy. The rusty fence does not block the love there. You see, the town's soul is in the people who live there. The ones who came and went in my family's home acting like family, sometimes with more ease than family. And, Brooke, they're still there, strong as ever, open as ever, waiting to meet people like you with a kiss on the cheek. With all that's changed, they're still making room at the table for guests. So I will never forget where I come from, never forget what they gave me because they're right here." She put her hand over her heart. "They never let me down. I can't let them down. I'll die trying or at least get audited on my taxes each year from a government trying to bully me into silence."

Brooke hugged her. "That's loyalty for all the right reasons." She was reminded of her conversation with Maureen on the ship. She too talked about giving back to those who touched her life as a child, which made Brooke think of her grandmother. Brooke wondered why she never thought to give back to the elders, why that connection to the wise ones died with her grandmother.

They drank more water and stretched out on the

rock. Brooke wondered if they should leave, but Gail was settling in.

"So I've been babblin' about my town and history for a while now. We'll need to move on, but first you should tell me something of your past. Tell me what day you would choose if you could go back and repeat any one day of your life."

"Interesting question." Brooke was caught off guard.

"Noncommittal response."

Brooke paused. "I would go back to the day my grandmother died. It happened suddenly, unexpectedly."

"I'm sorry, Brooke. Did something regrettable happen that day? I mean, between you two, did you argue?"

"Regrettable, yes, but there wasn't an argument. Grammie was not the type of person anyone would argue with. No, there was nothing bad between us that I feel a need to change. We started the day with breakfast in the kitchen nook. It was delicious. We talked and laughed about our weird neighbor. Grammie had a wonderful laugh. If you got her going, it was like she would laugh all day. Later that morning, I combed her hair while we watched her favorite morning show together. Then I ran a couple of errands and went back home. We had a light lunch. Chicken salad and sun tea. Talked a bit more. Then she took her usual afternoon nap. Unlike other days, I went back to her room for a kiss and told her I loved her. She never woke up from that nap. Her heart stopped. No one knew she was even sick.

"So nothing bad happened between us on what turned out to be our last day together. It's how I used those mundane moments that I regret," Brooke continued with the conviction of someone who'd had these thoughts for a long time. "I'd go back, and instead of staying so long in my room in the morning with my work thoughts, I would have joined her earlier for breakfast. Instead of the breakfast nook, we would have eaten on the patio by the pool. I would have held her hand more and told her how much I love her and what an inspiration she was—her strength, her humor, her casual insights into the world and the way it works. I'd thank her for the most wonderful gift she gave me when she gave up early retirement traveling plans and stepped in as a mother and mentor to me and filled those roles with love to spare. I'd say all those things while looking at her so she could see in my eyes they were more than words, that they were gifts that are part of my life, part of the things that sustain me in her absence. And then I'd sit with her and feel the reassuring power of her silence."

"I'm sorry for your loss. The two of you were lucky to have each other while you did. I'm sure she's proud of you." Gail was so sure of what to say.

"I hope she's proud of me. I keep thinking that one day I'll get a sign to let me know for sure. You know friends talk about seeing their passed loved ones in a dream or smelling them in the house. I don't have any of that to tell me she's still here with me. Why does it happen to them and not me? I miss her as much, more. Some people call it a heartache, a heavy heart, a broken heart. I can feel my heart drop in sadness and strike each nerve in my being. Then I think about how much I love her and what a difference she made in my life, and I feel so blessed to have known such a genuine, caring person. How can that be? How can I have so much of grief's sadness and love's joy simultaneously occupying the same spot in my soul? And with all of that, why can't she visit me in one dream? Where's my sign?"

"Some signs never come, some things we'll never truly know, some moments will never be captured in our sciences. That's why they call it faith," Gail said.

"Do you have faith?"

Gail smiled. "It's not my strength that gets me through working to save the rights of people who many consider throwaways. I don't have that strength. But I do have that faith. So since you can't go back and you're not getting a dream visit, how do you manage sadness? Are you hard on yourself about not doing more than having what sounds like an incredible relationship with your Grammie?"

"Surprisingly, not as hard as I know I'm capable of. It would be easy for someone like me to overanalyze the whole thing. But in other ways, it would be difficult because I know that would be the last thing she would want. And as much as I need and want it, I can't go back and redo that day or any other. But I can make more of the days I do have, put that lesson to use and honor her legacy instead of betraying it with regrets and self-pity. I think this trip awakened me to that no-brainer, which had escaped me in my grief."

"Now I'm sure she's proud of you." They both sat there for a while looking homesick, only both of them knew it wasn't the kind of feeling that could be cured by a quick trip home.

"Must be time to get to the waterfall. The others must be there by now. Are you ready to join them?" Gail asked.

"Not completely. But I think we should. Thanks,

Gail," Brooke said and gently touched her hand, which Gail took as they ascended to the waterfall. They walked hand in hand the whole way like two young best friends who had promised to be bridesmaids at each other's weddings when they grew up.

✦✦✦✦

Some women talked about the waterfall as if it were a sacred place. It provided most of the fresh water on the island. There was a natural pond that was much closer but less appealing for drinking after it became the popular place to wash up, or as they found, to rinse off without the benefits of soap. There were desalination tools in the lifeboat, which they sometimes used, but it took too long to purify the sea water, and it couldn't produce enough for everyone. The women put much time into their water walks and made efforts to keep a lot of it available all the time. They were keenly aware that many of them would not be there without that fresh water. The extra hike was worth all it gave them. The spectacular view was a bonus.

Brooke quickly understood that when they got there. For a moment, she was like Zeus looking out over the island and water. "This is glorious," she heard herself say out loud. "I didn't think I could see this far." Her thoughts continued as she followed her panoramic view.

I'm at the center of everything right here on this spot. The island's dense green vegetation moves out away from me until it hits the glossy white sands, the sea pouring out into the distant sky. Is this the best I can do with this profound view? Better not quit the day data job if that's it.

She laughed at herself. The women gathered quietly as they waited for others to catch up.

"Not everyone is here yet, but let's start the report out," Gail said. "How much did everyone cover today?"

"Madam Senator, we're definitely on an island," Joey joked. "Really, we haven't seen anything new."

"Including that joke." Tracy snickered.

"Same here, it's the same-old, same-old, only much fucking hotter."

Claire and Nina finally joined the group. "It may be something or maybe not," Claire called out.

"Tell us what you found, dear," Gail said.

"It may be another sign other people are or were here—like the ring that resembled a fire—I can't tell for sure, and if it is, I can't say how long ago. We found a pit in the thick of the trees. Creepy, ya know, lots of snakes and yuck. Anyway, it looks too perfect to have been made naturally." Claire panted.

"We marked a trail so we can show you it on the way back home," Nina added. "I agree with Claire, it looks man- or person-made. We'll show you on our way home, uh, back to the gathering place."

"Okay, we need to rest for a while longer. Then we'll head down and all take a look. You may be our good luck charm." Gail nodded at Brooke.

"I like the way you call it home," Leslie said, almost oblivious to the new find. "This is like a fantasy I've had. I've always thought if we ever got to colonize another planet, it should be a place solely for lesbians, a place to live together, love each other, and die. They'd have to rocket in more lesbians, or it would be a short-lived colony, but it would finally be a place to thrive and enjoy our time."

"Sounds great to me," Gail approved. "I like the

idea of being a senator on Planet Lesbo." They all laughed.

"You and Brooke don't seem as worn as the rest of us." Tracy was always ready to detract and agitate the women. "Did the new scout have difficulty today?"

"No, it was me who couldn't keep up with her," Gail said, coming to Brooke's defense. "Besides, I didn't feel like hiking all over the place today. The fucking island isn't going anywhere. Brooke and I used more of the time to get to know each other."

"Well, I'm jealous," Joey joined in. "How about we do the same before we go kill ourselves trying to get to the new find? It's not going…" And they all joined in "…anywhere," as if that was their motto.

Gail instructed, "Okay, ladies, let's take time to tell Brooke who we are. But do so quickly. I do want to get back sometime this afternoon."

"Oh," Tracy snapped, "as long as you had all the time you needed."

"That about sums it up." Gail refused to be pulled into her cat fight.

Madison began, "I was, I mean I am, an accountant. Nine-to-five-type of things except around tax time when I make rich people giddy, and then they make me richer than I was the year before. I enjoy working with numbers. They never lie, and when you're done, you're done. It satisfies my need for completion."

Brooke thought she and Madison had a lot in common. They both made a living through analytical jobs. But do I hold myself that stiff? She seems almost awkward with herself, unbending. I hope I'm more comfortable. Am I? If not, I guess that's okay, too. Marie doesn't seem to mind.

"Well, I'm as much of a people person as you're

ever going to find," Joey joined in. "I run a day care center with my business partner. It's called Watch Your Own Child Day Care."

"Do you get any business with that name?" Brooke smiled. Something about Joey allowed Brooke to think it was okay to tease her a bit. Perhaps it was the playful sense about her. She looked so bright and open to things going on around her. Obviously, the day care business was a good match for her. She still had energy from childhood.

"Yes. Much more than we can manage. There are kids on our waiting list for the next two and a half years. Our center has a video camera in it, and parents can log on through the internet and check in on their kids via their computers at work or wherever they are. The other benefit of the cameras is parents can also buy a tape of the day, so they can see what their little cuties did that day, what they said, who they played with, etc. Initially, it was a security system to weed out pervert staff. You know, you do criminal background checks, but the majority of perverts out there have never been caught, not to mention put in a database. This lets parents know I'm watching. Parents love it, and I love working with kids. I'm lucky. I have a wonderful staff and clients who can afford this type of day care."

"What does your staff think of it?" Claire asked.

"Bothered at first, like they work for someone who does not trust them. Then I explained I started it thinking it would protect them. If one predator gets in our work, it puts a shadow over all of us and the great work we do with kids. And they also see how it helps parents stay close to their children. They appreciate all that or find another job."

"I'm a people person also," Lillie joined in. "Only

thing is they're not alive. My family owns several mortuaries in Florida. My business specializes in female caretakers by request."

"What does that mean—female caretaker?" Nina asked.

"A nice way to say undertaker. There are a lot of widows and other single elderly women in Florida. Over the years, we found two consistent themes and fears from them as they planned for their resting place. First, they were adamant their dead bodies were not to be touched by male staff. So we trained and certified a wave of women caretakers, more than any other morticians provided. We can guarantee a woman for anyone who requests one. Second, they seemed lost to take care of those details their husbands used to attend to like the house budget, home repairs, car buying. Not all of them, of course, but for many, there were too many unknowns and too few family members around to help. This makes them easy pickin's for less honest groups. There are a couple of house repairmen we've run into that I swear check the obituaries for widows. So we offer transition support with home needs like accounting, connecting with reputable handymen, and all that kind of stuff."

"Wow, you all must make a fortune off of all that. No wonder you can afford these cruises." Tracy tried to punch holes in their altruistic business.

"Our business is successful, but we don't rake it in off their vulnerability. Actually, we charge a sliding scale for the transition support. I asked women who can pay to sponsor women with fewer financial resources. Several women have established ongoing scholarships as thanks for the way we helped them during their time of need. And if any of them need ongoing help, we put them in touch with other services."

"Lillie and I have several things in common," Claire said. "I spend my time in search of otherworldly knowledge and peace. It's my 'job' to find harmony in this world. Something I believe we're all born with, but that gets confused in the anxiety and stress of this world."

"And you get paid for that?" Tracy asked.

"No, I live off a trust." Claire temporarily put Tracy in her place.

"I live off a simple but adequate income from my woman's bookstore and sex toy shop," Naomi added. "It's in Idaho."

"Idaho?"

"Yes, they buy sex toys in Idaho, but they don't talk about it like they do in, well, almost every place else in the world," Naomi answered.

Brooke was surprised, but she hid it as she did her embarrassment at the assumptions she made about Naomi. It was strange to Brooke to think of Black women in Idaho, and she had to pause at this reaction of hers. It was one of her brief encounters with humility. She knew her assumptions were naïve, which she could forgive. It was not okay with her life's code, however, to notice such thoughts and not be responsible for them.

"I'm sorry, Naomi," she said. "I feel stupid here. I realize you surprise me."

"You mean the whole sex shop thing?" Naomi was confused.

"No, I wish it were that easy," Brooke stumbled. "I caught myself off guard by Black lesbians in Idaho. I hu—"

Naomi helped her out. "It's okay, Brooke. Me and my sisters are often shocked we live there, too. But if you visited, you'd understand. It's not like the whole state is one big Aryan national hotel. Many people there are cool. Laid back. Open. It's not what you're imagining, but I admire you asking about it. I think you'll make a good scout. There's bravery in that little white frame of yours."

"I'm always amazed at this manner of talk," Shavoon bashfully joined in. "Okay, Brooke, get ready for the cliché of the year. I'm a P.E. teacher for a junior high school in Sacramento, California. That's right, a black P.E. teacher," Shavoon kindly teased Brooke.

"Well, you carry the cliché wonderfully," Brooke answered while admiring Shavoon's athletic body. Brooke thought about how Shavoon wore her shaved hair better than most could get it on the island with the makeshift blades. It made her so regal-looking, with her long neck and proud face. It seemed to Brooke that she was a mix of an Egyptian princess and New York dance teacher. Brooke briefly thought about saying something of her lost partner and decided it would be bad timing. But her eyes gave her away to Shavoon's perceptive senses.

"Yes, it has been hard without her, but life has other plans for me," Shavoon said, looking into Brooke's eyes.

"Brooke, I know you know Nina, but I don't think you know about our thespian Cody." Gail introduced her with a bow.

"You're an actress?" Brooke didn't remember ever seeing her in anything but realized the island had changed their appearances. Still, she searched Cody for anything recognizable. Cody was attractive in the "girly girl" way, but Brooke didn't recognize her as being famous.

"Yes, but these bitches are giving me a hard time, making me sound better known than I am. I make a living at it, just not in too many things most people would know me from."

"Well, what type of acting do you do?" Brooke was curious.

"Nothing as kinky as you're thinking, though I considered it. My girlfriend never liked the idea of me pursuing lesbian lust films. Wow, it's a tough job, but someone has to do it. Unfortunately, my girlfriend has never seen it that way." She laughed. "My claim to fame began with training videos. Mostly for bank and hotel workers. Then I got my big break as a re-enactment artist."

"A what?"

"You know those shows that play back some real-life story. You get shots of the real folks telling their stories, then the actors who resemble them play out their story. There's Miracles Really Happen, True Ghost Stories, I Came Close to Death, or Saturday at the Emergency Room, all those. I was a female cop in that one. You know the reality shows. They're on every station. Hell, I think they're starting the re-enactment cable channel so folks can watch real-life stories twenty-four/seven."

Brooke tried to be polite. She knew what Cody was describing, but she never watched those shows.

"Well, I saw one of those miracle shows a couple of times. It was heartwarming. But I don't watch enough to recognize…sorry."

"No need to apologize," Cody reassured her. "There's enough interest in 'em. So a couple of non-converts don't make a difference. Though I find it interesting that few lesbians watch them. Anyway,

I've found a lot of work in that genre lately. And it's good acting experience. I've played a young woman, an old man, a boy, a thin person, a chubby person, one of a conjoined twin, you name it. A few might say it's slumming, but that usually comes from the 'serious' actors waiting on tables, hoping to be discovered. I guess some folks would rather dream of the perfect acting job than act in the less perfect ones. Whatever, I have fun."

"What's the strangest real-life story you've re-created?" Brooke asked, fascinated.

"The strangest story never got past the script phase, they wouldn't air it. It was about this woman, she must have been thirty or so. Anyway, she was rushed to the hospital choking on a dildo that got lodged in her throat."

"What! Was she practicing or what?" It disgusted Nina.

"If she had bought it at my store, we would have given her better instructions. Please, don't tell me she was one of us!" Naomi was so matter of fact.

"No, she wasn't, and she wasn't alone, either. Her boyfriend was with her. The two of them liked to use sex toys on each other and in a lot of different ways. Of course, I'm not that fluent on the sexual practices of straight guys, but ya know, I only thought gay guys liked it that way. How naïve of me. Anyway, one of their experiments went south. I mean sour. The two of them wanted to help write the script. It gave them both a creepy kind of pleasure."

"I can't believe they wanted to tell other people about this," Brooke frowned.

"Yes, to put it in their words: 'If our story can prevent another couple from this type of tragedy, then something positive would have come out of our frightening ordeal.'"

When the laughter abated, Brooke told Cody, "Well, I think you have an admirable, honest job."

"Thank you. I'm worried some shows hinge on 'spectator entertainment.' If I feel like that's where it's all headed, then I'll go wait on tables, too."

"What do you mean?" Brooke asked.

"It's that the popularity of these things is scary. It's so 'gladiator and lion.' I can imagine what's next. Viewers will all have their TVs connected to the internet. They watch one of my re-enactment shows. The narrator will say, 'A boy became stranded in the woods after he wandered away from his parents during an afternoon hike.' Then he comes face to face with a mama cougar protecting her cubs. You see the freckle-faced little cherub, then you see the cougar. Then the scene switches to the parents sitting in their living room. 'We were so frightened and felt guilty. We only let him out of our sight for two seconds.' Then, the shot goes back to the boy and freezes on his frightened face. The narrator asks you to hit the blue button on your joystick if you want the boy to survive or to hit the yellow button if you think he should be taught a lesson for not listening to his parents and get bitten or the red button for a mauling. Everyone votes, and then they show what actually happened. But wait, there's more: They fly people with the most correct votes over a year to Las Vegas where they have a face-off, and the winner gets a million dollars."

Cody added, "It amazes me to think of what some people will do. I mean, there are probably thousands of humans out there who would eat maggots for a million dollars."

Tracy said, "What I find frightening is that there are hundreds of millions of people who will pay to view someone eat maggots for a million bucks."

"Stop, stop, okay. I hope we never get off this island," Shavoon begged. "And if we do, I'm going to change my occupation. No more P.E. teacher. I want to be a TV show critic. I'm so tired of having middle-aged and older, upper-middle-class white men telling me what I'd like in a TV show or a movie. The mere fact someone gets that amount of money to tell me what I like is insulting."

"I find it more insulting that our peers can recite their movie reviews. Let's face it, if women didn't watch those guys on the tube, they wouldn't be so popular. Don't blame the guys for thinking they're contributing something worthwhile by telling us what we want to see. Blame your sex for making them so popular," Tracy said, and it scared Brooke to agree with her.

Shavoon answered, "I'm not saying these critics, as they call themselves, don't have an audience, they obviously do. I'm saying I'm not one of them, and I don't think more progressive straight women or lesbians do. So it's not that they need to go away, the choices need to be expanded. People like me should provide a woman's point of view on movies, a smart woman's point of view."

Tracy said, "We'll see which one makes an actual living at it. How many people do you think are going to watch your review of Miss Congeniality?"

"Hey, I liked that movie," Shavoon challenged her.

"Regardless, the lesbian thing is good for sweeps week. That's when you're most likely to see a kiss between a female star and a hot-lookin' dyke or a show about our cruel judicial system taking kids away from lesbian parents. But lesbians aren't talking about TV or movie ratings or even caring about your political point of view. Now that's the job I want." Tracy turned to the subject again. "I want one of those jobs on those shows where they do all that political verbal fencing. 'My idea, your counter idea' kind of thing. Now that world is about as male and white as it gets. Oh, every once in a while, they throw a woman in, mostly to see how she stacks up to the guys. For the most part, it's all the same cookie-cutter guys who try to be unique by wearing a bow tie."

Brooke interrupted her tirade. "What do you do, Tracy?"

"I'm a director of a social service agency. Doesn't matter which one. They're all pretty similar."

She runs a helping agency? Go figure. I should have guessed. Another wounded healer.

"Friends, are we rested up enough to examine this pit?" Gail asked.

"Anything is better than this depressing conversation," Nina mumbled.

As they descended, Gail noticed a woman sitting alone on the side of the hill.

"You shouldn't be here alone," Gail warned her.

"I know, I needed to sit someplace away from the settlers for a while," she called back.

The sound of her voice caught Brooke's attention, but she didn't want to believe what she heard. She slowly turned toward the familiar tone, to make sure the face did not match that voice. But it did. Heather? Heather.

Brooke looked again to confirm her cruise lust crush was sitting less than fifteen feet away from her. Brooke was too shocked to monitor her own reaction.

A chalky white flushed the color out of her face, and sweat beaded on her forehead.

"Are you okay?" Nina checked in with Brooke.

"Sure, I think so. I guess the maggot talk didn't settle well. I just need water." She tried to regain control.

Brooke's mind raced. Is it really? Yes, that's her, right here on my island. Seems like she was a dream from long ago. I haven't thought about her…out of sight, out of… I have wondered how she was, but not much more. Now there she is, and here I am still finding her so attractive, pulled right back into that crush. Even in that ripped-up outfit, she is so beautiful. She's like living art…captivating, warm, welcoming. What am I doing? This is not like on the boat when I first met Marie, I can't be having these thoughts, these feelings. I don't want this now. I know what's going on. Only one thing can explain this. It must be… This isn't an enchanted island, after all. Shit. I must have died on that boat. That's it, I'm dead, and this is my hell. Hell would be like this. First deceivingly offering pleasures of a tropical setting filled with lesbians, but it holds emotional horror in its true form. That's it. We're the ones who died on the boat. Maybe the sharks ate us, whatever. I'm dead, this is hell. Nothing else could explain this timing. Now hell reveals its true intent—torture me with the crush of a lifetime when I'm at last enjoying my life. Go away, crush, go away.

"Did you say something?" Nina asked.

"Maybe, I guess I got distracted," Brooke barely replied.

"Okay, is this a heat thing?" Nina was worried.

"No, I don't think so. I hope not," Brooke murmured.

"Should I ask someone to check?" Nina asked.

"No, I'll do a quick test. No headache, no dizziness or chills. Actually, I feel…" She looked over Nina's shoulder to catch the last glimpse of Heather.

My head says stop looking, run away, but every other part of my body says run to her, talk to her. Oh, no, I'm trapped inside a country song that does a crossover and hits the top ten of the pop charts, then drops to number fifty-five after everyone finds out a lesbian sings it.

"No, I'm just pissed," Brooke finally blurted out.

"Pissed, did you say pissed?"

Brooke answered, "No, no. I did not, in any way imaginable, expect this. And it makes me mad. I realized there's no way to let one or two wonderful emotions out of an unearthed tomb. After it's opened, they're all going to resurrect."

"What?" Nina put her hand on Brooke's shoulder.

Brooke looked more desperate than Nina had ever seen her. "Nina, I'm going through a weird moment right now. That woman sitting on the hill, I didn't know she was here on the island, although how could I not after this amount of time? Another evil trick, and it causes some…"

"Some of the most turbulent angst I've ever seen," Nina finished for her.

"To put it simply, yes." Brooke took a breath.

"How can I help?" Nina was much more relaxed with Brooke's emotions than she was.

"Walk next to me and make sure I don't do anything stupid," Brooke said, sharing her only plan.

"Stupid patrol reporting for duty, my pinky swear friend." Nina saluted.

"Let's get to that pit," Gail yelled and then called out to Heather.

"Well, you can get that alone time, but someone needs to stay here with you. She'll wait part way down the hill, so you get the view to yourself. Not like I'm tellin' you what to do. Well, I guess I am, but it's too unsafe and unknown to be so out of contact with at least one other person. Okay?"

"Okay," Heather called back.

"Any volunteers to stay with her?" Gail queried.

Brooke's hand raised as her mind raced. Don't. Be quiet. Take a deep breath. My hand is still raising. Tell Gail—

"I will," Cody said.

Good, I don't want to know what was at the end of my sentence, Brooke thought as her mind quieted down. She wasn't thinking, nothing racing around in her head. A dull numbness moved her into silence as they walked away.

"Yuck, I saw another snake. What's with those things anyway? I get so creeped out by them," Lillie said as they walked into the forest.

"Good thing you're a dyke. You'd be freaked out by your guy's baby snake all the time." Joey laughed.

"I said I hated snakes. You're talkin' about inchworms," Lillie came back.

They all laughed except for Brooke, who wasn't tracking the simple joke.

The scouts walked in silence except for the sound of breaking branches and foliage being pushed out of their way. The island seemed bigger to most everyone on the scout team when swallowed by the thick of it. There was no beach line as a point of reference. Light surrounded them, but they were unsure of the sun's direction. They walked with a trust that they would never get lost but were not sure why they trusted that.

They drank often and splashed water on their baking backs. Someone softly sang one of the most popular Rosewater songs. Brooke wondered what happened to the singers and felt heavy guilt for what she once thought about them.

"I love that song," Tracy said, and Brooke took note of the first positive comment from her.

"It's not too much farther," Claire instructed. "I think it's behind that tree we marked, or was that the second-to-last tree? I hate when this happens."

"You're right," Nina confirmed. "It's right here. It feels like we're in the heart of this island. Like any time, our feet will vibrate from its beating."

Lying before them was a large, almost perfectly square pit. It was perhaps thirty feet wide, but no one was sure about how deep it went. Entangled vines with thick leaves covered the bottom, so no one knew if it was a few feet deep or if it stretched miles into the ground. Vegetation had partially grown over the pit's outside. The most telltale sign was the mound of dirt, leaving no question the pit had been intentionally dug. The mystery even grabbed Brooke's attention away from the confusion of her feelings.

"Like I said. Someone dug this thing," Claire restated.

"Well, it ain't going to talk to us, might as well jump in and have a peek under the vines," Shavoon said, ready to end the unknowns.

"I like your idea, Shavoon," Gail responded. "But let's find a way to pull the vines out first. It might be a giant snake pit by now."

"Oh, I loved that movie." Claire drifted, and some of the other women nodded. The women lined up on the side of the big hole, looking into it as if an answer would jump out at them.

"Gail, look at this pile of dirt," Madison observed. "If all that came out of the hole, I bet it's not as deep as it is wide."

Before Gail could confirm Madison's notion, Joey said, "Okay, tie the rope around me. You all lower me in and pull me out at the first sign of anything."

"I'll go," Shavoon offered.

"No, Shavoon, you're always volunteering for the butch stuff. I want to do more of that, okay. I can do butch, too." Joey stood with her hands on her hips, which made it hard for the group to take her seriously. She had that playful look in her eye even when volunteering for this somewhat scary job.

"Is this what you teach the kids at your day care?" Shavoon laughed, and Joey looked down. "Sorry, I didn't mean to suggest that you couldn't handle it." Shavoon smiled.

"Oh, it's not what you said, it's just me." Joey took her hand.

"Ladies, could we process this a little later?" Gail announced. "I want to get us back to the gathering early, so you all have a chance to rest before dinner."

"I'll help tie the rope around Joey," Shavoon decided. "That is, if it's okay."

"It's more than okay." Joey blushed a bit. "I'll feel safer knowing you're holding the other end of the rope," she whispered in Shavoon's ear.

The group lowered Joey into the hole. The sound of the rope straining against the dirt and Joey's breathing was all that guided them. The rope tightened around Joey's stomach quickly and was out of her control. She tried to get slack in her hands to reduce the increasing pressure on her waist. Her breath shortened, and her nose wrinkled at the smell of moist dirt lining the pit. Spiders scurried up the pit walls without moving a speck of dirt. The day's heat waved over the cooler pit. Joey watched the vines reaching up to her dangling feet as she got closer to the bottom. It was as if she were standing still, and the entire pit was closing in on her. The tropical breeze did not reach inside the pit. The leaves on the vines lay motionless like a lion before the pounce.

Joey called out, "Hey, someone get me a stick, get me a large stick, hurry."

Joey didn't notice who passed it to her. She grabbed it and swung it wildly at the leaves encroaching her body. She erratically swung at the vines waiting right below her feet. And then her feet hit the bottom. The pressure released its grip from her waist. She started to swing at the leaves, moving them out of her way. A light scurry ran across the back of her neck, and she repeatedly swung the stick at the invisible culprit.

"What is it? Did something bite you?" Shavoon called down.

Joey did not answer but continued to swing at her own body. The vines easily moved back as if they were not at all anchored to the bottom. She beat them back with the stick, stopping only to shake a darting bug off her ankles, exposing most of the ground.

"Hey, what's that?" Shavoon called out, and Joey darted across the pit, trying to get away from what she could not see.

"What? What do you see?" she asked.

"It looks like…" Shavoon started. "The ground is a different color over in that corner. Is…is that a pool of blood?"

Everyone scanned the pit, trying to see what Shavoon had discovered. They leaned forward in curious fear.

"No, it's funny colored dirt. The ground would have absorbed blood," Gail informed everyone.

"Would it, all of it? It looks like dried blood to me." Tracy joined the group.

"Get me out of here. It looks enough like blood to get me out of here—now!" Joey tried to calmly call up, but the panic was obvious.

The team got behind Shavoon and pulled Joey up much quicker than they had lowered her into the pit. Joey tried to help by running her feet along the pit walls, but each wild step made the dirt crumble at her feet. It made it more difficult to lift her, but in their hurry, no one noticed the extra effort. Shavoon grabbed Joey's hands and gave her the final lift she needed to get out of the pit. She helped shake the dirt off Joey's shaking body, and they both made sure nothing had nested in her hair.

"Friends, look around, see if you see a body or anything laying here." Tracy's voice was scared.

The team rallied into action. Brooke, Madison, and Naomi were exploring the area around the pit and into the immediate surrounding jungle. Lillie and Gail were carefully investigating the pile of dirt. Tracy leaned into the hole as best she could, straining to get a better view of what she thought was blood. The others were meticulously searching the surrounding area. Gail periodically checked in with each of them. Her goal was to keep them focused on what was factual evidence as opposed to hurried assumptions birthed by their bored imaginations. After about an hour, they got back together at the pit.

"I'm rather certain that's blood in the pit," Gail announced. "Then there's those vines in the pit and all over the mound of dirt. So the blood may be old. On the other hand, we really don't know how fast things grow here. These vines may take off," Gail pondered out loud.

"If it's new, we may not be alone. Is that what you're thinking? Lillie asked.

"Either that or someone came to this island, walked into the middle of this jungle, dug a perfect pit, poured blood in it, and left," Tracy snapped.

"Or something between the two," Gail said, trying to keep her sanity.

"Maybe the person who dug it got hurt and left," Joey suggested.

"Maybe he or they hurt someone else and left," Tracy countered.

"This place could be a hideaway for a sick cult. Some kind of place where they do sacrifices or something," Joey half joked.

"Okay, friends, let's come back to planet Earth." Gail raised her hands. "Madison, Brooke, we haven't heard much from the two of you."

Madison answered with the matter-of-fact review of an accountant. "We have a pit dug by someone or someones, and it has something dried in the corner. It is most likely blood. That's the depth of our knowledge. Anything else is speculation. What I know about speculation is, the more you feed it, the more it grows."

"I agree with her," Brooke added.

"Okay, that's enough for today. Let's take our half-fed speculations and go refuel, relax, and relax, relax, relax," Gail said.

They were much quieter on the trail home. Gail tried to strike up a conversation. "Brooke, what do you think of your first day?"

"It certainly was one for the books" was all Brooke said.

Chapter Ten

The food patrol brought back a feast of snake meat, fish, and fruit for dinner. And the scouts hauled enough water to wash it all down with leftovers. There were berries for a special dessert. The scouts were feeling better now that they were nourished and out of the jungle. They sat by the bonfire and intermingled with the other women. Almost everyone had gathered this evening. They were holding one another, talking, and laughing in the early evening's humid air. A small group threw berries at one another and tried to catch them in their mouths. Others rested their heads in one another's laps. There were couples doing the finger comb through each other's hair or rubbing leaves and coconut juice on their faces. The gathering's chatter was louder than most nights, raucous with laughter and stories of the day or jokes to pass the time.

"Hi, friends," Shelby called out. She stood tall against the ocean backdrop and appeared more masculine than ever. "Let's do the announcements and move on. I'm sure you've heard about the newly discovered pit, and for those of you who haven't, here's the deal. The scouts found a pit in the middle of the jungle. The rumor about it being filled with blood and body parts is bullshit. There was dirt with discoloring to it. It was unusual looking, and no one knew for sure what it was. We're adding it to our list of lesbian mysteries. The scouts will look for other clues about this in a couple of days. In the meantime, stay away from it. It's in a somewhat dangerous place and not worth the hot trip to see a hole."

"Any trip to a hot hole is worth it," someone called out.

"You all are nasty," Shelby called back. "Just nasty as nasty can be. Oh, one more thing. I heard the food group needed help. If interested, go talk to, to…"

"Me," someone yelled and stood. "I'm Valerie and do most of the coordination with the food gatherers. A couple of the women want to take a break, so we need others to fill in."

Shelby waved. "Thanks, Valerie. Are there any other announcements?"

"Thanks for the great grub, you hunters and gathers!" a deep voice called out.

"Thanks to the carvers for the toys. I thought I was going to go crazy without my batteries!"

"Hey, where do I get one of those?" an older woman asked.

Her partner responded before anyone else had a chance. "I thought you said you liked it the old-fashioned way. You know, reach out and touch someone?"

"Oh, I do, honey, I do. You're great, but a toy is a girl's best friend."

"Hi. Sorry I was running late." Marie sneaked up to Brooke with a kiss.

"It's okay. I've been entertained by the group." Brooke smiled.

"So how was the first day on the job? Like the new boss?" Marie sat by Brooke and held her closer.

"It was fine."

"Fine? Just fine?"

"Yes, we walked and talked. I got to see the pit. It was hot."

"Okay, fine," Marie echoed her.

Brooke sensed Marie looking at her to see if there was something else going on. Brooke looked into her brown eyes. That country beauty of Marie's deep tan brought out more freckles than she had when they met on the ship. While searching for the right words, Brooke ran her fingers through Marie's hair. She saw the gentleness in Marie's face, all the things she had fallen in love with. Then, as she pulled away, Brooke turned her attention to the evening's discussion, hoping it would soothe the awkward moment.

Brooke looked over the large group of women gathered at the clearing, but instead of absorbing each nuance and every exchange between women, she was doing a superficial scan of the group and not letting her eyes rest to take in her surroundings.

"It's kind of nice, isn't it?" Marie asked Brooke.

"What's that? All the lust talk?" Brooke guessed.

Marie looked surprised. "No, that's so common now. It's almost not as fun anymore, although some of the jokes I've heard reach a new level of decadence." She smiled. "I was referring to that smell in the air. It's that dripping smell when heat meets moisture. It's announcing the storm. It reminds me of late summer in the Midwest. I travel so much on the circuit, I've found my favorite places based on the time of year and sometimes by the time of day. Fall on the East Coast with the smell of changing colors. Now that's spectacular. I'll take you there sometime. Then, of course, it has to be winter in the Southwest, unless I'm skiing in Colorado. Spring, just about anywhere, and summer in the Pacific Northwest. Except for the early mornings. If it's early morning in summer, then it's time to be in the Midwest. Sometime between four thirty and seven o'clock. During those hours, it feels like time captures a piece of each season in a single moment. There's the smells of spring's rain, summer's heat, a dash of autumn's changes, and a cool memory from winter. It's the best aromatherapy I've ever found."

"Sounds romantic." Brooke took her hand.

"Yes, it is." Marie squeezed back. "Speaking of which, I've been thinking about your visit this morning. About our time together tonight. It made today special but not as special as tomorrow." Marie paused, seeing Brooke's blank look.

"Brooke, your silence is, well, weird. I know we haven't talked in a couple of days, but this feels weird to me."

"Sorry. It is. I mean, I am being weird," Brooke confirmed.

"Want to talk about why?"

"Only if I know the outcome before I say anything." Brooke stumbled to find the right thing to say and questioned whether to even say anything at all.

"Well, I can't help you there. Has something happened?"

"Yes…no. It's so dumb. I don't want to say it out loud because I know how silly it sounds inside of me, and I'm sure it'll sound stupid out loud. Besides, I don't even know if there's something to say. It may be nothing. I'm not even sure there are words to describe it, it's nothing." Brooke put her hands on top of her head as if to push back a headache.

Marie said, "I'm getting dizzy. Obviously, you're not sure about something and even less sure about talking to me about it. That leaves me with little to contribute. But whatever it is, it's sitting right here between us."

"You're right," Brooke admitted.

"I'll leave you for a while to work things out," Marie told her.

Brooke was quick to respond. "No, don't go," she begged. "This thing is going to sit between us until I move it." Brooke did not want to finish this conversation. Even as she talked, she was thinking of ways to back out of it.

Brooke's thoughts scrambled for a decision. Just forget I ever saw Heather. Forget she's on the island. I can't do that. I can't stop thinking of her since I saw her again. She's stolen my thoughts. Look at me, sitting here with this wonderful woman, and part of me is looking for another in the crowd. Wait until I see her again, see if I still feel that way. Of course, I'll feel that way. It's still with me, getting worse. Don't tell Marie now, wait until I actually talk to Heather to make sure. Get a reason to believe there's something real there. Don't hurt her unless I absolutely have to. I must be honest with her, she's always been with me. I love her, and she deserves to know. Stop acting like I want it all.

"Back on the boat..." Brooke hesitated. "Back on the boat, I told you about a woman I saw. Someone I barely talked to but had an...an unexplainable crush on. No, not crush, a fascination. Do you remember?"

Marie leaned back on the palms of her hands and stretched her legs out as if to take a sunbath. "Yes, I remember," she responded simply, though Brooke sensed there was much more.

"Well, I saw her on the island."

"On our island?" Marie sat up and crossed her legs. "Please consider that my contribution to stupid comments."

"Yes. She was up by the waterfall today. Just

sitting there."

"Have you seen her before, has something happened? What are you trying to tell me?"

Brooke slowed down, trying to pull Marie out of her assumption.

"Today was the first time I've seen her on the island. She's staying with a group of reclusive women up on the mountaintop. I just learned about that group today, just as this is the first time you noticed something strange between us. Had I seen her earlier, you would have noticed it earlier, and I would have told you earlier. That's how it is with the two of us. Real and honest. That's why we've gotten as far as we have."

"And how far is that? Are you saying this woman, this crush is…is…what are you saying about it?"

"I haven't thought through much more than that, no more than knowing that I've seen her, and when I did, I felt something. A curiosity, an infatuation, something mysterious to me. It doesn't change my feelings for you, Marie."

Marie's tone changed. "Brooke, you're telling me two different things in the same breath. Your feelings for me haven't changed, and you have an unnamed feeling for someone else. Those don't go together. If your feelings for me haven't changed, there wouldn't be feelings for someone else. Not even a curiosity. My feelings are clear. I've never been so comfortably in love with anyone the way I am with you. So I'll ask again, what are you saying? What do you want?"

Brooke looked in her eyes, trying to be more responsible for what she was sure sounded like irresponsible feelings. "I'm saying I don't know what to do with all this. It confuses me. I need to figure it out so I can give you a specific answer to your questions. So I can be clear with both of us."

"From this seat, it sounds like all we have together can't stand the test of a substandard crush. That hurts and scares me. What the hell are you expecting of me? You want me to say go after this magnetic pull, and I'll sit on the sidelines until you figure it out? Well, I can't and won't. And hearing it out loud, I have to say that I'm glad I can't do that. I don't want to become one of those women who throws self-respect in front of a moving love train, forgetting everything that was once important to me in a relationship for a relationship. Brooke, know this, if you decide to go after this, I won't wait for you. And the fact that you're even considering this makes me wonder if I want to be with you at all." The confidence in Marie's voice rose as her words ended.

"I can see why you'd feel that way, but that's not at all how I feel. That's not at all what I think. It's because our relationship is so important to me, it's everything to me, that's why I'm questioning this crush. I don't want it to be that thing in the back of my mind for all our years together. I have to know. And this is not a common thing for me. If it were, I'd shrug my shoulders and say, oh, there's that stupid crush thing again, it'll go away in a few days. But I'm not like that. I don't know why this is here with someone I've exchanged less than ten words with. But I don't want that to be how I move into a lifetime with you."

Marie placed her head in her hands, trying to push back the tears. "My gosh, Brooke, how do you do that? Talk about all this so I feel like someone special. Damn you for that. I want you to make me feel special because of your uncontrollable feelings for me. Damn you! And let's at least finish this pretending. You and

I both know what you're going to do. You can't do anything else. I do love you so much, but what you've said doesn't change things. There are no guarantees about where I'll be when you're done, whether this is the first or fiftieth time you've been through this."

"Two more things I'd like to say," Brooke almost begged. "I've been thinking about them during our entire conversation but feared if I said them out loud they would sound like hollow words instead of the deep feelings I have for you. I love you, Marie. I love you, and I'm sorry."

"They don't sound hollow, but it's not exactly what I had hoped to hear from you. And, really, tonight, Brooke. On what was supposed to be our first time as lovers." Marie cried as she walked away, lost among castaways.

"Love you," Brooke repeated as Marie walked away.

Brooke was pulled down by a sinking feeling so powerful, she wondered how the women around her escaped its force. How were they all smiling and laughing, not at all aware of the weight resting on her? Part of her wished she was still naïve and could be part of their joy. And if she couldn't be part of it, why didn't she leave? But she lacked the motivation to get up and move. Instead, she just stared. She half heard what they were saying. She was falling inside, falling through the paradise beneath her feet and was only superficially aware of the women around her. They were involved in the nightly ritual. It satisfied several needs, like storytelling, sharing their thoughts and their unspoken need for predictability.

"Okay, Martha has an idea for tonight's visit. Today, she heard women sharing their coming out stories. Would anyone like to share that moment of truth with your fellow islanders?" Shelby asked.

"As long as no one writes this stuff down and sells it to some real-life freak show miniseries," someone called out.

"We all agreed a long time ago," Shelby reassured her, "no one repeats anything that takes place on the island unless they have permission from those it concerns. And we have the strictest rule about selling our stories once we're rescued. Anyone who breaks that trust will suffer the consequences."

"Which are?" someone else called out.

"The witches have created it but won't give details. They say it will be unpleasant, unpleasant for eternity, to be exact."

"Okay, that's good enough for me. Well, my name is Natalie. I'm from a pretty small town in Georgia," she began. Natalie often looked down while talking, only occasionally glancing up at the group. Brooke thought she looked like she was in her late twenties. She heard Natalie talking but looked almost through her. It could have been anyone standing there.

"I know what you're thinking," Natalie continued in her sensual Southern accent. "Small town in the South, surrounded by Southern Baptists who'd just as soon kill a lesbian before Sunday services as they would want to hear a coming out story. You'd be right on that one. Right, that is, except for my mama's love for me. I knew she'd understand. At least I thought she would. I waited until after I turned twenty to tell her. In my mind, that meant I was no longer a kid and could talk with Mom like an adult, not her baby. 'Course Mama would say that I would always be her baby. It didn't matter how old I was. But to me, it mattered. Anyway,

I had returned from a season away on our cousins' farm in Tennessee. See, I have this gift with farmin'. My family says I have a type of magic in me that makes things grow. I don't believe it, but I know we've been able to hold on to our family farm when everyone else was having theirs taken by the banks. We're not real wealthy or anything. After all, they say I can make magic, not miracles. But we survive, Mom, Dad, my two brothers, and me. And when any of my cousins' farms looked like they might be in trouble, they would have me spend a spell working there. I think it was just coincidence, but each time the farm where I was would turn around. Whatever. All my cousins have been able to keep their farms, too. And they all think it's 'cause of me.

"So I had come back from a time at my cousin Martin's in Tennessee. I had found a special woman while living there. I knew it wasn't a phase I'd been going through all my adolescence. This was the real deal, and I knew I'd have to share this with Mama. Oh, not all of it, of course. The details would make her sick. I remember once when I was a kid and reading that magazine they put inside the Sunday paper, there was this article on oral sex, and I asked Mama what oral sex was. To me, asking wasn't a big deal. She had given me the sex talk. I thought it was something she left out. She looks at me kind of mad and says, 'You know what oral means, right?' and I said yes. 'And you know what sex means, right?' I told her yes. 'Well, just put them together. Okay?' I said sure, and for years, I thought it meant talking about sex. So when I came out to her, I knew better than to share everything. What I meant to say was that I shared about me being a lesbian."

Natalie raised her head and saw the crowd staring

at her, which made her a little more nervous, but she continued with her story.

"Before I went to bed, I told Mama I needed to tell her something in the morning. I thought it was a good way to help prepare her for big news. But it backfired. I guess she stayed up most of the night thinking of all the things it could be. She sure was ready for me the next morning at breakfast. We ate…or tried to. Mostly, we picked at our food. I noticed her hands shook a little when she poured coffee. It seemed strange. Mama had nerves of steel.

"Again, I said I had something important to tell her. Immediately, she worried that I was sick or maybe I found a lump. I assured her that wasn't the case, and this was good news. At least, it was for me.

"She said, 'You've found someone, haven't you? I could tell by that look on your face. You walk a little lighter. Oh, honey, you're not with child, are you?'

"I told her there was no baby, but I did find someone. Now she was concerned that I had gone and fallen for a colored. She said this one will be harder on my dad, but they both love me.

The story made the group quiet, more silent than most. They all faced her as they sat or stretched out on the sand. Some obviously angered at her mother's worry that she was with a person of color. Others were secretly connected to the fear of talking to a parent who was miles away from the subject and the difficulty of how best to piece together the right words, those that would create the softest reaction.

"I told her I'm not with a Black man. I'm with a woman. I'm a lesbian.

"She sat there for a while like she was waitin' for a translation. Then she stuttered. 'Oh, well, you sure?

I mean, I guess you must be. You've never been unsure of anything. A lesbian. A lesbian.' She drifted off saying that over and over.

"Then I started to cry, which made her compose herself a bit more.

"'Oh, Nat,' she said, 'you know I love you. It'll be okay, baby. Sure, it'll be fine. But maybe we should keep this between you and me for now. No need to talk with your daddy just yet, okay, honey?'

"Sure, I thought, as long as I don't have breast cancer while pregnant with a Black man's child, what's the need in worrying Dad?"

"Did the old guy ever find out?" someone called out.

"He always knew. One day, after I had moved out, he called and asked why I hadn't come. Said he was worried I wasn't coming home because I didn't want to bring them friends with me and wanted me to know that he wanted to see me more than he cared about who came home with me. 'Them friends,' as he called my lovers. But no funny business while in his house. That was probably the best gift that guy ever gave me."

"My name is Tamara. Guess you'd never bring me home," a woman called out.

"Yes, I would have, and I did date a Black woman for a while. My parents often had us over for dinner. Like I told you earlier, they're Southern, they're Baptist, but they also never let me forget that they love me. Not gonna lie, it was hard for them. But they found a way. They loved me. And after their journey, they loved her, too."

"Hey, what's the deal with the race politics?" another voice called out.

"What race politics are you talking about?"

Tamara asked, ready to defend herself.

"Well, I don't know much about it all."

"You've already shown that," Tamara suggested.

"No, wait, there's a genuine question here beneath my ignorant introduction to it."

"Sorry. What is it you're trying to ask?"

"I don't pretend to know all the issues of this, but there's all the interracial stuff I hear a lot about but admit I don't know jack shit about. Like how straight Black women don't want men to date white girls. Right?"

"Right. In many ways, the sisters feel betrayed and much more," Tamara confirmed.

"Well, does that carry over to the lesbian world? I mean, do they get upset if you date a white lesbian?"

"Upset? They'd dance in the streets over it. I mean, that would mean one less black woman competing for the brothers. And as limited in number as they are, I'm surprised straight black women haven't been at the forefront of lesbian marriages. Now, if you're asking me, does a lesbian sister get an attitude if I date a white woman? Well yeah, some, but for the most part, we're aware of the small pool of lesbian prospects. We're not going to make it smaller by restricting too much to race. But staying together will always be an unwritten preference."

A strong wind broke through the otherwise gentle sea breeze. Women in the crowd looked up as if to see what caused it. Brooke was mostly untouched by it all. She got up unnoticed by the rest of the group and walked toward her sleeping area, barely aware of the change in climate. Then the wind became violent, which made the trees and shrubs rustle so loudly it sounded like the jungle was screaming.

"Okay, everyone," Shelby yelled. "This is what we've prepared for. Go to your ground shelter or the cave. We practiced this, now help each other out." The wind muted her voice. Women were holding on to one another with one hand and using the other to help block sand from their eyes. The wind fired each grain at them, like glass splinters attacking their legs. They reached down, trying to block their unprotected skin, but then the attack turned its attention to their hands and arms. They tried to help one another move against the force of the air. Then the rain came, but instead of it starting with a warning by light sprinkles, it came in a single, crushing downpour. Women bumped into one another while running with their heads down, as if that would protect the rest of their bodies. Soaked and exhausted, each woman finally scrambled into her assigned shelter.

࿔ ࿔ ࿔ ࿔

Brooke was one of the last ones to stumble into the cave. A hand reached out to help guide her there. The cave was large enough to fit about half of the women, but it was a tight fit. They lay elbow to elbow. A few sat up against the smooth lining of the shallow cavern. The storm planning team gave priority to the older and sick first, which left room for more. Next, they had the younger and healthy women count off, and "odd" numbers got a space in this den. The even-numbered women were supposed to go to the storm shelters they built in the jungle.

But that was not the end of it. None of their decision-making was that simple or easy. Any cave woman could trade places with a shelter woman if she wanted to give up her preferred spot to help someone else out. If she gave up the spot, they'd give her two extra water rations per day. If she kept her cave spot, she only got it for three consecutive storms, then the even numbers were allowed their time in the cave for three storms. When Shelby called out these instructions several weeks ago, Brooke was sure they would never keep it all straight. But somehow, everyone knew where to go and honored the system without question.

Brooke had tried several times to give her cave place to one of the odd-numbered women, but most of them were comfortable getting their turn in a couple of storms.

She looked around the cramped area and saw several of the scouts she met that day, like a family gathering. She smiled at Shavoon and Gail sitting by the cave entrance. The reassuring feelings they brought her were subdued by her own knotted feelings of guilt, worry, and shame—guilt for what had happened with Marie, worry about not seeing her in the cave when she was supposed to be there, and shame that she was also looking for Heather. After the brief check-in to make sure everyone was all right, it grew quiet. The smell of perspiration and moisture from their wet bodies filled the air, which gagged some women. There were sounds of panting and wheezing from exhausted women. The cave was dimly lit, as the total darkness was too frightening for most of them.

Brooke curled up, trying to keep herself warm. She noticed Claire, who had been staring at her for a while. Claire gently worked her way over and around a couple of damp bodies to sit next to Brooke. She put her arms around Brooke and gave her a compassionate hug. "You've had a disturbing day," Claire whispered.

Even after being chased by the island storm, her voice was calm and clear.

"Do you ever have a bad hair day?" Brooke blurted out with a smile. "I mean, you always look great, and even after the storm of the century is hurled at us, it's like a stylist met you at the cave entrance. Not just the hair, but all of you is so poised and refreshed while I'm running around like island of the living dead."

Claire smiled and blushed a bit. "You do not, Brooke. You're beautiful, and you should know that by now. Your eyes have a blue in them that reminds me of the ocean. It's breathtaking. And your lips, do you know how much my friends pay for that crowned look? Your full hair with that youthful bounce, like I had way back when I was half my age. All that would be enough, but you throw in those striking cheeks to top it all off. Now that's the part that's not fair. Me, I got good genes. And while all this is fun talk and rather excites me, it doesn't answer my question. You seem upset, and I don't mean by the storm or this place. Something in you has changed."

Brooke spoke her unchecked thoughts. "Sometimes you comfort me, and sometimes you scare me."

"And now?" Clair asked.

"Now, a little of both, I guess." Brooke looked over the lightly lit cave and the women seeking refuge there. "Not sure I'm ready to bare my soul to our island witch. Ooh, sorry, I didn't mean…"

"No problem. I rather like the title myself. And it's a little late, you know, deary, you've already borne your soul by the look on your face. Not much left but to put a few words to what's burdening you."

Brooke turned to her and couldn't help but smile.

"I guess I'm hoping it'll all go away without talking about anything. Can you do that, make it all go away?" Brooke asked like a young child talking to her favorite aunt.

"Some say I've done that for them. But you know, I haven't done anything for anyone that they couldn't do for themselves. I just somehow get credit for it. How strange. I'll give you this. Whatever all those feelings are I see churning in your eyes, you need to be more responsible for them." Claire's face stayed soft, but her words seemed out of character and certainly not typical of her delicate approach. It caught Brooke off guard, and she responded with anger.

"More responsible, more responsible? Claire, I was born fucking responsible. I've been honest and look where that's gotten me. Responsible. Next life, I want to be without guilt or conscience. Fuckin' responsible." Brooke got up but realized there was nowhere to go.

Claire ignored her anger. "Honesty doesn't stop the chain of events, it starts them. Now you've got to see them through. You can do that with more honesty, integrity, and determination, or you can do it while whining about the circumstances you're in—or, I should say, the circumstances you've created. There's no easy way through this. Either way is difficult. But those are the paths lying before you, each leading to the same goal. Do you want to reach that goal with your honesty and integrity intact, or do you want to reach it feeling depleted of all your emotional energy? You know, that's what happens when you whine through the entire journey. That is, if you're lucky enough to actually reach the goal. Self-pity usually disturbs the soul's compass and throws you off course. But if you're lucky and obtain what it is you're searching for, you're too exhausted to enjoy the triumph. Self-pity always does that, leaves you too tired to enjoy it or so drained you can't even realize you're there. You know, you risk walking right by your destination when you're so focused on yourself. That's not good for you, and it's certainly not good for the rest of us here with you."

"Is this the encouraging speech, Coach?" Brooke tried to joke or at least change the conversation a bit, but Claire was talented at staying on track.

"Somewhere in all that, I hope you'll see that I'm thinking of you, Brooke, but in a broader sense, I'm also thinking of those of us here who will benefit from an emotionally, physically, and spiritually 'fit' you. These people need you. They need your clear, quick thinking. I've watched you. You can talk with a lot of different people. In your own analytical and calculating way, there's this genuine person who enjoys women, and they sense that. That makes you a bridge builder. Things have gone well for us so far, but we'll be put to the test soon. And if we divide, we'll need women like you and like Shelby to remind us of our connections. That's what you see and remind us of—our commonalities. So, again, whatever you're going through, take care of it the best you can, be responsible for it, and be present for the rest of us. Leave that, 'oh, what will I do with all this confusion, poor little me' to Tracy. It's more her style than yours."

Brooke looked over at Tracy. She remembered hearing her negotiating for someone's cave spot. Tracy had gone right to the women who always complain about not having enough water, knowing the extra ration would be the perfect incentive for them.

"Thanks, I think," she whispered back to Claire.

"No, you know exactly what I mean. That's why

you've given me this much time. Now spend whatever time you need to cry. You're welcome to cry on my shoulder. Get angry. Get sad. Then dust yourself off, hold your head up high, and take commanding steps on your journey, dear one. I have high hopes for you." Claire kissed her forehead.

Brooke placed her head on Claire's shoulder and cried while shaking. Then she fell asleep for a while. Claire did not leave her side. When Brooke awoke, she kissed Claire's cheek, and then, without saying anything, she worked her way over to one of the wise women who looked ill. The elderly woman had her hand on her stomach and her knees pulled up. She was softly rocking back and forth. She wore a frown and squinting eyes. Brooke made a spot by her, took her hand, and whispered something in her ear. The elderly woman turned to Brooke, and they both smiled slightly in their silence.

❧ ❧ ❧ ❧

Not too far from the cave were the other women. They were in the homemade storm shelters constructed by the space engineers, several construction workers, a couple of athletes, and about seven women from quilting guilds back home. They each contributed the tools of their trades: physics, grooves and joints, strength and endurance, and the most vicious knots anyone had ever seen. They cleared a space about thirty yards into the thick brush and constructed three buildings, which looked less like tents and more like jungle-quilted huts. They used remaining trees from the cleared space to build elaborate protections around and above the shelters. There wasn't much time to test their strength before the storm hit.

"Okay," Renee called out to the women in the homemade shelter, "it looks like everyone is doing well. I know the wind sounds cruel, but its howl is much worse than its bite, or something like that. Pair up and stay close to each other. It'll help keep you warm. I'm sure none of us thought we would have a problem with that on this humid island, did we? But here we are, so now try to stay warm."

There was nervous laughter.

"Call out if you need help and pray or send out white light or meditate or whatever it is you do when you ask for help and ask now for these fine walls to stay up."

"Of course, they'll stay up. I helped build them," someone called out.

"So if something happens, you're the one my lawyer should call?" another joked.

"Remember," Renee added. "There are no lawyers on this island. That's why we call it paradise."

"What's with the lawyer bashing? Give it a rest already. I'm a lawyer, and I've helped many like you with wills, partnership contracts, and the paper maze through adoptions so your kids can legally have two moms."

"Good point, well taken. I'll retract my comments to say, there're only lawyers like you in this paradise. Okay, let's hug up and be safe," Renee finished and made her way over to Marie.

"I thought you were going to be in the cave with Brooke. She told me she wouldn't let you trade your spot unless she also found a trade."

"I guess there are some things she can't make me do," Marie snipped and then softened when she saw

Renee's confused look.

"Sorry, Renee. This hasn't been a good Marie and Brooke day. It would be strange for me to talk to you about it much, you being her best friend and all."

"Of course. Let me know if there's anything I can do."

"For now, you can help me check the knotting on these vines."

"Sounds good," Renee answered. When they finished looking at each connecting knot, Renee announced to the group, "Friends, we've done a final shelter check. Things are great. But we need to douse the lights now, which means total darkness. It may get a little freaky, but that's better than the risk of fire in here. Hold on to your friends."

The wind slashed at the structure, which shook and rattled throughout the night. The women lay mostly in silence. There were occasional gasps of fear or worry. Sometimes, they tried to comfort one another, but the dictating wind silenced any attempts to communicate. They were at the storm's mercy.

❧ ❧ ❧ ❧

It wasn't until late morning the next day when the storm finally broke. Without discussion, women immediately took inventory and began their work. They checked on one another, reworked the shelters, cleaned the gathering place, collected food, replenished water, and overall, they made ants in the ant farm look lazy. Brooke spent most of the day working with the water group. They had put together tubs of sorts to collect the rainwater and were now looking for ways to store what they could. Brooke noticed an uneasiness among the women. At first, she thought it was just her projecting her own discomfort on to everyone else. And that may have been part of it, but not all. They were quieter than usual, only talking when they needed to work through problems with their task. They moved with uneasiness and kept their gazes lowered a bit. There was much less physical contact, fewer hugs, or reassuring pats on the back or butt. Then she noticed something that had all but escaped her until that point. The women who usually went topless had clothes on for the first time in weeks. For a moment, Brooke was upset with herself for being so self-absorbed that she had missed the obvious that had surrounded her for most of the day. The storm had again forced the women through the unknown. It damaged the false security they had built around the island's sense of predictability. They weren't visibly upset or panicked, but they were altered.

Upon realizing this shift, Brooke checked in with the women. She asked how they were doing, how they got through the night. She touched them lightly on the shoulder and looked them in the eyes with each question or remark. As soon as the first woman gave her account of the stormy night, others joined in with their experiences. They talked about how the trashing rain mixed with sand hurt them, how the threatening jungle winds howled at them. It was like nothing they had ever heard before. They wondered when the next storm would get there. When they finished their work, they went to the gathering with extra water for the evening's dinner. By then, some of them were holding hands and laughing.

❧ ❧ ❧ ❧

They gathered for a brief dinner, and Shelby announced that regular work groups would start in the morning unless the storms continued. The mention of returning to their routine was rather pleasant for Brooke. She was finishing her dinner when she thought she saw Renee walking through the crowd looking for someone. She left early in case someone was her. She was not up for a probing conversation with her dear friend. Brooke wanted to tell her about the dyke drama in her life but decided to wait until she found the words for her feelings. At least, that was what she told herself. But deep inside, she knew she couldn't get out of a talk with Renee without exposing what she was going to do, and Brooke was still pretending she hadn't decided yet.

Brooke walked up the path the scouts made on the small hill behind the gathering place. The early evening sky looked washed from the rain, and there was still light for her to walk by. The path twisted and turned with the shoreline, so Brooke was soon out of sight and sound of the gathering. By the time she reached the small peak above a cove, she heard a few women talking and giggling. She turned to see who had followed her, but no one was there. Then she looked down to see two women lying on a blanket in the sand below her in an area dubbed "Lover's Lane," where Brooke and Marie had shared some serious necking. It was set in a bit, which created a sheltered area, and the cove setting made it easy for women to investigate the area around the rocks to see if the space was occupied or not.

Brooke kept staring, even though her thoughts were telling her not to. She continued to think even as she kneeled in the brush and placed her hands under her chin. She grinned with vicarious pleasure as she saw the woman on top rotating her hips on her girlfriend. Or at least Brooke thought it was her girlfriend. They were kissing on the lips and neck. The woman on top moved down to kiss her girlfriend's breasts. The girlfriend leaned up and whispered something in her ear, which caused the woman to turn her girlfriend over on her stomach. She ran kisses all over her girlfriend's back. Then the woman dropped her head and guided the tips of her hair up and down her girlfriend's back, which encouraged her girlfriend to spread her legs and raise herself on her knees, welcoming the woman to do whatever she liked.

Touch her already. She's definitely ready. Or lie down on your back and slide under her raised hips.

Brooke watched the woman continue to run her hair along her girlfriend's back.

No, I was wrong. Don't hurry, enjoy the tenderness.

Her girlfriend turned back over, and they shared a long, impassioned kiss. The woman kissed each part of her girlfriend's body: her neck, her shoulders, her arm, her stomach, her thighs. And when Brooke thought she was going to put her in her mouth, the woman slid her body over her girlfriend and moved back up to kiss her mouth again. She did this several times, going down as if to take her in her mouth, only to tease the woman with her knees bent, legs spread, and hips moving up and down, begging to be touched. Just when it looked like her girlfriend could not wait any longer, the woman reached down and placed her hand between her legs, stroking her girlfriend with the same rhythm of their kisses. Her arm moved back and forth as she slid her fingers in and out of her open body. They moved in this rhythm like two dancers who knew each other's steps. The girlfriend reached down to touch herself until her legs shook with pleasure.

Brooke noticed her own breathing was short and rapid. She thought about touching herself to ease the excitement in her own body. She felt her hard clit but decided that anything more would surpass her already stretched voyeurism boundaries to an unacceptable place of a threesome with only one consenting person. Feeling a little ashamed of herself, she got up and slipped on the brush. She caught herself before falling over the hill but not without letting out an unplanned yell. The women in the cove looked up at Brooke, who was mortified at being caught in the voyeur act.

What the hell do I say now? I didn't plan on watching you two have an early evening fuck. Oh, I've never done this before, really. No. What do I say? The one woman is going to beat the shit out of me. Shit, it'll be the talk of the gathering. I can't even watch without getting caught. I have to say something.

Then one lover waved at Brooke and called out, "Hey, you up there! Do you want to join us?"

Brooke smiled. Do I want to join you? Okay, not what I expected.

Brooke yelled back, "No, no, I was passing by and I…"

"It's okay. We like to perform. But I wish we had known you were up there. We would have livened it up a bit."

Brooke waved and thought, "What else could they have done?" Then said, "Thanks for the offer. I'll be moving along and letting you get to round two." Brooke tried to get away as soon as possible without bringing more notoriety to herself. She moved through the brush as best she could until she found a resting place, which seemed safe enough. She lay there smiling and thinking about the beach bunnies.

What if that were me and Marie? Me and Heather? Just me? Just Heather? Heather and Marie? Heather? Marie? Heather? Marie? Thanks, my unknown young strangers, for bringing some humor to this whole thing. Nice change of pace. Nice fuck.

That evening brought no rain. Instead, there was a beautiful star show in the freshly washed night sky. Brooke spent the night back at her own sleeping space and rested more than she ever thought she would have. She woke up feeling more hopeful and even looked forward to the day. She still hadn't admitted that she knew what she was going to do. But that didn't matter much that morning. Between Claire's words of wisdom in the cave and last night's voyeuristic romp, she walked with a lighter step. She went to the scout meeting place where Gail, Cody, Shavoon, and Joey were waiting. Shavoon and Joey were stroking each other's hair. At first Brooke thought it strange for Shavoon and Joey to be so close.

It hasn't been that long since Shavoon's partner—what was her name?—died. It seems soon for them to be…be…not sure what they are. What the hell am I thinkin'? Me deciding what's right with love and timing. Not my place at all to judge how Shavoon deals with grief, and I'm certainly not in the book of how to treat a living lover, not to mention the memory of one who's passed. Be glad she's happy. It was wrong of me to have wondered about it in the first place. Sorry, people who will never know the struggles in my head. She smiled.

"The storm made some interesting bedfellows: a day care owner and the P.E. teacher of the month." Brooke heard a familiar voice. It was Tracy, being even uglier toward Shavoon and Joey than Brooke could ever have come close to.

"Hi, little T. We thought the island goddesses had smiled on us, and you had dropped out of our little group," Shavoon answered.

"Okay, let's keep the rough welcome backs to a minimum," Gail said, putting an end to it.

Lillie, Claire, Nina, and Madison came toward the group. Madison was walking with her stiff accountant stride. She had bananas for the entire group.

"I love it when someone brings treats for the work group," Shavoon said.

Several other women joined the group that morning. Brooke had talked to most of them before. Fortunately, none of them were the two from Lover's Lane. Brooke was hoping not to run into them so soon after their provocative meeting.

"Okay, friends, it looks like we have a full group today. We've collected a lot of fresh water, so no need for a waterfall trip. Basically, we're going to focus on getting supplies to reinforce the storm shelters. Team up, and let's get started."

Brooke moved to Nina's side. "Mind if I walk with you today? I want to talk with you about something," Brooke told her.

"Sure, I'd enjoy your company."

They walked for a while, working with several crews to get vines and extra tree switches. Brooke waited for an opportunity to talk, but the physical nature of restoring the shelters postponed that conversation. The work required their full attention. Several women had to hold the switches while others tied the vines. Finally, they stopped for a lunch snack.

"Good work this morning, friends." Gail smiled. "It helps when we're larger in numbers. Eat up and take the rest of the day off. Swim, eat, rest, fuck, do whatever it is you all do." They cheered and laughed, hugging one another.

"Well, my curiosity is high. What is it you wanted to talk with me about?" Nina turned to Brooke.

Brooke lowered her head in slight embarrassment. "Remember the other day when we found the pit?"

"Of course."

"Do you remember that woman sitting by the waterfall? Before we all went down to the pit?"

"Yes. I remember her."

"She said she was getting time away from the settlers. Do you know her? I know you spent time with that group."

"Her name is Heather. I know of her," Nina said.

Brooke continued, "I'm wondering about her. I don't see her during the gatherings. Hell, except for that day, I haven't seen her at all on the island. Why does she stay with the other group? When you were with them, did she say anything important about herself?"

Nina looked at Brooke and responded as though Brooke's questions and her look gave it all away. "Important? Wow, how things change by one storm. What about Marie? I don't think I want to be part of something that will hurt her. Have you two broken up, or is this a side show you're after?"

"Whatever is going on, I'm being honest with Marie. At least as honest with her as I am with myself, but I need to know something, and I can only do that if I talk with Heather. Sorry, I didn't mean to make you feel uncomfortable or put you in the middle of something."

"No one can put me in the middle. I'll share this, Brooke. She does live with the settlers on that mountain toward the other side of the island. They're a kind of self-exiled group. I'm not sure why she's there. I didn't talk with her as much as I did with the others."

"Thanks." Brooke took a deep breath in relief now that the conversation was over. She knew she had managed it poorly but was still glad at the outcome.

Nina, however, didn't let her go without a final word, "For what it's worth, I think you're making a mistake. I wasted a lot of time not being honest with myself or with Amber. We lived in the same town for so long. All those trips up to Tucson to visit the bars, and there we were in the same town. We could have been with each other instead of pretending like we both weren't interested. Now I can't do anything about it except hope she's safe and back home thinking of me while she's teaching her elementary kids long division. I hope she's thinking of me coming back to her, not as the best friends we parted, but as the lovers we should have always been."

"She's there as sure as hell fuck." Brooke mimicked the irreverent language Amber had used that night on the ship.

"Hell fuck is right. Now you be careful, Brooke. Just be careful."

"Not sure what that means anymore, but thanks." Brooke kissed her on the cheek.

Brooke executed a plan she didn't remember formally making. She talked with Gail about needing a couple of days away from the scouts and apologized for taking leave after only a few days of work. Gail felt better about letting her go when she heard Brooke wanted to go to the settlement.

"There's an uncharted cave on that side. It's hard to get to. I've heard rumors it has something in it. Maybe more clues about the island. I may be grasping at straws, but it would be helpful to get a report on it. I'll make sure you have some strong rope and other makeshift tools to help your climb. Sound okay?" Gail requested.

"Sure. I'd be glad to," Brooke said. I know it won't be this easy with Renee. But she knew she had to take care of that quickly while she still had the nerve.

Brooke found Renee sitting alone on the open beach and explained as much as she could about Heather and going to see her. Renee sat in silence for a while, staring at her hands. She was sieving sand through her fingers as if it might leave a chunk of gold in her palm. In some ways, Brooke was looking at her best friend for the first time. She didn't remember when Renee's short hair had grown so long. She wondered which specific day it was when Renee became this muscular woman. And that mischievous, playful spark in Renee's eyes had matured into a thoughtful light of strength. Renee had changed on this island, and Brooke knew the maturity in her now flourished more from her love with Adair than from anything else she had been through in getting here.

"Come on, it's not that bad, Rinkie."

Renee looked at her with a blank stare before responding, "No, of course not. It sounds like you haven't decided to pursue Heather, yet all your actions say you are. Maybe you should pause for a moment. It took you so long, like a lifetime, to get to experiencing deep feelings for another woman. Maybe you should make some use of them. Don't think about what it is you want to do. I wish you would take a minute to feel what's happening in you without rationalizing things. Tell me what your heart says, what are your feelings saying?"

Brooke looked out over the ocean as if it would provide the answer. She struggled to find the words. "When I think of Marie, I feel like I'm sitting next to a spring river. The kind that rises from the melted winter snow on the mountaintops. The water is cool and clear. I'm sitting by its bank on a sunny day. The sky has a couple of those fluffy clouds floating around but never crossing the sun's path. The surrounding trees are tall and scattered enough to see the ground. I feel relaxed and happy to be there. Like all is well with the world."

"And when you think of Heather?" Renee probed.

"I feel like I'm sitting next to a dam that broke. The water is rushing over the bank. It's churning things up from an unseen depth. It hastens past me. It's still a sunny day, but I'm so taken by the vigorous flow of the current, I don't notice the sun or anything else at all."

"So you prefer an uncontrollable current to all the peace of that spring river?"

"It's not about preference. I'm not choosing Heather over Marie. It's about needing to know what it's like to get close to that energy. The energy called to me."

Renee looked at her. "Maybe you don't think it's a choice, but it absolutely is. So please stop lying to both of us. And more importantly, to Marie. Honey, you have no idea what she'll do if you leave her to chase this wild oat." Brooke's face hardened, and Renee saw how the words affected her. "Sorry for that comment. I'm trying to be the objective friend who helps you to sort through things by leading you to your heart's desire instead of telling you all my biases. But I can't do that. I can't do that because, honestly, I love Marie for you. The only rush Heather will give you is to keep you from something good and real and long term. All the things you're scared of. That's the only reason you're doing this, Brooke. You've never known all the way close, and now when you can have it, you're in some revolving-door mindfuck convincing yourself you need to see something meaningful through. You don't. It's not meaningful. It's a lie. You wanted a hand holder. Well, Marie is it and much, much more."

Brooke sat next to Renee and calmly told her, "I want the hand holder, and I also want that woman who I search for when I smell her perfume in the air."

Renee became more upset. "And Marie isn't both? Did you hear a word I just said? Heather may be dreamy, granted a throb-producing dream, but a dream just the same. She's a dream waiting to turn into the nightmare that will keep you from true love. You don't even know this person." Renee stood and reached her arms out to Brooke as if to coax her away from this decision.

"Do you realize how ridiculous this sounds? From the outside in and the inside out, it's ridiculous. It's like you've invented reversible ridiculousness. That's it, you've gone and invented reversible ridiculousness, that's what you've done." Renee stood there with her hand on her hips, trying to appear like she said something more profound than what came out of her. But Brooke remained unchanged. She continued with her steadfast responses and even became somewhat lighthearted.

"That's part of it—not your fashion analogy—

reversible ridiculousness. Hmm, who would have ever thought I would do that? Brooke tried to lighten the conversation, but both knew that wasn't possible. "But you're right about me not knowing Heather. And worse, I don't know the 'me' I would be with her. How can I go on with Marie and always wonder what I would be like with Heather? How?"

Renee didn't hear her point. "How can you expect someone to be with you if it means she'll never know when you need to chase after another crush to see what that means?"

"You know I'm not like that," Brooke tried to reason with her.

Renee countered, "Well, you're like that now. Do you think this is an exception for Marie? She's wondering what the hell will happen with the next dam burst. She has a mature love for you that doesn't include that type of unpredictability. Don't throw away true love because you're scared of another loss. There, I said it. Brooke, you want to beat the Fates from ending this by sabotaging it yourself. We're all scared of life's waves of impermanence. I know you, your fear is held in the hands of a kid whose parents didn't come home and whose grandma didn't wake from a nap. But you're not a kid, and fear shouldn't keep you from enjoying every moment with the real thing. Marie is the real thing. This is it. Everything ends. The only thing permanent is the way we love."

Brooke drifted into her own tangent. "True love. Everyone says they found their true love, their soul mate. Then they break up or someone dies or something, and in another two months, they're with their next true love. I always thought true love meant one person. But most people we know are on their fifth true love."

"You know what I mean. Few of us get what you have—that scene you described with the river, the sun, trees, and the sunlit path all at the same time. Don't do this. Don't fuck this up. Just because it's good doesn't mean it's going to be taken away from you. It's okay to get close to Marie and stay close to her. You deserve this." Renee was begging. Her determined eyes said it, her hands waved it as she made repeated gestures to Brooke to stay. Even the light wrinkles around her tan face showed they wanted Brooke to change her mind.

"I'm not proud of all of this. I do love Marie. It's not like I don't see how wonderful we are together. Any other time, you and I would not be having this conversation. But meeting Marie has happened at the exact time I'm just getting to know myself, and I can't turn my back on that anymore. I know you won't believe me, but this is not about my fear of losing someone close to me. It's about my being true to myself.

"I'm not acting out my past losses anymore. That put my life on hold. I'm not hiding in grief's shadows or being so buried in work I didn't even notice how Grammie tired more easily in the months before she died. Now my name has been called. I've stepped up to the podium and someone gave me time and said, 'Here, this is yours. You've always had it, but now you're aware of it.' It scares, worries, and excites me all at the same time. Do you know what it's like to have the pleasures of a new love, the weight of unspeakable grief, and the excitement of the unknown as constant companions? Well, I do, and somehow with all that I'm still thinking about moving forward. And I'm being honest about it with myself, you, and Marie. I will tell her. That will feel like death to me, Rinkie. But not telling her is not living. Not pursuing this is not living, either. I'm finally listening to me. I hope I'll do it in a way that makes me proud when I look in the mirror. I hope I'll find a way through this that embraces grace and humility that honors the memory of my family. I hope I'll minimize the hurt to others while trying to be true to myself. And if not, it's not like I don't fucking know what I'll lose."

Her words pulled Renee out of her combative stance. She sat next to Brooke and softened her words as she spoke to Brooke, who was still shaking from her own convictions.

"Perhaps it won't be as much as you've gained," she finally said. "Sorry, it took me so long to hear what you were saying, to see who you are now instead of who I've known for some time. For what it's worth, you'll always have me as a best friend. That's something you'll never lose, no matter how much you fuck up. Like you've been there for me on some of my less than optimal decisions. We're sisters of different mothers, you know. Best friends for the ages.

"And this friend really thinks you should give this more thought. I can tell it's not your logic that needs to see this through. It's something still attached to your loss that's driving this. But that's not for me to change. I love and accept you as you are. So hear me with that love. The you you're discovering is beautiful and evolving. It's also someone, Brooke, who I don't believe is emotionally ready for Marie. This isn't an honorable way of seeing these feelings through. It's simply about you not being emotionally ready for her. You still have healing to do. Go ahead and do what you need to, but for heaven's sake, let her go. Don't drag her love for you through your issues!"

"I love you so much. You're like a sister to me. You've always been there for me even when I couldn't be there for myself. How do you do that? You've held my hand through so much. I've always felt you with me. Supporting me. Reminding me of all the fun there is to have in life. Pushing—no, dragging—me to be my best self. No one has ever heard my silence the way you do. And while your words are hard for me to hear, I do hear them. Thank you, Rinkie, but, umm, who said you were my best friend?"

"Bitch." Renee smiled.

Brooke pointed her finger at her. "That's 'about-to-fuck-everything-up bitch' to you."

"I'll keep that in mind, your royal fuck-up."

"Okay, I'm tired of this. They're about ready to start tonight's discussion. That should be a pleasant diversion."

"Yes, I'm liking this more than karaoke night at the bar. Let's head to the gathering."

❧❧❧❧

Like most evenings for the past five months, the women gathered for the nightly talk. Renee and Brooke sat side by side with arms around each other's shoulders and slight grins on their faces. It had been a while since the two of them sat without Marie and Adair around. Brooke liked having her friend back. Though, they weren't the same. They'd both grown as women and as friends.

"Debbie suggested tonight's talk," Shelby announced. "But first, I want to acknowledge that this month represents several winter holidays back home. While we all agreed religion is a taboo subject at the gatherings, I want to remind you all that this is the night we're having holiday sharing. Anyone who wants to talk about your traditions or give thanks or whatever the will, the facilitators are meeting down by the sharing hut. They will help bring us together under that intention."

"I almost forgot it was the holidays," a voice called out.

"It just makes me sad to even think about it," another said.

"I want to acknowledge my religion by something this month. Why do we have to be all or nothing about it?" a third asked.

"Okay," Shelby continued, "stop. Just stop. If you want to be involved, please go to the sharing hut. If you don't, please make space for those who do. And if it brings up a lot of difficulty in you, I'll hang around here with some of the healers to provide comfort tonight.

"On a totally different subject, tonight's discussion is around building stronger bridges with our gay brothers. Debbie mentioned that she has talked with some of you who belong to a productive alliance with them, and we thought it would make for a positive discussion. Who wants to start?"

"Why? Are there gay men on the island?" Tracy called out.

"So much for the 'move away from the holiday vortex discussion and into something positive,'" Renee whispered to Brooke.

"That question doesn't deserve an answer," Shelby said. "Next comment."

"Without the sarcasm," Tracy tried again, "why are we discussing this? It should be one of those taboo topics like religion." She stood. Brooke noticed how out of place her hard face was among the warm looks from other women.

Shelby responded, "Just a reminder. Religion is not taboo as long as everyone agrees to have the discussion. Besides, I understand the Unitarian Universalists have incorporated a variety of spiritual beliefs and practices into beautiful and inclusive services. So, to my knowledge, religion is not tabooed, it has been inspirational to all of us on spiritual paths. Are you saying you don't agree to this discussion?"

Tracy continued, "I'm saying I'm tired of this topic. We beat ourselves up wondering how to work more with gay men, but what does it get us? Division among ourselves about their role—or lack of it—in our lives and more guilt about what we need to do to bridge the gap. More meetings, negotiating, and begging them to be more united. Well, I'm tired of it. Let them bridge the gap. But wait, we know when that will happen. Never. Let's face it, straight men only tolerate women as much as they do for sex. With gay guys, they don't even need us for that."

"I disagree with you." Brooke became less of a spectator. "That kind of talk is part of the problem, not the solution. Many gay guys are working to help our rights—"

"No, they're working to help their rights. We get the leftovers." Tracy didn't let anyone interrupt her this time and quickly explained, "I'll give you a good example of what I'm talking about. In college, I was studying sociology with a wonderful gay guy who I loved from my class. He was visibly upset. I asked him what was going on. He had gone for an HIV test, which he did every six months. We talked about how difficult that must be, the friends he lost, his fears, ya know.

Then he looked at me and said, 'I hope if anything this devastating ever happens to women, I could be there for the lesbian community the way you all have been there for us.'

"I almost fell out. I looked at him and said, 'Well, what do you think rape is, what do you think breast cancer is, what about the fact that after graduation I'll make so much less than you even with the same degree?' It went on and on. The point is, he couldn't see me through the needs of his immediate life, and none of them do."

"None of them?" Brooke repeated. "You talk about him like he represents all gay men. You would have a battlefield blowout if he talked about you like that. Besides, he was trying to be kind while under extreme distress and worry about his health, perhaps his life. He was not the problem. You were. How could you try to decide his values in life based on a statement he made to you while in crisis?"

"And women who fear rape all the time aren't under distress?" The tense topic fueled Tracy. "I've seen it over and over, even gay guys not under distress act like this. Let's face it, the day they find a cure for AIDS the first thing on their agenda will be to reopen the public bathhouses, and women's issues will be somewhere on the bottom of the list if we make it on the list at all."

"How can you talk about AIDS like that? After all the deaths, the loss, you can't be that cruel. Geez, Tracy, where's your compassion?" Brooke said.

Renee whispered in her ear, "Way to go."

Tracy wasn't backing down. "Your judgment of me is premature and inaccurate. I donate blood for AIDS patients, I give money, time with children, I volunteered during the quilt display in my community. And I volunteered at hospitals to sit with patients when their own families wouldn't show up. Their own families, Brooke. This plague needs to be stopped. And I care deeply for the dear gay men affected by it and their lovers and their families. But what I don't do is kid myself like the rest of you. I don't believe my work is bringing me and my lesbian sisters closer to our gay male counterparts in a union of compassion and understanding. This is another example of men in need and women rolling up their sleeves to take care of them. And we do so with the false hope that they will return it, that somehow helping them during a time of tragedy makes them equal and ignores the fact we are once again in the helping role. It's a one-way street, lady. This isn't building bridges, it's just giving us more bandages to wash, and we do it like the good little caretakers we were raised to be, and they let us help, like the good little boys they were raised to be. So, of course, I help. And you may not believe this, but I also care. I know the realities of working with men, any men. We give. They take."

Some of the other women clapped. It was the most support Tracy had ever received. Brooke knew the danger of being pulled into the argument rather than the solution. She proceeded with caution.

"I don't know what groups you work with, but you're not talking about my experiences. I know gay men working against violence against women, and these aren't guys with big jobs and lots of money. They're working hard to make ends meet, and in their spare time, they escort coeds across campus at night. They call me when I'm sick to see if they can bring me anything. They were the first ones at my house when my grandmother died and the last ones to leave, only after making sure I was okay," Brooke argued. "So do not, do not, try to spin a web of political issues with any group. It's endlessly more statements about your disappointment in the world not meeting your needs. Stop spewing that on others like they deserve it."

"Let's not forget our history, friends," another woman joined in. "Back in the witch-burning days of Salem, they'd throw gay men on the burning pile of wood beneath the mostly lesbians witches' feet to fuel the fire. We've had division among us through the generations, but we aren't in Salem. We're not being burned, and the only one who screams 'throw another faggot on the fire!' is the extreme right-wing coalition. That's the true enemy and haters against us. If we divide among ourselves, then they've won. The only way we can defeat them is through the strength of our unity." Many more cheered.

But Tracy seemed ready for those comments. "I agree. What I'm saying is we don't get to unity when one side is doing all the work. Actions speak much louder than words. Our gay brothers' actions are saying they're more interested in themselves than in us."

"And I'm saying you're wrong and misrepresenting gay men the way queer persecutors attack all of us. You're not working against gay men, you're unknowingly working for a larger agenda to keep our unity a myth," Brooke added.

"I wish I were, but part of you, part of all of you, know I'm right," Tracy said.

Another screamed, "Then what the hell do you suggest we do?"

"What we have been doing. Don't change who we are. Just stop with the false illusion that this is a reciprocal relationship. We're still doing all the work, and if anyone is going to be there for us, it needs to be us," Tracy stated.

Another woman joined in, "Way wrong. I'm from a state where voters defeated anti-gay measures in four separate elections. That didn't happen with only the gay vote. It happened from the straight vote. From men and women, some of them highly religious people, who don't believe in hate and discrimination of any kind. People who act on their beliefs."

"You've made a case for my argument. As lesbians, we'll find more support for our right to be who we are from straight Americans before we'll get it from gay men."

"Twisting words. How very old-fashioned. You know that's not what I mean. But you don't have a response for my point, so you twist it."

"Mean it or not, it's a reality." Tracy was verbally corralling some other women into her cynicism. She seemed to get more pleasure from this than anything else Brooke had ever seen. It was like a kind of drug for her, a drug that gave her false bravado. Brooke knew that continuing with the argument would only divide people more and give Tracy more opportunities to incite them. She saw the wave of tension shaking over the crowd. Shoulders rose and chests puffed up. It had all the markings of a pre-fight grooming. The division was making its way around the evening, gathering like a wave of discontent.

Brooke knew there was only one way to change the course of this downward spiral. "Well, I haven't heard anything new tonight." She stood and placed her hands in front of her. "If we're going to get caught in a recycled conversation, then we've gone nowhere during this time, and everyone agreed they wanted more out of our talks than the same-old, same-old, and if we can't do that, then at least we want to have fun. This, well, this is neither. I don't know about the rest of you, but even if you accept Tracy's argument, it doesn't have to mean there's nothing else we can do. There's always something else we can do. There's always another choice.

"How often does this happen? You know, when someone cleverly maps out two or three choices to a problem and emphasizes the choice they want you to make? There's always a benefit to them in that choice, but they don't tell you that. They make it seem like the problem is legitimate and choosing one response over the other is all you have. But you don't like any of the options. Still, you spend immense energy reviewing each of them, trying to find the best choice out of the worst available?" Brooke noticed a lot of women nodding. She could see Tracy slumping down.

"Now imagine that same situation. But instead of being sucked into having to pick from among what doesn't work for you, you said you wouldn't pick any? Instead, think what could happen if you took that energy, mixed it with your creativity and intuition, and came up with an entirely new option. Another that not only gives you what you need, but also doesn't create an additional problem in the meantime. There are people who use their intellect trying to convince you that you have to pick from the choices they present. It's limited because you allow it to be. So I ask you, what are your other choices? That's how we should spend our time. Looking for the way out of this maze, not building more tunnels in it. Remember, we're women. Hell, we're not just any women, we're lesbians. We can do better than this petty negative discussion." The women clapped again, this time louder and with whistles.

"I guess you have the answer then," Tracy said and tried to subdue the enthusiasm Brooke created.

"We do have the answer, Tracy. Working together, women always do. And that's what bothers you most. You can't stay in a cycle of getting attention by stirring up all that doesn't work in this world. Like hate. You can't do that if the rest of us work together to find more pleasing options."

"Love is the answer?" Tracy responded. "Sounds like some religion to me. Is that part of your new enlightenment?"

"No, it's part of me just not liking you." Brooke smiled and continued. "What pain do you carry so much that the rest of us have to constantly feel its weight?"

"Oh, I was abused as a kid, raped as a teen, left by my only love. Pick a victim rationale, any rationale," Tracy snipped.

The crowd, and even her cautious supporters, became defensive and angry. She spit on almost everyone there or at least someone they knew. But Brooke was quick to fend off what she sensed were town villagers on their way to kill the monster in the castle on the hill.

"Tracy, thanks for your insights. What about the rest of you? Any ideas on how to build bridges with our gay male friends?" She gestured toward Tracy. "Sorry, I mean to say, any ideas on how to build bridges with our gay male friends and not take on the role of caretaker?"

There was a pause. The tension focused intensely on Tracy. One more painful opinion from her, and the crowd would do damage. They were giving her one last chance to say something stupid so they could go wild. But the female spirit prevailed as one lone voice by the fire took Brooke's challenge.

"Instead of getting angry at them for not coming up with it on their own, let's tell gay men what we need and see if they don't rise to the occasion. While Tracy is greatly over-generalizing things, there's some truth in what she says, truth we don't want to accept because it affirms our place on the proverbial totem pole. But I have more faith and even love for our gay brothers. Let's face it. This is all just talk, our different perceptions. And actions do speak louder than words. If there are those of us here who think our relationship with gay men could be more balanced, then let's ask them to work with us in ways that create more support for lesbians. We could come up with a list, 'Fifty things gay men can do to help lesbians,' and see what they do with it."

Her comments didn't completely stop the town villagers, but it caused them to put down their weapons for a while. Attention moved away from Tracy to the simple voice by the fire.

Brooke and others breathed a quiet sigh of relief. Brooke watched the mood change. This is what women do best. Just when it looks like there's no way out of a situation or you're running in circles around an issue, someone comes up with a simple idea. It raises everyone above the confusion. It dissipates the pungent lunacy into harmless droplets. Women are so wonderful.

"Okay, what's number one? A complete package of C batteries," the first woman called out.

"I'd like a better rate for my home loan."

"How about Ellen's home phone number?"

"Now this is the fun part," another yelled.

Brooke watched the group move from disgust with Tracy to having fun with their fifty ways. She smiled at their ability to reject Tracy's invitation to argue into the evening. Her goal to get folks to ignore Tracy and find more creative solutions to her contrived argument was working. One by one, they called out:

"One, how about the million gay man march for women's health and safety?"

"Two, gay men contribute to counseling scholarships to surviving children of woman killed by domestic violence."

"Three, gay men raise funds for more affordable day care."

"Four, gay men give respite care to single lesbian moms."

"Five, a gay man visitation program with elderly lesbian widows."

"Six, a gay men's scholarship program for poor lesbian students."

"Seven, a gay men's 5K to raise funds for breast cancer."

"Eight, gay men build shelters for abused women and kids. Better, they work to change the current culture so it's batterers who must go into shelters and the women and kids get to keep their homes!"

"Nine, and you can all thank me for this one—we adopt their practice and make it our own!!"

"What practice are you talking about?"

The woman responded, "Well, given all this tension, lesbians obviously need to hold our own circle jerk parties!"

As they continued, Adair joined Renee and Brooke. Brooke saw her kiss Renee in a loving and tender way. She was happy for her friend. Renee deserved this attention and had been looking for it in all the wrong places. Brooke had moments of fear when thinking of not having Renee's attention in all the ways she used to. But then she remembered it was a loss for a good reason. Finally, she got to the selfless point of realizing it wasn't a loss at all, but rather, having a new part of Renee, the part of someone who had found magical love with someone.

"I should go talk with Marie," Brooke whispered to Renee.

"I'll see you off in the morning. I love you," Renee answered.

"Be with me before my dead-woman-walking trip?" Brooke asked.

"No, just your trip to the unknown. You've been on a couple of those with me."

Brooke kissed Renee on the cheek and made her way over to Marie, who was sitting outside the gathering.

"Thirty-three, food drop-offs for weeks after a lesbian has surgery," Brooke heard as the crowd continued through the list.

"Hi," she said as she approached Marie.

"Hi, Brooke." Marie got up and kissed her on the cheek.

"We need to talk," Brooke told her.

"I always hate it when someone starts a conversation with either 'Look, we need to talk' or 'do you have time to talk about something.'" Marie said.

"Then I'm glad I didn't say, 'Look, we need to talk, do you have time right now?'"

"Oh, stop, that hurts. You're going to the settlement tomorrow, aren't you?"

"Yes. While talking to Renee, I realized that to you I must seem like some out-of-control midlife lesbian who erratically chases someone she doesn't even know."

"It doesn't just appear that way, Brooke, it is that way."

"But it's not. This isn't something I've done all my life or will do for the rest of it. This has happened at a time in my life, though, when I can't ignore it. I have to find out. And talking to Renee made me realize something else that I've ignored. I've talked to you about this as something that is rare, I've never seen in myself. That's completely true. I've talked about it as something that I need to see through so it's not in the back of my mind when I'm with you. Also true. What I've ignored is that if I see it through, there won't be an us. I've selfishly wanted both—to face what this means and to be with you. That entanglement tells me one very important thing I've not wanted to accept. I don't believe I have the emotional maturity for what you're offering me. I'm not there yet. I don't want to hurt you, Marie."

Marie was fiery in her response. Her fingers were pointed and hitting the other hand's open palm. "Not ready for me? I can see that. But everything up to your seeing her here said you were ready. Where is that person? How did she just disappear in the blink of an eye? I want her to show up right now and tell me she's decided to ignore this because that's how important I am. Tell me that you're going to wait it out with me until it passes like a tornado that takes an unexpected last-minute turn and avoids the small, unprotected town. Tell me that because right now, I am dead center in its path. How do you get to do this? How do you get to become a stranger who all of a sudden isn't emotionally ready for me? Were you disingenuous until this point? I don't believe that. You're too authentic. How can you make me feel so important and then—poof—not?"

Marie was shaking more with fear than anger. Her confusion expanded with each question. They stared at each other. The once loving gaze was empty with hurt and disbelief. It seemed like an hour before Brooke finally responded.

"I am a genuine person who can only be as honest with you as I am with myself. I know nothing of this woman except she is traction bringing me closer to things inside of me that still need my attention. Things that, with or without her, will hinder me from getting emotionally raw with you. I can't do that now. Obviously, there are things in me that will not allow it. She's just that—traction, a compass pointing to where the shadows live in me. I think finding her and following through with what she brings up in me will get me closer to their meaning. And more importantly, what I need to do about them."

Marie's fervent tone thinned as she finished, and she looked at Brooke with the love she felt for her. She placed her hands on Brooke's shoulders and looked at her with softer eyes. She barely nodded. "You're right, you're not ready." Marie kissed her cheek and walked into the island's darkness.

The crowd was oblivious to their torture as they wrapped up the night's verbal frolic. "Forty-nine, tutor young girls in math and science."

"Fifty, promise to watch an all-women cable station at least one day a month and not just on Barb's biography night!"

Chapter Eleven

Brooke awoke before the sun started to show its dawn colors. She sat on the beach looking at the thinly lit ocean and recognized a new theme in her life: searching her heart while gazing out over the sea. She thought it would be a dawn showdown between the beckoning in her heart to go to Heather and the logic in her head telling her to run to Marie and beg temporary insanity. But to Brooke's surprise, her endless thoughts and conflicting emotions had taken a morning hiatus. She was filled with an undisturbed silence. She sat and noticed the color of the ocean, its smell coming off the early morning air, the cool sand beneath her body and how it gave her chills, the sound of the light breeze rustling through the trees—experiences of briefly living in the now. Like the promise of the sun rising behind her. There was a brief analytical moment that interrupted it when she wondered if she had finally numbed out on her own thinking. But that passed as she returned to her mind's holiday.

The sun showed more of itself as it rose and changed the color of the sea. Brooke heard women waking and greeting one another and the chants of early morning spiritual gatherings. Her silent retreat was gone, along with any chance for her to reconsider her actions. The early light hinted at a shadow beside Brooke, which she immediately recognized. "Grammie, is that you?" And on the tip of that second, she believed it was her grandmother standing there. A wave of memories followed her conviction: how it felt when Grammie put her arm around her, her touch, her laugh, the smell of her perfume, her comfort, her love.

"Morning, dear one."

Brooke turned her head with disbelieving hope. "Grammie?"

"It's me, Renee. Were you asleep, dreaming of Grammie?"

"Yes, something like that. Why are you here?"

"Remember, I told you last night I'd show up. You didn't think I'd let you go without seeing you off. You are still going, right?"

"Yes, we…I am."

"Have you ever thought maybe you're mad at me?" Renee looked away, afraid to see any hint of an answer in Brooke's eyes before Brooke responded.

"Mad?" Brooke asked.

"Yes, for talking you into this trip in the first place. After all, if I hadn't begged you to come on the vacation, you never would have found and then left the perfect partner."

"Hmm, you're right, you bitch. I hate you." Brooke smiled. "Of course, I never thought of it that way. But if we had to do it again, I'd say yes to the trip."

Renee smiled back. "I haven't heard that good of a lie since 'While you may not have voted for me, I still represent you.'"

"No, I mean, I wouldn't want anyone to have died in the ship's explosion. That I would change if it were mine to do. But in terms of what I've been through, this has all been good for me, Renee. It was long overdue. I don't know if I would have found so much of me in my Phoenix safe place. I was walking around with all the answers, and I thought I had it together. Turns out, I didn't know shit. I like that. Now I keep finding pieces of me I never knew I lost. I know that sounds weird, but it feels more real." Brooke half grinned.

"Okay, glass is still half-full, friend. Take care of yourself. It's a torturous hike to the settlement. Why they chose an isolated bluff to take up as home, I'll never know."

"Thanks. Hey, do I look okay? Never mind, I can't believe I even said that out loud." Brooke smiled.

"I can't believe it took you this long to ask," Renee joked.

"I love you, Renee. You and Adair take care. I'll be back when there's answers to my questions."

"I hope they get answered," Renee said as Brooke walked toward her new traveling companions. About twenty women gathered to make the trip over to the settlers with supplies. Brooke recognized the weavers who helped make the storm shelters. They packed some extra food and water. One woman was guiding the rest, telling everyone what to do and what to expect on the trail. Brooke barely heard a word of what she was saying.

❦❦❦❦

The group tried to stay on the trail for as long as possible. The cliffs were covered in thick vegetation and not welcoming even to the skilled hiker, not to mention the want-to-be mule team using it today. They stopped as much as they needed, but whether walking or taking a rest, they stayed mostly silent. Brooke's thoughts shifted between walking a safe course and meeting up with Heather. Her mind was moving faster during this day's travel.

Hi, I'm Brooke. No, way too boring. Hi, Heather, I remember you from the ship. We talked briefly on the deck about what we were discovering about ourselves while out at sea. I remember you were looking for insights into your breakup. No, don't remind her about the painful ex. Hi, can I help you with…with…what type of work do they do at the settlement anyway? What does someone who's about to ruin my life do anyway? Can I help you find that herb you were looking for to grind into that special medicine you're making for the sick women on the island? Great, now I've made her into a grand healer. Hi, we talked briefly on the ship, and I haven't seen much of you. Why is she on the reclusive side of the island anyway? Why didn't I wonder that before? I was so fixated on seeing her, talking to her, looking in her eyes to see any hint of the passion brewing in her like I feel in me. A drug addict, is she going through withdrawals? No, maybe a counselor helping the women. Or maybe she's so broken up by her break-up, she can't be around other people. Maybe she'll be so preoccupied by that last love, she won't even be able to talk to me. Will I have gone through all this to be rejected by the memory of a stupid ex? I like the counselor version of her better.

Brooke erratically looked for the perfect introduction as if it were going to either create or destroy every moment to follow the chance encounter she was creating in her mind. She didn't talk much to the other women, preferring the company of her rambling thoughts. They stopped for food and water but otherwise kept a constant and cautious pace.

"Okay, it's over there, nestled on top of those hills," the leader called out.

"We'll be meeting with Joyce, or JJ, as friends

call her," she informed the group.

Brooke had heard about JJ, who was a type of counselor legend on the island. Women talked about the way she jumped into the most volatile situations of women arguing and yelling at each other and defused them in a loving versus patronizing way. She didn't try to play the mom or auntie role as had been adopted by a couple of the more maternal women. She was a down-to-earth mediator extraordinaire. Of course, that was only what Brooke had heard. She'd never seen her in action or even known what she looked like. Brooke imagined her as a large woman with a somewhat squared-off face, flatter than round. She thought JJ would have a powerful presence and a soft voice.

"Welcome to the other side of nonreality," a voice called out.

"Hi there, Joyce. Sorry it took so long. The shuttle was late," the leader called back.

"Like I've never heard that before. You must get new material." JJ's loud voice roared among the tired group.

Brooke was surprised. Joyce walked over in short, fast steps. She wasn't over five feet tall, with a round face and a full, round body to match. She had a youthful bounce in her approach and a smile that introduced her welcome.

"Hi, everyone, I'm Joyce or JJ, whatever you wish. Thanks so much for giving your time to our home over here." She got straight to the point. "Most of you are familiar, but I see a couple of new faces. For you new gals, forget whatever you've heard. We're not harboring a bunch of foaming-at-the-mouth monsters in detox. No one here is foaming at the mouth, okay?"

They all laughed and tried to catch their breath

a bit. They walked closer to the living area of this place called the settlement. A couple of women had gathered to greet them. Brooke noticed Heather was not among them. Then JJ called out, "Okay, food and water carriers, this is Margaret. She'll show you where to go and what to do. Counselors, thanks for the walk over, but we've got too many of you already. Seems like no one at this point wants to switch places. Sorry for the extra walk. Next time, check your email first. Shelter builders, we need your help. Our lean-tos were worth crap in the last storm. Not much else up here to protect us. I hear we have a scout all to ourselves. Which one is…?"

"I am," Brooke answered and moved through the small group to shake JJ's hand. "Scouts R Us right here. My name is Brooke. It's good to meet you, JJ."

"Thanks, you too, Brooke. The big settlement mystery is in a cave down on a secluded beach. It's hard to get to as our home is right on top of this kick-ass bluff. Too steep to walk down, you see. You have to do the switchback trail, and I use that word kindly. It's a day's journey or so, depending on the weather. A couple of women did it once—they wanted to see the beach below and found this enormous cave under the bluff. They thought they saw something in it, but most of us have had many experiences of thinking we see something. Anyway, they didn't plan for such a find and had a lack of light and an abundance of fear. So they came back full of possibilities in terms of what's down there. Personally, I don't think shit about all that. We've chronicled most of the area here and haven't found crap." She put her hand on Brooke's shoulder and, with a wink, finished by saying, "But if you find something truly amazing, we'll name it after you."

"Then I hope it's a large boat hidden in the cave.

I've always wanted to sail on The Brooke." She smiled back.

"It won't have to be large," JJ confirmed. "Most of the women here have declared they're staying. Except for me, of course. I can't wait to leave this bunch of whining dykes lost at sea," she joked. Brooke liked her immediately. She may not have wanted to stay, but Brooke thought she seemed right at home, like some crusty old sea captain trying to hide his love of his shipmates.

JJ had one last instruction. "Okay, the rest of you will have to figure out what to do as the day goes on."

Brooke smiled and wondered about the accuracy behind the stories of JJ, the great mediator who would have made a wonderful air traffic controller.

The hiking group dispersed as the women tried to find their places at the settlement. Brooke tried to help the shelter builders organize their materials and take stock of what they still needed. A couple of women from the settlement helped them, but most stayed away. Brooke was not sure where. As Brooke took better notice of the surroundings, she understood all the "dark side" jokes about the settlement. While the bluff's meeting place provided more exposure to the almost constant blue sky, the light was muted here. There was something uncharacteristic in this otherwise tropical place. Where's all the chatter? The free-floating laughter? This doesn't even feel like the same island. This is like suspended animation.

As evening approached, Brooke jumped in and

helped with the meal. She could be at ease and capable in situations where she felt awkward and unsure. Her lighthearted approach toward the pitfalls of making a fool of herself guided her through those times. She could flounder and laugh at herself with the best of them, and most of the time, she could do it before anyone else had the chance to do it for her.

Women gradually came to the bluff, most alone, others in pairs. The largest group had only five women in it. There were gentle hugs and kisses. Little talk occurred, but there was a lot of what Brooke thought was disinterest—indifference to the food, the surroundings, and to the new women who had joined the settlement. If a new face had shown itself back at the clan gathering, there would have been questions and hugs, and they might have made it part of their evening sharing ritual. Out of the settlement's fifty or so women, fewer than five came up to Brooke to introduce themselves, although everyone she extended herself to was most welcoming. So she knew it wasn't a group of rudeness. Something else was going on, and it caught Brooke's imagination.

I feel like a social worker visiting an impoverished neighborhood, a community that has seen many social workers come and go, making promises but having to leave before they were fully actualized and leaving with more lessons from the residents than the worker left behind. Another face of helpers passing through. There were those who left more, a lasting impression or real contribution. Point is, they all leave the neighborhood at one point or another. They're looking at me and probably wondering what I'm going to do during my brief stay. What will I do? My motives have been so selfish. Fuck, how many times do I need to relearn this?

It's not just about me, but about those around me. What am I giving? This is another opportunity for me. What will I do? Not just coming to my Waterloo. What about the bigger need, where am I in that? I'll put more effort into mapping this area for the scout group.

Brooke watched the settlers. In some ways, they reminded her of the women in the clan group, but in important ways, they were so different. Their clothes were similar: torn, tattered. Their haircuts were clumsy. They had those tans—tans on top of old sunburns. They showed the new bleached blonds and new grays, all similar to the clan women. It was their faces that carried the difference. There was no effect, no animation, no wonder, no pain, no worry, no hope. Only blank faces with female features. And they were so quiet, which Brooke found the most bizarre.

"Okay, you all have met our new settlers," JJ announced. "Most are workers. Three have opted to live here for a while. Then there's Brooke. Brooke, wave your hand. She's the scout who will explore our mystery cave. Let her know if you're interested in joining her."

Someone calmly said, "Who would do that? Penny was there and said there's something in that cave. Who wants to be bear chow?"

"I don't know," JJ bellowed, talking louder than anyone Brooke had ever heard. "I've never heard of a tropical bear." There was a slight giggle from the women.

JJ continued, "Oh, we also have a couple of people who came to do a vision quest. Marty, you've become famous with the clanswomen. They've heard about your extraordinary ability to prepare and take someone through that inner journey. I guess you're the queen of the quest."

Marty yelled back, "I like that much better than what they called me back home, given my profession. Yes, 'vision guide' is much better than 'street walker.'" The joke flew over the visitors' heads, and only the settlers laughed.

"Sounds like a plan. Anyone want to add anything?"

"Yes, many thanks for the extra help the clan brought," someone called out.

JJ responded, "We'll give that message back. I know they'll appreciate our gifts of fishing arrows and other tools. I hear the shaman Claire is extremely thankful for the herbs we've found up here. In other words, ladies, the trade business is doing great. Oh, just a reminder, the clan has invited us for a full island dinner. Anyone interested in the trip?"

"Perhaps more so than in the past, but I still don't have a calling to be around that many people," someone replied.

"Same here. Even the thought of a group meeting makes me hyperventilate. Please extend our thanks again for the invitation and ask them not to take our position as a sign of our lack of appreciation for them. It's too much for me," another voice added.

JJ reassured the group, "They don't take our isolation as a reflection of what we think of them. I'm sure many of them don't even know who we are or why we're here. I bet some don't even know there's a settlement or more women on the island."

How do these women make it at home if they can't make it to a dinner on the other side of the island? What is the pain here?

"It's a reminder that one day we'll be home, and this small dinner get-together on an island where you can get away at a moment's notice may be an excellent test," JJ tried.

Brooke's eyebrows rose. Heard my thoughts? Nah. It always freaks me out when that happens.

Someone answered, "We've been there before, and we'll do it again. In the meantime, it's nice to have the choice. I don't always have that. I can't stay home every time I'm overwhelmed by my day."

"Sure, you can, trust me. You lose a lot of jobs that way," another voice said matter-of-factly.

An unfamiliar voice joined in, "You're right. And I've certainly been there before. But as I was trying to hold on to this last job, well, I guess that's no longer an issue. But I really was trying. I didn't call in every time I couldn't handle the stress. I forced myself to work on those days. Now this place, well, it's the ultimate timeout. I don't have to force myself to do anything, and that in and of itself has reduced my anxiety. I guess some of us can think of this as a safe place for trial get-togethers. And I appreciate the occasional suggestions, JJ, but it's not for me. I'm not in therapy here. I'm not testing what I can and can't do. I'm here and letting myself have the social limitations, which seem to bother others more than it does me."

"You don't bother me, deary," another said.

"I don't mean you all. I mean the well-meaning friends back home who are sure that if I only had enough to drink, I'd loosen up. They don't appear to care that alcohol makes the anxiety worse for the next several days. I mean the endless ads in magazines and on television on that little pill that will stop social anxiety. Never mind, the side effects are worse than the isolation. I want to be left alone. I enjoy staying home. I like going out while others sleep, and I'm fine the way

I am."

"Then you go be that way. Not all of us want to work on it. Like me. Not with the drugs and stuff, but I would like to go to work without having to force myself. It would be nice to see a movie without the room moving, my palms sweating, gasping for breath while my head spins. Sometimes, I feel like we haven't come further than that old movie The Snake Pit. Women's health care is barbaric."

JJ jumped in. She made a large circle with her hands and placed it on her forehead. "See this O? You all are over-sharing. Besides, I stopped using leeches as therapy last year."

Brooke stayed quiet, but her thoughts didn't. I had no idea. They all suffer from anxiety. This is like panic attack island, hell, to be sure. They're so blank, even when talking about their strong convictions, it's without effect. Blank faces, dull eyes, eyes that look down for the most part, eyes that can't rest from their pain, eyes held up by dark circles under them. Such torment. When they talk, it's as if they're shaking on the inside, making their faces look unstable. Even their voices sound shaky. Heather? Heather has panic attacks. She wasn't uncomfortable at dinner on the ship. Maybe she uses some of those drugs to help. Who would hurt her so much to cause this? And where is she?

JJ continued, "I'm not telling you what to do or how to do it, I'm making a dinner suggestion. Can we all please focus on that? Does anyone here want to have a joint dinner with the clan? We don't all have to do it, but if you want to, for whatever reason, then I'll arrange it. If not, I'll say, 'thanks but no thanks,' just like all the other times."

"I'd like to," a slight voice said that a couple of

others joined, "but I'd rather do it here. I guess that doesn't make much sense given there's more of them, and it's a difficult walk."

"It would be a difficult walk for us, too," someone added.

"I'll find out how many of them would like to make the trip for a bluff-top dinner," JJ said, ending the conversation. Not much was said after that, though Brooke would not have noticed, even if it had been. She was drawn toward Heather, who appeared without fanfare and moved through the crowd hugging and kissing each woman before she took her own small meal. She stopped to talk with a few of them like old friends, her hands resting on their shoulders or gently stroking their arms. With that same air of comfort and ease she had on the ship, she moved with a graceful maturity, full of purpose, while the shine in her eyes looked more like the lighthearted dreams of childhood. And her smile set off a comfort all but absent from this gathering.

She was like magic to Brooke's eyes, making her so grateful for the gift of sight. It brought up memories of experiences Brooke did not remember having: a connection to someone she thought she knew before, knew for a long time and somehow lost. Looking at Heather reminded Brooke of her life's truest possibilities. She awoke feelings in Brooke that made her realize she was wrong by having called it a "crush." This was more profound than that word suggested. These were life-altering feelings, the kind people wait forever to feel but spend no time planning how to react to them.

Brooke noticed her heart starting to do the teenage dance. That unannounced surge of excitement ignited in the center of her belly and moved inside her body with a glowing thrill. And as she thought it had filled her, it found new parts of her body to titillate. The loud pounding of her heart embarrassed her.

Get a grip. At least act a little fashionable, a little more like my real self and not this goof. She looked down, trying not to be too obvious.

"Hi, I'm Heather. I understand you got here today," she said and stopped by Brooke.

"Yes, news travels fast here."

"As fast as I can walk around the circle. You haven't been to the settlement before, and you're visiting our mystery cave on your first try. You're either brave or have a complete absence of any sense."

"Both. And the fact that I love a good mystery. I'm like that cartoon dog that solves mysteries."

"Mystery Rex, my hero." Heather smiled. "I know this is your first visit, but I thought we had talked before."

"I recall you and I spoke briefly on the ship one night," Brooke answered. Well, it's only a small lie, and it came out before I thought. Don't do that. Don't betray my ethics for this.

"Everyone I spoke with was brief. I guess I wasn't exactly the belle of the ship ball. I remember you. It just took me a minute. So have you had any volunteers to make the trip with you?"

"No, I didn't realize the cave had such a foreboding reputation."

"Every place needs its legends. This is ours. I'd like to go. Okay with you?"

Brooke's mind raced. Okay with me? Okay, oh, shit. What's keeping me from jumping up and down like a damn fool right now? Focus. Try more at being honest with her and less at being cute. Relax already.

"Sure, I guess even Mystery Rex needs a suitable partner now and then," Brooke finally said.

"Rex roves a mystery," Heather joked about the cartoon, and they both laughed.

⁂

Heather sat close to Brooke while eating her dinner. In some ways, she reminded Brooke of Marie—natural, country girl looks, unpretentious. But Heather did not have Marie's athletic presence. She was softer and more feminine. Though it wasn't Heather's looks that Brooke found captivating. It was the familiar feelings Heather stirred up in her. Sitting there with Heather made her feel like she had found her way back home, home to someone she never meant to leave. And now she had a second chance to amend the time they were apart.

"How is it being a scout with the clan?" Heather asked. "I imagine it as difficult but intriguing. Have you found any telling clues on the other parts of the island?"

"Clues, yes. Telling, no. The most interesting things have given us more questions than answers. There's this large square pit in the thick of the jungle. We determined it was hand dug and had discoloration in it. Some thought it was dried blood. We know someone, or someones, was here, and perhaps not too long ago. But that's about it."

Brooke was sinking in a surreal moment, sitting right next to the woman who found her way into Brooke's thoughts. The woman who made it difficult for her to concentrate on what she was doing. The woman she was jeopardizing everything with Marie for.

"Well, it means more than that. If people were here and now they're not, they found a way out." Heather was oblivious to Brooke's infatuation.

"Or they died, and we haven't found the bodies," Brooke added.

"Now there's a lovely thought. But if that didn't happen, then they got off the island. Now that's something."

"Yes, it would be if you're one of the few who want to go home," Brooke said.

"I don't care much about the home part, but what I'd give for a Quick Day Burger." Heather pushed the food around the large leaf holding the fish and fruit.

"I thought you were in the printing business, not a food critic."

"I told you about my work?" Heather was confused.

"Yes. That night on the ship," Brooke answered, and her thoughts slipped into their own world of anxiety.

Shit, what a stupid slip. Now I sound more interested than a casual first meeting should be. It's like I remembered every word she said. Well, I guess I did. I didn't want to show her that right away. That'll be like I'm interested. Well, I am. Why else would I have remembered that small detail in a passing conversation between two people who talked for five minutes? Maybe she won't make the connection. Like hell she won't. If my words don't give me away, my blushing cheeks sure will.

Heather kept talking, "Well, scout, you must

have one of the best memories I've ever witnessed. I'm on the average side. It used to be exceptional, but you know…or maybe you don't." Heather paused and looked Brooke over, trying to guess her age. "You pass forty, and the memory begins to slip. Is it age? Or is it all the pot we did in our teens? Maybe all that stuff they warned us about was true. You know, all that stuff about getting a cheese brain in our midlife. There are days when I swear I'm a certifiable Swiss cheese brain. Back home, I would go to the fridge, open the door, and spend the next five minutes trying to remember why I was there. It was as if opening the door created a vacuum that sucked the reason for being there right out of my head."

Brooke laughed and touched her arm like she would an old friend. "I know exactly what you mean. But for me, it was closets. Open the closet door and hope something in there would remind me of why I was there. At least that was in the privacy of my home. The worst was at work. Once it was so bad while I was presenting during a meeting. I was starting an important point, and part of me was praying I would remember the words at the end of my sentence," Brooke said.

"Oh, how wonderful to be female and forty." Heather smiled. "Though one of the significant benefits is, we get to relive moments and think it's for the first time. That's a hopeful thought." Heather continued, "I've also noticed it's not as bad on the island. I guess there are fewer things here to take up our dwindling memory chips. Well, I'll get together supplies for the next couple of days for our adventure. We'll need the ever-popular and often-coveted flashlights, ropes for the hike, bedding, and all the good stuff."

Bedding? Oh, shit, did I say that out loud? Did it set off a blush rush again?

Brooke finally answered, "Great, I'll work on the food and water supply and meet you in the morning. Thanks for the offer to help. I wasn't looking forward to doing it by myself." Oh, now I didn't mean it that way.

"Glad to help. It'll be fun. See you in the morning, scout."

Chapter Twelve

Waking up long before the sun, Brooke awaited her rendezvous with Heather. Everything had come down to this day, and she was determined to be part of every second of it. She sat at the edge of the steep bluff. She was giddy. Sitting there in silence, Brooke had an affinity for the birds around her, as if she too could take flight at any time. "Hey there, you're up early," JJ said, stating the obvious. She approached Brooke while rubbing her eyes.

"Yes. I had a hard time sleeping."

"Hell, if you can't get a good night's sleep here, you really are in trouble. Now back home, that was the place to lose sleep." JJ sat next to Brooke. She rested on the palms of her hands, which were stretched behind her. She looked rested, as if she were going to lean her head back and stare at the pink sky. Instead, she turned right at Brooke with an intentional stare.

JJ's early morning intensity intimidated Brooke, and she searched for lighter chitchat.

"JJ, what did you do back in the real world?"

"I worked for the police department."

"Police?" Brooke asked in a tone that implied, "in your condition?"

"Not as an officer. Not in my condition," JJ said.

Shit, she did it again. Her words pick up where my thoughts leave off. Too friggin' weird.

"I worked for a special group that dealt with domestic violence calls. It can be one of the most dangerous situations an officer walks into, you know. Angry couples, many times on alcohol and drugs or too often with weapons in the house. He beats her, in walk the cops, then the married couple joins forces and turns on the police like some well-trained attack team." JJ talked about these dangerous encounters as if they were another part of a typical day. All the while, she had her head turned and was looking into Brooke's eyes.

"The situations were ugly. Gosh, do I have stories I could tell you. I rode along with them and served as a mediator. Sometimes, I helped work on issues between the abuser and the victim. Other times, I helped victims deal with the police. Sometimes, here, I miss those guys, imagine that."

"The guys?" Brooke thought for a moment she was talking about the abusers.

"The cops. I loved working with them. Actually, I thought I'd miss them more. When I do, it's sad for me. But like I said, those moments are rare. In fact, I'm surprised at how little I consider them and at how little I miss men in general. I didn't think I had a separatist bone in my body, and maybe I don't. Separatist sounds so political, and that's not how I feel now." JJ scratched her head a bit.

"It's hard to describe. I get along great with guys. And I miss my close friends, but no way do I miss all that male stuff we live with back there. And I didn't even notice all of it until this place. Being around all women has highlighted all the compromises I make each day, most so subliminal I didn't even realize that I was doing it. This is weird for me. I'd expect these words from the younger or more radical lesbians, but here I am, a born-again, just-want-to-be-with-the-chicks dyke.

"And I've always been the one in the group to talk about how men have been as victimized by society as women have. I've advocated that it has been worse for them. At least women are encouraged to seek help, share their feelings, explore themselves. Guys have had to deal with being good little boys who keep their feelings to themselves. No wonder they explode, all that pent-up emotion. And I still believe all that. I still feel for them. They're so out of touch with their center. But I've got to say, in the same breath, I have loved being in a place where I don't have to deal with their socialization residue. All that space consumption they do. I mean, I don't have to sit somewhere, like a restaurant, and have to listen to the conversation from the guy across the room because he has to make sure everyone in the place hears him. I don't have to deal with them at work during a meeting where they spread their files and papers out across four places. But most of all, I don't have to be artificially swept up in conversations that almost always have to be steered toward centering on them. Hell, you can be talking about the earthquake in South America, and somehow, it becomes about them, and I don't think that's just true for cops. No, I don't miss that residue at all. So what are you doing here?" JJ sneaked that into her tirade while looking sharply at Brooke.

"Me? I'm waiting for Heather to come with the—"

"No, on this side of the island. Why are you here?"

"Mostly to scout."

"And the other reasons? Come on. Since we met, I could see the activity behind your eyes. Something's going on. What is it?"

Brooke didn't even try to pretend. "I'd rather not discuss it."

"Too bad. I've worked hard to establish normalcy here, and I will not have someone I don't know with secret motives come over here and hurt any of these women."

"Hurt? Who said anything about hurting someone?"

JJ's stubborn stare stayed locked on Brooke's eyes, "You haven't said anything—anything. How else should I interpret your secrecy? As admirable intentions?"

"I'm not here to hurt anyone, JJ." Brooke became relaxed and confident. She knew JJ's words were not an attack on her, but rather a defense of the women in the settlement, and Brooke admired that. Besides, telling her story to anyone but Marie had to be easier than what she'd been through. "There's someone here I saw on the boat, and I want to get to know her better. She's here. My intentions are admirable. I'm planning on telling her why I'm here and see what happens. That's the main reason. The second is to scout the cave."

"Who is she?" JJ put her hand on Brooke's shoulder.

"Heather."

JJ moved back for a second, but it was a second easily caught by Brooke. "Heather? Are you sure?"

"Yes, why?" Brooke asked.

"Nothing I can say. Just be careful. Sorry if I was rough on you. I'm the bear. These are my cubs."

"They're lucky. Can I ask more about them? So I don't do something stupid while I'm here. At least can we talk about them in ways that you're comfortable sharing?"

"There's quite a mix here. As you heard last night, some suffer unbearably from anxiety," JJ began.

"Yes, I was wondering about that. How did they even get on the cruise ship?"

"Drugs and therapy. It was part of a sensitivity group. A way to get them out into the world in as safe a way as possible. They spent over a year working on the trip. The plan was to stay on the ship for a short while, get dropped off at a port, then the ship would pick them up on the way back for another quick trial. The doctor who developed the treatment was on the ship. She believed being around all lesbians would lessen the anxiety because the women could be themselves." JJ looked down for the first time and tugged at the grass a bit. "We don't know where she is."

After a few moments, JJ proceeded with her description. "Then there were other settlers who were tired of processing everything with the clan. We do some of that, but it's short. I make sure of that. Many of these women are internal processors. Internal, and many times, incremental processors. They have large hurts in their lives, wounds they don't want to revisit every time a sensitive woman senses something amiss with them. They want to escape all the mental health specialists, counselors, and otherwise empathic clan women's great intentions and be somewhere where they have privacy. I guess that sounds funny, having to move up here to find privacy while we're all on a deserted island."

"No, actually, I know exactly what you mean." Brooke thought of her own efforts to dodge Renee when she was feeling the need to keep things to herself.

"We have the reputation of housing drug addicts

and alcoholics at the settlement. True, some women are in recovery. Of course, not necessarily by choice but by lack of access. All are hurting," JJ said.

"It feels like they're missing something," Brooke wondered aloud.

"They are. For some, it's their voices, others the sparkle in their eyes, and for most, it's the spirit we're all born with. The genuine tragedy is each one of them knows, somewhere inside, they didn't give those things away. Someone had to steal it all from them."

"Steal it?" Brooke asked.

"Sorry, it's hard for me to remember there are women who don't know what that means. Try to imagine it's you or your sister or friend who had your voice silenced by a vise-like hand over your mouth from a date rapist in junior high. Or had the sparkle in your eyes dimmed after too many viewings of your mother being beaten by a man you called dad. Or the cruelest—the spirit thieves, you know, the drunk dad or visiting uncle, who violated your childhood innocence during your sleep, leaving scars so deep you don't believe they'll ever heal. Most of those women know that helplessness. It echoes in their childhood nightmares of familiar monsters in the night. It's a fear that perspires out of each pore until they lay in a coating of sticky terror. Only now, the monster isn't that father or uncle who manipulates them into a night of secret stealing. It's anxiety left from an event that happened a lifetime ago. But knowing that doesn't change things. Being frozen by fear is part of their childhood keepsakes."

"How do they heal? They do heal, right?" Brooke cried.

"Yes, they do. Their voices aren't gone, but the

pain muffles them. The sparkle isn't missing, it's been dimmed. And the family thieves didn't take their spirits, but there are parts of their souls that jumped out of their youthful physical beings to hide from the horrors of the night."

"How do they get it all back?"

"How do any of us? On some level, all women have experiences that cause them to feel desperately less than they are. I gave you extreme examples that happened to these women. But for others, the loss is more subtle and constant in their lives. What do any of us do to get beyond that? Learn we're not alone and look for ways to repair—revive, move on, help others for those who can. Those who don't heal usually become our worst enemy," JJ said.

"Tracy," Brooke whispered.

"No names, please. But it sounds like you can recognize them. You know, they're the ones who say, 'I'm so tired of these whining women, why don't they just'… fill in the blank. Harsh words are always spoken by someone whose pain is buried somewhere inside, like a rotting growth that makes them hard on the outside. They have to be. Softness would allow them to see how much we have in common as survivors, but that would mean they would have to step too close to what they thought was out of their memory and sight.

Anyway, the question isn't how do they move on, it's more a question of why don't more of us get stuck behind? We're the most resilient bitches known to any species, you know." JJ stopped.

"And Heather. Is there anything special I should know?"

"I wish I could say, but you know I can't. I can talk generally but never about specific people. Besides, you'll find out in time. She's as honest as you."

"You know I needed to try." Brooke smiled.

"Yes, those junior high days sure do bounce back at us with a new crush. Don't they?"

"There you are, scoutmaster," they heard Heather say. "I brought extra food in case you didn't have time for breakfast. Sound good?"

"Sounds great. Thanks. And thanks for the talk, JJ." Brooke watched Heather, who had the energy of an entire scout team. She was more animated than the woman in the shadow on the ship where she made herself almost invisible. Her vivaciousness was also adorable.

"You both be careful. Don't act too much like adventurous heroes." JJ stood while listing her warnings. "And drink lots of water. It's not as humid the last couple of days, but that pre-storm heat is still with us."

Heather kissed her on the cheek. "You're such a worrier, and we all love you for it. We'll be back in a couple of days. If a week passes, give someone my sleeping spot."

"Give it away, hell, I'll take it myself, you brat." JJ's eyes teared up. Her love for these women was pure and simple.

❧❧❧❧

Heather and Brooke stood at the peak of the bluff, looking down at their destination. It was almost a straight drop to the beach hundreds of feet below. They had to take a longer route covered in thick vegetation and sporadic trails. In some places, the vegetation was so dense, Brooke thought they might have to turn around. This was a hike for experienced climbers with sophisticated gear, not a couple of dykes with shoes that didn't match. If it wasn't for the company, Brooke wondered if she would even make this trip.

But the trip's perils could not shake Brooke's ability to enjoy the beauty of the hillside. Nature always filled her with her own religion. And this nature rested on land where time began. The open sky and ocean embraced its greenery. The cool breeze could move through her, and birds sang as if they were teaching her their songs. This beauty turned her thoughts to Marie. It was like her—unassuming, gentle, and loving.

"Sorry, I have to slow our pace down," Heather said.

Brooke answered, "I don't know how we could go any faster. This is the safest way to do it. I'm glad about the thick vegetation here. This soil is so loose, it gives way underneath me. Without all these vines and leaves, I'm thinking I'd be..."

"Yes, I'm trying not to think about that too much. It's a long way down there, and that long way is right there, to the side of me." Heather avoided that discussion.

"Good time to take up a religion," Brooke smiled, "especially one that promises something great after death. Although, I already believe in that myself and in some type of divine creator caring for me. That and a bit of born-again pagan."

"You too? I've leaned much more that way since the shipwreck. The women here have created calmness through meditations and live a spirituality I've only read about. But it's more than pagan, it's women's magic. And what impresses me most is how the medicine women live by their beliefs. Those ladies can spin good health with a couple of herbs and funky teas. Do you know them, Claire and Lillie?"

Heather didn't have to say another word, for Brooke knew exactly what she meant. She was thinking of Claire and Lillie herself and how they nursed her back to health. Brooke thought it was much more than a coincidence that her first conversation with Heather would be on a topic so personal to her. Brooke felt the two of them were uncovering commonalities that were always there. Although she tried not to compare the two, Brooke thought of how that was different with Marie. Marie had always been easy to talk to, easy to get to know, while Heather was someone she had always known.

"Yes, I know them. Claire a bit more. The two of them helped me after the wreck. Check out this scar." Brooke tried not to lose her footing while showing Heather the mark on her calf.

"You can barely see it," Heather noticed.

"And it was a long, deep wound," Brooke told her.

Heather reached down to run her sweating hand along the scar. "Those two, if only I could find a way to package them. I can tell you, I know they practice herbal medicine back home, but I sure hope they make a larger business out of it when we all get back."

"That would be great. Have you talked with them about it?" Brooke asked.

"Not directly, but it's not out of the question. I know many women here, both at the settlement and with the clan, have had time to think about our lives and work back home."

Brooke jumped on the conversation as an opportunity to learn more about this woman for whom she had so many feelings and knew so little of. "What about you? Do you want to do things differently when you get home?"

"Sure, very much so. The printing business has been good to me. But it's 'flat,' you know. Advertise, go to work, fill orders, find out what works and what doesn't, improve on your product, advertise, go to work. And I'm not about to give it all up from a tropical island epiphany. I like being able to pay the bills, my mortgage, and take trips. Heck, I'll even take another cruise someday."

Brooke had to hold herself back from asking too many questions. Like what epiphany she was talking about. Or why she was so sure she would take another cruise. And what other work she wanted to do. But as each interest occurred to her, she quickly waited to see what Heather wanted to share.

"Anyway, I'm not giving up my bread and butter. It's a job that has been good to me. But this place has taught me to take time for other things. To listen to the things my heart is saying about my life and how I'm spending my precious time. And when it's all said and done, I don't want to say, 'Wish I would have,' like most of the women I've talked to here. We all realize the power of action. So I hope to go home and write those children's stories I've been thinking about since I was a child myself."

"What type of stories?" Brooke had to ask.

"Stories about feeling different from everyone else, then learning that the difference comes from some special powers that one day will help the world or even help a few friends, but to a kid, that is the world."

"Sounds like you have a calling," Brooke said.

"Yes, I do, and it took me getting to a place of

pristine silence to hear it. What about you, any changes in your job after we're rescued? Has this place helped you to find your calling, or have you always heard it?"

Brooke felt like she was at a coffee shop with a dear friend she was attracted to, the two of them talking about their future plans instead of walking on a life-threatening trail.

"No, no new jobs for me. I've decided that I want to go back to my old job but do it in a new way."

"What did you do back home?"

"An analyst for the city manager in Phoenix, Arizona."

"What type of new analysis are you imagining? I mean, how many different ways are there to do that type of job? Sorry, I didn't mean to negate your wish, I guess I don't understand what you do."

"Actually, you do get it. I analyze city problems and provide recommendations. I mostly work on issues related to public housing. This will sound corny, but I've always loved being a public servant. I'm proud to think that what I do can somehow improve people's lives and contribute to my community. But in my 'old way' of doing my job, I was too focused on people at work who caused problems. That made it difficult for me to get things done, you know? I've spent more time trying to figure out how to deal with them than with the issues of public housing. So I want to go back to my job with a new focus. I'll seek colleagues who are doing great work and find ways for us to work together. I want to be part of a positive team. And I know they're out there. That's what I forgot. For every jerk at work, there's literally hundreds of dedicated people with great ideas and a high work ethic. And I want to work with and learn from them. I want to be part of a team that says, 'We can do better for people in our community, and here's how.' And I want to connect with the elected officials who have that attitude about them. The kind who wants more than the status quo while on 'their watch.' I met a senator on the island who reminded me of that. And I can do that in my city where I know local politicians similar to her. I want to find ways to be part of their team. A team that wants to be responsible stewards of the public's work. Corny, huh?"

"Not at all. I think it's admirable. But why don't you run for office yourself? With values like that, we need more politicians like you."

We're here just talking, talking about things that matter back home. And I'm telling her things I've only partially thought about myself. She seems like a good listener. After all the high hopes and wondering, I'm here with her, but she doesn't even know what it means to me.

Brooke answered, "I do research. The only thing I know how to run for is help." And they laughed. "Besides, there already are politicians with more expertise than me and who share my hopes of improving the quality of life in our community. I know that may seem hard to believe because we're so bombarded with media messages about the lack of integrity in their profession. But I know differently. Sure, the bad are there, they're in any profession. But the majority of politicians I know care about issues and people. They are trying, more than most people will ever see and certainly more than the media will show, to make a difference for the people they represent. How cool to work for them! At least I used to think that until this neurotic jerk at work got to me. I focused more on him and the things he said about me, the things that fostered doubt instead of action. People in my community don't have the time for that diversion. No more. I need to be who I am, and I'm going to do that when I get home. I'm going to find help from others at work who share my convictions, and we'll do good things together. And if we do it well, no one will know who to thank. It's the kind of work you can't put one person's name on."

Heather smiled. "We'd make a cool team, you and me. I'll write fun stories that help kids realize their special gifts and how to use them to be whatever they want when they grow up, and you'll be part of a political gear that creates a community where they can realize those dreams."

They stopped and looked into each other's eyes with respect. "We should stop here," Brooke said. "Even though we don't have much farther, we should rest and rehydrate."

"I don't feel tired or even thirsty." Heather tried to brush off the suggestion.

"The humidity is getting thicker, if that's even possible. Besides, the best way to prevent heat exhaustion is not to wait for it to start. It's the way of the scout."

"You're funny." Heather grinned.

The compliment was an emotional hug for Brooke. Brooke watched Heather looking at the ocean, flicking bugs off her smooth, partly tanned, partly sunburned legs, brushing her hair behind her ears in matched timing to the waves. Wait, smooth legs. This woman is so femme, she's one of the few with a razor. How the hell did that happen after all this time? I didn't realize how much I missed seeing a woman's bare legs.

The women took deep breaths in unison, smiled, picked up their water bottles together, and drank, and finally, without talking, both got up at the same time to finish the trip. They had more in common than chance could ever explain.

"Thanks, you've got a pretty good sense of humor, too…for a settler," Brooke jabbed back.

"I thought being with the settlers was a good place for someone like me," Heather said.

"Someone like you?" Brooke wanted to know more. "Or is that too personal?"

"Not more so than anything else." Heather smiled. "Someone who needs to keep a low profile and not affront others."

"Affront? You couldn't offend the other women. You're certainly connected to the other settlers, easy to talk to. I don't get it."

"There are women here who would be offended to find out I'm a stowaway. I was on the cruise, but I'm not a lesbian. I'm straight." She spoke so matter of fact with words that sliced through Brooke's fantasy and stopped in the center of her heart.

I did not hear that. I did not hear that. Don't be too crushed or desperate. Think. Say something to get a good pause.

"Boy, did you get on the wrong cruise." Brooke forced a smile.

"No, I chose that one on purpose. My boyfriend…"

Brooke's thoughts raced while Heather continued with her story. Boyfriend, boyfriend. Just announcing out of nowhere you're straight is one thing—one horrible thing—but don't tell me you were with a guy. On the ship, she talked about her partner, not boyfriend. Straight people shouldn't be allowed to use our code words, it throws off the whole lesbo balance.

"…and so, I felt betrayed by his lying, even if

it was one time in a weak moment. What's with guys anyway, that 'other woman thing' really makes them feel wanted or what? All the long weekend trips I took included guys trying to pick me up. I needed time to myself. I figured an all-women's trip would be safe. I've told all the settlers, but I don't think the clan women know. Anyway, the settlers get me. They understand my need to be around women's energy, though they were somewhat disappointed by my undercover choice. I thought it best to lay low. You're not saying much, are you one of the disappointed ones?"

Brooke shrank into the vegetation and was waiting to be flicked off into space. The small island on the large ocean became a vast island with a small person on it. Everything stopped. Her thoughts, her breath, her smile.

"Are you okay, Brooke?"

"Sorry, you…you threw me off guard a little. No, I'm not disappointed," she finally answered. Not disappointed, I'm mortified. No, I'm a speck on mortified's shoulder.

They were closer to the beach than Brooke realized, and she was glad to see it so close. They walked in silence for a while except for brief chitchat about the hike and things they missed back home. Then the hike ended on the white sandy beach.

"Let's take another notice of this place," Heather said, even with her shortness of breath. She dropped her gear and twirled around with her arms spread out. "This is the most beauty I've ever seen all in one place. The fine white sand greets us, the crystal-clear waters. I can see the bottom of the ocean wherever I look. And we're here alone, no one else in the universe is here. Is this the stuff of tropical paradises or what?"

"Yes, all that and what," Brooke answered and whispered, "all and more." Brooke stood still while a range of feelings hid in her. She'd wait until she could take them out in a timing that protected her. This wasn't that time. Brooke turned her attention to the nature surrounding them. She looked up at the bluff of truth they had just descended, and the striking beauty of that spot helped her feel as if she were standing right above the center of the universe.

Nestled at the bottom and set far underneath the bluff was an arched mouth to the cave. Brooke felt like crawling in and hiding. She senselessly tried to shake it off, but her sadness and shame were finding their way to her attention, and her thoughts raced with what-ifs.

What if the initial conversation with Heather hadn't turned straight? What if we had continued to uncover our parallel thoughts? What if we had continued to use humor to mask our flirtations? Those were flirtations. Straight or not, I know when someone is flirting with me. Then we'd be standing in front of this mysterious place and perhaps holding each other out of slight fear. Perhaps this is where we would have kissed for the first time. Somewhere between the ever-present ocean and the cave of the unknown. Shit, Brooke, get a hold of yourself. Wake up, the dream is over. Even when you hear it, you're still dreaming for something that is never going to happen, but it sure felt like something was going to. There was something there, not like when I'm with other straight women. Renee will give me shit about this until the day I die, 'So you gave up the love of your life to have an attractive straight woman blow you off, and you walked how far to hear this rejection? You went down what kind of bluff?' Maybe there's something important in that cave. A promise of help to get these women back to their homes, reasons for being here other than to screw up my entire life, hurt my dear Marie, and give Renee enough ammo to keep me humble from here to eternity. Yes, maybe this cave holds help to get women back to their homes and their families. Of course, they have families to go home to. I have two failed loves—or one failed love and one failed fantasy."

"There it is," Brooke finally said while pointing to the cave. "I know that because of my keen sense for the obvious."

"It sits like it's about to pounce on us, doesn't it? Should we head in and get this over with or eat something first?" Heather walked closer to Brooke, a little unsure of it all.

Brooke answered, "We should have water, perhaps a light dinner. I'll get the flashlights and hats ready."

"Hats?"

"In case of bats."

"Oh, I'll take two." Heather squeezed Brooke's arm in a familiar way.

They sat on the beach. It was a quiet and quaint time. They helped each other find the best thing to eat. They pretended to set up a formal sitting area in the middle of the white sand. They sat close and in silence and passed each other food. At one point, Brooke spilled her water, and it ran down Heather's shirt. Heather pretended to throw water back at Brooke, and they chased each other, laughing and threatening to carry each other into the ocean. When short on breath, they faced the cave and knew it was time to check it out.

While the entrance was large, it was also shallow. There was an immediate turn that led to a larger area and closed off the day's remaining light. They stopped to search the walls of the cave with erratic movements of the flashlight, guided by their nerves. Brooke tried to slow her movements and focus on the large cavern.

"I don't think it's inhabited by large creatures, anyway," Heather finally said. "Look there." They walked closer to a strange pile. "It's clothes. Pants, shirts. This is bizarre," Heather said while staying close to Brooke.

"Not too," Brooke said, almost expecting the find. "It confirms there have been other people on this island, and not too long ago from the looks of these. The cave isn't as deep as I thought. Looks like this giant room and the one we passed through are it."

"I guess this is what scared the other women. Just some clothes."

"They said they didn't have light." Brooke turned off the flashlight. "What would you think that was if you touched it?"

Heather hugged Brooke's waist. "Okay, I get the point. Turn the light back on."

"We're lucky. This will be a great shelter. I'll get something to make a fire. Let's set up someplace to sleep by the entrance."

They worked quickly as they both noticed the sky darkening and the smell of rain on the way.

"Wow, I'm beat," Brooke said. "This is a great place. Too bad the settlement didn't come here. They would fit in here."

"Too hard to get to this place," Heather said.

"True, you either find the right new home that has no yard or a great yard with a small house."

Heather laughed. "Then you have to ask yourself if you can afford the smaller home and the addition you'll have to build to make it exactly what you want."

"Or do you keep on looking?"

"You're so tired of looking. Just buy and refurbish."

And they summarized it in unison: "Then you'll be house poor."

"Remembering all that makes this island seem all the better," Brooke said again.

They made up the vine-woven bedrolls and crawled in for the night. For Brooke, they were uncomfortably close. Should I tell Heather about my admiration for her? Why? She's straight. What the hell difference would it make now? I should shut up, go home, beg Marie to… No, I blew that one.

Brooke took a couple of long, deep breaths, the type of breathing that slows down the earth's rotation. Then she said it without a plan of where it would lead.

"I need to be honest with you," Brooke blurted out.

"No, you don't. I like it when women lie to me." Heather laughed.

"Part of why I'm here is to do the scout thing."

"And the other part?" Heather turned on her side and looked over at Brooke.

Brooke became short of breath and dry-mouthed. She took several secret deep breaths, though she was sure Heather heard her.

Heather placed her hand on Brooke's stomach. "It can't be that bad. You're not with the IRS or something, are you?" Her humor eased Brooke.

"The other part, the main part, was to get to know you better."

"Me?"

"Yes. When I saw you on the boat, I felt…well,

I'm not sure what it was for my age group. But I know I didn't feel that way without a reason, and I knew I had to find out that reason. I decided to meet you and see if there was anything more real behind the 'across the room' infatuation. I'll shut up now because I feel silly. I mean, falling for straight women is something that happens in college, not when you're old enough to know better."

"I didn't know there was an age limit on good taste," Heather was quick to reply. "It's not dumb. It's adorable. It's the most honest thing anyone has ever said to me." She held Brooke's hand with care instead of like someone repulsed by the idea, which was what Brooke expected.

They heard the storm breaking on the beach, but Heather stayed engaged in the conversation. "That genuine part of you is one of the loveliest parts of being with women. I'm sorry if I misled you by being here. I tried to stay away from women, keep to myself, but as I get close, I let them know as soon as possible."

"I guess that means we were getting close." Brooke wouldn't let it go.

"Yes. I've found this beyond flattering."

Flattering. That's how graceful people turn you down. I must admit, that was the nicest rejection I've ever had. But how will I walk away with this weight in my heart?

A part of her deep inside knew she should consider Marie, but she wasn't. She was still thinking of Heather, thinking about their talks and the way Heather was resting her arm on Brooke. Brooke remembered each of their meetings. The first look on the ship. Wondering if she was real or a dream. Then their brief talk, finally seeing her on the island. How easily she talked to Brooke at the settlement. It was so natural. Like they had done it before. And how about the way she kept touching Brooke? Not a tease, but not like a casual friend, either.

"Sand dollar for your thoughts," Heather finally said. Brooke took it as an invitation to settle the thoughts inside her head. She had more courage now because she thought she had lost everything worth keeping—a genuine relationship with Marie, the possibility of one with Heather. The nervousness was gone, and she was acting like the mature woman she knew she was growing into no matter how awkward it was happening.

"I was wondering, of all the places to go to recuperate, you chose a lesbian trip. And I'm hesitant to bring this up because I don't want to invalidate your sexuality. I know how much I hate it when the straight world does that to me. They assume it's because of a poor relationship with my father. You know, if that were the case, there would be many more of us. Or one of my favorites, they wonder why a woman so pretty is a lesbian, which is such a back-handed compliment. What they actually mean is many guys would find you attractive, so why be with women? Their subtle reasoning is only homely women should be lesbians. It's so ridiculous. But here I am, trying to do, or not do, the same to you and still make my point, but in a gingerly way."

"I think you've set the record for qualifiers," Heather teased.

"It's just that I've been around flaming straight women before, and I know the energy level between me and them. It's inert. That's not what I've felt from you. I did feel something between us, didn't I?"

"Are you sure that's not your overconfidence at work?" Heather became serious.

Brooke was brave all the way now. "It's either my arrogance, and thanks for the polite way of saying that, or it could be my sensitivity. I have rather good antennae. And I've learned not to ignore what they're telling me. For a woman, that's the ultimate, and only real, betrayal, you know. Anyway, you didn't answer my question. Was there something between us, some kind of 'more than friends' energy?"

There was a long pause. During it, Heather lay back on her bedding and ran her fingers over it, desperately searching for a loose thread to play with.

"Damn thing is made too well," she cursed.

"What's that?" Brooke asked.

"I said I haven't been completely honest with you." Heather repeated Brooke's introduction. "I guess I haven't been honest with myself. I have been with one woman before. We didn't do everything, but we did a lot."

Bisexual. This gets worse and worse. There's nothing more frightening to me as a true blue dyke than someone who switches. It's one thing to lose your partner to another woman, but to have her slip off the fence on you is almost unrecoverable. Alert, alert, back up from this conversation. Get out while you can!

But the other half of her brain took over, and she repeated, "So was there something there?"

"Yes, there was something, something that scared me. Okay, here's the whole sad story. My brief gay past was in college with a roommate. We had been drinking, of course, at home after a frat party. Which I guess makes sense, if anything is gonna make you want to run to a woman's arms, it's the frat experience."

Somehow, during the hopeful discussion, Brooke moved closer to Heather. The tone of the conversation had changed, as had the environment. They didn't notice the rain was now a full storm. It masked the sound of the waves. The wind whipped around the cave's entrance, but their natural bungalow stayed dry. Its side entrance kept the water from coming in. The air got cooler, and the glow of their small fire dimmed. One of those two things brought them closer. Brooke did not know which one, she knew only that their bodies were now touching.

Heather continued with her story. "…she had had more experiences than me. At some point, she said she was attracted to me, then she leaned over and kissed me. It wasn't like any kiss I had had before. And the way she touched me, I felt her in parts of my body that only another woman would know about."

"So telling me you were straight was…?"

"Was my lie to myself, and I think, trying to avoid this conversation with you. I thought I was…"

Thought, past tense, keyword.

"I always thought it was a college drunk thing. But the truth is, I never forgot it. In one way or another, I compared that evening to every other intimate experience I ever had, always trying to convince myself that the men were better, that I wanted them. I even lied to myself about this trip, just the way I have lied to you. I even question my reason for volunteering to come with you, but I've assumed enough already. This trip, it wasn't about being safe, it was about being with other women. There, I said it. And yes, there's delightful energy. How can you want something that makes you so scared?"

"Sometimes, the feelings between fear and

excitement are too close to separate. I'm scared, too. Scared of someone who has drawn me here. Of making so many changes and not sure for what. Of what I may have missed."

"Yes, but at least you know what it's like to, and in a sober state, be with another woman. I have a memory or the echo of a memory. And a masked ache to go back there," Heather whispered.

Brooke took her hand, and Heather responded with a wanting touch. Brooke said, "Well, if this is headed where I think, where I'm hoping, then I'll tell you what it will be like. It will be whatever you want. We'll go slow so we're both comfortable. And if you like something, let me know, and we'll do more of it. And if you don't, at any time, just say so, and we'll stop and find a way to be friends. But at least we'll know. We'll both know, finally know."

The light was out at this point, and the darkness made it difficult to tell for sure, but Brooke thought Heather was smiling. She leaned over and delicately kissed Heather, who sighed and wrapped her arms around Brooke in a timid but welcoming way.

Chapter Thirteen

The storm finally ended, and it washed the air clean. Brooke and Heather lay side by side at the cave's entrance. They were lying on their stomachs with their heads propped up by their hands, smiling at their conversation. Heather's knees were bent, and her feet pointed straight up and wiggled every once in a while.

"Seems like I've been talking for days." Brooke was embarrassed.

"I enjoy our talking and listening to you. I enjoy so many things I'm learning about you. But still, it's weird. That feeling we both have, like we've known each other for a while. This place is so beautiful. So quiet...except...what the hell is that noise?" Heather was puzzled.

Together, they ran outside the cave and then halted. Brooke raised a hand over her brow, trying to block out the sun's light and focus on that thing out at sea. She squinted and visually confirmed there was a large boat offshore and a smaller one making its way to the beach, with what looked like a single person in it.

They stood there as if they were watching a movie in a foreign language. The kind that if you watch long enough, something sounds familiar, but mostly you feel one step behind the storyline. The person in the boat, who looked like a young man, was staring back, trying to make sense of the two women he saw on the beach. The boat bobbed up and down in the otherwise calm water. He approached with purpose, though, not like someone lost. It was indeed a man, and a rather handsome man in his early twenties, Brooke guessed. He was slender and tan and wobbled a little when he walked, struggling to get his land legs while trying to hide his uneasiness from the strangers.

Brooke stared in disbelief. No, not this, not now. Give me more time. Do things have to unravel so damn quickly? I still have to—

"Hello, ladies. I have a thousand questions. Like, are you okay? Who are you? What are you doing on Mr. Pearson's Island? And, well, who are you? I guess I asked that twice." He was nervous and made assumptions about the women. "If it were me, I wouldn't care about you escaping to this place, but the boss and his more uptight staff would be mad as hell."

"Hello, man," Brooke answered, trying to be composed and to remember how to talk to a man. She talked like the professional she was back at work while explaining the details in a monthly report. "We were on a cruise. It was an all-women's trip, and it had an accident at sea. We're survivors. There are more than a hundred of us all together, and I don't believe any of us know Mr. Pearson."

The young man stood there for a moment in recognition of her. "Oh, that bombing of the lesbian ship. God, that was sick. Yes, I know of you. Everyone does. It was all over the world news. How did you get here? The attack happened hundreds and hundreds of miles from here."

"Attack? Bombing? What are you talking about?" Heather was lost in his explanation. Brooke searched her thoughts for a plan to deal with this situation, but instead, she uttered soundbites of complete thoughts.

"You said bombing. Are there other survivors? We traveled for hundreds of miles. You said bomb, right?" His words came out from nowhere, and she wanted to swat them away like bugs in the jungle.

The young man walked closer to them so they could see directly into his eyes. He took Brooke's hand. "Yes, your ship had a bomb on it. It was set to explode while you were out at sea. A sophisticated attack, it was. And, yes, there are many others who made it. They were found within about two weeks of the disaster. I remember because the news carried the story every day. But, no, not everyone made it. I know the news reports mentioned fatalities. I think, shit, I don't remember how many. One hundred and fifty alive or didn't make it. I'm sorry. I'm not being much help here and am probably scaring you more than needed. And, well, this is a tough conversation for me." He looked down at the sand, searching for help from the silent grains.

"You may want to prepare yourselves because a super-religious right-wing group bombed the ship. I think it was God's Righteous Federation. They wanted to rid this world of sin. I'm sorry to have to greet you this way. Oh, shit, I'm so thrown off by all this. My name is Guy. I'm Mr. Pearson's get-things-ready guy. I'll go back to the boat and radio for help. You two can get the other women over here." Heather grabbed Brooke's arm, holding it so tightly it hurt.

Brooke answered, trying to collect herself and make sense of all this. It was hard, but she could tell from Heather's grip that it was harder on her. Heather fell to her knees, crying. Brooke reached down to help her and calmly informed him, "It would be difficult to get the women down here. They're up on that bluff. We should go to them and bring them to the other side of the island, where most of the women are." She saw the need to be in charge and responded to it the way she had been raised. "Oh, I'm Brooke, and this is Heather," she finally said as they held each other.

Heather's voice was shaking. "Brooke, why don't you go with him? You need to introduce him to the clan. I'll head up to the bluff and gather the other women, if they'll come."

"No, it's too dangerous for you to go alone."

Guy interrupted their caring conversation. "Not sure what you mean by 'if they'll come.' I don't want to sound like a real jerk, but you all are on a privately owned island. Mr. Pearson's next client will be here within three weeks. We're here to prepare the island. You all don't really... um...you don't have a choice about this. Sorry again, but I agree with Heather. It sounds like this kind of news would be better coming from you two. I'll help however I can, but, gosh, ladies, I just work for him."

Is there no end to this?

Heather took a stronger stand. "It'll be easier coming from me, Brooke, and the other women will need you to deal with Mr. Sid here."

"It's Guy. Please, let's not do the 'stick it to the messenger,' okay? I'm trying. His other staff can be real assholes about all this, and most likely, they will be. I don't want to go there."

"Sorry about that, Guy, this is not what we thought about in terms of a rescue and hearing about the other women. We'll work with you on this. Heather is right. I'll go with you to the other side."

Brooke hugged Heather and kissed her on the cheek.

"I can't believe this." Heather cried and whispered

in Brooke's ear, "What's happening?"

Brooke's tone became more urgent, though she wasn't sure why. "I'll catch up with you with the clan. Hurry to the bluff. They've probably seen the boat. They'll need to know what's going on. Be extra careful on your climb. We'll cry later." Brooke kissed her again and motioned for Guy to take her to the boat.

Brooke stayed alone on the boat's stern while Guy talked with the other staff. She couldn't hear what they were saying but knew it had to be unfriendly given the raised voices and flying of hands. Whatever magic Guy had was working as they all finally calmed down. The men's obvious discomfort bothered Brooke, but she was so overwhelmed with news that some things just didn't get her attention at that moment. The shipmates' issues with her and the other women were one of those things. She sat there rocking in the boat and staring at the island from the sea. It was actually the first time she had had this view given her unconscious condition when they'd landed on the island. The island wasn't as big from this view. But big things happened there. And for Brooke, it was where more things occurred than in all the years she lived in Phoenix. Her happiness was lost, found, lost, found…it all occurred on that chunk of land sitting in the ocean.

"Here's tea and a sandwich. We don't have gourmet food here or anything, but it should be more than what you're used to," Guy said.

Brooke became lost in circular talk. "Who's Mr. Pearson, and what do you all do here? Did they get the fuckers who bombed the boat? How many survivors again? Who's coming here? A group of famous people who want to get away? Or do they do one of those Survivor shows here or something equally dumb? Who bombed the boat again?"

Guy placed a hand on each of her shoulders and looked directly at her.

He is too young to have to do all of this, but I'm surprised at how well he's handling it. Especially how he looks right at me to communicate this hard stuff, poor boy. I must remember to thank him.

"Okay, Brooke, first the part about the bombing, then I'll tell you about my boss and the island. A group of religious fanatics in the U.S. claimed responsibility for bombing the ship. They said they believed it was God's will to cleanse the earth of the unwanted. And they named the unwanted as gays, lesbians, and pedophiles. They are also responsible for several other bombings in the U.S. Do you understand me?"

"Yes, where?"

"At gay bars and abortion clinics mostly, and a shooting attempt was made at a gay family picnic in Miami."

"Oh, no. How did all this happen? Did they catch those responsible?" She put the sandwich down.

"No, they haven't. But there's been a worldwide response. The U.S. has been in a flurry with gay allies and advocates condemning everything they feel contributed to this hate, from various states' positions on same-sex marriage to the Youth Scouts' position on homosexuality."

"If only it were that easy to find the root of these actions. How short-sighted," Brooke said.

"I see what you mean, but the point is, folks are not being quiet about this. And the attention lasted more than just the first week or two. Even now, every day, there's info in the media about how states are reviewing their laws, especially same-sex marriage laws.

Scandinavian countries are offering U.S. gays asylum if they give up their U.S. citizenship. Canada has made it clear. Their slogan is, 'Be here, be married, be safe.' Or 'Canada, the melting pot you won't get burned in.' That's one of my favorites. And it's just the beginning. So much has happened." Guy talked as if these positive actions would help focus Brooke.

"Religious terrorists bombed us? From our own country?"

"Yes. Though there's a lot of speculation about who is arming them. And I wouldn't use the term 'religious.' I'd call them terrorists who hide behind their dark hatred. Brooke, there's something else."

Her eyes told him she didn't have room for more, but he continued. "There was another attack in New York about two months after your ship."

Brooke was almost speechless. "These lesbian haters also attacked New York?"

"No, it was an attack from outside our country. Much different group. Different hate."

"That's a lie," Brooke softly said. "All hate is the same. They just package it differently."

Guy noticed Brooke trying to make sense of it all. "Do you need more time on your own?"

"No, you sweet man, I don't. I need time with you. You're my gateway to home, and whether I like it or not, I find myself standing in that gateway. A place where I really need you right now. Also, it may surprise you, but I'm having a harder time believing people have come to the defense of us than I am in believing religious terrorists attacked us in our own country."

"Now that's the fucking saddest thing I've heard yet about all this," Guy responded. "But there's more, you haven't heard it all yet. And this is good news. People are banding together in response to this hate. Millions of Americans, straight couples, have recently canceled their weddings and filed for divorce in protest of gays not having the right to also marry in America. I tell you the whole thing isn't going away. It's growing. And now, this latest move from the masses in our country has the current administration dumbfounded, as if it needed any help. But can you imagine, the crusader of family values, our president, faced with causing the greatest divorce rate in our history, in any history? And the best part. Couples put their plan into action the same day the president officially signed into law the National One Man/One Woman Marriage Act. He spearheaded the act, which includes two billion in funds to improve marriage longevity. Some of the money is for counseling to help couples stay together. Which sounds harmless, but most of the money is being used for penalties. Like funding a national database to track divorced couples. They take extra penalties on their taxes the year after their divorce. They also slipped in penalties for people on welfare, which affects the poor who divorce.

"But can you fucking imagine it all? The same day he announced this national act, over fifteen million people canceled their wedding plans or filed for divorce. That story gave the media their biggest hard-on ever. They played it twenty-four/seven. That, that's what makes our country great! We may have our hate groups, we may have our religious fanatics, but we have the best timing of any people in the world. I love that place." Guy's face showed excitement.

Brooke cried, "I can't believe this all. I remember that day on the ship. The explosion. To know that it all came from a small group that hates us, and now all this from a large, courageous group who cares about us. It's too much for me." Then she placed her head on his shoulder while he rubbed her back.

Brooke grabbed Guy by the arm, "Guy, oh, my God, oh, no. The women who didn't make it. We buried many on this island. We can't leave them here. Their families will want their remains. This is not their resting place!"

"No, we can't and won't. We'll make sure they're taken back home."

"With care and respect?"

"With that and more. You and the others can tell us how you want that done. I'll make sure of it."

They sat in silence for a while until Brooke was ready to hear more. She took a deep breath before speaking as if she knew there would be more ugliness to their conversation.

"Guy, tell me about this place we've called home."

"Hunters" was all Guy said.

"Hunters?" She lifted her head.

"Yeah, he rents it out to big game hunters. They pick their hunt, we bring it to the island, and it's just the two of them for as short as a couple of days to several months. One on one, as they say."

"Now you're kidding me. You have a wild animal on this boat now?"

"No, we're the check-in crew. We make sure the last group hasn't left any signs of human existence on the island. That's part of the experience. Mr. Pearson leaves more than a year between hunts, so the island goes back to its most natural state before renting it out again. That's what the other guys are most upset about. No one can figure out how we're going to clean this all up. But I made a few calls, and we're going to bring in an extra group and garbage ship. But that's our stupid minor problem. The important thing is that I've called the U.S. Coast Guard. I guess there's a ship in the area that will be here in a couple of days to get you all. Lucky, huh?"

"Luckier than some animal stuck on the island with an armed hunter. Don't get me wrong, I eat meat. This isn't a political speech. It's hard to think of the place where we all…where the clan was…as a place for trapped animals." Brooke struggled.

"Many people react that way. I won't make excuses for it. Mr. Pearson enjoys hunting and wanted to do this. It's a sideline. He's the man, the computer man—you know, 'Pearson's Software: Open the Door Past Tomorrow,' that stuff. I don't mind the business myself. Clearly, if I did, I'd be somewhere else. And to tell you the truth, it's not just the animals who are trapped. The hunters are, too. Over ten years, we've lost three of them to the animals."

Brooke cocked her head as if to hear those words differently. "And other hunters come here knowing about the deaths, or didn't your Mr. Pearson tell them?"

"Of course, we let them know. Actually, it brought more customers. It's become an extreme hunting experience for the ultimate risk takers. It's part of the attraction for some. Back to nature and all." He changed the subject. "I think the news folks will hear about you all. You'll have quite the homecoming, you know."

"Yes, homecoming." For the first time, Brooke was tired. "Guy, if I forget, please remind me to thank you properly after I get my wits about me," she said while looking at the clan women on the beach, running and waving their arms.

Brooke and Guy took a smaller boat to the shore. Brooke could hear the women's screams of joy as they got closer. She wished she could be as excited, but she had heard too much reality for one day. How will they take all this?

"Do you mind if I head to shore when we get close enough? Perhaps you could go back to the boat with the other staff and allow me to talk to them?"

"No, I don't mind at all. We'll come ashore when the rescue ship gets here. That will give you all time together. It's the most I can offer."

"Yes, and thank you again, Guy. You've been refreshingly kind."

"This is an important thing for me, to be the one," he said, and his eyes teared. "My sister is a lesbian. When I heard about the bombing, well… How could someone want to hurt a person like my sister? A person like you. She wasn't on that trip, but what's next? I wish I could do more. I do tell those lug heads I work with to fuck off with their jokes. You know. It's not much, but—"

"It's a lot. Your sister is lucky." Brooke kissed his cheek and wiped the tear from his face.

"No, I'm the lucky one. She helped to raise me. No one talks badly about my sister. No one. I radioed my boss and explained the situation."

"Did he have a cow?"

"No, he's a sensitive guy, really. You can't lump all hunters together like that now. He canceled the next trip and called the Coast Guard himself. He gave everyone direct instructions on how he wants you all treated."

"He owns the Coast Guard, too?" Brooke tried to make fun of Pearson's extreme wealth.

"No, he's used to getting his way. Though I don't think the Guard needed his influence. They, too, will be proud to be part of the rescue. To know so many more of you escaped that group's hateful intentions." Brooke looked skeptical. "They're a good group who's coming for you. Don't worry about that at all. It's the Guard, remember, not the Tailhook ship. They're used to rescuing and helping. I've always been impressed with those folks. But I know a lot of this will be personal for them. Some of them were quoted in the paper as losing sleep because they didn't get to the wreck soon enough to find more of you. So many wanted to help, to show they didn't approve of the violence, even those who don't approve of your lifestyle. Many rented boats and planes with their own money and continued the search long after the government called it off. It's been an un-American type of reaction. People were brought together by this tragedy, but none as close as the survivors and families of the victims."

The conversation reminded Brooke how much the outside world had had no meaning on their island, how spoiled they had been by their isolation. Though, it began to seep into her brain that she was about to rejoin that world. As they got close to the beach, Brooke jumped out of the boat and ran through the shallows to the women on the beach. It looked like almost everyone from the clan was there. She ran up, and they all hugged her and hugged one another. It was a spontaneous expression of love. Renee ran up and pushed her way through the barely dressed women.

The truth will kill this moment. When will I tell them? How will I tell them?

Renee hugged Brooke and said in her ear, "My friend, how I missed you! Only you could go on an adventure of the heart and come back with a boat. Pilot and all."

"No, they found us. Okay, everyone, listen up, here's the deal," Brooke called out, wanting to hurry through her unpleasant task.

"A rescue ship has been called and is on the way. We'll all be leaving in a couple of days. That's right, all of us. For those of you who were seriously thinking about staying here forever, if that was more than a fantasy, you'll need to rethink your plans. Apparently, we're on a private island. That's right, we got shipwrecked first class." They all laughed. "So we need to give it back to its rightful owner. Take our memories, our plans for a better home, and take them home."

All the women shouted and cheered. It was easier to talk about staying when they couldn't get home. But the reality of it was, they were relieved to be rescued. It took several minutes of hollers and hugs before someone called out, "What happened, Brooke? Are there other survivors? Who else made it?"

Brooke only wanted to tell the tale one time, and she knew that must wait for the settlers to join them.

"There were other survivors, but I don't know how many. I'll go over all the details tomorrow at the full meeting. The settlers will be with us then. Let's find time to get things together now and say our goodbyes as we need to."

Renee whispered to Brooke, "What about the crush woman? I've been dying to find out."

"And I'll share it all with you after I talk with Marie. She needs to hear this first."

Renee looked at Brooke like the sister she was to her. "You found something over there. Even if I don't know what it is, I can tell it's good for you. There's something different about you. Not so much a glow, but maturity. Anyway, telling Marie first may be hard.

She drifted into semi-isolation. I'm sure she saw the flare and should be here shortly, though."

❧ ❧ ❧ ❧

Brooke spent most of the next day fruitlessly looking for Marie. As she searched for her, she walked by all the places they visited together, places spent in silence and in endless conversations and in deep and passionate necking. She saw parts of the beach where they swam together. Brooke could almost see them in the water, and she remembered what it felt like when their bodies slid over each other in nature's bathtub. She remembered Marie's soft smile and her powerful arms around Brooke's waist. She sat by the still waters and cried. In her solitude, she found room for her sadness, and she shed crowded tears. She was filled with sadness at the pending goodbyes, with joy at the rescue, and with fear of the hate that attacked their ship. It ripped at her stomach with the same sudden explosion that had hit the ship, coming at her from unseen directions with an endless force. She bent over as if to stop its burning tears, but the pain only found new places to hit her in her failed defensive position. It wailed on her body, knotted her thoughts, and crushed her otherwise prepared heart. How would she tell the other women about something she was trying to unhear herself? She decided to warn JJ, so she could be prepared to help the settlers deal with this anxious news. If only Marie was there. They could talk about what had happened. She could explain things differently now. More decisively. And maybe in their talks, she could absorb some of Marie's steadfast courage. How vain to dwell on my needs. Even now. Brooke rejected her intentions.

Besides, she doesn't want to talk to me. She's cleverly hidden from me.

❧ ❧ ❧ ❧

It was their last night gathering. Brooke tried not to think about it that way, but it kept coming back to that single group passage. It was the first nighttime they were all together—the clan and the settlers, minus a couple who could not be in the crowd. But even they stayed by the not-too-distant trees. Everyone was within earshot. There were long speeches, short statements, and goodbyes, words of thanks and of love all shared.

Shelby made what she thought would be her last comments. "Well, now we know how Dorothy felt as she said goodbye to the Scarecrow. It sounds like the end. But we know it's not. We developed a lot of ideas here, plans, new job focuses, ways to deal with old problems, and a new view on what we need to ask for—sorry, what we need to insist on. Hell, we could put this all together as some type of How to Live Like Lesbians Without Really Trying book. Now let's not make it all for nothing. That's what will happen if we don't take these ideas and turn them into action. Make it happen. Claire and I offered to be the clearinghouse to keep us all in touch. She'll be the main contact. I understand she'll set up a web page. Stay tuned for details. Now the answer to many of our questions. Brooke, what news do you have for us?"

They turned to Brooke with their eyes bright and hopeful. She looked over her new family. All their attention was on her at that moment. She looked over the sea of smiling faces. Kate huddled with the other wise women. Renee and Adair had their arms around each other. Tracy leaned against a rock all by herself. The athletes were sitting together, finally resting. Gail, Shelby, and JJ stood tall, allowing others to be in charge of the goodbye, for their survival goals were accomplished. Claire winked at her as if she knew of her difficult mission. She wanted to soak in their glowing faces before the darkness fell.

Brooke began, "I wanted to wait until we were all together because I don't want to say this more than once. There are other survivors. I'm not sure how many, but they picked up others. There is bad news. The wreck was not an accident. A hate group tried to hurt us because we're dykes. The good news is there has been an outpouring of support for lesbians and gays back home. Many groups in America and the rest of the world have rallied in support of us. They're demanding more rights for gays and a safer world for everyone." Their faces showed that they needed more. "You should all prepare yourselves for this difficult information," she said, not realizing how Guy taught her to use that phrase.

Immediately, their bodies reacted to her words. They leaned forward, slightly shaking their heads, trying to push off her warning. This wasn't a night for bad news. Brooke could see their smiles turn to blank looks. They were confused about the direction of her message. She didn't want to leave them waiting any longer.

"A fanatical right-wing religious group bombed our ship."

She saw many women turn their heads toward those beside them, trying to hide themselves from these spoken words. Most of the athletes stood with puffed-up chests and raised shoulders. The wise women looked at one another with a call for someone to make sense of what they just heard. Many women placed their heads in their hands. Then the screams started.

People yelled, "No, no." It reminded Brooke of the screams in the ship the night of the bombing. Now she had a reference for that noise. It was the sounds of disbelief and fear crashing into each other. It was a deep pain, the kind only women and men of war could understand.

Claire and Shelby took center places again, realizing their work was not over. JJ moved by the group of settlers as soon as Brooke talked. She huddled them together. Clair and Shelby whispered in each other's ears, but before they addressed the shocking news, they went around the group hugging the women. And their lead spread across the gathering. The women cried, talked, and held one another for hours. And when the time was right, when Claire noticed the group beginning to look for answers more than for comfort, she and Shelby addressed the crowd. But her own shock was more in charge than the leader she had been.

"In all our dreams of what happened, this was never part of the picture. This attack upon gentle women is outside the vastness of our mind's own resources to consider. How can you prepare or react to something you can't even imagine? I love all of you. I thought my place here was helping to keep us all safe. Now we're all headed back to the most unsafe place of all—our homes." Shelby spoke the first negative thoughts the group had heard from her. It had always been her place to bring them out of that dark space. But she taught them all too well, for this time they came to her aid.

Someone yelled out, "You know they'll expect a

statement from us about what we've been through here and about the attack on our lives. We should be ready to respond—no, to do more than respond. We should be ready to take whatever rallying is going on and move it in the right direction. We can move in a direction that stops this insanity of hate."

Tracy was in familiar ground now and reacted. "Don't you think they all said that? Don't you think the Jewish people talked about never again. Do you, in any way, think antisemitism is over? Don't you think Black people said never again when the shackles were removed? At least the physical ones? Other types are still there. We just can't see them from our white seat. The only thing different is they stopped using the Bible as a rationale for slavery. Friends, is racism over? Has the hate ended? How many 'take back the night' marches do we need to have before we realize we do not have the night, we have not been safe during the night for a long time, and we will never have it again? This is our world now. Just saying so will not make it end here."

"Words never have," Shelby rebounded. "But we're much more than words. And if you haven't learned that by now, then you really have missed this life here with us. Okay, what do we need to do?" she yelled with an authority that said anything less than a plan would be unacceptable. Her voice offered a reminder that she truly believed they could be safe again; they could even have the night back if they worked for it.

Brooke answered, "Tracy, you're wrong. We're not just talking about words, we're talking about action. Real action. And we won't be alone with this, my friends. I told you that groups around the world are showing they don't tolerate this hate. But what you haven't heard yet and you do need to hear is this. Millions of our fellow Americans are coming to our defense. Straight Americans are protesting by canceling their weddings and even divorcing to show their support. They say that if we can't marry, then they won't. They're saying the hate must stop, and they believe in us. Now we must tell them it's not all for naught. Our survival will be like a huge harness to collect their supportive efforts and make real change. We'll be a grand model for change because we're alive, we're strong, and we're women who've been pissed off. But we need a response to what has happened and a plan for where to go from here. We must be that plan, a plan we're all committed to. A plan they can't divide us on. Any disagreement happens at home between us, but out there, we work as one. Because this is not my world, Tracy. It may be yours. But this is not my world, not now, not ever." Brooke took her place.

There were cheers, and Heather yelled from the crowd, "I'll be the point person. Find me on the rescue ship. The work starts there. Come to work. And, Tracy, come too if you like. You see, my goals are greater than taking back the night. I'm so bold, I think we can take you back, too. Back from whatever took your hope away."

For the first time, Tracy didn't have a comment. Brooke wasn't sure if it was Heather's comment or knowing that millions of straight Americans believed in her more than Tracy believed in herself. Regardless, the group finally saw her breaking point. Brooke looked at Heather and winked.

Again, the volunteers came forward, and the hugging continued.

Claire ended the talk. "Let's take intentional time

to remember those lost and to find the compassion to rise above this horror thrown on us. Let's try to find a place in our hearts that's stronger than the hate they believe their God has given them. And let's never forget we know a divine creator would never allow this hate on any group of people, it's just their thinking that makes it so. And we have thoughts, too! And our thoughts and actions of love and compassion are greater than anything they have in their arsenal."

The women continued to console one another. Brooke worked her way through the group to Heather. She saw women introducing themselves to Heather and offering help. They were all trying to be hopeful and consider the possibilities that would come of it all, but it was too early for that. Mostly, the shock and pain needed its due time.

After Heather met with as many of the women who wanted to talk with her, she moved off suddenly before Brooke could catch up with her.

"It took a long time for me to find you," Marie heard someone say. She was close enough to the group to hear what was going on but not to be seen.

"Sorry, I'm usually good with names, but—"

"I'm Heather. I lived with the settlers. I'm the one who—"

"You're the traction. Why are you here? How did you find me? Never mind, I've heard enough for one evening." Marie started to walk away.

"It wasn't easy—to find you, that is. I had to ask several people. I'm good at finding people. It helped when living with the settlers. I'm here because I need to talk to you."

"No offense, okay, but I don't need to talk with you." Marie said.

"Probably not, but you do need to listen to me. And if you don't hear anything else, hear this. Nothing happened," Heather said.

"Oh, you turned Brooke away. Is this supposed to make me feel better? You weren't interested, so now I'm supposed to forget everything?"

"No, I was interested. I was very interested. I got a glimpse of why you're so angry with me. I'd hate the person I thought took her away from me, too. But I'm not that person. There was a dream of someone, I think a dream to keep her from facing what you have to offer. Something that scared her. But enough psychoanalysis. We both thought something was there. Until we kissed."

"Oh, is that the 'nothing that happened'?" Marie was angry.

"No, what followed the kiss was nothing. I wanted there to be more. But Brooke stopped. Something was wrong, missing. Something she shared with you that was far beyond a kiss with a stranger. Sorry if that sounds kind of corny, but it's true. The dream, you see, didn't match up to what she knows is the real thing. Something, ironically, she didn't want to lose."

"That's not what it looked like from my view."

"Of course it did. It's all too easy to manifest something we so desperately don't want to happen. For some women, they're drawn to that lesson over and over again until they make peace with what stirs that mess. For her, like most of us, it's about loss. Something she ran from. It's the epicenter of how she hurt you and herself. Marie, she spent our time together talking about you and her grief. Her grand gaffe."

"Gaffe. It's not like she used the wrong fork at a dinner party. Shouldn't she be telling me this?"

"Hell, yes. But I'm afraid she won't. I'm afraid

she'll miss happiness out of regret for what she did to you. She's on some stupid self-punishment thing. She gave me something: an honest look at myself. This is my attempt to give back by being a total buttinski with you. And believe me, that's not my natural place in the world."

"It's not? You're pretty good at it." Marie almost grinned.

"Well, I've always lived by 'friends don't let friends get off the island stupid' motto. It was coined by Mothers Against Sabotaged Relationships. Don't let her go. Don't turn this into a dyke soap opera. Be honest and direct."

"What if I am being honest? What if I'm done with the whole thing?"

"Then everyone gets hurt with nothing to show for it. That's against our nature, you know. Usually when women hurt each other out of love, they leave some redeeming reason for it all. You won't even have that because this is something that doesn't have to happen. You two were meant for each other. Give her another chance. Give yourself another chance."

Marie looked at her blankly.

"It was nice to meet you, really. Good luck to you when you get home. And thanks for the effort" was all Heather said before slipping into the night.

Chapter Fourteen

The castaways stood next to one another on the Coast Guard's rescue ship as it moved toward the dock. Brooke and JJ were standing side by side, leaning on the ship's railing. Brooke looked at the large mob of people waiting for them. Their faces were hopeful, curious, and scared. Sprinkled throughout the crowd were reporters, cameras, and photographers. Helicopters with more reporters swirled overhead to the point they almost hit one another. People in uniforms began to move the crowd back behind the brightly roped-off area.

The welcomers were crammed on the dock's perimeter allowing for a large clearing in which to greet each woman. Brooke noticed many of them were holding signs. Some had women's names on them. Others waved signs that welcomed the women home. Their messages found a way to mute the hammering pain in Brooke's head, the pain birthed from hatred's hands. She read each waving sign as if they were her personal hug home.

Our religion didn't do this—our God loves you, too

Welcome home, we love you

Our prayers are with you

You're always welcome at our synagogue

Hate sucks

Priests for gay rights

Christians against hate

Parents of lesbians welcome you HOME

Chicago welcomes you

Gay men of New Orleans love our sisters

Nieces and nephews of lesbians welcome you HOME

NY says come on home

Springfield, Oregon, says welcome back, Shavoon, we love you

Buddhists for gay rights

We will never forget the lesbian heroes

Police Response Team supports our lesbian buddy— We missed you, JJ

"Hey, JJ, is that the group you worked with?" Brooke asked while pointing to the men holding up that sign. But she quickly saw that JJ had already noticed them. She was jumping up and down, yelling and waving at them. Brooke could not help but tease the woman who once put Brooke in her place. "Aren't those the guys you said you didn't miss so much? The ones you thought took up a lot of physical space. Did they come all this way to see you off a ship? Just to greet you and welcome you home?"

"Okay, I get the point. Yes, that's the team, that's my team. And I love the way they take up all that space because that's who those big lug heads are. Big guys with big hearts. Can you believe they came all this way for me? I was so wrong about them. And one day, I may even apologize to them. But for now, I just love those guys. Did you hear that, you bunch of cops? I said I love you!" JJ yelled with her hands up to her mouth like a megaphone. But no one could hear anything above all the cheering.

Then music started to play, and Brooke almost didn't believe what she heard. The Coast Guard band was playing the lesbian's battle hymn of the seventies. And the artists who wrote it, Rosewater, were standing behind the tall microphones and crying as they sang their song, the one every lesbian knew, I'm Taking Me Back. It was a song Brooke once thought she never wanted to hear again, but as she looked at the lesbian singers and the rows of Guardsmen and women all at attention, all saluting, she thought it was the most wonderful song she had ever heard, and she began to sing the words with everyone else. She sang with the pride and love that she was sure Rosewater had intended. She knew this day would not end without her giving Rosewater a huge, stray-eyed fan hug. They had made it.

The Coast Guard stood in a straight line wearing their crisp white suits, and in unison, they saluted each castaway as she walked off the ship. At the end of these beautiful men and women standing at attention, was Guy in his plain T-shirt and dress pants. He too stood at attention. As Brooke approached him, he saluted her and smiled. She placed her hands on his cheeks and lightly kissed his lips. "Don't go away, Guy, we need men like you," she whispered in his ear.

The women waved and blew kisses at their rescuers as they walked off the ship. They didn't all rush off. Instead, they walked in pairs with enough space to give each pair who exited enough time and space to be greeted by friends and family. The cheers quieted down so everyone could hear their names being called as they entered the crowd. Some women fell to their knees at the sight of the welcoming. Others ran into the crowd and were immediately lost. They began to gather with their loved ones.

Brooke stood in the middle of it all as if it was

just revealing itself around her. She saw Nina run up to Amber, jump in her arms, wrap her legs around her waist, and give her the "beyond friendship" kiss that Amber did not stop to question. Gail was over by the cameras, giving a senator's view on the survival and the attack. Adair was introducing Renee to a group of people, who kept kissing and hugging Adair. Brooke smiled.

Brooke saw Kate surrounded by a group of elderly women. Most of them had their heads down except the one with her hand on Kate's shoulder. She was looking her in the eye and talking slowly, until Kate put her head in her hands and cried. "Goodbye, Millie," Brooke whispered. Shelby and Claire walked around, making sure everyone had someone to hold. Brooke sighed. What a time to do my invisible thing.

Shelby approached Brooke with a child in her arms. "Brooke, this is my daughter, Allison."

"Hi. Allison. I love that name! How old are you?" Brooke smiled.

"I'm six and a half. My mommy said you made sure she came home to me. I wanted to say thank you 'cause I love my mommy, and I missed her lots."

Brooke looked somewhat puzzled at Shelby. Shelby answered her unasked question. "I know you're the reason the lifeboat went back for me. You're the reason I didn't become shark lunch. They told me how you stood up to Tracy, even though you were so hurt and out of it, and you heard my cries for help and made them go and get me. I didn't say anything on the island because, well, I'm not sure why, but when I got here, I knew Allison could say it better," Shelby said and cried.

"You're right," Brooke said. "You couldn't have said it anywhere near as good as this six-and-a-half-year-old. I hope I get an invitation to celebration number seven."

"You're at the top of the list. I'll be in touch," Shelby said and kissed Brooke right on the lips.

Brooke watched the mother and child reunion with more pride than sorrow.

"Did you find what you were looking for?"

Brooke turned to see Marie. "I found the me that exists behind the fear of loss, of abandonment. The demons I denied in myself to the point of hurting you."

"That's not a quick journey. Not something that can be answered in one trip to the settlement," Marie said.

"No, it's not. I'm sure I'll be looking at it for the rest of my life. Unfolding all that exists behind those damaged shadows. But that's not all."

"That sounds like a lot to me. What else was exposed in your vision quest?"

"The act of peeling back that pain doesn't magically transform into healing. I need to also cultivate who I am without that fear. And no, that's not done in one trip. Hell, it's a lifelong commitment and one I'll need expert help with, at least for this leg of the journey. But even at this early stage, Marie, I feel a small budding of some peace. Not because I have it all worked out, but because I have a sense of what needs my tender attention and professional help. My instinct about it says that I need to stop ignoring and pushing down the grief and actually make friends with this fear and anxiety. When I know how to care for it, for me, when I reach that juncture, can I give you a call? Maybe go out and get reintroduced?"

She saw Marie was ready to answer but wanted one last thing to be heard before she heard her heart's fate. "Before you answer. Regardless of what you're going to say, I want to start this journey with a sincere apology to you. I know I hurt you, and you didn't deserve that. I was wrong. Is there anything I can do to begin to make this right?"

"No. I don't need anything from you. No, you won't be contacting me in the future."

"I understand," Brooke said as she fought back tears.

"Don't wait till then to call me. I'm not stepping out of your life as you work that hard to make peace with yourself. I'm not abandoning you. I'm not getting super close to you either right now. But I think somewhere in between will be good for both of us. Let's stay in contact and see where this all goes."

"What did I do to deserve this?" Brooke's tears flowed freely now.

"I've seen enough to know there's more about you than the harm life forged upon your young heart and the way that hurt came out on me. I'm not emotional exercise equipment, Brooke. I'm not here for you to work your shit out on, and I definitely need to be treated differently. But I also see how you care enough about yourself to seek help for your healing. I also feel your apology to be true. I'm not saying there's a relationship for us in the wings. But I've experienced enough with you to know I want to be in your life as we both figure this out. One step, a breath, one step…"

"A breath," they said together.

About the Author

Ari Basil Wagner lives in the Pacific Northwest, where she finds beauty in all things nature, even the rain. She writes novels about the lives of lesbians and the people who love them, showcasing the diverse ways women love and learn from each other. Ari's work invites readers to find hope, healing, and self-discovery through her characters' journeys. As a gregarious introvert, she enjoys meeting people but refreshes her spirit during solo adventures in nature. When not writing, she can be found hiking, kayaking, snowshoeing, or snowboarding. She has an adult child, Mika, who offers endearing inspiration. Proudly lesbian and out her entire life, Ari embraces authenticity and gratitude for this precious life.